"I'm going to check it out…"

"Hier," Sierra commanded her dog. *Here.* The dog whined then moved close to Sierra.

Sierra grabbed Bryce's arm and squeezed, tugging him back. "Bryce, be careful."

Her tone was intense, and something else in her voice told him she did still care deeply about him.

Gunfire exploded.

The bullet whizzed by his ear even as he shoved Sierra to the ground.

"Nein!" They crept behind a van they could use for a temporary barrier. Sierra kept her dog close.

"Cover me." Bryce prepared to dash across the street.

"No, wait!" Sierra whispered. "Don't go out there."

"This is our chance to get him, Sierra."

"You're not law enforcement anymore, Bryce. Remember? You can't arrest that guy—Raul or anyone else—even if you catch him."

They'd have to work together then.

Because as much as he didn't want her in the line of fire, he knew she wasn't going to back down…

Elizabeth Goddard
and
Mary Ellen Porter

Trained to Rescue

Previously published as *Fugitive Trail* and *Into Thin Air*

LOVE INSPIRED
INSPIRATIONAL ROMANCE

LOVE INSPIRED®

INSPIRATIONAL ROMANCE

ISBN-13: 978-1-335-41859-3

Recycling programs for this product may not exist in your area.

Trained to Rescue

Copyright © 2021 by Harlequin Books S.A.

Fugitive Trail
First published in 2020. This edition published in 2021.
Copyright © 2020 by Elizabeth Goddard

Into Thin Air
First published in 2015. This edition published in 2021.
Copyright © 2015 by Mary Ellen Porter

This edition published by arrangement with Harlequin Books S.A.

For questions and comments about the quality of this book, please contact us at CustomerService@Harlequin.com.

Love Inspired
22 Adelaide St. West, 40th Floor
Toronto, Ontario M5H 4E3, Canada
www.Harlequin.com

Printed in U.S.A.

CONTENTS

Elizabeth Goddard is the award-winning author of more than thirty novels and novellas. A 2011 Carol Award winner, she was a double finalist in the 2016 Daphne du Maurier Award for Excellence in Mystery/Suspense, and a 2016 Carol Award finalist. Elizabeth graduated with a computer science degree and worked in high-level software sales before retiring to write full-time.

Visit the Author Profile page
at Harlequin.com for more titles.

FUGITIVE TRAIL

Elizabeth Goddard

The God of my rock; in him will I trust:
he is my shield, and the horn of my salvation,
my high tower, and my refuge, my saviour;
thou savest me from violence.

—*2 Samuel* 22:3

Dedicated to all those who put themselves
in harm's way to protect us—
both two-legged and four-legged creatures.

Acknowledgments:

Thank you to my new editor, Shana Asaro, for asking
me to write a K-9 mountain rescue story! I've always
loved these stories from LIS and this gave me a
chance to showcase my own dog (though not a K-9)—
an English mastiff named Solomon. As always, I so
appreciate the encouragement and support from my
writing friends—we've journeyed long and hard to
get here! All my gratitude to my agent, Steve Laube,
for believing in me. It goes without saying,
but I'll say it anyway—thank you, Dan,
Christopher, Jonathan, Andrew and Rachel
for your patience with this novel-writing mom.

ONE

Southwest Rocky Mountains,
Colorado

The wind picked up and whipped big snowflakes around Deputy Sierra Young's head as she followed Samson, her K-9 mountain rescue English mastiff, up the densely wooded incline. She maintained a steady pace but her heart rate increased along with her breathing.

She hoped the small plane hadn't crashed too high in the San Juan Mountains. That could make it impossible for her and Samson, as well as the SAR—search and rescue—volunteers, to reach the site before nightfall or the snowstorm grew worse. But they had to find the plane before they could rescue anyone.

Two snowmobilers had returned to the small tourist town of Crescent Springs, Colorado, earlier this afternoon claiming they'd seen the prop plane go down but they hadn't been sure where it had crashed.

She'd brought Samson as far as she could before releasing him to find any human scent. Samson had been trained to find humans, whether air scenting for anyone in the wilderness or tracking a specific person. He was smart and used his skills to find whoever he was searching for. The other SAR volunteers searched downwind from Samson. It was important to spread as wide a net as possible. The victims could have escaped and gotten lost in the mountains, or they could be trapped in the plane. Or worse.

She couldn't think about *worse*.

Lord, please let us find and save them, whoever they are.

Before the weather turned too harsh or night took over. Sure, Samson could work through the night, but not in this weather. The terrain and elements during the winter months here in the Rockies were currently too harsh for searching at night. Sierra worked as a part-time deputy and K-9 mountain rescue handler for the county. She knew that Sheriff Locke would protect the volunteers, and if it became too dangerous to search, he would call it off.

Samson's massive two-hundred-pound form plowed up the hill through the deepening snow, giving credence to his aptly picked name. Snow could tire out some breeds of search dogs and limit their time searching, but mastiffs were the stronger working-breed dogs, and Samson hadn't tired yet.

An old friend—Bryce Elliott—had given Samson to her when he was a puppy, and had even named him. After the attack when she'd been a detective in Boulder, she'd wanted a big dog, and Bryce had surprised her with the English mastiff. A pang of regret that she'd left her friend behind when she'd moved from Boulder stabbed her at the worst possible moment. She missed Bryce. But she needed to focus on this search.

The sheriff radioed he was calling the search, bringing her back to the present.

At the same moment, Samson alerted her.

"Wait, no. Sheriff," she said into her radio. "Samson…he's found something. Let me check it out."

"All right. I'm on my way to you."

Her leg muscles burned as she tried to keep up with the big dog scaling the incline until they topped it, then to a terraced ridge and a well-over-a-hundred-foot drop.

Sierra stood tall and caught her breath. Her heart lurched.

A red Cessna rested on the ledge—halfway on, halfway off. The banged-up plane looked partially crumpled on one side. She could make out a figure inside the cockpit, and another one outside, beside the plane. Both were utterly still.

Sierra radioed the sheriff. "I found it. I found the plane. I see two—" *Bodies*, but she didn't want to say the word. "We need to check and see if they're alive."

"Good work, Sierra," he said. "Wait there while I let everyone know to head your way. And…be careful."

"Always," she responded.

If the two people she spotted were still alive, it would be a difficult rescue at best, getting them down this mountain. The most difficult part would be saving the person inside that plane that teetered on the ledge. In the snow and cold, even if they had survived, hypothermia most likely would kill them if the SAR team didn't get here quickly and get them medical attention.

She signaled for Samson to remain then she hiked closer to the wreckage in the deepening snow. A man rested face down in the snow and would soon be completely buried. Sierra removed her glove and brushed the snow away then pressed a finger against his neck. His body was cold and he had no pulse. Sorrow bled through her.

She released a heavy sigh. SAR missions with Samson always started with the hope of rescue. Of finding a lost hiker or helping someone who'd fallen by bringing them to safety. Always the hope that she would find survivors and the day would end well. But more times than she'd like to admit, the searches ended in tragedy when they found victims of an adventure gone wrong.

The wind whipped around the mountain blasting the snow at an angle and causing a near whiteout. Not good.

She eyed the small plane and from here couldn't see the other person. Should she get closer and see if she could help?

She hoped the rest of the search team arrived soon. An eerie metallic sound resounded from the plane. Its position was precarious at best. Could the howling wind push it over? She spared a moment to wonder what these people had been thinking, taking the plane out on a day like today. The plane probably shouldn't have been flying in this weather, and she guessed that the weather had everything to do with the crash. But she wasn't here to question them; she was here to save them…if she could.

She crunched through the snow to get closer to the plane and look inside the cab.

The pilot remained inside, his body hunched over. It was possible that his position meant he'd remained warm enough, if he was still alive.

"Can you hear me? Are you all right?" She crept even closer to the plane.

The sheriff had said he and the others were coming. What was taking them so long?

The pilot shifted. Her heart jumped. She radioed. "Hurry, sheriff. The pilot is still alive. He's going to need medical attention…"

Metal scraped.

The plane shifted. Fear skated across her nerves. "The plane is in a precarious position. It could fall from the ledge at any moment. I'm not sure what to do!"

The radioed squawked but a burst of static meant she couldn't understand the sheriff. Panic built up in her chest. Sierra eyed the plane and the junk scattered around the crash site. She searched for anything she could use as a rope. Samson whined, sensing her growing anxiety.

"It's going to be all right, Samson. You found the crash site. We're going to save the man who's still alive." What was she saying? She had no idea if she could actually save him, but she could hope. And she could try.

God, please help me!

Was there anything worse than finding someone and then being completely helpless to save them?

The man groaned inside the plane. She had to reassure him so he would hang on to the will to live.

"Hold on! Help is coming."

She peered at the wreckage. It would be too dangerous to try to get in and get him out with the plane shifting on the ledge. She had to find a rope.

The snow was quickly covering the scattered wreckage—duffel bag, sheets of metal, clothing articles. Then she spotted what she needed—a wire rope used in aviation.

She eyed the airplane then the top of the slope. Something must have held the SAR team up. She couldn't risk waiting if they weren't going to make it in time.

She found a boulder on which to secure the rope and tied the other end around her waist. Then she edged slowly to the plane.

Sierra ducked under the broken wing. Nothing about this was safe. The plane was completely unstable, but that was the whole reason she needed to act—and act *now*. She had to get this guy out, even though, depending on his injuries, that could also be dangerous for him.

The mangled door creaked when she pulled it open and then toppled to the snow-covered ground. Sierra yelped and jumped out of the way. She could enter only on the passenger side because the other side of the plane was hanging near the ledge. She couldn't reach it.

"Help," the man called from inside.

Fear tried to seize her but she had to remain calm and focused, especially if she was going to have to do this alone. She leaned into the cockpit and inched onto the passenger seat to get a better look at the man. Blood covered his forehead and temple from a gash. It oozed from his lips. He likely had internal injuries.

"Can you hear me? If you can, give me your hand."

Maybe she could grab onto him and pull him out through this side of the plane. Medical personnel would go at this much differently, but there wasn't time to wait.

The man's eyes popped open. Those eyes. They peered at her and into her and through her. His face was almost unrecognizable under the blood and bruising but she had never forgotten those eyes.

Sierra froze. Damien Novack. Air whooshed from her. She couldn't breathe.

No. It couldn't be. "What… What are you doing here?" The question squeaked out of her making her sound feeble.

Afraid.

Somehow, even though he was injured and probably dying, he managed to offer her a sinister, bloody smile. To her horror, he lifted a weapon. Aimed it straight at her.

Screaming, she ducked as gunfire exploded then froze in place. Where was the sheriff? She glanced up hoping she'd see him coming over the ridge. Instead, she spotted footprints, barely visible as the relentless snow continued to bury them. The prints led away from the plane and tracked along the ridge until they disappeared completely.

Someone else had been on the plane.

Then she heard what sounded like the weapon tumbling from Damien's hand. She could hardly believe he had been able to shoot to begin with, given his obviously severe injuries. His anger and need to see her dead had been enough to drive him.

Heart pounding, Sierra peeked inside the cab again and Damien's eyes tracked her. "Doesn't matter that I missed. He's coming for you," he said.

"Who… Who is coming?" Dread filled her.

"You know who. He came for you before. This time he won't fail."

Raul Novack, Damien's brother.

Moments ago, she thought there couldn't be anything worse than losing someone she was trying to save. But now she realized that wasn't true. There *was* something worse. Indecision warred inside of her. She truly did not want to help this man. He'd perpetrated countless evils and if she helped him to survive, there could be more victims down the road.

But she couldn't serve as judge and jury. She couldn't

take a life or refuse to give her best to save someone in danger—God would know, even if no one else did. She grabbed the weapon he'd tried to kill her with and set it aside.

Regardless of the fear that tried to strangle her, Sierra reached for him. "The plane is going to fall. Take my hand or you're going to die."

He coughed up more blood. "I'm as good as dead anyway."

Then his face went still. His eyes blank.

He was gone, and she knew it. He'd known he was going to die and he cared only about attacking her with his gun and his intimidating threats.

Samson barked. The plane shifted. Sierra reached for the man she knew to already be dead, but it was no use. She couldn't free him. The plane moved and she realized she had only seconds to escape.

She backed out of the open doorway and ducked just before the remaining broken edges of the wing could hit her. Still, metal scraped her body, eliciting a cry of pain, and snagging her coat. If she didn't get free, the plane would try to take her over the ledge too, causing serious injury when the wire rope wouldn't release her.

"I got you!" The sheriff appeared and slashed the arm of her coat away from her body and gripped her arms. "I got you," he said again, breathless.

She slumped to the ground, the adrenaline whooshing out of her body.

Samson licked her and whined, warming her frozen cheeks, and comforting the icy cold fear that had stabbed through her.

Damien Novack had been here. And he hadn't been alone.

She let her gaze follow the tracks and, in the distance, along the tree line, she noticed that a man stood watching. Damien's brother, Raul—

He's coming for you...

Bryce Elliott checked into his hotel across the street from the Crescent Springs Toy Store—the reason Sierra had given for returning to her hometown. Her father had been struggling to keep up with the store, and needed her help. Bryce had suspected health issues were involved too but Sierra hadn't said.

That wasn't the only thing she hadn't said. Bryce believed that her father was only part of the reason she'd given up her detective job with the Boulder police department. He suspected that Sierra had never gotten over the night Raul attacked her, even though she had been given the go ahead to return to work.

But no one else knew her as well as Bryce. She'd needed to escape Boulder, and maybe even escape Bryce. The place and the people served as reminders to her of what had happened. He was glad she had found a way to move on. Before she'd made that physical move from Boulder to Crescent Springs, though, she'd made an emotional move when she pushed him away. They'd been close and had been growing closer every day. He'd taken a risk with her, putting his heart on the line for the first time since being utterly rejected by Rebecca, a woman he thought he loved a couple of years before he met Sierra. But with Sierra, he'd been ready to try again. Then Raul and the night of violence happened. After that, everything between Bryce and Sierra had changed. He had sensed her slipping away from him, and had experienced the pain of rejection all over again.

He cared about her and was here for her, but that didn't mean he would let himself fall for her. Definitely not. None of what had happened between them should matter now.

What did matter now was that she was in danger, and Bryce wouldn't let her go through that alone.

He sucked up his nerve and crossed the recently plowed street in the throes of an ice festival, presumably the biggest event of the year for the small out-of-the-way town in southwest Colorado. Other than ice climbers, most people opted to visit Telluride and Purgatory in Durango to ski. Crescent Springs offered an ice park to celebrate the ice climbing sport—beginners and professionals from around the world came to the small town to climb the frozen waterfalls of the gorge.

Moisture surged on his palms as he drew near the toy store he'd seen only on the website before this moment. Bryce drew in a deep breath and pushed open the door. How would she react when she saw him? That question had kept him company as he traveled here from Boulder.

The smells of plastic and cinnamon and peppermint wafted over him. He had no idea if he would actually find Sierra here, amongst the toys, but it was a start. Aisles of toys blocked his view, but as he browsed, he noted the store was relatively crowded. An older man's voice offering customer assistance drew his attention to the cash register and counter at the back of the store. A young woman he didn't recognize stood next to the older man he assumed was Sierra's father. She took payment from the customer and bagged toys.

"Can I help you?"

The voice. *That* voice. Turning to Sierra, he grinned.

In a flash he took in her bright blue irises, her lithe and petite form, and the perfect lips that often turned up in an amazing smile, but which now morphed into a huge O.

She gasped. "Bryce, what…what in the world are you doing here?"

"Ah. You're glad to see me." He instantly regretted his slightly sarcastic tone. "It's good to see you too."

A frown emerged on her face and seemed to war with a tenuous grin.

"Well of course. I mean…of course I'm glad to see you. Why wouldn't I be glad to see you?" She reached forward and hugged him. This was the Sierra he loved— well, loved to see. She was wonderful. Except he sensed her wariness.

When she released him and stepped back, he saw the fear flashing in her eyes. Her face shifted as though she was searching for the right response, though he saw a spark of amusement when she noted the section of the store he'd stopped in. "Any particular type of baby doll you're looking for? I'm guessing this is for a niece? Or do you have…um…a daughter?" Sierra handed him a doll.

Like a fool he took it automatically.

"No. I don't have a daughter." It had been only a year since Sierra had left Boulder, and they hadn't kept in touch. "I'm not married and don't suddenly have a young daughter." He put the doll back on the shelf. "Nor do I have a niece."

He jammed his hand into his pockets, wishing he could go ahead and shrug out of his coat. It had kept him warm outside, but in here he was downright hot.

Sierra turned and walked away, still lacking the usual

bounce in her step that he hadn't seen since she'd been attacked in Boulder.

"You still haven't told me what you're doing here," she called over her shoulder. Then she stopped at the counter. "Are you here for the ice climbing festival? I didn't know you were a fan. You might have said something back when I was in Boulder—we could have visited my hometown together." Sure they could have visited her hometown together while they were still "together." A pain flitted across her features. Had she forgotten that in Boulder, after Raul's attack, she'd distanced herself from him? No. And that made his appearance all the more awkward.

He stared too long, struggling to find the words. "I came to check on you."

A deep bark resounded from somewhere inside the building and rattled through him. "And Samson. I... missed him." *And you, Sierra.*

I'm worried about you. But he kept that to himself for now.

She eyed him, then walked around behind the counter. The man he'd seen earlier stepped from the back room. "Dad, this is Bryce Elliot. I used to work with him in Boulder. Bryce, this is my dad."

"Nice to meet you, Mr. Young."

"Call me John. It's nice to meet you too. My daughter told me about you. You had her back when she was there in the city. Thanks for taking care of her for me. You can stick around if you like and keep up the good work." John winked at Bryce then grinned at Sierra.

She gently elbowed her dad and scowled at him, though love poured from her expression. "Dad. I'm perfectly capable of taking care of myself."

"And me. Your daughter took care of me too," Bryce said. They had, in fact, saved each other from certain death. He had no idea how much Sierra had shared with her father about what really happened. Bryce suspected she would have kept most of it from John, choosing to spare him the pain of knowing what his daughter had gone through.

"You want to see Samson?" she asked.

"You know I do."

"Come on back." She led him through the door past an employee area where boxes of toys were waiting to be stocked. Then through another door into a kitchen where Samson popped up to greet them. "We have an apartment at the back of the store. It takes up two floors. It's enough for the three of us. Me, Dad and Samson." She rubbed Samson's head.

Wagging his tail, he barked and lumbered over to Bryce. "Wow, he's gained some more weight."

"It takes about three years for them to be full grown, and he's about four now. He could still get bigger, but I train him often and keep him in good shape."

"I'd say that I named him appropriately."

"Well, I kind of liked your initial suggestion of 'Tiny' for a name, but I think you're right. Samson suits him."

Bryce leaned toward Samson and ran his hands around the dog's ear and enormous head. "Hey, buddy. How're you doing? Did you miss me?"

He received a wad of drool across his face and shirt. Bryce smiled to hide his inward cringe.

"You're the one who got him for me." Sierra's tone told him she was thinking about the reasons why.

"You said you wanted something big." He pet Samson, then glanced up.

She crossed her arms and gave him a pointed look. "Why are you really here, Bryce?"

His stomach sank as he noticed something in her eyes. "You already know."

"You're here because Raul and Damien escaped prison."

He nodded. Should he tell her that his thoughts went immediately to her when he heard the news? "I wanted to make sure you were okay. Did Captain Stephens call you?"

"I called *him*." She gestured for Bryce to have a seat at the kitchen table. She grabbed mugs and poured coffee without asking. Sugar and nondairy creamer were already on the table.

"Why did you call him?"

Sierra took a seat and then placed her elbows on the table. She pressed her face into her hands. "A plane crashed yesterday."

"Oh, no."

"Samson and I found the crash site. The state is working to recover the bodies. One died before I arrived. One survived only minutes after I reached the plane. But before he died—" horror crept into her eyes "—Damien tried to kill me. He shot at me. I dodged that attempt, but then…then he told me that Raul was coming for me."

"Oh, Sierra… I don't know what to say." He'd heard about the escaped convicts on the news like everyone else in Boulder and immediately contacted his old boss and BPD captain for the details.

"That's not all." Her voice cracked and, though she tried to appear unaffected, he didn't miss the shudder that ran over her. "I saw footprints in the snow from a third person—someone who escaped the plane alive. Then I saw him, Bryce. I saw Raul. He was on the edge of the tree line. He just stood there watching. If the sheriff and SAR team hadn't caught up to me, I don't know if Raul would have come back to the plane and tried to kill me."

She rubbed her arms and stared out the window to the woods. "As soon as I saw him, I tried to point him out to the sheriff, but Raul had disappeared. It was snowing hard so you could barely see anything. I wanted to go after him, but the sheriff wouldn't let me. If the sheriff hadn't seen the tracks in the snow before they were buried, I'm not sure he would have believed me about the presence of another man—and I'm still not sure he believes it was Raul."

"Why not?"

"He might have thought I was seeing things. I failed to hide how shaken I was at seeing Damien."

"What did the sheriff do? I hope he took action."

"He sent a couple of deputies to search the area, but the storm and nightfall forced them to return before they found anything. They did retrieve the body of the unidentified deceased man though. My understanding is that a team will try to retrieve Damien's body today. I hear they suspect the other man worked for the brothers on the outside and helped with their prison escape. I guess Raul and Damien escaped prison and thought they'd get revenge before they disappeared forever. But Raul… He's out there somewhere, Bryce."

And Sierra was terrified. She wouldn't say the words, but Bryce could see the truth she tried hard to hide. She was tough and trained to protect others as well as herself, but anytime you became a target, even as a member of law enforcement, there was nothing wrong with a little healthy fear.

It was all Bryce could do to remain in his seat and not rush to her. Take her in his arms. He'd missed her since she'd walked out of his life. He'd been such a fool to let her so easily slip away.

"Sierra. I'm so sorry."

"You didn't have to come all this way to tell me that," she said. "You could have called."

He continued to pet Samson, rubbing his neck and behind his ears. "I don't have your number anymore." She'd changed her number—and she hadn't given him the new one. And besides, he'd wanted to do much more than say he was sorry.

"Fair enough, but you knew where to find me. You could have called the toy store."

Bryce cleared his throat. "I *did* call." And left a message that it was important and to please call him back.

"Oh. Okay. I didn't get that message. It's just Dad, me and Jane, our part-time help, working the store. Whoever took the call must have forgotten." She shrugged.

When she'd first seen him, she'd hugged him as if glad to see an old friend—glad and yet edgy. Now she seemed downright irritated, like she didn't want him here at all. He partly understood. He was a reminder about what happened. But then, Samson served as a daily reminder too, since the dog's sole reason for being in her life was a result of the attack in Boulder.

As a detective with the Boulder Police Department, Sierra had been instrumental in putting notorious killer Damien Novack in prison. Damien had headed up an arms and drug trafficking organization and had committed numerous heinous crimes and murders. After

Damien's conviction, his brother, Raul, had come to extact revenge on Sierra, and attacked her in her home. Bryce had barely made it in time to save her. Raul had tried to kill him as well, but Sierra had saved him too.

Bryce wasn't sure either of them had ever quite gotten over that violent night.

"Doesn't matter." He could shrug too. "I'm here now."

"And so you are." She arched a brow again.

He resisted the need to shift away from her piercing gaze. Was he prepared to stay even if she didn't want his help? He wasn't entirely sure how to take her reaction to his presence, but the fear in her blue eyes over the news of Raul remained.

And Bryce knew then that he would remain too—until the threat on her life was eliminated.

TWO

Sierra rose from the table and moved to dump her drink so she could hide her trembling hands. She was still working to get over what had happened yesterday—the image of Damien's dark eyes and his intimidating words still fresh in her mind. Yesterday's experience would have been traumatic even if the man hadn't been an escaped prisoner who had come for her. Trying to save a man and watching him die like that had felt like a fist squeezing her heart tighter and tighter, crushing her.

And then to see Raul watching her from the trees...

As if that wasn't enough, Bryce apparently thought he could walk back into her world and she would welcome him to save her again—as if he was her knight in shining armor? On the one hand, that he would do such a thing warmed her through and through. But on the other hand, she didn't want to feel that way about his sudden appearance. They'd been through enough already.

Before Bryce, she'd cared deeply about someone on the Colorado State Patrol, but he'd been killed after he'd pulled a speeding driver over on the highway. His death had been senseless. It had been hard for her to get over it, but time had eased the pain enough for her to be ready to try. She had been close to letting Bryce in when Raul's attack came. He'd almost died.

Sierra wouldn't let herself care deeply or love someone in law enforcement again. There was too much pain to be had, something she knew from experience.

She sighed heavily. She truly had no idea how she really felt about Bryce's appearance. The moment she'd seen him in the aisle next to the baby dolls, her heart had stumbled, then begun to beat erratically until she'd calmed herself and reminded herself why she had to guard against caring too much. But that had always been hard for her when it came to Bryce. His sturdy form, strong jaw and huge dimples when he smiled had always made her heart jump around, but adding to that, he could be tough as steel one moment, then instantly turn gentle and sensitive and caring the next. She was surprised someone hadn't snagged and married him already.

"Listen." He remained at the table, toying with his mug. Samson lay at his feet, taking up half the space of the nook.

It was a picturesque moment, one she wouldn't easily forget.

"I know my sudden appearance today is a surprise to you. But I couldn't stay away. Not when I heard about Raul and Damien."

That news hadn't filtered all the way to the small town of Crescent Springs—not until they'd found the crashed plane. That Bryce still thought of her, and that some part of him had remained committed to her, could melt the cold places in her heart. And that wasn't a good thing. She'd tried to forget him and now he was here.

She'd hurt him before. She'd hurt the both of them. Could she really turn around, face him and ask him to leave? Washing the mug off, she tried to figure out what to say.

She continued to rinse the few remaining dishes in the sink. "So, what are you going to do?" she asked.

"I'm staying in town for a few days." His chair scraped the floor as he scooted it away from the table.

Oh. Okay. Hmm.

Facing him, she crossed her arms and leaned against the counter. "Don't you have a job? Did you take vacation or something?"

"I'm taking a few days off." He studied her as if waiting for her reaction. She kept her emotions hidden away.

Bryce turned his attention to the dog. Samson was a great distraction when one was needed. She totally got that.

"Is it always this crowded in town?" he asked. "Or is that just because of the ice festival?"

"No, it's not usually so crowded. The town becomes an ice climbing mecca during the festival." The timing of the prison break couldn't have been worse. The tourists and fans that flooded the town—so many strangers here—could make it easier for Raul to hide in the chaos and get to her.

If only…

Bryce glanced up at her. Not even the hint of a smile curved his lips. And why should there be? There was nothing to smile about under these circumstances. Bryce showing up because of the Novack brothers only served to emphasize the way the horrors of the past were coming back to threaten her again. Maybe even threaten Bryce again too. Still, the look in his eyes—He wanted to know how she felt about him being here—of course, he would want to know. But she wasn't sure herself.

"You know." She smiled. "I have this amazing guard dog, compliments of you. Samson wasn't there before, when the attack happened. But he's here now so you didn't need to come for me."

A pained look skittered across Bryce's face. Had she imagined it? At the sound of his name, Samson lifted his head. Bryce ran his hands through the dog's fur. "And I missed Samson, okay? I needed to come see my buddy and make sure you were treating him right."

Bryce's grin ignited memories in her. She'd adored his grin before. She couldn't let herself adore that grin again.

"I appreciate you coming to check on me, Bryce. Really. But there's no need to worry about me. I'm fine—and I'm sure Raul will be captured soon."

He crouched to get a better angle to rub Samson's enormous belly. The dog was really too big for this kitchen.

"Yeah. Maybe. In the meantime, why don't we have dinner tonight? You can tell me about life back here in Crescent Springs."

Dinner. Two friends catching up. Not a date. As long as they were both clear on that point. "And you can share what you've been up to. Catch me up on the Boulder PD." Wistfulness washed through her. While she loved working here and being close to her father, there were aspects she missed about the daily grind of detective work in Boulder.

Bryce stood to his full height, his silver-blue eyes taking her in. An old, familiar stirring hit her, and she realized how much she'd missed this man. She'd always felt drawn to him. But then, that was why she'd been deliberate about putting emotional distance between them.

"I don't have any inside scoops for you. I don't know what's going on with BPD."

She glanced at him. That didn't sound good. "Why don't you know what's going on?"

"I'm not working with BPD anymore."

Okay. That surprised her. "Why didn't you tell me?"

"I'm telling you now." He winked. "I've been a private investigator for a year now. That and working security."

She nodded, taking it in. "That had always been your dream." She remembered that much. "Good for you, Bryce. I'm glad."

Bryce held her gaze captive for a few breaths longer than necessary. There was so much more she could say to him.

He approached her and, in two easy steps, he stood much too close. Samson, who had stuck by Bryce's side, decided to wag his dinosaur tail and it thumped against her leg.

"Just so you know, I'm here until Raul is back in prison. I'm here for as long as it takes."

Sierra stared into his eyes. If only she could send him away. It would be safer for her heart. But his proclamation had the strange and unbidden effect of reassuring her that she would be safe as long as he was here. Between Samson and Bryce, no one would get to Sierra. And maybe it was okay to accept his help. After all, it had been only yesterday when she'd looked into Damien's vengeance-filled eyes right before he died. Only yesterday she'd seen Raul watching her.

Bryce suddenly took her hand. "Breathe, Sierra. It's going to be okay."

She hadn't been breathing? She slowly drew in air along with the hint of his musky cologne. "Is it? You didn't see what I saw." She hadn't meant to show him how scared she was. She didn't want to be scared. But this situation made her anxiety impossible to ignore. "You didn't see the hate in his eyes. He wasn't even afraid of the fact that he was about to die. All he cared about was getting to me. His last words were nothing more than evil. His brother is no different than him, and Raul succeeded in getting to me before."

And both she and Bryce had almost died.

A shudder rolled through her.

She tried to hide it but Bryce didn't miss the effect Damien's words had on her. Without a second thought he wrapped his arms around her. As a friend. Nothing more. Someone who cared for her deeply—and platonically.

"It's going to be okay. I hope some part of you knew that I would come. We've been through so much together. We faced off against Raul before. If he comes for you, we'll face him again and win—together, Sierra. That's why I'm here. To face him with you if it comes to that."

Though uncertainty about his decision to come had plagued him, now Bryce was more than glad he'd decided to head to Crescent Springs. Whether she had realized that she needed him before, he didn't know. But the way she held on to him now told him she would accept his presence, at least for the time being.

He eased away and gripped her arms. "I'm here for you."

In her eyes he could see that she didn't *want* to need him. He took a step back even as she did too. "See you at dinner?" he asked.

She nodded. "Okay. Sure."

"How about the Crescent Springs Café just across the street." That should be easy.

"It's going to be crowded." She shrugged. "We could eat here."

"We could. But then your father would hear our conversation."

She nodded. "Right. I don't necessarily want him to know all the danger I've had to face or am facing now. I haven't even told him the worst part about yesterday." She rubbed her arms. "I need him to know. He needs to be safe and remain cautious, but I know how much it will hurt him to learn all the details of what I went through before, and that it followed me here."

"I'll be praying for you," he said.

Her eyes widened. "Looks like you have a lot to share with me, then."

Right. He'd found God. Or rather God had found him since Sierra had left Boulder.

"So the café it is."

She smiled. "I'll call and let them know to save us a table. I'm friends with Miguel, the owner."

"Sounds good." He left her standing in the kitchen petting the gentle giant he'd given her four years ago. She'd remained in Boulder for three years. When Samson had been old enough she'd trained him for K-9 work. Just before Samson had become an official part of BPD, Sierra had moved to Crescent Springs. Bryce got the feeling that the timing wasn't a coincidence. Sierra hadn't wanted to put Samson in harm's way or lethal situations.

He headed out through the toy store and gave a small wave to her father and the young woman Bryce assumed was Jane. She didn't look a day over twenty. As he exited the toy store, he realized the anticipation he felt about tonight's dinner with Sierra felt so much like a date when it shouldn't. She'd hurt him before, and he knew Sierra well enough…she would hurt him again if given the chance. Regardless, Bryce was only here to keep her safe. Sierra was in danger. That he found himself wrapped up in protecting her against a Novack brother again seemed surreal. But he would see it through until the end.

If only he could shake the feeling that it wouldn't end well. They had survived the last time. Could they survive this time?

He hesitated before crossing the street and leaving the toy store. But he reassured himself that while Sierra was at the toy store and surrounded by people, she should be safe. He walked the growing crowds to see if he spotted any familiar or unwanted faces and called his old boss from the Boulder PD on his cell.

"Bryce." The man was breathless. Traffic resounded in the background. "Good to hear from you. Since the Novack brothers' escape, we've been trying to find out everything we can. Where are you?"

Three steps ahead of you. Bryce leaned against a storefront and watched the toy store across the street while he talked. "Crescent Springs, Colorado."

"Oh, you're staying close to Sierra then. You obviously know about the plane crash."

"Yes. And I'm here with her until this is over."

"Don't forget that you sent them to the penitentiary too. You could be in as much danger."

"I'm well aware of that, don't worry. But I don't think that I was their primary target since they headed straight for Crescent Springs."

"But now that you're there, it's easier for Raul to get at both of you. That said, I don't blame you for being concerned about her." A car door opened and shut. "You're a good man to make sure she's all right. I'll stay in close communication with Sheriff Locke there in Crescent Springs as the state and NTSB work through this so we're all on the same page. I don't need to tell you to watch Sierra's back, but please watch your own."

"I will, don't worry. I'm sure someone will spot Raul soon. He couldn't have lasted long in the elements so my guess is that he would have made the closest town."

"Crescent Springs."

"Which is hopping right now for a local ice festival. If he's hanging around, someone's going to see him."

"On the other hand," his old boss said, "he's smart enough to know that, with the plane crash, we're onto him. He might get as far away as he can rather than trying to get to Sierra."

"Whatever the case, let's hope he doesn't get to Sierra." The state was searching and local law had been called in, as well. Sierra wasn't out there searching for the criminal for obvious reasons. Bryce was glad that Sheriff Locke hadn't involved her.

"I'm with you. And Bryce? It's good to be working with you again. I wish you would have stayed with the BPD. You're always welcome to come back. We could always use another good detective."

"Thanks for the vote of confidence, Captain. I'll keep that in mind." At the very *back* of his mind. He ended the call.

Bryce leaned against the wall to watch the tourists entering the shops or merely window shopping.

Across the street, next to the toy store, he spotted a big man, his hood covering his face. The guy's build was the right size. He could be Raul.

Sierra appeared in the glass doorway of the store, stepped out onto the sidewalk and turned left to walk up the street. Where was she going?

His gut tensed. Bryce started across the street. The big man turned and walked away from the store as if to follow Sierra.

Bryce trailed him, picking up his pace. If this was Raul gunning for her, Bryce couldn't let him hurt Sierra. Nor could he let him get away.

The man increased his pace and headed directly for Sierra.

"Sierra! Watch out!" Bryce shouted but he wasn't sure if she could hear him over the bustling crowd and the traffic.

Sierra jerked around at the same moment the man was on her. He grabbed her, then threw her against the wall. He wielded a knife, but Sierra dodged his strike.

"Hey!" Bryce called out as he weaved through pedestrians and sprinted toward Sierra and her attacker.

The man jerked his attention to Bryce then threw Sierra down hard as if she was nothing but a rag doll. He pushed his way through the tourists to escape, bumping shoulders with people as he passed, and knocking a man and his child over.

Bryce caught up to Sierra and tried to help her to her feet.

"Go, get him!" She pointed. "I'll radio the sheriff."

Bryce ran after the man, but the attacker climbed onto a motorcycle and sped away. The chase wasn't over yet though. The traffic and tourists would slow the motorcycle and that would be Bryce's only chance of catching him. Bryce pushed himself, dashing between cars and people, shouting that he was coming through. The motorcycle turned right at the corner, away from the heavy traffic in the town's center. When Bryce made it to the corner, his legs slowed. He was good for a marathon but not for a sprint. Up ahead, he spotted the motorcycle speeding out of town.

There was only one main highway out of town, but there were numerous forest service roads. Bryce would never catch up to the man he suspected had to be Raul, but once notified, the Colorado State Patrol would ramp up their search. Bryce wanted to believe that Raul would be captured. The fact that the convict had stayed around the area this long knowing that law enforcement was searching for him didn't reassure Bryce about Sierra's safety.

Catching his breath, Bryce turned to make his way back to Sierra.

What would have happened if Bryce hadn't been there, watching the toy store when she was attacked? Would Raul have gotten the best of her despite her defensive efforts?

He couldn't bear it if something happened to her. Bryce would camp out at her place if that's what protecting her required. He had the feeling the hotel across the street might not be close enough.

THREE

That night Bryce had dinner with Sierra as planned, in spite of the events of the afternoon. In spite of Raul's attack on her in broad daylight. The guy had no fear.

That alone had shaken Bryce to his core, though he tried to hide that fact from Sierra. He'd also tried to dissuade her from dinner at the café.

"I won't let him ruin my life here," she'd said.

After chasing after Raul and failing to capture him, Bryce had found Sierra in her kitchen, calming her nerves by petting Samson.

And now here they sat across from each other in a booth, trying to pretend everything was normal. Trying, and failing.

He'd been relieved when the waiter took their barely eaten food away. Neither of them had much of an appetite, and in that way, Raul was succeeding in ruining her life, as she put it.

Add to that, here in the café, they were probably too exposed.

"I'll see you back home," he said. Maybe if he stuck close to her Raul wouldn't be so bold. And maybe law enforcement had chased him far from here after today.

In the meantime, he'd seen an increase in state law enforcement in town, adding to the county sheriff's meager presence. Sierra was as well protected as she could be.

But until he heard that the criminal had been caught, he would remain on high alert.

Nodding her agreement, she eased from the booth. "I'll need to take Samson for a walk. Want to come?"

"Of course. I wouldn't mind spending more time with him." He hitched a grin. "Oh, okay, and you too."

He kept the conversation light, but neither of them was feeling it. The heaviness of Raul's escape and pursuit of Sierra was pulling them both down.

"You know, walking Samson could be a problem if Raul is still here in town." Walking a dog was one of those daily routines that tended to follow a predictable pattern—and that could be dangerous, even if the dog was a massive K-9 mountain search dog.

"It's not like it can be helped." Her eyes glistened in the low lighting of the café. "Samson has to be walked."

"Maybe I can do that for you instead."

She shook her head. "I won't put you in danger like that."

He knew, like him, she hoped it would be over soon.

Sierra paused at the door to thank Miguel, the café owner. The man's smile and warm gaze told Bryce that he was interested in Sierra. Bryce swallowed the shard of jealousy that surged up his throat. Then he escorted her across the street and through the store. Samson's deep throaty bark could be heard through the walls.

"It's easier to go through the store than to walk all the way around the building and storefronts, through the alley and then back around, especially when the snow can get too deep and isn't always plowed or shoveled. It's a weird setup, I know. But living at the back of the store is super convenient for Dad."

In the living room, her father sat in a recliner and flicked through television programs.

Bryce peered through the blinds at the dark woods. The light coming from the windows chased away few shadows. "It's convenient, true, but it certainly isn't the best setup for your current situation."

Sierra grabbed the leash off the hook. "Good thing I've got my K-9 and my handgun."

Right. Good thing. "Better keep the gun with you at all times then." She certainly hadn't had it with her today.

She nodded, but didn't acknowledge his comment any further, turning to her father instead. "How was dinner?" she asked. To Bryce, she said, "He insisted on warming up leftovers—fried chicken tenders and green beans—in the microwave."

"Probably better than what you ate at that restaurant." Her father chuckled.

"Right. My cooking isn't the best, I know, Dad. But the café's food is definitely better." Sierra attached the leash to Samson's collar—more a formality than an actual restraint, due to Samson's size.

She started to open the back door. Bryce touched her arm and leaned in to whisper. "I think it's a good idea to avoid going out this back way for the foreseeable future." He wouldn't say more in front of Sierra's father. He wasn't sure how much she had shared with the man.

She frowned and nodded. "What was I thinking? You're right."

She led Bryce and Samson back through the storefront. She unlocked and then once again locked the door. Anxiety settled in his stomach. He shoved through the deepening snow and a snow berm to get to the plowed street. "I'll be here first thing in the morning to shovel this away so customers can get to you."

"It's a problem, to be sure."

Snowflakes coated them both but being with Sierra seemed to add warmth to Bryce's layers, despite the cold dread that coursed through him.

As they walked, keeping to the freshly plowed street as opposed to the un-shoveled sidewalk, he didn't want to break the silence but he needed to say the words. "Samson is a deterrent, but be cautious even when you're out walking him. His protection isn't foolproof."

"And yours is?" She arched her brow again.

He almost smiled at that—he'd missed seeing her feistiness on a regular basis.

"You know what I mean," he said. Someone bent on harming her could shoot Samson and then Sierra too.

"I didn't thank you for today. You distracted Raul, pulling his attention from me and then he ran from you. Not me. *You*. If you hadn't been there maybe I could have won the fight, but I can't be sure. Just like before, you were there in time, Bryce. I owe you. But today drove home that you're putting yourself in danger by being here." Sierra turned to him, her breath puffing out white clouds. Snowflakes clung to her lashes.

"Don't tell me that you're worried about me?" Okay, that was just plain wrong—it sounded like he was asking her to say how much he meant to her. He wasn't going to flirt with her.

Sierra didn't answer.

That's because she probably knew he didn't want

to know the real answer. Either way. He ignored the painful memories of their past and his attraction to her. Samson's low growl drew his attention to the animal and then the woods just beyond the line of buildings. He had suspected those woods were going to be a problem.

The beast continued his growl then barked.

"Easy, Samson," she said.

"Can you control him?" Bryce asked.

"Warten!" She commanded Samson to wait.

Sierra had used German words for her commands when she trained Samson because it was easier for Samson to differentiate the commands from her every day communications. The dog did as he was trained to do but he continued to growl.

"I'm going to check it out," Bryce said. "Get behind that nine-passenger van."

"Hier." Here, she commanded Samson. The dog whined then moved close to Sierra.

Sierra grabbed Bryce's arm and squeezed, tugging him back. "Bryce, be careful."

Her tone was intense, and something else in her voice told him she did still care deeply about him.

But neither of them would act on that, each having their own reasons.

Gunfire exploded.

The bullet whizzed by his ear even as he shoved Sierra to the ground. She held firm to Samson who wanted to take off. *"Nein!"*

"Sierra, we could use his help here." Bryce edged away from her, preparing to make a run for it and get this guy.

"I won't send him in there to be shot and killed," she said. "I've seen that happen before. I won't do it."

"Then don't. Let's take cover." They were still too exposed.

They crept behind a van they could use for a temporary barrier. Sierra kept her dog close. Bryce could breathe a little easier now that they had some protection—but they weren't out of danger yet. He didn't want to get pinned here. "Contact your sheriff and let him know we have an active shooter."

Sierra nodded and tugged out her cell. She wasn't wearing her radio. She spoke quickly into the cell letting dispatch know about the shooter at the edge of town. Good thing the festivalgoers were mostly at the other end of town near the vendor booths.

Bryce and Sierra had both pulled their weapons out. Another shot rang out and Samson was eager to work. If he weren't well trained, he would already have taken off.

"Cover me." Bryce prepared to dash across the street.

"No, wait!" Sierra whispered. "Don't go out there."

"This is our chance to get him, Sierra."

"You're not law enforcement anymore, Bryce. Remember? You can't arrest that guy even if you catch him. I'm the deputy sheriff. I need to come with you if you go."

Bryce wanted to give her a piece of his mind, but this wasn't the time. They'd have to work together then. As much as he didn't want her in the line of fire, he knew she wasn't going to back down.

Another shot rang out, this time from a different position. Pain stabbed through Bryce.

"Bryce!" Sierra shouted. Fear coursed through her. He'd been shot. Bryce stumbled back. Then grabbed his upper arm. He lifted his bloody hand to stare at the wound. "It's just a graze. I'm all right."

"How do you know that? You can't tell by looking at the blood on your hand."

He moved his arm, though with a grimace. "See? It's just a graze." They moved out of harm's way and he peered around the vehicle, his weapon at the ready.

"Well, the sheriff knows where we are, someone should be here soon." Sierra's voice shook.

"Stay here with Samson. You're not going with me. Raul wants you dead, remember? I don't need to worry about you or Samson getting shot."

Oh, that was a low blow. Bryce knew she would want to protect Samson.

"Does he have a command for guarding you?" Bryce asked.

"Of course he does. I'll be fine. I just need *you* to be safe too, Bryce."

Wind whipped around the vehicles and sliced through her like a frozen knife, and of course—the snow had to pick up.

And just like that, Bryce disappeared around the vehicle and ran across the street.

Grrrrr!

Sierra got on her cell again for dispatch. "Where's the sheriff? Is he on his way? Or a deputy or something. One of those state officers. Bryce is chasing after the shooter."

"Aren't *you* a deputy?"

"That's beside the point. I don't want to put Samson at more risk from a bullet by chasing after the shooter." She didn't use him as anything but a SAR dog. And sure, if someone broke into her home with intentions to harm her, then Samson was there to guard her, but that didn't mean she'd deliberately put him in harm's way. And yet, it didn't sit right to let Bryce face whoever was out there by himself. Apprehension warred inside—Sierra wasn't sure if she was doing the right thing.

"Sheriff's on his way."

"Okay. Tell him to hurry."

Samson yanked on his leash, pulled her away from the van. He wanted to follow Bryce to track and find the threat per his original K-9 training. That, and Samson was protective like any dog, wanting to neutralize the threat.

"Sitzen!" Samson followed her command and sat next to her, his huge form giving her warmth. *"Zei Brav,"* she said, then again in English: "Good boy."

After a few seconds ticked by, Sierra tightened her hold on Samson's leash. *"Hier.* Come on. I'm taking you home. I need to go after Bryce." Just what Bryce wouldn't want. "From now on, you're wearing your vest when we go out."

Because of his enormous size, Samson had to have a special vest created for him. That had been back in Boulder—over a year earlier. Now that she thought about it, his vest probably wouldn't fit him anymore. They made their way quickly down the street back toward the toy store. Only a few people were out visiting restaurants in this cold. The vendor exhibits still open were at the far end of town.

No one reacted as if they'd heard gunfire.

Samson barked again, letting her know his displeasure. He was well trained. Samson could track the shooter, but she knew what could happen to him as well.

Raul would shoot and kill Samson.

As for Bryce, she couldn't control him. He was a grown man—and he was fully trained in dealing with dangerous criminals. Samson couldn't shoot back or protect himself against a deadly bullet. She pushed through the deepening snow, heading back toward the toy store as fast as she could. And away from Bryce.

Lord, please, please keep him safe.

She didn't like that he'd run off from her, and later on she would scold him for it. But only after he was back and safe. She started around to the back, which was the entrance she usually took with Samson, then remembered the woods—the same woods Bryce had probably entered to find the shooter. She'd assured him she wouldn't take that route.

Sierra took Samson through the front of the toy store to the apartment in back and found Dad still watching his program. He glanced up at her. "That was a short walk. Did Bryce go back to his hotel?"

"Dad, didn't you hear those shots fired?"

He turned the television down. "What'd you say?"

Right. "Never mind. I have to go back out. Keep an eye on Samson for me, okay?"

"Always do."

Samson growled then barked at her. He wanted to come along. He nipped at her gloved hands as if he would keep her from going back outside without him. She pressed a kiss on his massive forehead. "You're a good boy. You know what's going on, don't you?"

Her weapon tucked away, she exited through the front, locking all doors behind her. The sheriff met her at the door. Great timing, but she nearly ran into him.

"I got the message about the shots fired. I couldn't find you so hoped you were back here," he said.

"Where's Bryce?" she asked.

"I didn't see him. Tell me what's happened."

"Walk with me while we talk." The snow was growing deep enough to slow them down, filling her with frustration. "Someone took a couple of shots at us while we were out walking the dog. Bryce went after the shooter."

"And you let him go by himself?"

"I tried to stop him. He wanted me to take Samson back home, which I did."

"The dog could find the shooter. Maybe take him down too."

"Yes, and the dog could also get shot and killed. I don't have Samson for these kinds of circumstances, Sheriff." Even though the fear of an attacker was the exact reason she'd wanted a big dog. "Samson is trained for mountain search and rescue."

In response, the sheriff merely offered her a severe frown. Clearly he didn't agree with the way she used her dog. Sierra didn't care what he thought.

Samson wasn't an employee of the sheriff's department. No one other than Sierra had any right to say what he should or shouldn't face.

She tugged her weapon out. She hoped the shooter hadn't taken Bryce out already. Her heart ached at the mere thought of it. And if Bryce got seriously injured out there—how much of the blame lay with her?

"Now are you going to help me then?" she asked. "Because I'm not sitting this one out."

Sheriff Locke readied his own weapon. "That, I am."

FOUR

Bryce continued following the footsteps through the nearly thigh-deep snow. With the way the snow was falling, soon the tracks left behind would be completely gone.

The snow was to his knees, and hip-deep in some places. He tried to step into the shooter's steps to ease his efforts, but it was still slow going. Without snowshoes, he had no hope of picking up the pace, and this kind of exertion was going to exhaust him too quickly. He wasn't out of shape but navigating the snow-covered rocky terrain took all his effort and focus.

Bryce stopped to catch his breath and take in his surroundings. It was pitch black out here. The only illumination came from the town lights that reflected from the clouds. That reflection helped him to see the way, but it wasn't nearly enough to let him track down the man who had shot him.

What was Bryce doing out here?

This seemed like a suicide mission.

Standing beneath the low-hanging branches of a spruce tree, he considered his options. If he didn't silence his gasps for breath they would give him away—

that is, if someone was watching and waiting for the chance to take Bryce out. Except Bryce had no doubt the shooter had come for Sierra specifically and taking Bryce out would simply be a bonus.

Anger coiled in his gut. He couldn't let Raul get to Sierra. His efforts might fall short, but he wouldn't stop trying.

He drew in a sharp, cold breath. Bryce wouldn't give up so easily.

Even though Raul wasn't the typical perp.

Shoving from the spruce tree, Bryce continued following the tracks before it was too late and the shooter was gone for good.

He pushed harder and hiked farther than he thought he could. Finally the snow clouds thinned, allowing the moon to illuminate the forest into an eerie, foreboding scene.

Glancing back, Bryce noticed Crescent Springs was growing smaller. He was putting himself in danger by going deeper into the cold without proper clothing. He wasn't prepared to face off against the elements.

But he'd only been thinking about getting his hands on Raul, ending this once and for all so Sierra could be safe.

He caught a glimpse of the mountains that stood watch over the small tourist town. Bryce flexed his cold fingers in both hands to shake the stiffness away. He wished he'd worn ski bibs instead of jeans layered with thermals. He hadn't thought through what having dinner with Sierra would look like—and he certainly hadn't expected the evening to end this way, with Raul taking a shot at her.

Bryce should have been better prepared.

Regardless, he couldn't stay out here much longer.

The clack of tree trunks rustling with the wind drew his attention to the south. A crunching sound followed. Was Raul pushing on too now that he knew Bryce would follow?

Frustration boiled through him and warmed him—good.

Just a little farther. *God, the tracks are here for me to follow. Help me find this guy before he hurts Sierra!*

He allowed the hot anger to fuel his steps.

A shadow moved in the trees ahead of him.

Yes!

Bryce was catching up. His weapon ready, he prepared to pull the trigger.

He aimed at the silhouette of a man in the trees. "Stop, police!"

Only he wasn't the police anymore. Old habits die hard.

His prey fled deeper into the woods. He was so close! Bryce would get his hands on Raul. Adrenaline pushed him farther and deeper.

A force slammed into his body. The breath whooshed from him. He crashed face-first into the biting snow that rushed into his mouth and nose.

Bryce fought for purchase, grappling with the snow. Reaching for something, anything, to push the weight from him. He twisted around to face the barrel of a weapon.

Reflex kicked in.

Bryce rolled as gunfire blasted into the space where he'd been mere seconds before. Using his training, he knocked the weapon from the man's hand. Kicked his attacker to the ground as he twisted away and scrambled to his feet, despite the snow impeding his efforts. Bryce searched, digging through the snow and found his weapon. Gasping for breath, he shoved the fear down.

Aiming his weapon, he turned in a circle looking for Raul.

No.

No, no, no.

Bryce had lost him. He'd fled into the night again. Bryce could follow the tracks farther, but the cold was making him numb and slowing both his moving and thinking. Grousing that he'd let the man get the best of him and get away on top of it, he decided to follow the footprints left behind. The cold seeped through his inadequate clothes all the way to his bones. From now on, he'd dress for unexpected treks through snow on cold winter nights. Maybe even drag snowshoes around with him so he'd be prepared.

He took one more step.

A crack resounded directly under his feet—a familiar and terrifying sound.

He stilled and listened. Gurgling water. A river? A stream? Whatever it was, he'd just stepped on the thin layer of ice covering moving water—thin and dangerous.

Another crack and then his foot plunged into the icy water.

Sierra heard the snap and the plunge into water that came after.

Oh, no!

"Bryce!" she shouted.

Gasping for breath, she pushed forward through the snow, following his tracks. She'd seen a man standing there not fifteen yards away through the trees. She had just decided it was Bryce at the moment he'd stepped on the ice.

Now she couldn't see him at all. "We have to hurry!" she shouted to the sheriff who trailed her.

"Bryce, I'm coming." She pushed faster, breathing cold hair into her lungs.

"We're on our way!" Sheriff Locke shouted. "Hold on!"

Holding on when you fell into a frozen river wasn't always an option. *Oh, Lord, please let us reach him in time!*

She hiked as fast as she could, wishing she could push faster. "Answer me, Bryce!"

Another splash of water resounded.

"No!" Sierra cried out.

Then she was at the river that weaved through these woods. It was wide and deep enough to be lethal.

Bryce was clinging to a frozen branch as more ice gave away again beneath him. He held tight...for now. She knew that he would soon succumb to hypothermia and would no longer be able to hold himself up on that branch.

"Stay back." His voice was commanding, but she heard the hint of fear. The shivering in his words.

That sound shook her to the core.

"No." She crawled along the thick snow-covered branch and scooted along until she reached him. The sheriff found a boulder nearby so he wouldn't risk stepping through the ice. Together they hefted Bryce up and out of the river.

They dragged him away from the riverbank.

"Are you okay?" she asked. "Scratch that. It's a stupid question. Let's get you back."

He wasn't out of danger yet.

Shivering, he gasped for breath. "Thank you. But you shouldn't—"

"Let's get you back." Sheriff Locke's voice was authoritative. No nonsense.

As was Sierra. "Of course we should have. Now, let's go and get you warm."

"But he's still out there. Raul is still out there." Bryce teeth chattered. "I can't let him get to you."

What was it about Bryce that made him feel personally responsible for protecting her from Raul? It confounded her and warmed her heart at the same time. But she needed to stick to the no-nonsense attitude. Experience had taught her it was the best way to push past his stubbornness.

"I'll get more deputies," the sheriff offered. "We'll follow the tracks until we find him, Bryce. In the meantime, you're going to freeze to death if you don't get out of those clothes."

"Sheriff Locke," she said. "It's too treacherous to go after Raul at night. You see what happened to Bryce. He almost got swept away in the river. You can't send deputies out there after him."

The sheriff growled. "I'll let the state boys know and we'll see if they want to join in the search tonight. He's too close to let get away. We all know the risks. Leaving him out there is also a risk."

"I agree. That's a big risk to Sierra." Bryce forced the words out through his shivers.

Sierra didn't want to argue with the two of them. They had a point, but the danger was real to anyone who was going to search for him in this terrain on a cold snowy night.

She kept her mouth shut as they hiked the rest of the way back to town, Bryce between them. His legs weren't moving too well—numb and cold—and he was unstable on his feet.

What if they hadn't followed him? What then? Bryce would have died out there tonight.

"Are you sure it was Novack?" Sheriff Locke finally asked.

"I fought with him. But I didn't get a look at his face. It was too dark and happened too fast. But it must have been the same man who attacked Sierra today in town. Who else could it have been tonight?" Bryce's words slurred as his body grew colder. "I shouldn't have let him get the best of me."

"Need I remind you that you're not law enforcement? You should have waited on me and my men or the state officers in town."

"Do we have to talk about this now?" Sierra asked. She wanted to get Bryce somewhere warm before it was too late and frostbite took his legs or worse. The sheriff could wait until later to dress him down. But he seemed to disagree as he continued his scolding.

"You can't go chasing people through the woods and think you're going to detain them."

"I might not have the power of the law behind a badge," Bryce said again through chattering teeth. "But you can bet I'll detain them."

Sheriff Locke finally chuckled. "At least you're single-minded. I wouldn't stand in your way, honestly. Just doing my duty to remind you to keep it legal. I can't really say I object to you trying to keep our town safe. My department is spread thin with this ice festival. And we certainly don't need a shooter scaring off tourists from our one claim to fame."

Sierra thought they would never make it to the toy store. The cold had seeped into her bones so much her hands shook as she fumbled to unlock the door.

"I think we should get him to the clinic," Sheriff Locke suggested.

"They're not open this late."

"They are with the festival. Let Doc make sure he's okay."

"I'm fine, I'm fine. I just need to get warm." He started to cross the street.

"Where do you think you're going?" she asked.

"To my hotel room."

She grabbed him and swung him back around. "Oh, no, you don't. Not until I've made sure you're going to be okay."

The sheriff took this opening to back away. "Call me if you need anything, Sierra. I'm going to let the other agencies know about what happened tonight. We might start combing the woods soon. But you stay here. I don't want you out there. Understand?" He gave her a pointed look.

"Sure." She focused back on Bryce as the sheriff left them.

"I'm soaked through," he said. "I need new clothes and those are in my room at the hotel."

Despite his protests, he let her lead him through the store and into the back apartment.

She ushered him next to the fireplace. "Dad has a pair of pants you can borrow while we dry those," she said. "And I'm going to take a look at your arm. If it's more than a graze, then you are going to the clinic after all. Do you hear me?"

Bryce said nothing. Concern crawled over her. She should force him to go see a doctor anyway.

Dad rose from the recliner. Samson sniffed Bryce and released a low groan.

"What happened?" Dad asked. "Don't tell me you—"

"He took a tumble, that's all," she said and gave Dad a warning look.

"You don't need to sugarcoat it," Bryce said. "I fell through the ice."

Dad's eyes widened. "You—"

"Dad. Will you please get Bryce some clothes?"

Dad nodded. "All right. Can you follow me?"

"Sure," Bryce said through gritted teeth.

Was he trying to hide the chattering?

Dad led him upstairs to his bedroom. Now that both men were out of sight, Sierra collapsed into a chair, pressed her face into her arms on the table.

"Oh, Lord," she whispered. Raul was in town and closing in. He was after her.

Samson nudged her and whined. She weaved her fingers through his fur and held on tight. Held on for dear life. Would this ever end?

If and when it did, would she survive? Would the people around her get hurt—or even killed? Bryce shouldn't be here putting himself in harm's way for her. Somehow she needed to find the strength to push him away for his safety, and that of her heart.

FIVE

Sierra's dad had laid out a few pairs of jeans and shirts on the bed for Bryce to try. Bryce held the clothes up and looked at them. They would do. His limbs, hands and feet were finally starting to feel normal again, though he still shivered. He wished he could take a hot shower first. That's why he'd wanted to go back to his own room.

Woulda. Coulda. Shoulda.

But he took Sierra's urging him along with her into her own home as a sign that she didn't want him to leave her. He shared the sentiment. Raul was still out there. He'd come close again tonight. More worrisome was that Raul had made two attempts on her life in one day.

That would be enough to set anyone on edge.

Sierra wanted protection though she wouldn't admit it. And it certainly seemed like they were safer when they were together. She'd saved him—pulled him from the icy river. She and Sheriff Locke—for which Bryce was grateful.

It was like before. Bryce and Sierra had saved each other.

He shook off the ruminations, the reassurances that

he was doing the right thing by staying, and focused on getting ready and back out there to protect Sierra.

In the bathroom in John's room, Bryce washed up the bullet graze and found bandages in the cabinet. A couple of millimeters in the wrong direction and he would have needed a medical professional's attention. He could only be grateful it hadn't come to that—that he hadn't been left with an injury that would take a long while to treat or heal, something for which he had no time. He couldn't get distracted.

His coat had been ripped so he'd need to patch it or replace it soon.

Finished dressing, a look in the mirror told him what he already knew—his lips were a little blue, and he was still much too cold.

A knock came at the door. "How you doing in there?" John asked.

"I'm almost done. Coming out."

He opened the door.

Crossing his arms, John eyed him. "Sierra made some hot chocolate. Go sit by the fire. She said you're not going anywhere tonight. I don't know if that's because she wants to make sure you're not going to die from hypothermia, or if it has to do with the gunshots she mentioned earlier. Sooner or later, one of you is going to tell me what's going on. I try not to interfere because she's a deputy here and was law enforcement back in Boulder. My girl can take care of herself, but there's something more going on this time. Sooner rather than later, I'll need some answers."

"That's a deal." Bryce followed him downstairs where he took a seat next to the fireplace and let the warmth wash over him. Finally. Comfort.

Exhaustion warred with his need to remain on high alert. He spotted the English mastiff sitting like a sentinel near the back door that opened up to those woods. Anger burrowed deeper at the thought of Raul, still out there—getting the upper hand and getting away. Bryce wanted to go back out and track through those woods again until he hauled Raul in, but Bryce knew his limits. He was in no condition to do anything else for now. The sheriff made mention of others looking for Raul tonight. He hoped they brought their own tracking dogs and made short work of it, considering that Sierra wouldn't put Samson out there for the task.

As for Samson sitting next to the door as if guarding it, Bryce understood how the dog felt. He wanted to do the same. Right now, the hotel room across the street felt entirely too far from Sierra so he was glad she'd wanted him to stay.

She approached and offered him a mug. He took it and felt the warmth, letting it seep into his palms. Sierra eased into the comfy seat across from him.

Neither of them spoke for a few moments. He must have freezer brain because he couldn't formulate any words. He fought the need to drift off to sleep. He was here with Sierra. He would stay awake for this moment with her.

She peered closely at him. "You're looking better. Your color has improved. I wish you would have let me take you to the clinic."

"You're right. I'm better." Being here with her was all he needed.

"What about the gunshot wound? Was it a graze like you said?"

"Yep. I bandaged it up. I promise, if I need a doctor or the hospital, you'll be the first to know."

Her smile told him she liked what he'd said. She turned her attention to the fire for a few moments, then looked back at him.

"Go ahead and sleep," she said softly. "Samson's here. He'll warn us if anyone gets close. Besides, I don't think Raul is going to try anything tonight."

"Why not?"

"He's only human, Bryce. He was running from you. He has to be numb with cold too. He needs time to recover. I wonder where he went? Does he have some hideout? Some cabin out there? Maybe he got on a snowmobile and took off and is miles away by now. Who knows. But while you were upstairs, I talked to Sheriff Locke. He said the state will be bringing in dogs again tomorrow. It takes time to get fresh and rested dogs here—unfortunately, this terrain wears them down quickly. But until they arrive, law agencies are all on high alert. So for tonight, Bryce, I think we're as safe as we're going to be."

He wished he could fully trust in that. Then again, this might be the last decent rest he got for a good long while, and he needed to make the most of it so he could be at his best. "I should go back to—"

"No. You can sleep on the sofa right there. For tonight. You and Samson. I know you won't sleep if you're not here."

"You know me that well, do you?"

Her eyes shimmered in the firelight and an emotion he couldn't quite pin down surfaced in her gaze. His heart melted a little.

"I do, actually." She kept her voice low. "I know you have a protective nature."

Sierra held his gaze for a few heartbeats, then she suddenly stood and broke the moment. "I'll bring down some bedding. Sheets, a pillow and comforter. Samson will stand guard."

Funny that she'd let Samson do that now when she sure hadn't wanted him tracking a shooter. But Bryce understood that. It was the whole reason she'd broken things off with Bryce to begin with.

She didn't want anyone else she loved getting killed.

After getting ready for bed, Sierra fluffed her pillows so she could sit up and read her Bible, hoping the comfort of the words would wipe out the events of the day. Her Bible fell open to Second Samuel and she started reading the prophet, her gaze holding at chapter twenty-two, verse three. "The God of my rock; in Him will I trust: He is my shield, and the horn of my salvation, my high tower, and my refuge, my savior. Thou savest me from violence."

The words were just what she needed to read, what her heart needed to hear. She closed her eyes and meditated on the scripture.

You've saved me from violence before, God. Please save me from Raul.

She hated that the man's proximity could set her on edge and fill her with fear.

Sierra wanted to trust God to save her, but images of Raul wouldn't leave her mind. She set her Bible down and turned off the bedside lamp, then she crept to the window to peer out at the street below. Her second-floor room was right above the toy store so she looked out onto Main Street. At this hour a few street lamps stood lonely in the night illuminating snow piled high in the street and on the sidewalk. Early in the morning a snowplow would wake her up, creating berms along the sidewalk. She would need to get out there and shovel it away so potential customers could get to the store.

Dad had pulled her aside after she'd left Bryce downstairs with Samson. Her father had wanted full disclosure about what was going on, and she'd shared what she could without including the sordid details. Just that someone she'd put away was trying to get to her.

Seeing the pain on his face had nearly done her in. On the other hand, she needed to tell him so he could be on alert. It was one thing to be attacked in Boulder. Quite another to have the Novack brothers come here to her home. What if Damien had survived and both brothers had come after her and caught her off guard? Dad could have gotten hurt too. Anyone close to her.

A chill crept over her and she rubbed her arms.

Sierra climbed back in bed and thought back to Bryce's face tonight as he sat by the fire. She'd always found him attractive and so caring. He'd come here for her.

For me...

Why did he still have to care?

She didn't want him to be caught in the crossfire of Raul's attempt to get at her. Sierra was scared for Bryce. As scared for him as she was herself, Dad and anyone else close to her.

She knew how to stay safe and now she had a guard dog that weighed more than the average man. But Sierra didn't want Samson hurt either.

God, what do I do?

She wasn't only confused about the dangerous situation. Bryce walking back in her life stirred all sorts of long-buried feelings in her heart. She wanted him here, and yet she wished he hadn't shown up.

She'd gone to a lot of trouble to put both time and distance between them.

Her reasons for coming back home and leaving Boulder behind were many. Dousing the remnants of feelings for Bryce was among those reasons. Did he know that?

An image of an exhausted Bryce relaxing in the chair by her fire stayed with her much too long, until finally she felt herself dozing and she allowed sleep to take her.

There was a noise. A subtle nuance, or a feeling, she wasn't sure, but something stirred her from a deep sleep. She blinked her eyes open. Turned her head to the right. The clock on the table read 2:30 a.m. She slowly reached toward the drawer in the bedside table where she kept her Boulder PD–issued weapon—a Glock 22. She slowly and quietly slid the drawer open and reached in. She felt no cold plastic against her fingers. She felt around the drawer. Her pulse jumped.

Her gun was gone.

Heart pounding, she pushed up from the bed. She always put the gun right there in the side table and now it was missing. What was going on? In her mind she retraced her steps last night. Exhausted, she'd dragged herself to bed much too late and after a little while of tossing and turning, she'd taken something to help her fall asleep. And yes...she'd put her Glock in the drawer like always.

Alarms resounded in her head. Realization dawned as fear corded her neck and tightened, choking her.

She had to breathe. Had to get air.

Someone was in her apartment.

Had that someone taken her weapon?

She grabbed her cell to call 911 and slipped over to the corner to get the baseball bat she kept there. It was her dad's weapon of choice and had been her protection for many years. That training had never left her. She reached for the bat to slip her fingers around the slender neck.

Arms grabbed her from behind and squeezed hard.

A raspy voice whispered in her ear. "You put my brother away and now you're going to pay."

What to do. What to do. Push away the panic. Stay calm. *"I don't know what you're talking about."*

"Damien Novack is my brother. He asked me to take care of you."

Sierra twisted out of his grip only to look down the muzzle of a gun. Her gun. It was loaded, too—she knew because she kept it loaded. The gun was of no use without bullets. And it was of no use to her in someone else's hands. She could think about her failures later. Right now, she had to survive.

"What... What do you want?" A stupid question to extend her life only a few moments more. She knew what he'd come for.

Raul punched her in the face. Dazed, she couldn't respond as he threw her onto the bed. He aimed her own weapon at her. She rolled as he pulled the trigger, the sound firing off in her ears, hammering forever in her head.

Sierra shot up in bed, a noise startling her awake. Gasping for breath she saw the lamp on the floor. Had she knocked it off? Was that the noise she'd heard? She couldn't be sure. She reached for her weapon.

Her door burst open and she screamed. Bryce and her father rushed in, both of them wielding weapons. Air whooshed from her. Samson rushed into the room, a vicious warning bark escaping his maw. She reached for him and his wet tongue licked her face. "Shh. It's okay."

"Are you all right?" Bryce lowered his weapon.

"Yes. It was just… It was just a nightmare."

A vivid memory from that night. She'd never been the same.

"All right. Somebody want to tell me what's going on? And I mean the whole truth this time."

Oh, Dad…

SIX

Bryce put his weapon away and exhaled. He scraped his hand over his eyes. He wanted to rush to Sierra and hold her, but he held back. Instead he locked gazes with her.

Understanding passed between them and he read it clearly in her eyes—she'd had a nightmare about Raul and what had happened the night that he had broken into her home and accosted her. Raul had targeted her because she'd been instrumental in securing Damien's incarceration, with a life sentence.

What Bryce couldn't know was if she'd been having this same nightmare all along since that night years ago. Or had recent events triggered the nightmare tonight?

He could understand if they had.

But hearing her scream when he'd finally nodded off had been like a stab to his heart. He could have died from a heart attack at the panic he'd felt before he'd gotten upstairs to her room. It didn't help that he'd been in the middle of his own dream. He couldn't recall the details only that it had left him disturbed.

John stared at them both now, waiting for an explanation. Bryce wasn't at liberty to share more than Sierra wanted her father to know.

"I'll leave you two alone," he said. "Come on, Samson."

Samson understood Bryce's command, but he didn't seem happy about it. The dog whined and refused to budge. He was loyal to Sierra not Bryce.

Bryce looked at Sierra. "You want him to stay? You might feel safer with him in the room with you."

"I'd feel safer if Samson was guarding the entryways." Sierra sighed and urged Samson to leave with Bryce. "*Aus…* Out, Samson." She stood and urged Samson out the door with Bryce, leaning out the door to whisper, "I guess I'll have that talk with Dad now."

Bryce nodded. "I can stay if you like."

"It's okay." Grief filled her eyes, concern for her father's reaction obviously overshadowing any remnants of the terror her nightmare had ushered in.

The bedroom door shut. Bryce stared down at Samson. The dog's massive forehead was wrinkled as if he was worried about John's reaction too. Bryce rubbed the dog behind the ears. "I know, boy, I know. Let's go downstairs to make sure the bogeyman doesn't get in."

He followed Samson as the big dog plodded down the steps. On the first floor, Bryce checked the windows and the doors to make sure all remained locked, then poured himself a glass of milk. Samson's water bowl was filled with water, so Bryce poured milk in a separate small bowl for Samson too.

While he finished off the milk and Samson lapped his up, Bryce thought back to the years Sierra spent raising and training Samson for work as a K-9. Strange how things had unfolded—that despite all of Samson's training, she was afraid to put him in harm's way.

The milk finished, Bryce washed up the glass and bowl, and then he sat back on the sofa and gave Samson some more petting and attention. At the same time, he thought about the conversation Sierra was having with her father, and prayed for that discussion to go well. Her father had to realize as a police officer and then a detective, Sierra had faced some life-threatening situations. But how would he react to the severity of the danger facing her now?

The big dog tried to sneak up onto the sofa with Bryce. His size wouldn't allow for that. From the guilty look on the animal's face, Bryce was sure that Sierra had trained him to stay off the furniture.

"You think you can get away with it because I'm a softy?" Bryce rubbed Samson's ears and prevented his slow climb onto the couch. Samson finally settled on the floor at Bryce's feet.

Bryce had almost nodded off when Sierra appeared at the bottom of the stairs and drew his attention.

"You're still up." She came all the way into the small space. "The fire is almost out."

She bent to grab more logs.

"Leave it. It's fine. Tell me. How did it go?" He ran his hand through his hair.

Samson was spread out on the floor now and sighed.

She crossed her arms. Instead of moving closer or sitting on the sofa next to him or the chair, she kept her distance. "As you would expect. He was angry and hurt about the whole thing."

She swiped at her cheeks. "I'd wanted to protect him from all that. I'd wanted to escape to a more peaceful way of life and now Raul has brought the fear and chaos here to Crescent Springs." Anger edged her tone.

Bryce understood just how she felt. He hated that this had happened. It was why he'd wanted to catch up to Raul tonight. If he had, maybe this would all be over, and Sierra and John could get back to their lives. "Sierra, I need to talk to you about something. I don't want to keep you up too late, but now seems like the right time."

"I don't think I'm going to go to sleep anytime soon anyway." She finally eased into the chair across from the sofa. "What's wrong?"

"It's not so much that anything's wrong, but tonight, when someone was shooting at us, you wanted to protect Samson. I understand that. But he's a big dog. He's trained to do many things—including protect. Remember you trained him to become part of the new BPD's K-9 unit. Tonight you were afraid to let him protect you or to let him go after Raul." He wasn't telling her anything she didn't already know.

He wanted to better understand her reasons.

Sierra stared into the dying embers as though gathering her thoughts, or softening angry words she might have said. "I just couldn't put him in danger, Bryce. I know it sounds ludicrous. Maybe I should have let him go. I'm sorry. I put you in greater danger instead."

"It's all right. That's not why I'm bringing it up. I'd just like to understand."

"Samson and I trained with another dog—a German shepherd named Jackson—and his handler, Officer Kimmie Tombs. We worked hard with them and learned so much." Then the tears came and she once again swiped at her face. "Jackson become a K-9. He and Kimmie were called upon that very first week that he was official. He... Jackson was shot and killed."

Sierra looked at him then.

Bryce understood better now. He'd known about this, of course, but not how much it affected her. "It was that next week you resigned."

"And moved to Crescent Springs."

Samson stirred and sat up, then shifted his big head over to Sierra. She grabbed him around his neck to hug him. "Here he works as a SAR dog only and we train every day. Twice a month we get with other handlers and their mountain rescue dogs for training. It's been good for both of us. He's still useful, still helping people—just not in the way we thought he would back then."

She pulled Samson's face up to look at her. His big tongue lolled as drool spilled out both sides of his mouth. Sierra wiped it away with one of the drool towels she kept on the side table. "He loves it here. You love it here, don't you, boy?"

He barked.

Sierra chuckled. "Shh. Don't wake Dad. I hope he could even fall asleep after what I told him. But now he'll appreciate Samson that much more."

Not if Sierra didn't allow the dog to protect her.

Her gaze slid to Bryce. "We won't let Raul come after us or cause us to live in fear, Bryce. We're going to find him and bring him in."

"We are?"

"Yes. You, me—and yes, Samson. We'll go out and search for him. We know these mountains pretty well, don't we, Samson?"

"That could be dangerous, Sierra. Raul is after you.

That might be just what he wants—for you to come out after him."

"Better than letting him come here and get me. We'll have the element of surprise as our advantage."

While he liked the way she thought, it didn't make his self-appointed task of protecting her easier.

The next morning Sierra struggled to stay alert as she helped her father get ready to open up the store. She set up the cash drawer in the register while he arranged building block sets from a shipment they'd received last week. They were so behind!

She yawned and rubbed her eyes, unsure if they would ever catch up. But she could do only so much. What would have happened to the store if she hadn't come to help Dad last year? He was too stubborn to hire more help than Jane, thinking he could do it all himself. When Sierra had come home for a week to visit him after the K-9 dog Jackson had been killed, she'd been devastated and brought Samson to Crescent Springs. When she got there, boxes of toys were actually in the aisles, left there to be dealt with who knew when. Add to that, Dad couldn't seem to balance the drawer at the end of the day. He wasn't worried about it, but Sierra had been. That week-long visit had been the nudging she'd needed to leave Boulder. Leave it all behind. That's when she'd decided to stay.

Save Samson from a similar fate to Jackson.

Help Dad with the store.

Dad needed help and Sierra had needed a big change.

A grunt from the aisle brought her attention back to the present. She should finish up the drawer and help Dad with those boxes.

This afternoon she was on deputy duty. What task would the sheriff assign her given the ongoing ice festival? She'd been here in Crescent Springs as a deputy during the last festival. A couple of guys had gotten rowdy after too much to drink—spectators rather than participants—but other than that one incident, things had gone smoothly.

Sierra sighed and shoved the cash register closed. Her hands trembled. She stared at them. Squeezed them closed. Opened them. Squeezed. Opened.

Still shaking.

The nightmare last night had prevented much-needed sleep and set her on edge when she needed to stay sharp until Raul was behind bars once again. Instead, she was irritable and cranky. And Dad had hardly spoken to her this morning.

After all, she'd told him the whole story last night.

She wasn't sure if he was upset with her or just needed time to process what had happened in his own way. As for Bryce, he'd insisted on taking Samson for his morning walk, and had returned the dog already, before leaving her at the store with her father so he could head across the street to his hotel room to shower and dress.

All of this before the store opened. Jane should be here at any moment to help.

Sierra moved to the storage room to bring a few more boxes of toys out. She hefted a box and tried to maneuver through the door but failed and the box toppled, spilling fidget toys everywhere. Sierra pressed her forehead against the wall and groaned.

The Novack brothers' escape and plane crash had

certainly turned her world upside down, and now she wasn't sure which end was up.

She knelt and reloaded the toys in the box as she thought about Bryce. She'd been stunned to see him in the store yesterday. His sudden reappearance in her life left her confused. After all, she'd put enough time and distance between them with her move from Boulder to Crescent Springs, she should have doused any remnants of feelings she had for him.

Maybe if he'd stayed away, those feelings could have lain buried forever, but it was as though they had simply been dormant and all it had taken was his presence for them to stir back to life.

For a few moments last night she'd watched him sitting on the sofa dozing, Samson at his feet, as the fire died. Warm sensations and longing had flooded her. She would be the first one to admit that she was definitely missing that kind of warmth in her everyday life, but she'd denied herself that relationship with him because of the danger. She wouldn't love a cop or anyone in a dangerous line of work again.

Sierra hefted the refilled box of fidget toys on her hip and lugged the merchandise through the store in search of Dad.

The sound of boxes toppling caught her attention. "Dad?" she moved to the left of the store. Boxes had spilled into the main aisle. "Dad. You okay?"

"Yep," he grumbled from behind a display. "Sorry."

"No reason to be sorry. I dropped this box all over the floor just a minute ago. Looks like we're both having the same kind of morning." She set her box down and blew out a breath. "We could wait until Jane gets here. She can arrange the toys and stock the shelves."

"I can do it." He didn't even look at her. Just started picking up the toys. So he was upset with her after all.

Sierra couldn't take it. "Dad, I'm sorry, okay? I'm sorry I didn't tell you. I just wanted to spare you. Please don't be mad at me. It just makes everything that much worse."

She helped him gather all the toys and stack the boxes in silence. Then Dad straightened to his full height, finally looking her in the eyes. "I'm not mad at you. Not anymore. I just wish I could help protect you. I feel…helpless."

Sierra started to reach for him, grab him up in a hug. She needed to know things were okay between them, but the door jingled, startling them both. Hadn't he locked the door after Bryce left for his hotel earlier?

Oh, Dad… She wanted to comfort him. "We'll talk more about this later," she whispered.

She started to move, but he grabbed her arm. "Let me see who it is first."

Sierra frowned and shook her head. "You—" Then she caught herself. If this was what he needed to feel like he was protecting her, then she wouldn't deny him.

Dad stepped from the aisle as if he would defend her from an attacker. She told herself that there wasn't really anything to worry about. Raul wouldn't actually walk through the front door of a toy store to come for her… Would he?

A chill ran over her. She heard the footfalls but could see Dad's shoulders relax.

"Who is it, Dad?" She hoped it wasn't a customer. The store wasn't due to open for another half an hour and she sure needed that to compose herself.

"Morning, Sheriff." Dad left her standing in the aisle while he stepped forward to greet her boss.

"Morning. I need to see Sierra."

Dad turned to stare at her where she'd remained in the aisle. "Any news on that escaped convict?"

"That's what I came to talk about."

She spotted a fidget toy they'd missed, and grabbed it and held on to it. Maybe she could use it to keep herself awake, despite the fatigue digging deeper into her bones. Sierra moved to the counter. Sheriff Locke was making his way toward her.

His gaze landed on her.

He looked her up and down, taking her in, and she didn't think he'd missed the look of a woman who hadn't slept much. The sheriff frowned. "Where's your bodyguard?"

"Samson's barking in the back, don't you hear him?"

"Samson should be up here with you. Wherever you are, keep the dog with you. But I wasn't referring to Samson."

"Oh, you mean Bryce." Had the sheriff figured she knew whom he'd meant to begin with? "Sheriff, I don't need a bodyguard. I'm trained law enforcement, which you already know."

"Even a trained law enforcement officer is vulnerable with a target on her back. I don't want to feel like I neglected one of my deputies, but you know the ice festival is our busy time so between you and me, I'm glad he's here for you. Take advantage of that."

She sighed. "With law enforcement coming down around these mountains to look for Raul, surely he'll be caught soon."

"For all our sakes I hope you're right."

"Where could he possibly hide?" The question sounded ridiculous. She risked a look at the sheriff.

He'd arched a brow and she sent him a wry grin. The San Juan Mountains region was filled with millions of acres of forest, old mining camps and probably a few deserted cabins. No one knew that better than her and Samson. But Raul didn't know this area. Could he find his way around that and hide well? She doubted it.

"You said you'd come by to talk about Raul. Do you have any news?"

"Only that the dogs are here." He frowned and scraped his hand over his mouth. "That is, dogs to track the fugitive. In the meantime, I had hoped I could convince you to take some time off. Go on vacation. Leave Crescent Springs."

Sierra couldn't withhold her stunned look.

"At least until this is over, of course."

"You can't be serious." Samson nearly knocked her over as the dog rushed from their private apartment in back. Dad closed the door and gave the sheriff a smile and a nod. He'd let the dog up into the store. Sierra groaned. Samson was massive and the shelves were heavily stocked. Just one walk down the aisle could end in disaster.

Giving herself a reprieve from the two sets of human eyes pinned on her, she squatted to rub Samson's head and behind his soft floppy ears, focusing her attention on him. Was the sheriff right? Should she leave town? She didn't want to bring danger here to Crescent Springs.

Frustration boiled to the surface, but before hot tears could spill out Samson licked her. She wiped her face with her sleeve. Then finally she stood to face the two men who seemed to be staring her down.

"Look. Maybe I ran from Boulder." Sure she'd used the store and her father's need of help as her excuse, but she knew the real reason. "I'm here now. And I'm not running again. Staying here is the right thing to do. I can't let Raul think he has me running scared." She hoped the men understood. "I won't let what happened in Boulder force me from Crescent Springs as well. You've got my back, Sheriff."

"And the people of this town have got your back too," Dad said. She appreciated his support. At the very least, *he* understood.

Concern for the tourist population that came for the snow sports and ice climbing competition skittered through her, but Raul was here for *her*. Not them.

"Good. That settles it then. I'm staying here in Crescent Springs. For the short-term and the long haul."

"Fine, but you're off duty until this is over and Raul is caught. I don't want you facing off with him under any circumstance if that can be avoided."

Her jaw dropped. A few breaths passed before she composed herself. "Why, Sheriff? You said yourself that we're stretched thin with the festival. You need me to help you. You need me."

"I need you to be safe. This is *me*, protecting you. Since you won't take a few days away from here, I'll do my best to help in other ways and maybe even find this jerk too." He stared at her. "Don't look so surprised, or so grim. It isn't the end of the world, Sierra. Stay safe. Let Bryce help protect you, along with your father, and maybe you'll even consider letting your K-9–trained dog protect you."

"What about… What about SAR? If someone needs—"

"That's different. If someone needs to be found, you and Samson are close. But deputy duties are on hold for now."

Sierra wanted to protest, but she recognized the hard set of Sheriff Locke's jaw and knew he'd made up his mind. She almost wished she was still in Boulder because maybe there, she would be allowed to keep working.

Still, coming back here had been the best decision. The only thing she'd missed about Boulder was Bryce.

She hadn't realized how much until he'd walked back into her life yesterday.

And that kind of thinking would lead nowhere.

The door jingled, startling all three of them—the store wasn't open yet. She or Dad should have locked the front door after the sheriff came in. But they were both much too distracted.

Bryce stood at the entrance for a moment as if to let his vision adjust, then his gaze found hers and seemed to drill through her. With a somber expression he made his way toward her.

Her heart pounded. Why did she react this way the moment he walked into the room?

SEVEN

Bryce got the impression he'd interrupted a private conversation between Sierra, her father and Sheriff Locke. But he trudged forward anyway with every intention of inserting himself into the thick of things.

He wouldn't be left out. Not as this juncture.

As he approached the counter, he forced a grin. "You guys are getting started without me?"

Frowning, she shook her head and straightened the pens and cards on the counter. She didn't seem happy with whatever had been discussed. He didn't wait for an explanation and instead gave Samson the attention the dog required. Or rather, demanded. Bryce thought Samson's eyes were scolding him for not staying here this morning after Bryce had taken him for a walk. Like the dog wanted Bryce to stay and help him protect Sierra. "I know, boy, I know."

When he stood, John had moved over near the door, preparing to open it for customers. Someone had already shoveled the sidewalk in front of the stores, and would need to keep at it all day long.

"What did Samson say to you?" Sierra teased.

"He implied with his eyes that he didn't like that I

had left him and John here to protect you alone. So he was scolding me. I was just telling him I understand that you need to be watched and protected from Raul." Sierra's eyes had narrowed as he spoke. He lifted his palms in surrender. "I'm just telling you what he said."

Sheriff chuckled. "You two are ridiculous."

"Maybe it's you who needs protecting, Bryce," she said.

"Yeah, from you. I see that look in your eyes," he said. "You want to kick me to the curb right now. But even if you do, I'll stand out there in the cold." He wouldn't let Raul get another chance at her like he had before in Boulder, and then twice already here in Crescent Springs.

Sheriff Locke actually rolled his eyes. "Well that's my cue to leave you two to protect each other, but please remember—I want to know if something suspicious happens. Anything odd or strange or out of the ordinary. Don't take any risks. Let's keep in close contact."

Hmm. That was an interesting way to put it. She was a deputy. Why wouldn't she be in close contact? Bryce didn't miss Sierra stiffening at the sheriff's words.

"Thanks, Sheriff," she said. She didn't exactly seem pleased to see her boss in the store this morning.

Bryce would wait until the sheriff exited before he spoke. Sierra held her silence as well. He hoped she would tell him what was going on. Before she got the chance the front door signaled the sheriff's exit and that someone had entered. Jane came through bringing snow with her on her coat and boots. She coughed then spotted Sierra at the back and gave a sheepish grin. "Sorry I'm late."

"No worries," Sierra said. "It's hectic out there."

Sierra turned to him with a forced smile.

"What was that all about?" he asked.

"That depends on what you're referring to specifically."

After shrugging out of her coat, Jane hung it on a rack at the back wall. She rushed behind the counter and stuffed her bag onto an already overflowing shelf. Tugging off her knit cap, she turned and smiled at them while she finger combed her long black hair and put it up in a hair clip. She released a hefty breath. "There. Do I look like I'm together?"

"As always." Sierra's smile was warm and her gaze held respect for her employee.

Then Sierra turned her attention back to Bryce and grabbed his arm. "Jane if you don't mind working up front and—" she leaned in to whisper "—keeping an eye on Dad, I have a few things to do."

Jane scrunched her face and waved her hand. "Pfft. Go ahead. Please. You're the boss. I got this."

Sierra promptly ushered Bryce and Samson to the apartment. Bryce let her grip on his arm remain as she urged him back like he was a child. At the door to the apartment she seemed to realize she still held on to him and released him.

She opened the door for him. "Gentlemen first."

He tried to hide his smile as he entered her home. This was serious business and he needed to remember that.

Someone was out to kill Sierra.

Once inside, Samson rushed to his water bowl and Bryce stuffed his hands in his pockets. "What's going on? What did I miss?"

She paced frantically and shoved her hands through

her hair. "The sheriff first asked me to leave town for a few days. Then when I refused he said I'm off duty until further notice. What does that even mean?"

Good for the sheriff. Bryce approached and blocked her from pacing. He gently grabbed her arms. "Sierra, calm down. It means that he cares about you, and I for one am glad for that since I feel the same way. I came to Crescent Springs to be here for you. Protect you. Investigate. Everything that's needed to make sure you're safe." Oops. He'd said the wrong thing.

"You think this is about you? Me not working as a deputy makes it easier for you to watch out for me?" She shrugged free of his grip, a deep frown brimming with annoyance carved into her forehead.

He dropped his hands. "You're right. I'm sorry that I was selfish enough to think of it that way."

She covered her face with her palms. He couldn't be sure—was she crying? He didn't know what to say to appease her. Maybe he would just go stand outside the door and watch over her from a distance. Maybe that would be better for them both.

She dropped her hands, her face twisted into anguish. "I'm sorry. You're right. I didn't mean to lash out at you. You're only here to protect me. I just feel like the walls are closing in around me."

He approached and took her in his arms then. Sierra hugged him back, her face pressed against his shoulder. Bryce wanted to comfort her, but old feelings for her were stirring so easily the more time he spent with her.

Lord, how do I protect my heart? She'd hurt him once. He'd come here only as a friend, and didn't want to get hurt like that again. But it was becoming increasingly clear that the struggle with his feelings for her was far from over.

Sierra stepped away. "Well, at least this gives us more time to search for Raul. If I'm only working at the store part-time and then have nothing else to do, I have more time to fight to get my life of peace and quiet back."

In her eyes he saw that she wanted that more than anything. Terror was quickly beginning to reign in her life again.

Bryce frowned. Sure they'd discussed going out there and searching for Raul, but he was sure that wasn't what the sheriff had in mind when he'd taken her off deputy duties. In fact, Bryce imagined that what the sheriff had in mind for her was stay inside and wait for others to track Raul down—the exact opposite of what she was planning to do with her new freedom.

Now Bryce's job would be even more difficult.

The perfect distraction came later that day when a SAR call came in. A couple of snowshoers hadn't returned. Sierra had driven the mountain roads and finally parked at the trailhead. The volunteer searchers would follow, but Samson needed time to search the area without other people confusing the scents.

She hopped from the vehicle and opened the door for Samson to jump out. She kept him leashed for the moment. She was dressed in the typical search-and-rescue gear, along with a bright orange jacket over a Kevlar vest per Sheriff's request. Sierra studied Bryce, who had come along with her. She couldn't shake him so easily, for which she was secretly grateful.

He'd donned his own vest too, just in case. They

looked like they were going on a raid rather than searching for people lost in the wilderness.

"This feels so over-the-top," she said.

"You really think so? It seems sensible to me. You're not going out without protection, especially with a target on your back."

She got out the snowshoes and they each donned a pair. She preferred snowshoes to a snowmobile because clues could be missed as she searched.

She squatted next to Samson to release the leash. Looking into his eyes, she rubbed his ears. They'd been together and trained together. She knew his signals, and he understood her, as well.

Now… *"Zooch!"* Find. "Go find people."

Samson barked and took off, running through the snow.

"Wait," Bryce said. "What are you doing?"

Sierra angled her head at him. "We're in the wilderness. Samson is searching for people. He's following the smells in the air to find them. He's cross-trained for trailing which can include tracking from an article, but dogs are smart and finding someone can include tracking via the ground or the air. He's certified in avalanche searches, as well." She took off after Samson as quickly as she could in snowshoes. "So we're doing an area search now based on the scent. But he can air scent for humans without an article or an initial scent to go from." She scratched her head. "I'm sorry—you probably know all that stuff."

Bryce had gotten her the dog, but he hadn't gone through the K-9 training himself. Still, she hadn't wanted to insult him.

"Not at all. You sound like an expert to me." He

huffed a laugh. "I always knew he was a good dog, but that's impressive."

Sierra hiked along the mountain trail alongside Bryce, her self-imposed bodyguard. "So here we are. This is the high probability area where the subjects supposedly left to hike. Samson knows to find a human scent and then search."

"What if he finds the wrong person?"

"That can happen in a search like this. If it does, we tell him he's a good dog and then to find again. And we just keep looking."

"And he won't track the others searching?"

"Not yet. They're coming in behind us. That's why we go in first."

"What happens next?"

"We'll give him time to explore and he should alert me soon if he finds anything." They walked a bit farther, and Sierra couldn't help smiling. "I love the switch to wilderness from the city—it's refreshing in ways you can't imagine. Though of course it's challenging too. There was no question we would train for avalanches."

"Again, impressive."

She shrugged.

"How often do you train?"

"I like to train with him every day, but the last few days we've gotten off our schedule. We meet with others every other week and train together."

Bryce glanced at her intermittently while he hiked across the top of the snow. "This suits you."

Admiration clung to his silver-blue gaze and her heart tripped up. She stumbled forward then righted herself on her snowshoes.

"Careful there."

"I'm fine." She was the expert hiker here, but it didn't look like it.

Get a grip, Sierra. You can't fall for him. Time to redirect. "You said this suits me."

She wasn't sure she completely understood what he'd meant.

"Being here in the small town where you grew up. The mountains right at your back door sans the smog. And the dog." An emotion beyond mere admiration surfaced in his eyes.

Sierra wanted to pull her gaze away from his but she couldn't.

Samson's deep throaty bark startled her and broke the moment. She jerked around to search the woods. Through the trees she could see her big dog plowing his way through the snow toward them.

She worked hard with him all the time and could read him. As soon as she acknowledged him he turned around—his way of alerting her that he would lead her. He'd found someone.

Sierra radioed the sheriff. "We can't know if it's them. I'll let you know as soon as we're there."

Through the woods, she could see other searchers.

Samson barked and tirelessly tilled through the snow.

"Oh, no…"

"What is it?" Bryce asked.

"Up ahead, see? It looks like… It looks like there was an avalanche." She picked up her pace and radioed the sheriff again to let him know.

"Well Samson can find them, then. You said he was an avalanche dog now."

"If they were buried in that, they're dead by now."

Sorrow infused her but she pushed it away as she

caught up to Samson who had his nose to the ground, sniffing at the snow that recently collapsed from the mountain face looming above them.

His actions let her know that he might have found someone. Saint Bernard dogs were one of the preferred breeds for avalanche dogs, and they were descended from mastiffs. Still, she didn't doubt that no matter the task, Samson was the dog to get it done. He was faithful, hardworking and enthusiastic. Her heart warmed with love for him.

On top of the snow, Samson whined but seemed confused, then, with his nose in the air, he suddenly took off again and disappeared into the woods.

"I don't understand," Bryce said.

"Neither do I, but let's go."

A shout resounded.

Bryce grabbed her arm. "Wait, Sierra. I have a bad feeling about this."

She yanked her arm free. "Samson is barking. He found someone. It could be the hikers we're searching for."

"Over here!" a woman called. "Please help us!"

Sierra spotted someone in the shadows under the overhang of a rocky ledge. She hiked toward the area and, as she got closer, two people could be seen in the shadows. Sierra's heart rate jumped. Could it be the snowshoers?

She tried to pick up the pace, but moving quickly was difficult in snowshoes. Already she was gasping for breath. Finally she approached the woman on the ground. A man was sprawled out, but his head rested on her lap.

"Are you McKayla Markum? McKayla and Jim?"

"Yes." McKayla choked out the words. "I'm so glad you found us. Please help. My husband's been shot. I've put pressure on the wound, but—" Tears overcame her.

Samson sat close to the woman, panting and whining. He pawed the snow. Sierra took that to mean he was concerned too.

Sierra called the sheriff to let the others know that Samson had found the missing snowshoers and that medical assistance was required. A gunshot wound was a serious injury. Since he was not instantly killed, the greatest danger was that he could bleed out. If he was still alive, McKayla had done a good job of slowing the bleeding, and the cold could have helped too. But the temperature presented other complications since hypothermia would also be an issue.

"Help is on the way." Sierra dropped to her knees. The snow was packed where McKayla and Jim had been waiting. "What happened?"

Tears streaked McKayla's face. "An avalanche almost took us out. We made it out of the way, but then we came across someone. He acted like he was here to help us, but I…" Her teeth chattered making it difficult to understand her. "He wanted to hurt us. I don't know why. My husband fought him but was shot. Still, I got the weapon when the guy dropped it." Her hands shook and she pressed it over a gun next to her. "I would have used it, but he ran off. And I couldn't shoot him in the back no matter that he attacked us. I couldn't do it."

Fear corded Sierra's throat. "What did he look like?"

"His face was mostly covered, you know, with a cap, and sunglasses. He seemed tall and bulky. It's hard to tell with winter clothes and coats, but he seemed large. Jim tried to protect me." McKayla couldn't finish. She pressed her faced against her unconscious husband's forehead.

Sierra shared a glance with Bryce. An escaped convict was in the region. Was the man who attacked the Markums Raul Novack? If so, maybe he thought they'd recognized him and he hadn't wanted anyone to report his whereabouts. But his actions were counterintuitive.

Samson growled and paced. Bryce grabbed Sierra and forced her to look at him. "Raul could still be here which means you're in danger. Now's your chance to let Samson do what he does best. He can track a criminal. Raul is hurting others, Sierra. We have to stop him now."

Sierra looked closely at where McKayla still pressed her hands against Jim's wound in the side of his gut. "You can let go. I'll take over now. You must be tired. I'll keep the pressure on. Help is coming."

McKayla appeared slightly relieved, though deep lines of worry were carved into her thirty-something face. She was scared for Jim. "I… My cell… I couldn't get a signal to call for help."

"Give him the command." Bryce pleaded with Sierra.

"No. We'd send him to his death. Besides we have to stay here with McKayla."

Come on, Sheriff Locke! Come on, medical assistance.

She continued to press her hand against the blood-soaked scarves McKayla had used against the wound. "We don't know if this was Raul's doing."

"Don't we?"

"I'm not sure if Samson can even detect the scent from a gun that has had so many hands on it."

"You don't need that, remember? He can air scent.

He can find anyone. We know the man who shot Jim ran that way, though the tracks are gone now."

Sierra had noticed that too. McKayla and Jim had done well to find a place to keep out of the falling snow.

"May I?" She eyed the gun.

McKayla handed it over.

"No, just set it down there in front of the dog."

"Samson." Sierra forced the right voice and tone to come out. *"Verloren!"* Find whoever belongs to the gun.

The massive beast took off as if he'd been waiting for the chance.

Bryce started after Samson.

Sierra glared at Bryce. "I'm coming too!"

"No. Someone has to stay with McKayla, until help arrives."

She eyed the search and rescue volunteers, who'd left their snowmobiles behind in rough terrain and hiked toward them. Help was arriving soon.

Then she was going after Bryce and Samson.

EIGHT

Bryce followed Samson's tracks, huffing and puffing. If he was made to do this with any regularity, he'd have to train on snowshoes to get in the right kind of shape. The scent of evergreens filled his nose. His snowshoes crunched on the snow, the only sound in the quiet, white-blanketed wilderness.

He hadn't caught sight of Samson or Raul yet. But he watched and listened as he hiked and tried to catch up.

In the distance a vicious bark resounded. Deep and throaty—it must be Samson. Bryce hadn't heard that degree of hostility from the dog before, even when they'd taken gunfire. Adrenaline pumped through him.

Samson must have found his target.

A man shouted, the sound coming from the same direction as Samson's bark. Bryce was torn—if it was Raul, everything in him screamed he should tell Samson to attack. But he couldn't know for sure. Still, if it was the man who'd shot Jim then he needed to be detained.

What was that word in German? Samson might not listen to Bryce's command, but it was worth a try.

"Attack! *Fassen!*"

Samson wouldn't simply attack unless he sensed the man was a threat.

Gunfire resounded…

Bryce's gut tensed.

Oh, Samson… Oh, no…

He couldn't catch his breath but forced himself to keep moving forward. "Samson! Come on, boy. Come here." What word had she used to call Samson back to her again?

Suddenly Sierra was behind him, and almost on him. That startled him. She'd caught up? Apparently, she was more accustomed to hiking in this wilderness.

"Samson. *Heir!*" She shouted for Samson. "I don't like this," she said to Bryce. "I can't see a thing."

Bryce couldn't see through the dense trees, nor could he hear Samson barking. Dread rose in his chest. They followed the tracks.

Sierra left Bryce behind and jogged on her snow-shoes. "Sierra, wait. You could be putting yourself in danger. Wait for me."

But she didn't listen. He caught up to her through a copse of trees that opened up to a clearing. Samson was there, licking at his fur. Crimson spread on the white snow.

Sierra grabbed his head. "Good boy. It's going to be okay."

Bryce caught up to them. "What is it?"

"A gunshot wound." She glared at Bryce. Then tried to look at the wound but Samson nipped at her. "Shh, it's okay, boy. I need to help. Let me look, okay?" She shook her head. "I can't see. But I need to stop the bleeding."

Like McKayla had used her scarf on Jim, Sierra tugged her scarf off and folded it. She pressed it gently against Samson's fur, he growled and placed his massive maw over her hand, but didn't bite.

Sierra obviously trusted him not to lash out, but Bryce wouldn't trust any dog that much. Sierra got on her radio to let the search team know that Samson needed medical help too.

Bryce let his gaze roam the woods. "Whoever shot Samson is still out there, Sierra." *Raul is still out there.* "I thought McKayla said she got his gun, but apparently he had more than one."

"One that he couldn't get to without her shooting him, so he fled," she said. "But he could have killed Samson with one shot."

He felt her eyes boring into him so he finally looked back at her. "You're wondering why he didn't."

She nodded.

"He could have stumbled and missed. Maybe he wasn't really aiming—he could have shot at Samson and kept running, not realizing he hadn't killed Samson. We can't know. If Samson hadn't been shot, he could have brought Raul down."

Her frowned deepened. "Whatever. Samson could be down-and-out now for SAR. Other tracking dogs were brought in and haven't found Raul yet. But our team has spotted him now so maybe they'll scour this region and find him soon."

The sheriff had told Bryce the state had set up a command center at a ranger station outside of town so they wouldn't disrupt the ice festival. So far he and Sierra hadn't seen or heard the dogs looking for Raul, except for a couple in town. The bulk of the dogs were in the woods and up in the mountains far from where Sierra and Bryce were now. The terrain was treacherous and the region vast—even with dogs, it seemed impossible to search it all.

Samson whined and licked at his wound.

"Come on buddy, you're okay," she said.

"Maybe it's just a graze."

He wished he hadn't said the words. She pulled first aid from her backpack. "I'll see if he'll let me take a look."

Samson had finally calmed though he still whined. He lay across the snow, but remained alert. Sierra removed her bloodied scarf. "I think the bleeding is slowing." She peered at the wound without touching it. "I'm no expert, but it doesn't look like an actual hole in his body it… It's more like a slice over his skin. Do you think Raul cut him with a knife and this wasn't a gunshot wound?"

"I heard the gunfire."

Sierra gently placed gauze over the wound then taped it. It wouldn't stick well or hold tight on Samson's fur. "The vet will have to shave his fur. But—" she hung her head "—this could have been so much worse."

Right. The dog could have died. Guilt flooded Bryce—he understood Sierra's reservations much better now, though he'd known the danger all along.

"And it could still be that much worse. I think we need to get out of here. We're too exposed here in these woods."

"Okay, Samson. We need to try to walk back to the others."

"Come on, boy." She leashed Samson. He growled and barked, but got to his feet.

"Get down!" Bryce covered Sierra.

She kept a hold of the leash. "Get off me, Bryce."

"He's still here. Samson was warning us."

Gunfire rang out again. A bullet slammed into a nearby tree, shattering bark. Bryce covered her again.

"We need backup. Someone to help us here, and soon. Definitely not volunteers. Radio your sheriff to let him know."

Shouts rang out from the direction they'd come, along with more gunfire.

Sierra got on her radio to relay about the shooter. "Searchers are out here and this could be dangerous for them. Most of them are volunteers!"

Sierra shrugged away from Bryce's protection and brandished her own weapon. "The other deputies won't get here in time. This is up to us. You and me. Let's get him."

She started to rise and he pulled her down, keeping his grip on her this time and refusing to release her despite her protests.

Sierra stared at him, fury pouring from her gaze. "You agreed to help me find him."

"Not like this," Bryce said. "He has the advantage. He can see us but we can't see him. Besides, you haven't forgotten Samson, have you? He needs medical attention."

Samson panted, drool hanging from both sides of his mouth. At the mention off his name, he licked Bryce.

"I want to go after him too," he said. "But not like this." Not with Samson compromised. "There'll be another chance and we'll have the advantage." He was making promises he couldn't keep.

A deputy rushed forward. "Sheriff said you should be safe now."

"Wait." Sierra shared a look at Bryce. "What? How can I be safe? Did he get Raul?"

"We saw him crossing a river on our approach up the trail. So went after him. Then we lost him. The terrain was too rocky. We'll bring the dogs to this area today to search." The deputy frowned. "I see Samson is hurt."

"Yes. He's going to be okay though. Aren't you, boy?"

"We need law enforcement who climb too," the deputy continued. "The way he disappeared, he looks to be great at rock climbing."

Bryce frowned. "This time of year it's more like ice—"

"Climbing," Sierra said. "Ice climbing."

Samson whined as if in pain. Sierra reassured the dog, who had warned her and tried to protect her. The dog's injury was on Bryce, and Sierra would probably not let him forget it.

Back in the Jeep with Samson, Bryce drove this time so Sierra could sit in the back holding the dog. He steered back to town, following the directions she gave him for the office of the local vet. "Raul couldn't possibly be here for the ice climbing festival," he said. "That would just… That wouldn't make any sense."

"No, it wouldn't. I think he somehow got away. He's eluded the search dogs because he somehow knows his way around this terrain and he can go places they can't go. But that's just an assumption on my part," she said.

"But Samson knows his way around too, right?" Bryce glanced in the rearview mirror to get a glimpse of Sierra and her dog.

"I don't want to put him out there again before he's ready."

"Let's hope his wound is truly only superficial and will heal quickly."

"I hope that too, but he could have died today, Bryce."

Oh, Sierra.

The vet, after a long visit, patched Samson up and gave him an otherwise clean bill of health, commenting that after a day or two Samson would be as good as new. But to be certain—mostly to appease Sierra's concern—he would keep the dog with him overnight.

Bryce parked the Jeep around the side of the building and escorted her back to the toy store that had closed an hour ago. He'd had to drive around a few times to get that parking spot as the town had started to fill up with those coming to view the big competitions this weekend.

Sierra walked through the toy store to the back and then unlocked and opened up the apartment. "Dad?" she said as she stepped inside.

Then she looked around, and screamed.

The apartment had been sacked.

She pressed her hand over her mouth. "Dad!"

Sierra sprinted up the stairs and was practically yanked down as Bryce tugged her behind him. "Call the sheriff for backup."

"You're not—" She didn't bother finishing.

Bryce had already drawn his gun. "I'm getting you out of here."

"Not without my father you aren't."

"You don't know that he's here."

She brandished her own gun. Determination drove her to push past Bryce. "But I'll know soon enough."

"Then let's get to it, but I'm going in first." He started up the stairs.

Sierra called dispatch as they climbed the steps. She understood that Bryce trusted her as a deputy, but right now he was trying to protect her from Raul, and that changed the dynamics.

"John, are you here?" Bryce shouted the question.

At this point, they weren't trying to surprise whoever had broken into the home. But Bryce still wanted to use himself as a shield for Sierra.

"Dad!" she shouted.

She had never fully been able to be rid of Raul and now it was as though he had stepped right out of her nightmares. Fear for her father nearly paralyzed her but she and Bryce managed to clear the two rooms upstairs.

Catching her breath to slow her pounding heart, she leaned against the hallway wall. "If he's not here, then where is he?" She looked at her cell. "He didn't leave any texts to tell me where he is, but I'm texting him now. Then I'll call too for good measure."

Somewhere downstairs, shouts resounded.

"Must be backup," Bryce said. "Up here!"

Bryce put his gun away and leaned in close to look her in the eyes. "Sierra, you okay?"

"No. Not until I find Dad. You don't think—" Could Raul have taken him? *Oh, no. No, no, no.* Her legs grew weak and she leaned against the wall with her cell to her ear, praying Dad would answer her call.

Sheriff Locke climbed the steps. "Got your emergency call. I just returned from taking the statement of the two snowshoers. Looks like someone has done a number—"

"Sheriff," she interrupted. "My dad. He's not here."

Deputy Colfax stepped up next to the sheriff. "John's at the café across the street. I just left there when I got the call to come here. So far, it doesn't look like he knows there's any trouble."

"Oh." She pressed her hand against her chest and relief whooshed through her. "I was so worried. I thought—I thought something happened to him."

Or that Raul had taken him.

And why hadn't he answered her text or call?

"Jane!" She called her friend and employee on her cell. "We need to make sure she wasn't hurt," she said to Bryce.

Jane answered right away. "Sierra! Hey. What's up? Don't tell me I forgot to turn the lights off again."

Sierra eyed the men watching her. "No, nothing like that. I'm just glad to hear that you're okay. Where are you?"

"I'm at home getting ready for a dinner date tonight."

"Oh good. Is it with that Chuck guy?"

"I'm so over him. No. His name is Chris."

"Okay, well please be careful. Someone broke into the apartment and ransacked it. As far as I can tell they didn't touch the store."

Jane gasped. "Oh, no. You're kidding! This must have something to do with the man after you." Sierra had told Jane some of what was going on, and to let her know if she saw anyone suspicious in the store.

"One would assume that's exactly who's responsible."

"What do you think he was looking for?"

"I have no idea." Sierra eased down the stairs and looked around the apartment. The coffee table in the living room had been overturned. Chairs too. Books pulled from the shelves. And the kitchen… Her stomach soured. She drew in a breath. "I just wanted to make sure that you're all right. Please be careful."

"Why are you telling me this? You don't think I'm a target do you?"

"No. I just think it's common sense."

Jane chuckled though she didn't sound convinced. "All right then. Unless there's anything else, I need to get going."

"I do too. Text me when you get home safe and sound after your date, okay? I'll see you tomorrow."

Sierra ended the call. The sheriff, Deputy Colfax and Bryce all stared at her as if waiting to hear about Jane.

"I guess you heard she's safe," she said. "Which means that whoever broke in must have done so after Jane left, unless they came through the back. Working up front, she might not have noticed or heard anything coming from the apartment." Sierra hugged herself. "I need to talk to Dad."

"Miguel is with him now, escorting him over," Deputy Colfax said. "They should be here any second."

"We don't want to contaminate the scene," Sheriff Locke said. "But he needs to see this. Maybe he will see something missing, who knows."

"Does he know what happened yet?" she asked.

"Only that someone broke in and you're all right," the sheriff said. "Can you tell us if you've noticed anything missing? Though my gut tells me this wasn't a burglary."

"Exactly. We know who did this."

Deputy Colfax scratched his head. "I'm not so sure."

"What do you mean?" Bryce asked.

"Why would Raul ransack your home? He's after *you*, remember?"

"I think he's trying to shake Sierra up," Bryce said. "Intimidate her with fear tactics."

"If that was him out there today who attacked those two hikers, he's mixing up his tactics."

"That could have been a simple matter of him getting you out there with Samson to search for missing people. But his plans to hurt you didn't work out." Sheriff Locke rubbed his chin. "I hate to pull you from SAR too."

"Sheriff, please don't."

"He's right, Sierra." Bryce crossed his arms. "If Raul thinks you'll be out there with Samson searching for someone lost in the wilderness, he could try that tactic again. That puts others at risk."

She blew out a defeated breath. She hadn't thought about it like that. Raul was shutting her world down.

"Okay. Okay. I get it. But it doesn't look like staying home would keep me safe either. As far as him breaking into my apartment, he could do it again," she said. "Next time Dad might not be so fortunate as to be somewhere else."

"Which brings me to another point," Bryce said. "We need to figure out how someone got in and make sure that can never happen again."

Bryce kept fisting his hands. She understood his frustration and feelings of helplessness.

"I should get busy and see if there's something missing." She knew there wouldn't be, but this was all part of the investigative process.

Sierra glanced through Dad's room and as she suspected, found nothing missing—but what a mess. They all suspected Raul had done this when she and Bryce had gone to the vet. He'd come off that mountain and headed straight for her home to do this. To torture her. He was a sick, sick man.

She hated being in his sights. Exhaustion and wariness already ate at the edges of her composure as she moved to her own room.

She and Bryce had already cleared the room so she'd seen the mess, but she feared what she might find there upon closer examination.

A shiver crept up her spine. She'd been sleeping in this bed, this room last night and she'd had nightmares about Raul. It felt like he'd stepped from those nightmares right into her room.

He was here in my room.

She rubbed at the goose bumps, but they remained.

God, how do I get him out of my life? When will this end? I don't understand why it's happening.

She wiped tears from her cheeks, then moved to head out of the room.

A small slip of paper next to the bed caught her attention. She picked it up, then read the words.

"I'm going to finish what I started that night four years ago."

Her hands shook. The trembling took over her entire body. She couldn't show this to Dad.

"Sierra, what is it?"

Bryce rushed forward. She glanced up at him. "This. He left me a note."

Concern poured from his gaze, then he looked over her shoulder to read the note before taking it and laying it on the side table. Bryce turned her to face him. She looked into his eyes where emotion and concern for her trumped anything he might have said, and then simply pulled her into his arms.

Comfort seemed to exude from his every fiber and she soaked it up, but she knew that he was restraining his anger. Not at her, but at the circumstances. She understood he felt powerless to stop the events from unfolding. What could possibly happen next?

Finally she stepped away from him. She hadn't wanted to need him, but Bryce had been here for her just as he had that night when Raul attacked her. "It's like we've come full circle."

"We won't let this happen again."

Bold words. Sierra was unsure what more they could do to prevent it except call in the National Guard to surround her everywhere she went. "Please don't tell Dad about the note. I don't want him more upset than he already is. I'm going to distract him and you can show it to Sheriff Locke. Okay?"

Bryce nodded. She wasn't sure she could express to him how much she appreciated his support. But she thought he probably already understood.

She was on her way down the steps when Dad appeared at the bottom.

"Oh, Dad." She bounded the rest of the way down and hugged him on the last step.

She thought he would never let her go—and that was just fine with her. She'd been so afraid that she'd lost him. That Raul had killed him or taken him to get to her. "Somehow, this has got to end."

He released her then peered at her, overwhelming concern in his eyes. "How's Samson?"

His question surprised her. "He's going to be all right. The vet wanted to keep him overnight to be sure."

"I'd prefer it if he were here to protect you."

Now she understood why he'd jumped right to that.

Sheriff Locke approached. "The state's coming in to process the scene. See if they can get some fingerprints. We don't have the resources for that, so they'll take care of it."

Sierra stared at him. "So you're saying we can't sleep here."

He shook his head. "I'd give their evidence processing team a couple of days to get here and get it done, then you can come home again. The store wasn't disturbed, so you're good to keep that open."

"You've got to be kidding." Sierra scraped both hands through her hair and hung her head back. But then again, did she really want to sleep in that room where Raul had been mere hours ago, after eluding them up where the snowshoers had run into him?

Sheriff Locke moved away as he got a call on his cell.

"Bryce, what was he doing up in the mountains?" she asked. If he had been hiding somewhere up in that area, the searchers would have come across his hiding spot, and he would have to move.

"Maybe that's what Raul wanted," Bryce said. "To get you out of this apartment so he could take a shot at you, only he missed. He injured Samson, knowing you'd be at the vet, and came here to leave you that note. He loves this game of terror."

Sheriff Locke finished the call then approached Sierra.

"Sierra, you and John are welcome to stay at my place," Sheriff Locke said. "Barbara would be happy for the company."

Barbara was her boss's wife.

"Oh, no, I couldn't impose."

"The biggest event of the festival is tomorrow. You're not going to get a room at a hotel tonight," Sheriff Locke said. "Give me a yes and I'll let Barbara know. Bryce, I'll add you in to the count, and don't say you couldn't impose. Your protective services are required so I insist."

Bryce nodded. "I won't give up my hotel room, though, so I'll have a place to stay in a couple of days."

"Fair enough. Everything should be back to normal in a day or two. Who knows, maybe we'll have tracked Raul down and caught him by then."

One thing Sierra knew: she would have to come to terms with the fact that Raul had chosen to come into her room. He'd let her know that he could get to her whenever he wanted. He'd chosen not to kill Samson but had harmed him enough that she would spend hours at the vet, showing that he could also get to her dog if he wanted. He could hurt her in so many ways, whenever he chose.

And he would choose the time and place to end her life.

And…she had to come to terms with the fact that the whole reason Bryce had gifted her with the English mastiff puppy was for protection. Sierra had fallen in love with that dog and removed him from that role—to a point. Sure he could warn her of danger here at home, but she didn't want him to face off against a criminal holding a deadly weapon.

In her current situation, with a killer after her, how did she prevent that from happening again?

NINE

In his Subaru Forester, Bryce had followed the sheriff to what he'd been told would be a sprawling log cabin with a wraparound porch situated somewhere just outside of Crescent Springs. Sierra and John had ridden with the sheriff along with Samson. Sierra had been too worried that Raul would somehow try to get to the dog at the veterinarian hospital, so she'd gotten him released. The vet had agreed that Sierra could take her dog with her and that she would call him tonight if she noticed anything concerning.

Sierra had told Bryce all about the sheriff's dogs, Turner and Hooch, from the Tom Hanks movie by the same name, though these dogs weren't big dogs, but corgis. Somehow that totally didn't fit what Bryce would expect to see from the sheriff. But he understood better after learning the dogs mostly belonged to the sheriff's wife, Barbara. Turner and Hooch weren't K-9 or SAR dogs but were purely spoiled pets.

Sierra had mentioned her concern about bringing Samson with them to Sheriff Locke's place. Samson needed to take it easy and not get caught up in playing with Turner and Hooch, but the sheriff's wife had promised to make her pets behave.

So for a night or two they were going to be one big happy family.

He thought back to the whole family thing. He'd once thought that he wanted exactly that, and he'd allowed his heart to take that risk in caring deeply, loving someone, hoping for a future.

First with Rebecca.

He'd let himself, no holds barred, fall head over heels for her, and had been foolish enough to believe she had fallen in love with him in return. He thought back to that moment that he'd planned to propose. He'd planned to meet her at a nice restaurant. He'd walked in with a little black velvet box in his pocket. They'd enjoyed a nice dinner and as his hopes had risen and his palms slicked for that moment that would soon be upon them, ushered in with dessert, Rebecca had proceeded to explain how much and how deeply she cared about Bryce…but that she had met someone else. This other man, she explained, was a better fit for her because Rebecca hadn't wanted to grow too serious with a police officer.

Really? She could have said no to that first date then.

He followed the sheriff who turned down a winding drive. Bryce had gotten over Rebecca. Learned his lesson and his heart had grown a little bit harder. Then he'd met Sierra—a woman who was in law enforcement too, who understood the risks involved and wouldn't judge him for them. They'd connected in a way he could never connect with anyone else, especially considering their battle with the Novack brothers.

Bryce had… He'd loved Sierra. But he knew to take it slowly and not confess those feelings or consider proposing until he knew she felt the same. He had believed she was beginning to return his love.

So, yes, Bryce had been foolish again and let himself fall.

But after Raul had attacked her, Sierra had cut ties with Bryce. She didn't want to care too deeply, she'd said. He had known about her past and that she'd loved a highway patrolman who had been shot and killed on duty. Raul nearly killing Bryce had brought that back for her.

So with Bryce's track record, a relationship with Sierra, any relationship, seemed like it wasn't worth the risk. A happy family was a pipe dream.

He still cared about Sierra and was here for her now to see that she made it through this alive.

The sheriff finally parked his vehicle and out climbed the happy gang. Bryce exited his own vehicle and yanked his small duffel from the seat.

A slender brunette stood in the doorway of the cabin and let the corgis run out, barking and wagging their tails. Turner and Hooch.

Samson's deep bark mixed with their yaps.

Yep. One big happy family.

Bryce pulled his gaze from the joy and took in the surrounding woods. So the sheriff thought this would be a good idea. No wonder he'd made sure Bryce came along for the ride and stayed too. After he met the wife and dogs and settled in, he'd make sure to check the perimeter. This wouldn't be a vacation.

He never imagined it would be.

Not until Raul was out of their lives for good. Not until Sierra was safe.

Then Bryce would go back to his life in Boulder.

* * *

Samson snored loudly at her feet.

Turner and Hooch had been put to bed like young children. They slept in Barbara's room.

Sierra yawned, wishing she was already sleeping in the guest room offered by Sheriff Locke and the hospitable Barbara. Dad had long ago gone to sleep in one of the extra rooms. The day had been long and terrifying on so many fronts that it had left her exhausted. But instead of resting, hoping she could sleep without nightmares or fears of Raul preventing her, she sat on the comfy sofa across from Barbara, sipping the hot cocoa her hostess had offered. Bryce and the sheriff were outside making sure no one was stalking the house.

Neither of them believed Raul would find her here or dare to attack her while she was at the sheriff's house, but just in case, the state had loaned Officer Kendall to them for night duty, and the sheriff and Bryce were giving the area another once-over. The sheriff's home had become an unintended safe house—except that her whereabouts weren't exactly a secret.

"Thanks for letting us impose on you for a night or two, Barbara." Sierra watched her over the brim of her cup.

Barbara was about a decade younger than the sheriff's late forties, and she was a talented artist—her paintings and decor brightened the walls. She offered a soft smile. "We're more than happy to open up our home. We don't get guests nearly enough and, without kids, we can't expect grandkids in our future."

Sierra resisted the urge to suggest Barbara get a SAR dog and get involved in that kind of work. That would be so worthwhile, but Barbara spoke first.

"The way you and Bryce look at each other, one

could almost construe something was going on. I see by that flash in your eyes that *was* is the operative word."

Sierra measured her next words, then asked, "Do all artists read people so well?"

Barbara laughed, clearly pleased to learn she'd hit her mark. "Some do. But with you and Bryce, I think anyone could see that there's something more going on."

"*Was* going on. Yes, we saw each other when we both lived in Boulder."

"The way you look at each other begs the question— what happened? Surely you could work out whatever it was that broke you two up."

Sierra stared at the fire, exhaustion flooding her. Did she want to open up all of it to Barbara? She'd moved back to Crescent Springs wanting to escape and she'd done well for a year. But the least she could do was answer this sweet woman's question.

"Before Bryce, there was someone else." Sierra frowned at the thought.

"Oh, honey. I'm sorry if I overstepped. You don't have to tell me."

She was already in so she would finish. "No, it's okay. I thought I was in love. No, wait. I *was* in love with a guy named Buck Thomas. He was Colorado Highway Patrol. One day he stopped a driver whose taillight was out—a simple traffic stop. Oddly enough those simple stops are one of the most productive ways of catching the bad guys. The next thing you know, he was shot and killed. I don't think Buck knew what hit him. But I do. He'd pulled over someone who was transporting drugs. They thought it was worth it to kill him to try to evade justice."

"I'm so sorry."

"It's been five years and time heals most wounds.

I told myself I wouldn't care about anyone in law enforcement again. Then I met Bryce. He got under my skin before I knew what was happening and I became close to him. But…"

"What happened?"

Sierra hadn't meant to get this detailed. "Raul happened. He nearly killed us both. I knew then I needed to distance myself from Bryce. I couldn't bear it if he got hurt again because of me. I couldn't go through someone else I cared about getting killed. Someone I loved. Unfortunately, I also love my dog. Bryce gave him to me. I trained him for protection and to search for and detain those the police were after. But then a friend's K-9 was killed in the line of fire and that's when I decided I'd had enough. I couldn't let Samson die too, so I moved here. I cross-trained him for wilderness search and rescue and avalanche searches, so here we are."

"Yes." Barbara gazed into the fire too, as if lost in thought. "And Bryce is here too. Looks like you can't get away from those who care about you even if you try."

Barbara offered Sierra a soft smile, then she rose from the chair. Squeezing Sierra's shoulder as she moved past, she said, "I'm going to leave you to your thoughts and do a few chores before bed. Feel free to turn in if you want. Oh, and I see Bryce is already back."

He stepped all the way into the room from the hallway. Had he come in the back door? "The sheriff is in the mudroom cleaning up."

Sierra risked a glance his way and found Bryce studying her as though he had heard every word she'd said about him.

Oh, no.

TEN

Bryce edged closer to the sofa opposite Sierra, uncertain if she wanted his company.

Chewing her bottom lip, she watched him approach—with that look in her eyes. It was obvious that she wondered if he'd heard what she'd said to Barbara.

Should he tell her? Or spare her the pain? He'd come in through the back and padded down the hallways in his socks. Sheriff Locke had remained outside talking to Officer Kendall.

When Bryce had heard her voice and mention of Buck, he'd paused. He should have made himself known or headed the other way so he wouldn't eavesdrop, but his feet became cemented in the floor.

He didn't think he could bear the discussion of their past loves and their breakup himself, so said, "Do you ever wish you lived somewhere like Florida?"

She rewarded him with a smile and a burst of laughter. "Where did that come from?"

"Are you kidding me? It's cold out there. Brrrr." He rubbed his arms for effect.

She angled her head, her smile soft. He wished her lips didn't appear so inviting. He was positive she didn't intend that, but they did have a history, after all. He should good and well remember the other part of their history and why he was here at this moment.

Stay focused on protecting her.

"I guess I've never thought about it," she said. "Growing up in the mountains, I couldn't see living anywhere else. Maybe Florida or some warm beach with palm trees would be a nice break and make me appreciate my home even more. But I can't think that far into the future at the moment."

He heard in her tone what she hadn't said—Raul was consuming all her attention.

"Uh… Bryce?"

Uh. Oh. "Yeah?"

"I've been thinking."

He leaned forward until his elbows were on his thighs. "I'm not sure that's such a good thing."

She threw a pillow at him and he caught it. "Hey."

"Hey, yourself."

"So what have you been thinking?" He rubbed his chin. This was going to be a long night on multiple fronts.

"You and I discussed going out there and searching for Raul ourselves. Samson and I know the area better than the state police and their dogs. We could come across an obscure place—a cabin or a mine—out of sight. Some place he could be hiding out. It's far better than waiting around here for him to come and get me. That he's crazy is obvious, but—" she shivered, even sitting close to a crackling fire "—being targeted and obsessed over by a sick person like him is unnerving in a thousand ways. We have to get him before he gets us. We have to find him."

"But you don't want to take Samson out there until he's ready for that." And that was only if she would allow Samson to search for Raul, at all, especially after what happened today. But he wouldn't bring it up.

"Exactly where I was going with this. Tomorrow is the mixed climbing, one of the main competitions in the festival, so it's going to be über-crowded. Raul knows his way around. He must have some skills in mountain climbing. Maybe ice climbing, like we discussed. We should go to the event and see if he makes an appearance. He'll think he can hide in the crowd."

"I don't know, Sierra. Your safety is the most important thing." Should he tell her? "Tonight when we checked the perimeter, the sheriff and I discussed you potentially staying here through this—as a sort of safe house."

"Dad and I are here only until the state has processed the crime scene and released our apartment. I can't stay here beyond then, Bryce. I've already texted Jane to let her know that Dad and I will be back in town in the morning in time to attend the ice climbing festivities and watch the main event with you tomorrow."

"So you won't stay here even for your dad?"

"That's a low blow and you know it."

"It's like you're *asking* Raul to come and get you."

"Maybe I am. This time I'll be waiting." Sierra shoved from the sofa and headed toward the hall. She called over her shoulder, "Be ready early—the events start at eight." Sierra nudged a sleeping Samson with her toe. "Come on, boy. Time for bed."

She disappeared down the hallway, Samson on her heels. Bryce heard the telltale sound of her door opening and closing.

Well that settled it. She'd made up her mind and all Bryce could do was follow her to the crowded event and stand in the cold until his nose froze off. He'd grown up in Florida and he'd never quite gotten used to the cold here. Still, he'd do his best to protect her while he worked by her side to bring down Raul.

In a way they were a team again, and this time, he hoped Raul would finally get put away in a place that he could never escape—somewhere far from Colorado would be optimal.

Sheriff Locke rushed into the living area. "Bryce. Rick thought he saw movement. Could be an animal, but we're going out to investigate. Bryce, you remain on guard in the house."

"You got it." Bryce immediately got to his feet and brandished his weapon. It was going to be a long night. He moved quietly through the large home, checking all the locks on the doors and windows. He came across Sheriff Locke's master bedroom and softly knocked on the door. The sheriff had entrusted him with the inside of his home, so he wouldn't make any exceptions when it came to checking things over.

Barbara answered with a concerned frown. "Is everything all right?"

"We're not sure. Will you please make sure your windows are closed and locked?"

She opened the door wide. Folded laundry was on the bed and a television program played quietly on the wide screen. "To tell you the truth, we usually do sleep with the window cracked, even in the winter. We love to sleep with lots of covers piled high."

Barbara showed Bryce the windows—they weren't

locked, but Bryce secured them. "Thanks. I'm sorry to disturb you."

"No problem," she said. "I was just getting on top of laundry."

Turner and Hooch barely lifted their heads to acknowledge his entrance as they slept on big dog pillows by the wall. She'd trained them well. He left Barbara to finish the laundry. What must it be like after a long day of police work to come home to a nice log cabin in the woods and spend the evening with the woman you loved next to a big fire? Sheriff Locke had carved out a good life for himself here, though Bryce knew it wasn't entirely without its dangers. The sheriff could be called upon any time of day or night.

Still, somehow, Bryce's bachelor lifestyle didn't measure up. He was on his own because he'd resolved he wouldn't allow himself the pain of heartache again. And yet there was heartache nonetheless. The endless pain of loneliness. He brushed off the melancholy. Now wasn't the time to think about what he could have had. What he still wanted.

Next, he knocked softly on Sierra's door. Of course she would lock the window, but Bryce hadn't expected Barbara's windows to be open either, so it was better to check every single one of them.

Sierra cracked the door and peeked out, a meager grin on her face. "What do you want?"

"I'm doing a window check. Are yours locked?"

"Well of course they're locked. Why wouldn't they... Hold on." She opened the door and then moved to the window and opened it wide, letting a cold breeze blow through. Then she closed it hard and locked it.

Sierra jerked her face to him. "Is there something going on? What's happened?"

"I don't know. Kendall thought he saw something. He and the sheriff are checking it out."

Samson was snoring per usual. He didn't seem too disturbed. "Do you think he's too drugged from whatever the vet gave him to warn you or protect you?"

Her brows pinched as she stared at him. "I'm not sure."

Sierra moved to the side table and pulled a weapon out of the drawer. "I might as well just sit in that chair with my gun all night. I'm not going to get any sleep like this."

Bryce gently took the weapon from her, surprised she so easily gave it up. He gripped her arms and peered into her eyes. "I'm here to protect you. I did it before. Please trust me to do that again for you. Tonight and for the next many days and nights until this is over." More emotion than he'd intended resounded in his words, but maybe she needed to understand the depth of his commitment.

He could see in her eyes that she wanted to trust him. He didn't miss the longing there and the images of previous kisses they'd shared crept softly across his mind and heart. That same longing coursed through every artery and vein, through his soul.

Sierra...

Then Bryce caught himself. Now was the absolute wrong time for this. There was a killer out there—maybe only a dozen yards away. And even if there wasn't, this moment could never happen for them.

He hitched a half grin and stepped back. "Besides, you're a mess when you go without sleep."

* * *

Sierra blinked her eyes open. *Where am I?*

The familiar rush of fear sent her heart rate into her throat, then she exhaled.

No nightmare had woken her up.

She stared at the ceiling for a moment before she got her bearings. She was in Sheriff Locke's home. And she'd fallen asleep. She'd actually slept hard. Maybe that was because Bryce had made her feel safe. That man she'd once thought she'd fallen for was here for her until this was over. She trusted him with her life, but she knew to steer clear of him in matters of the heart. She didn't trust herself when it came to her feelings for him.

But Sierra couldn't figure out why Bryce would be here for her in this way when he had his own life and business to run back in Boulder. Why would he put his life on the line for her like this? He wasn't here for some romantic dream that they might rekindle what they had been growing toward in the past. They both knew where they stood on that. She had her reasons. He had his.

They were friends, yes, or tried to be while ignoring their attraction, but Sierra hadn't realized the depth of feelings for her. Still she knew in her heart that if Bryce was in some sort of trouble she would probably rush to his aid as well—no matter the cost. Right? Friends did that for each other.

Except she'd never had that kind of friendship with anyone else. And she wasn't entirely sure hers and Bryce's relationship was completely platonic.

In fact, she needed to face and accept the truth—tonight, if he had kissed her, she would totally have let him. She had *wanted* him to kiss her, even though she'd resolved not to let herself fall for someone in his kind of career. She shouldn't live in fear, and in this way, she didn't have to. Still, if something happened to Bryce—whether she was romantically involved or not—it would crush her. He held a big place in her heart and that had never changed.

Samson drew her attention in the dim lighting. He stood by the window and a low growl rumbled in his chest.

Could that be what had woken her up?

She sat up on the edge of the bed and grabbed her weapon on the table, her breath coming fast.

That night long ago, she'd woken up to find Raul in her room. He had already taken her gun while she'd been sleeping. If he was back, he'd find that she was ready for him this time.

Sierra got up and paced the small, warmly decorated room.

The blinds were closed so it wasn't like Raul could see into the room, for which she was grateful. But Sierra really wanted to see outside. She didn't want to disturb the household if it was nothing. The sheriff and Officer Kendall had gone out checking earlier and she'd meant to wait up and see if they'd found anything. Sierra had fallen asleep.

She glanced at the clock. That had been two hours ago. So the men would have come back inside by now.

Could Samson be growling at an animal? Maybe a mountain lion was roaming around out there in freezing temperatures.

Sierra crouched to eye level with Samson and rubbed his ears. "What is it boy? Are you hungry? Thirsty? Are you in pain?"

He moved back to the window and growled, then gave a deep menacing bark.

And with that bark fear curdled in her gut.

Okay. That was it.

She backed against the wall every bit the coward she didn't want to be, hadn't expected to be, but images of Raul nearly killing her swarmed through her.

Her throat constricted until she could hardly breathe. *He's outside the window. He's out there.*

"So get your act together and get out there and take him down." *Snap out of it.*

Sierra quickly changed into snow pants and pulled on a hoodie. In the mudroom she would grab her coat and snow boots. She would let Officer Kendall know that something might be happening.

Samson whined as she made to open the bedroom door. Even if Sierra was willing to let Samson face off against a killer, with his injury he wasn't ready. "Sorry, buddy. You need to heal."

She opened the door and found Bryce standing there as though waiting. "I heard him bark. What are you doing?"

"Raul is out there."

"How do you know?"

"I just know, okay?"

"And you're going out there to get him all by your lonesome?"

Sierra gave him an incredulous look. "Of course not. I knew you'd be standing right here. And we can get Kendall and the sheriff too. But Raul is out there. He was…" Her throat constricted again. She fought for air, then said, "I think he was at my window."

"Stay here." Bryce stomped off.

She trailed him to the mudroom. The blinds had been shut in there as well.

He found Officer Kendall putting his boots on. "It's time for my perimeter check."

"We think Raul's out there," Bryce said. "So I'm going with you."

"Notify the sheriff," Kendall said.

"Right." Bryce turned to her. "Sierra, you go let the sheriff know what's happening."

"Okay, but I'm coming with you when you head outside to search. If you leave without me, then I'll find you, so you'd better not leave."

Sierra rushed down the hallway to find the sheriff exiting his room. "We think Raul is outside."

"Because?"

How did she explain? She felt like an idiot. "It's a gut feel. Samson was growling at my window. Don't ask me how. I just… Know."

"Good enough for me. But you're staying here."

"Sheriff, I—"

"I need you to keep Barbara safe."

He left her standing there. This wasn't how she'd planned things to go down. But she couldn't leave his wife sleeping in her room—and her father, just down the hall—when Raul was outside.

Sierra stood in the hallway next to Barbara's door. Samson whined and barked from her room, wanting out. From here, she could see a portion of the mudroom and she watched the three men exit. Sierra headed that way, opening the bedroom door to let Samson come with her.

"Raul could come right through this door now that all three of them are out there, Samson. And if he does, you and I will be waiting for him."

"And me." Barbara emerged from the hallway and pumped the shotgun she held. "I'll be here waiting for him too."

Sierra couldn't help but smile, and almost wished that Raul would come through that door to face off against the three of them—Barbara, Sierra and Samson.

Barbara moved closer to the door. "I don't think it hurts to lock it though, in case he tries. We'll let the guys in when they get back."

A window shattered.

Turner and Hooch yapped, shrill and anxious, in the master bedroom.

Samson barked and ran toward the sound. Sierra commanded him to stay. Bryce's words to her about letting Samson do what he was trained to do surfaced in her mind.

But he's a big dog. He's trained to do many things including protect. Remember you trained him to hopefully one day become part of the new BPD's K-9 unit that would work with the Boulder County Sheriff's office K-9 unit. Tonight you were afraid to let him protect you or to let him go after Raul.

She already knew all of it, but Bryce's words stayed with her and unsettled her.

"I'll go check it out," Barbara said.

If something happened to Barbara, Sierra would never forgive herself. Samson acted as if his wound didn't affect him. She was being overly cautious.

"No. I have Samson for protection. He can also apprehend and detain a suspect. I'll take him to check it out. You stay here and watch the back door for the guys."

Barbara pursed her lips and nodded.

Sierra commanded Samson to guard. In this case he would apprehend an intruder if one existed.

God, please keep us safe.

He took off, an intimidating, ferocious beast of an animal.

She kept her eyes opened as she silently prayed. *Please keep Samson safe.*

Her weapon ready to aim and fire, she followed her K-9. They'd never gotten to officially work together in Boulder. How surreal this felt.

Samson sniffed at the master bedroom door and barked. Turner and Hooch continued to yap and growl, but the sounds were muted. Maybe Barbara had put them away in the bathroom to keep them out of harm's way.

Heart pounding, Sierra leaned against the wall and drew in two breaths. She prepared to come in low as she opened the door.

She flung it open, giving Samson the "attack" command. *"Fassen!"*

He dashed into the room as she aimed her weapon at empty air.

The curtain billowed with the rush of wind through the broken window. Sierra crept to the side of the window to peer out.

A shadow moved outside. "Freeze!"

"It's me, Sierra!" Bryce shouted.

She lowered the weapon and gasped. No wonder Samson hadn't jumped through the window—he'd known Bryce was there. But someone else had been there moments before.

Samson approached her. She knelt and rubbed his ears. *"Zei Brav!* Good boy."

Relief washed through her on the one hand that Samson wasn't in danger, and frustration gnawed her at the same time—how did they bring this man down?

She stood and examined the broken window. The sound of a snowmobile's engine growing distant mixed with the increase wind gusts. Raul getting away?

Would the sheriff make Samson search outside now?

Boots clomped in the mudroom. It was over. The men had come back inside. She bent over and pressed her face into Samson's fur.

A hand squeezed her shoulder and she looked up. Bryce. "We need to board up that window now."

"Did you see him?"

"No. Just tracks." But it's snowing like crazy so they'll be gone soon.

"And the sheriff doesn't want to use Samson to track him?"

He pursed his lips and crouched to look her in the eyes. "It's two degrees out there and a possible whiteout is in the mix. Neither you nor Samson is in any condition to track someone. If it was Raul, he's gone now. Just like earlier today, he shows up and, by the time we're on to him, he's already retreating. We aren't going to be able to follow him tonight. I want to know what he broke the window with."

Bryce looked around the room. Samson was sniffing at something on the bed.

Sierra gasped. "It's just a rock." She held her breath. Did it have a note attached?

Bryce carefully lifted the rock to find a slip of paper affixed, held within a Ziplock bag to make sure moisture didn't destroy it.

"What does it say, Bryce?" Raul was going to a lot of trouble to keep her in fear.

He frowned. "Let's let your sheriff look at this."

"Look at what?" Sheriff Locke appeared in his doorway, Barbara standing behind him.

He marched forward into the room with a big board. Barbara held the hammer and nails.

"Oh, I'm so sorry, Sheriff," Sierra stepped forward. "This happened because I'm here."

"Nothing to apologize for." The sheriff grabbed the rock and peeled the taped Ziplock bag off.

He carefully opened the bag and slid the note out. The fewer fingerprints on it, the better, even though they knew who'd thrown the rock—and he'd likely worn gloves, given the current weather. The sheriff quietly read the note, then cleared his throat. "It says 'I'm coming for you.' Just more intimidation tactics," the sheriff said. "He wants to win a psychological battle and keep you buoyed by fear."

"Before he makes his final move," she said.

Sheriff Locke handed the rock and note off to Officer Kendall who had entered the room. The state officer placed it on the dresser and assisted the sheriff with boarding up the window. Barbara slipped into the bathroom to reassure Turner and Hooch.

John stumbled through the doorway looking like he'd slept like a rock through the whole thing. "What's going on?"

"Oh, Dad." Sierra hugged him. "Go back to bed. I'll explain tomorrow."

He gave her a look and Sierra quickly explained what had happened. John's features sobered and he approached Sheriff Locke to engage him.

Bryce tugged Sierra out of the busy room into the hallway.

He lifted a strand of her hair as if cherishing her, then cupped her cheek. "Are you okay?"

"As okay as I can be."

"The problem is that he's not going to stop coming for you. Right now it seems that he's willing to go through a lot of trouble just to taunt you."

Sierra agreed. "Why would he come here to the sheriff's home and not finish the job? How did he even know I was here?"

That much evil in one person sent chills crawling over her.

"All good questions." Bryce dropped his hand. "Let's get you out of here. I'm staying with you while they board up the window."

Sierra followed Bryce out to the living room where he put more logs on the fire. "You're right when you say he's going to keep coming for me. So I need to find him first like we discussed. We're still going to search for a cabin or a mine or someplace to find where he's hiding out, aren't we?"

Bryce leaned his arm on the mantel and stared into the fire, concern etched in his features. "Law enforcement is already searching, Sierra."

"But don't you see, Bryce, most of the people searching are not local. They didn't grow up exploring the woods and mountains around here. Help me to find him before he gets the advantage."

His gaze flicked to her. "And Samson? Are you willing to let him do what he was trained to do?"

Her heart wasn't willing, no. "Yes."

ELEVEN

Tented vendor booths exhibiting ice tools, outdoor wear and gear lined the crowded walkway of the ice park. Spectators in coats and knit caps and beanies gathered to watch the ice climbing events featuring competitors climbing the frozen waterfalls of the gorge.

Bryce kept Sierra close at his side as they meandered through the exhibits, people on every side of them. If he weren't so focused on trying to protect her in this ridiculous scenario, he might enjoy actually watching the competitors scale the ice in the variety of contests including speed climbing.

But his priorities required he focus completely on protecting Sierra from Raul, and searching for the man in the process. State law enforcement was present as well, some dressed in uniform and others in plain clothes—everyone here to spot Raul Novack if he showed his face in town.

Like Sierra, Bryce couldn't help but hope they actually spotted Raul today here in plain sight so they could get their hands on him once and for all.

When the toy store didn't see any customers, Sierra and John had made the decision to close the shop for a few hours so that Jane and Sierra's father could watch the climbers. They would reopen for a couple of hours this afternoon. For now, all the excitement was here. Everyone wanted to see the action at the gorge or browse the vendor exhibits. No one was interested in shopping for toys at the moment.

Samson stayed behind with Barbara and seemed to be on the mend. Bryce was proud of Sierra for allowing the dog back into action—for the second time in one day. Sierra was slowly getting there. Bryce hoped Samson wouldn't have to protect her against Raul, but if it came to that, he would be glad for Samson's help.

He still found it interesting that Raul hadn't shot and killed the dog in the woods the previous day. Maybe he'd missed, but at close range, Bryce doubted that. Many criminals had quirks and maybe Raul was willing to kill people but unwilling to kill animals. Bryce wouldn't count on that though.

When it came to Raul, conjecture was just that—a presumption.

They made it to the gorge area just as the competition was starting, and maneuvered their way to a rail so they could watch as a woman used an ice pick and crawled her way up the frozen waterfalls. He kept thinking back to the way Raul had escaped them in the cold, snowy, icy mountains.

He glanced at Sierra who was smiling, and for once in the last few days, he thought she actually might have forgotten an evil man was coming after her. Her cheeks were rosy from the cold, and a few snowflakes clung to her lashes. Warmth stirred inside him.

Friends. You're friends and nothing more.

But the way he'd slipped his arm around her and the

way they held on to each other for warmth and protection might seem to those around them that they were much more to each other than mere friends.

Bryce planted a kiss on the side of her head. Oops. He'd acted without thinking. Sierra smiled at him as if she welcomed the attention.

God, what happened to us? Why can't we be together? Catch a break? Something?

He had no business thinking about it. Or even asking God. He knew the answers to his questions—this woman had hurt him before because she hadn't been willing to take the risk, and he wouldn't let her do it again. He'd heard her plain enough last night as she shared with Barbara her reasons for not wanting to be with Bryce. It was as he'd suspected all along.

He didn't blame her. She had a choice and she'd made it. He had a choice too—to protect her until this was over. Then he'd be gone before he fell head over heels for her again.

Her bright blue eyes flashed at him then at the climber scaling the ice, and his breath caught.

Bryce loosened his grip on her just a little. She'd be okay. He didn't have to hold her so close to protect her.

There. That was better. His heartbeat slowed enough for him to breathe.

"Bryce. Earth to Bryce." Sierra pretended to knock on his head. "You're a million miles away."

"Sorry." He refocused on the task at hand. Being this close to her scrambled his brain.

"Can you believe it's almost lunchtime? I'm hungry. Let's head over to grab food before everyone has the same idea."

"Sure thing." He held her hand—just so they didn't

lose each other in the crowd, of course—as they pushed through the crowd, bumping into a few people, but no one as nefarious as Raul Novack. One of the more permanent eating establishments was situated near the ice festival and crowds already gathered there, while others remained focused on the competition.

This town really exploded during this festival.

Hot dogs, fries and Cokes in hand, Bryce and Sierra found a table inside the restaurant.

"I don't think he's going to show up today." She said the words around a mouthful of hot dog. "I can't decide if I'm glad about that or mad. I mean, if he does show up here, then maybe we can get him and I can get on with my life and you can get back to yours."

Her brows suddenly pinched and she stared at the ketchup while she stirred a French fry, creating a figure eight. What was that about?

He wouldn't for one second imagine that she didn't want him to leave. But her words had that effect on him, as if she'd said she wanted him to stay. As for him—he wasn't sure how he would feel when it came time to leave her once and for all.

Time to change the subject. "I've been thinking I might like to get a dog and train him."

That brought her face up, her beautiful blue eyes widened. "But you're a PI now."

"So? Are you saying that since PIs don't have their own canine groups, I can't train a dog? Well, there are plenty of SAR dog rescue volunteers. I could get involved in SAR and other activities." It would be something to do. Something to take his mind off…everything else. Off Sierra. Then again, it might only be a constant reminder. "I see how you are with Samson, and

I've heard a few stories since being here of his rescues. That must bring you a measure of satisfaction and the sense of achievement. Like you're actually accomplishing something."

"Stories? Who'd you hear those from?"

"Well that guy at the café who seems interested in you. I grabbed coffee from there and he regaled me. He seemed very interested."

"Oh, I get it. He was fishing to see if…" Sierra seemed to catch herself.

"Right. If you and I had something going."

Sierra sipped on her soda until the straw made the gurgling noise. "There's nothing between me and Miguel. Would you excuse me? I need to use the facilities, but I'm not finished yet, so don't throw my fries away."

She got up from the table.

Why had she told him there wasn't anything going on between her and Miguel? As though she thought he would care?

He should follow her and stick close. He started to get up and then glanced down at her fries. She wasn't finished eating yet. Instead of leaving the food behind, Bryce watched her walk to the restroom, and kept his seat. He wanted to see her smile when she came back and saw him guarding her fries.

In the lady's room, Sierra washed her hands. *There's nothing there between me and Miguel.*

Her words to Bryce echoed through her mind. Now why had she told him that? It wasn't any of Bryce's business if she was seeing anyone. They'd parted ways long before she'd moved and she hadn't seen or heard from him in the year since she'd been back in Crescent Springs. So what if she'd changed her number?

Sure she'd thought about him.

A lot.

More than she should or had a right to. But she'd seen the question in Bryce's eyes when he mentioned that Miguel was fishing for answers—Bryce had been the one fishing. He'd wanted to know if Sierra was interested in Miguel.

She thrust her hands under the dryer as if the obnoxiously loud noise could drown out her thoughts.

If only.

Sierra shoved through the door.

A sharp pain jabbed into her back—unmistakably a knife. "Scream and you die right here."

The man belonging to the voice yanked her around the corner down a short hallway where the restrooms resided. The voice sounded raspy—was it Raul's? She didn't remember him sounding this way, but it had been a long time since that horrible night.

It all happened so quickly Sierra couldn't react to prevent it. All these people—it was so crowded that nobody noticed.

And Bryce!

The weapon pressed deeper against her shirt, just beneath her coat, making her wince. She had to do something now or the man would succeed in abducting her in broad daylight at the ice festival. At the end of the short hallway, he commanded her to open the door with the red exit sign.

How could she use this door, this hallway, her defense tactics? How could she get away? If she screamed he would kill her—she had no doubt of that.

Then as if anticipating she would try something, he jabbed her so hard, she almost cried out in pain. She was certain he'd drawn blood. The door opened up to an alley and cold air swirled inside the restaurant.

This can't be happening.

All those people in the restaurant. All the crowds swarming the festival and the vendor exhibits, and an alley was empty? But she understood—two dumpsters blocked off one end, and a van blocked off the other.

Sierra should have seen it coming. But she hadn't and now she was in the middle of it. She was law enforcement. She knew how to protect herself. And yet she couldn't use her weapon because he'd disarmed her with a knife.

A stupid knife!

In her peripheral vision she could see that he was wearing a ski mask. It wouldn't draw suspicion—it was cold outside, after all. But it succeeded in hiding his face from all the law enforcement officers searching for him. No one paid much attention.

She couldn't suck in enough oxygen and hyperventilated. Fear choked her.

God, help me!

Even Samson couldn't have prevented this. Sierra should be able to go to use the facilities without fear of an attack. But her dog could have at least warned her.

The man guided her down the alley, but instead of the knife, he switched to her gun, having removed it from the shoulder holster as he held the knife to her throat. She could feel the muzzle pressing into her side under her coat. Locked and loaded. Ready to fire. At such close range it would blow a hole through her.

She'd wait for the moment—that split second in time

that Raul's attention was somewhere else—and she'd go for the gun. What did that say about her that she lost her weapon to him?

She let the fury at herself and the situation course through her, hoping it would drive away her fear, so she would be ready to act when that moment came.

He urged her forward to approach the van parked at the end of the alley.

Whatever happened next, she absolutely couldn't let this man put her in that van.

"Look, I don't know what you think you're doing. I don't know why you think you can get away with this, but—"

"Shut up!" He jabbed her weapon harder into her side.

And that small pain was only a small taste of what he would do to her when he got her alone. He would torture her before he killed her.

She fought the weakness spreading through her limbs.

No, no, no, no...

They were fast approaching the van, but Sierra was losing control of her body—her mind going into shock.

"Don't worry, girl. You're not going to die. Not yet. I'll let you watch me torture that beast you call a dog first."

Anger surged through her, empowering her. Sierra threw her head back and head-butted Raul. Temporarily stunned, she took that moment to free herself from his grip.

She had to get that gun away from him. Her gun.

"You're not going to touch Samson!" She plowed into him, reaching for the weapon.

He brought it down on her head. Darkness edged her vision.

Raul yanked her up by her hair. Still stunned from the blow to her head, Sierra was powerless.

"Stop right there. Let her go!" said Bryce.

TWELVE

Raul had his filthy hands on Sierra!

Bryce pointed the weapon at the man, even as he pointed a gun at her head. The man yanked harder on her hair, but she didn't scream. Blood oozed from her head. What had he done to her?

Bryce saw red. He blinked to clear his vision, but he still saw red.

He should take the shot now and kill the man and be done with it.

"Lower your weapon or I'll shoot." Bryce allowed all the venom he held inside edge his tone.

"I don't think so," Raul said. "You put yours down or I'll kill her."

Bryce's body shook but his hands were steady, his aim was true.

"Mommy, Mommy…" A little girl ran around the van in search of her mom and ran right into Raul.

Oh, no! Bryce couldn't shoot. Raul was momentarily startled as well and lost his grip on Sierra, who slammed her elbow into his gut. He lost his aim and the advantage he'd had over Sierra and Bryce. Bryce had the drop on him and fingered the trigger, his aim true. Realizing he'd lost his chance, Raul shoved Sierra into the snow and took off into the crowd. He knew that Bryce wouldn't shoot him in the back, or shoot into the crowd.

Bryce was relieved he didn't have to shoot the man in front of the little girl, but he was ready to give chase.

A woman appeared and grabbed her daughter. Screamed when she saw Bryce's weapon and blood in the snow. Sierra's blood. How badly was she hurt? Bryce couldn't lose Raul. But Sierra…

He dropped to his knees next to her, his heart in his throat. "Sierra, Sierra. Are you okay?"

She grabbed her head and peered up at him. "He hit me with the gun. I'm okay. You go after him. I'll be all right. You can detain him for me. We have to get him!"

"I'm not leaving you." Bryce got his cell out and called the sheriff's direct number to inform him that Raul was indeed in town. "We have to close the roads, whatever it takes to get him," he said. "He almost got Sierra." *Almost took her from me.*

Bryce ended the call but he could hear in his head what the sheriff might have said to him. *"I thought you were supposed to watch over her."*

The guilt could crush him, and he would let it—later. After this was over. Now it was time to make amends.

He grabbed her arm and assisted her to her feet. She leaned into him. "What kind of cop am I, Bryce, to let him get the best of me like that?"

"You're a great cop." What kind of man, what kind of protector was Bryce to let Raul get to her?

He escorted her out of the cold and into Miguel's café. "Wait, what are you doing?" she asked. "My home is across the street."

"I'm getting you out of the cold while I call an ambulance."

"What? Bryce, stop it. You don't—"

But he was already calling. The ambulance might have a tough time getting through the crowd, but it would be easier than him trying to get her to a vehicle to drive her to the hospital.

"Can I do anything?" Miguel rushed forward. He peered at Sierra, his concern for her sincere.

"Yes. A bag of ice would help."

Miguel nodded and quickly disappeared. He returned just as quickly with a big bag of frozen English peas and handed it directly to Sierra. "Here, put this on that knot."

She eyed him. "Thanks, Miguel." Then she pressed it against her head.

Concern for her filled Bryce. Fury at Raul twisted through his gut.

Disappointment in himself could paralyze him. She might need someone else to protect her, but he knew she would never allow anyone else—he was fortunate she allowed him.

A siren sounded in the distance. Miguel explained the small ambulance service often had to deliver people to bigger hospitals, but the nearby clinic could look her over and then if necessary send her to Montrose or Telluride. Bryce feared that would be the case though.

EMTs rushed into the café with a gurney.

"Oh, please," she said. "I can walk."

The paramedic looked at her head. "Do me a favor and sit on the gurney."

Sierra sat and then she lay down.

The woman looked at Bryce. "She's going to be okay, don't worry."

Words of assurance spoken without any real knowledge. "I'm coming with you," Bryce said.

"Who's going to drive me home later if you don't have a car, Bryce?" Sierra was thinking ahead, even injured. She had to be feeling that injury now, not only physically but psychologically.

"The sheriff or your dad." Oh, that's right. Bryce would need to let her dad know what happened too. The gurney was moving and Bryce strolled along with it and held her hand. "Stop worrying, Sierra."

She closed her eyes, but the worry lines remained in her face.

They lifted the gurney up and Bryce made to climb in.

The paramedic looked at him. "Can't you just follow?"

"No. I'm protecting her. I'm not leaving her. A maniac is out there and tried to take her."

And Bryce had let that happen.

Sierra sat on the edge of the bed in the clinic.

Bryce stood against the far wall, but in the small space "far" didn't mean much. She could feel the concern and protectiveness radiating off him. She'd tried to ignore it while the doctor had bandaged the small wound in her side where Raul had drawn blood while forcing her out of the restaurant. She also had a mild concussion from where he'd smacked her on the head.

She would gladly take that concussion over all the other scenarios that ran through her mind of what he'd have done to her if he'd succeeded in taking her away.

Bryce was here with her for which she was glad. But

she knew that look on his face. He was contemplating, and it was something big that she wasn't going to like.

That, and…well, she was pretty sure he was berating himself on the inside. Neither of them spoke much because there were far bigger self-recriminations going on inside—and who wanted to speak those truths out loud?

When she could no longer stand the silence between them she drew in a breath, then said, "I'm not going to sit here and let you beat yourself up, Bryce. Just stop it. I agree that what happened today should never have happened, but—"

"Oh, you can read my mind now?"

"Of course I can. You're thinking the same thing I am. You're trying to figure out what you could have done differently the same as me. There's no time for this kind of examination."

Despite the pain in her head, she slid from the table and moved to Bryce, blocking him against the wall. In his gaze she saw that he felt trapped and for some strange reason, for the moment, she felt like enjoying the power she had over him. But she'd truly been hit in the head too hard if she was thinking that way. She took a step back but he snatched her arm and pulled her close again.

He held on to her waist as he inched forward and spoke, his voice shaky and barely audible. "I could have lost you."

He gently tugged her against him. Wrapped his strong arms around her. "I'm so glad you're safe. And I'm…so, so sorry. Please forgive me."

The tenderness and anguish in his voice nearly did her in, but she'd had enough of weakness for one day even if the reasons for that weakness couldn't be more different. Still, she allowed herself to stay in his arms.

Sierra inched away enough to see his face. He was much too close, but she didn't want to pull away. "There's nothing to forgive. Nothing. You hear me? I wouldn't want anyone else here with me in this, protecting me and helping me. No one but you, Bryce."

At the same time, she wanted him gone. He was in danger because of her.

Fierce emotion flashed in his eyes.

Oh, why had she said that?

Because it's true...

Sierra found the strength to take a step back. Then another.

That emotion she couldn't read in Bryce's gaze remained. "Let me take you away from here," he pleaded. "We can go halfway across the world if that's what it takes. Whatever it takes to keep you safe, Sierra, that's what I want to do. I can't..."

What would he have said? Lose her? Fail? She wasn't sure she wanted to hear. Her throat constricted.

"Look, I'm begging you."

Sierra frowned and shook her head. "I just can't leave like that, Bryce. What about Samson? What about Dad? I can tell you he won't leave his home or his store."

"Because he's stubborn like his daughter."

"Whatever the reason, leaving is something that's not happening. If you want to do anything to keep me safe then help me get Raul. Help me take him down."

A throat cleared.

Sierra turned to see Sheriff Locke. "If you two are done, I've come to drive you home. I didn't feel I could trust anyone else with the job."

What he meant was he wasn't sure anyone would be safe in Sierra's proximity because of Raul's determination to get to her. "Where is home, Sheriff?"

"You're welcome to stay at my place until this is over."

"Have they finished gathering evidence from my home?"

He nodded. "They have. Your dad already gathered his things to go home. I made him wait for you though. You decide what's best."

What was best was fewer people in her proximity so there would be fewer people in danger. Yet, she couldn't leave Crescent Springs either. Her father wouldn't leave, and leaving him here alone wasn't an option either.

"Okay, then. It's back to town."

Bryce's disapproval was clear in his gaze.

THIRTEEN

In the middle of the night, the town was finally quiet after today's festivities. Even the lights were out in hotel rooms.

Bryce finished hiking around the cluster of buildings that included the toy store and Sierra's apartment in the back, wishing not for the first time that Sierra would have stayed at the sheriff's home. Though Raul had found her there and quickly. He must be watching her somehow. Raul hadn't taken her out from a distance because he didn't have the sharpshooter skills. Or maybe he was just fixated on the idea that he wanted to torture her before he killed her.

Bryce had equally dark thoughts about what he wanted to do when he got his hands on the escaped murdering convict and menace to society.

As he considered their current situation, Bryce hiked through the deepening snow back around to the street with his hotel.

Since Sierra refused to go anywhere, Bryce wished that she lived somewhere else besides this property on the literal edge of the small town. Their apartment next to a big empty wooded lot connected to the National

Forest. In the dark, the location presented too many opportunities for someone to get to Sierra. And it was dangerous—as he knew since he'd tried to chase down Raul and had fallen through the ice on the frozen riverbank.

She would be safe when Raul was once again incarcerated—as long as he stayed that way this time.

Sierra was right, though—she and Samson might be the best ones to search for the escaped convict. He knew how hard that decision had been, and how torn she was—not wanting to subject Samson to danger—but in the end, he was the best dog for this job. His safety was ultimately tied to Sierra's, and she'd finally reasoned it out. They had to do this.

Tomorrow they would take Samson and go Raul-hunting. After the near-abduction today, Sheriff Locke had convinced the state to send Rick Kendall along with them, though he wasn't available to guard Sierra and John's home tonight. They were shorthanded and no one was available—except for Bryce. Tomorrow, he and Sierra would be just one of many teams of searchers looking for the escaped convict, but until now, the searchers hadn't been local to the area.

None of them knew the area like Sierra and Samson.

At the hotel, Bryce crept up the stairs and tried to keep quiet so he wouldn't wake anyone. For now he would make the rounds every couple of hours. He wouldn't get much sleep tonight, just grabbing cat naps as he could through this ordeal. If this continued through tomorrow night, maybe he could take Samson with him. That dog would smell trouble and warn him. But like Sierra said, Samson needed his rest if he was going to search and track during the day.

Inside his room, Bryce peeked out the curtains at the store below. Glanced up and down the empty street.

It was much too cold on a winter's night to imagine someone out stalking—except Raul had shown them he was obsessed with Sierra and that the weather and elements wouldn't stand in his way.

Bryce's concern was only tempered for tonight anyway because John had installed a top-of-the-line security system for the store and apartment—he'd had a friend come in and set it up this evening when Sierra insisted on going home. Bryce wondered why it had taken them so long to begin with?

Still, short of sleeping on her sofa or next to her bedroom door, there wasn't much more Bryce could do. Sheriff Locke had his other deputies changing out watching the town, the state had left a few officers here as others pursued Raul this afternoon, coming up empty-handed so far, but they still searched. And Sierra had a gun—though they hadn't recovered the weapon Raul had taken—an alarm system, a dog she seemed willing to allow to protect her, and she had Bryce across the street. Not nearly close enough for him, but there all the same. Physically.

But emotionally?

He sensed that she still cared about him in a romantic way and was fighting it, the same as he fought it. So tonight, there would be no late night chats by the fireplace that might end in a kiss. A kiss presented dangers of its own and could send them down a road where neither of them wanted to be. He shook off thoughts of kissing Sierra—he definitely didn't need to spend the night thinking about that.

Her life was in danger, and he wouldn't, he couldn't, let Raul get his hands on her again.

God, please help me keep her safe. Please let us find Raul before it's too late.

Bryce lay on the bed fully dressed, his alarm set for two hours when he would check the perimeter again. Maybe his footprints left in the snow would serve as a deterrent.

He bolted awake when his alarm went off, surprised he'd actually fallen asleep. He rubbed his face then peeked through the window. Immediately he spotted footprints not his own. Or at least he didn't think so. He hadn't tracked so close to the building, almost as if hiding in the shadows. It could simply be someone walking home or to their car, but his gut told him it wasn't.

Heart pounding, he sent up a silent prayer as he texted Sierra. He hated waking her but this could be life or death. He warned her about the footprints in the snow and to be on the lookout. To be cautious.

Then he pulled on his coat and grabbed his weapon. Outside, he glanced up and down the street. Peered into the shadows and obvious hiding places.

The snow had stopped and the moon shined bright tonight, giving off enough light for him to see. He set out to follow those footprints. If this was Raul, he must not care if anyone spotted his steps. Or this could be a trap for Bryce. He would remain mindful of that.

He wished he knew where the footsteps had started but at this point, he could only follow and hope he would find whoever had left them. If it was Raul he hoped he found him and took him down once and for all.

He gripped his weapon and held it at low ready. He

followed the steps around the end of the building and then behind it near the woods.

Not good. Not good at all.

Apprehension grew in his gut.

The footsteps did not lead to Sierra's apartment door. They veered sharply away just before the door which raised his suspicions. Bryce stood in the shadows and let his gaze search the woods.

He hadn't felt the telltale buzz of his phone to let him know Sierra had replied to his text.

But Samson's deep bark resounded from inside the apartment. Maybe he'd barked earlier and scared the lurker off. Bryce wouldn't be foolish enough to follow him into those woods again, especially since he was alone. But how he wanted to get his hands on the man. He almost couldn't wait until tomorrow and he hoped Sierra would let Samson loose. The dog should be recovered enough to track Raul and if Raul really was here tonight, his tracks should be fresh.

Surely the man knew that, but he'd succeeded in escaping the other K-9s brought in by the police.

His cell buzzed and he read the text.

Samson barked and growled. He won't let anyone get to me. Don't worry.

Bryce chuckled to himself. Yeah, maybe even including Bryce. Though it wasn't his intention to get too close to her, emotionally speaking. Unfortunately he had to keep reminding himself of that.

He responded to her text with a reply of his own about the tracks and a promise that he would stand guard out here for the rest of the night.

At least until he thought frostbite might take his nose.

The door swung open and Sierra peered out. "Get in here."

Sierra and Bryce snowshoed through the woods with Officer Kendall, following Samson as he trailed Raul with a combination of tracking and air scenting.

Sierra was so grateful to have Samson. And now, Samson's sharp olfactory senses searched for Raul—or the person who'd walked uncomfortably close to her door last night. Their tracks were now gone with an early morning foot of snow, but something of the scent remained and Samson would find him this time. She felt sure of it.

Their small three-person search team had dressed in protective clothing like the crowd of winter sports enthusiasts in Crescent Springs. The public was aware of the escaped convict and warned to be on alert, but it seemed to Sierra that news hadn't diminished the crowd or their passion for this event. Fortunately the competition was nearing its end and today would be the last day. This evening or early tomorrow morning tourists, spectators, competitors and vendors would pack up and leave town.

Then it would once again be peaceful and quiet.

The sun had come out and she felt entirely too warm inside her jacket, but taking it off was not an option—it was entirely too cold out without a jacket, and she'd have to lug it around anyway. Despite the business they were on, she couldn't help but think about the beauty of nature around her. God's creation was nothing less than spectacular.

And Bryce in this with her—God had seen to that, as well.

She wasn't exactly sure what to make of it since she'd worked so hard to distance herself from him.

A cold wind gusted over her face feeling much like the slap she needed. Sierra reined in her thoughts and focused on staying in tune with Samson. Training him had taken up so much of her life and they had to continue to train to keep on top of things. Now that she was sending him out to find a killer, she wished they hadn't fallen behind on training the last few days. If she had it all to do over again, she would have been especially focused on the attack aspects. She still feared Samson would face a gun and Raul would hurt him again—fatally this time.

She'd let that kind of training lapse since living in Crescent Springs and instead had cross-trained for search and rescue missions, and avalanche searches. Searching for criminals just wasn't a huge part of what they would normally see near Crescent Springs and the San Juan Mountains.

The evergreens' trunks clacked together as the wind blew again. An entire hour in they had traveled barely a mile and a half over the harsh terrain and deep snow, which, all things considered, was actually keeping up a decent pace. They had to move briskly in order to keep up with her working-class dog, Samson. But then his pace slowed. At the base of Carmel Mountain, Samson seemed to have lost the trail.

Would he find the scent again? She eyed the woods, the rocky terrain filled with fallen trunks and snow-covered thicket.

Finally, Samson started forward again. Relief whooshed

through her. Bryce pressed a hand on her arm. "Careful. We need to remain cautious. If we're closing in on Raul, he's even more dangerous."

True words. She patted her handgun in her holster just inside her coat and left her coat unzipped at the top so she could easily reach the weapon.

Samson started making his way down the edge of a ridge that left just enough room for him to descend. Sierra studied the drop. It would be a perfect "hidden" trail for someone looking to hide, but it wouldn't shake a tracking dog.

"Hold it," Kendall said. "Are we going to follow him?"

"Sure we are," she said.

"Do we need special equipment to safely get down there?"

"First, keep your voice down," Bryce said. "If Raul is hiding out somewhere near, we don't want him to hear our approach. As for climbing down, we can see what Samson does first."

Giving the dog a chance. Sierra appreciated that Bryce believed in Samson.

Samson still made his way carefully down, and Sierra took off her snowshoes, preparing to follow. She wouldn't leave him alone in this.

"What are you doing?" Bryce asked. "I thought we were giving Samson a chance to let us know if someone is down there."

"I need to be down there with him. Just in case." As she made the first step she eyed the bottom. Her throat tightened. "There's a mine down there," she whispered.

Bryce nodded. "Let's go then." Bryce looked at Kendall. "You coming? If you don't want to, then you could stay here and guard our exit. We'll signal you if we find anything."

Kendall wore dark sunglasses and Sierra couldn't read what he was thinking, but he gave a subtle nod—that and the fact he didn't budge from his position was answer enough.

"While we're climbing down, you watch the area. Watch if someone comes out of that mine," Bryce instructed the guy.

"I know how to do my job."

"Wasn't implying that you didn't. But we can't defend ourselves so easily if we're coming up on Raul."

Sierra missed any further conversation. She needed to stick close to Samson. Beyond the protection of a vest, K-9s had only their teeth and an intimidating warning growl. They depended on their trainers to keep them safe.

She stepped carefully. A quick glance up and she spotted Bryce treading carefully behind her. Samson made the bottom and shot toward the mine.

If she'd kept him on a leash she wouldn't have to shout. She tried to keep her voice down as she gave him the command. *"Hier!"*

Samson had heard her because he immediately turned and ran toward her. "Good boy," she whispered, knowing he'd heard her words of praise too.

Finally, Sierra hopped on the ground at the bottom of the gorge that was only about fifty to a hundred yards wide in places. Bryce wasn't far behind and he rushed forward then tugged her behind him. He pulled his weapon out and readied it.

Her heart jackhammered.

Could this be where Raul had been hiding out? In an old silver mine down in a gorge near Carmel Mountain?

They could all be in danger if they cornered him like this. At the same time, she would never be safe until he was caught.

Wariness curdling inside, Sierra swallowed the lump in her throat. She removed her gloves and ran her hands over Samson's soft ears. She looked into his big brown eyes filled with love and loyalty.

He looked eager with anticipation. He wanted the hunt. She could be sending him to his death.

"I never wanted to put you in harm's way," she whispered.

"Sierra…" Bryce said nothing more.

She considered what command she should give him, but Samson seemed to understand they were hunting Raul—the man who threatened his master's life. *"Zooch."* Find him.

Samson barked then dashed away. He ran another twenty-five yards then disappeared deeper into the mine. Bryce and Sierra followed him, their weapons out in front of them and ready to fire.

Her heart pounded.

God, please keep him safe. Please, keep him safe. Please, keep him safe…

He was on the front lines now. He barked, signaling her that he'd been successful in locating his target.

She wasted no time shouting her next command. *"Fuss-en!"* Attack.

Samson snarled. Bryce led the way into the depths of the mine, pushing past the broken boards that had been put up to seal it at one time.

"We're at a disadvantage," Bryce whispered. "Whoever's inside can see us, but we can't see him."

"Help!" A man yelped from deeper in the mine. "Help me. Call off your dog."

Samson had subdued him. But the dog was still in danger. He could still get shot. *Hold on, Samson.* Bryce rushed forward and Sierra followed, turning on her flashlight.

Deeper in the mine they spotted a tent.

Her heart jumped to her throat. This was it. They'd found Raul. The man whined in agony, his voice sounding unusually high.

She shined the light on Samson and the man he'd restrained, his maw securing the man's arm, subduing him with one bite, warning of more. Bryce aimed his weapon at the man as did Sierra.

The man groaned. "Please, call him off."

Lowering her weapon, she commanded Samson to release the bite. "You're not Raul Novack."

Sierra eyed Samson.

"He tracked someone all right," Bryce said, frustration in his tone. "All the way from the woods. So you were out walking around town in the middle of the night?"

The man held his arm and nodded. "Yes. Who *are* you people?"

"We're searching for someone. A killer." She stared him down, letting the fury wash over her in waves. Fury this man didn't deserve.

"I'm no killer. Your dog got the wrong trail."

Sierra approached him, tugging a bandage from her pack and she wrapped his arm. Samson whined and sniffed around in the mine.

"Did we?" she asked.

Bryce paced the small campsite and ran a hand down his face. "So we're off tracking the wrong guy meanwhile Raul is out there doing who knows what."

Realization dawned. "Wait a minute. That's it. Raul. He wanted—" She stuck her face close to the man's boots. "Are those your boots? Are these your coat and pants?"

He shook his head, fear evident in his gaze. "I don't want any trouble. I don't—"

"Then you should have thought about that before you agreed."

Bryce approached them. "Agreed to what? You don't think—"

"That Raul had this man wear his coat and boots so Samson would track him here." Sierra glared at the man. "What's your name?"

"Eric. Eric Green."

"Tell me what happened." Sierra planted her feet next to him but crouched where he remained cradling his arm after Samson's attack.

She wanted answers and now.

He leaned away from her as if she intimidated him. Good.

"A man offered me money to do exactly as you said and to stay here. This isn't my tent or my stuff. I had to stay here until you came. At first I refused. It was crazy talk. But he said he knew where my mom lived and… and… There was something in his eyes…"

"Why didn't you just come to the police with that information?"

"Because he scared me. I didn't want him to hurt

my mom. You guys are here now so that means I can go and my mom is safe."

Officer Kendall appeared at the entrance. Apparently he'd finally decided it was time to climb down, just in time to hear the man's confession. "You'll need to come in for questioning," he said as he continued into the mine. "Also get that bite looked at. The man you helped is an escaped convict."

"I didn't know. I didn't know. I was scared." He threw his palms up in surrender. "Look, I didn't even take the money. I did it to keep my mom safe. And well, I thought he might kill me too."

"He's telling the truth," Sierra said. "But how did Raul get away? There should be another trail leading out of the cave."

"How should I know? He approached me days ago."

Days ago...

Sierra struggled to wrap her mind around that news.

"Raul did this to throw us off. To drag us away... Oh, no. What if... Dad!"

FOURTEEN

"We need to check on him!" Sierra tugged her phone out. "No signal!"

She moved closer to the exit until she got one. Bryce did the same. Officer Kendall would take care of Mr. Green.

Bryce contacted Sheriff Locke.

Kendall contacted his superiors to let them know what happened and that they had items Raul had left behind, maybe for no other purpose than to throw them off. But why had he decided to put this plan into motion last night? What was so special about the date and time, if anything?

"Sheriff. Please make sure John is safe, will you?" Bryce relayed the information to the man including their concern about Sierra's father.

"I'm standing next to him," the sheriff said. "He's all right. I'll stay with him for now. You keep Sierra safe. I don't like this."

Bryce ended the call.

Neither do I.

"Let's get out of here," he said. "We don't know if Raul has planned something, or if he's watching us now."

"I've been instructed to wait here until I'm relieved."

Kendal's tone let them know he wasn't pleased about this new assignment. "Evidence techs are coming to collect Novack's things and search for anything important we might have missed."

"Did you explain that this could be some kind of trap?" Sierra asked him.

"I relayed the situation, but I don't see how it could be a trap."

Bryce looked at Mr. Green. "What can you tell us? Was he planning anything? Why would he go to the trouble to throw us off his trail?"

Mr. Green shrugged. "He didn't confide in me. Nor would I want him to. Since you called to check on her father, anyone care to check on my mom? He didn't leave me with my cell."

"Officer Kendall, let him come over here where I get a signal," Sierra suggested. "He can use my phone to call his mother."

Kendall escorted Mr. Green toward Sierra in case he decided to make a crazy dash out of the mine and this was all a charade on his part. After he contacted his mother and confirmed she was grocery shopping and having an ordinary day, he handed the cell back to Sierra.

"I'm sorry about your arm," she said. "Samson's really a good dog."

While Sierra made small talk with Mr. Green, Bryce pulled Kendall aside.

"I don't feel comfortable leaving you here under the circumstances. Nor do I like the idea of staying here with Sierra, but I can't send her back alone. Got any suggestions?"

"I'll be fine. Deliver her to safety. I shouldn't have

to wait too long for the evidence techs. I'll remain in communication and let you know if I see anything suspicious." Kendall had taken off his sunglasses in the mine and studied Bryce. "Look, I know the brothers escaped and they might be some kind of brilliant criminal minds, at least the one that's left, but I can't fathom what he could gain by doing this. Unless maybe he wanted to study your strategy and tactics. See you and Sierra working with the dog and go from there."

"And that would mean he was watching." Bryce had already come to believe that somehow, someway Raul knew what Sierra was planning next. He pursed his lips, making a mental note to check her cell phone for some sort of tracking app and her apartment and store for hidden cameras.

"I'll tell you what," Kendall continued. "I'll look around here some more first. Explore deeper in the mine. Shine the flashlight around before we make any decisions about who is staying and who is going."

Bryce nodded to Kendall. He couldn't risk that he would make the wrong decision in this so he found a signal and called Sheriff Locke again. The sheriff asked him for more details.

While he relayed them, Bryce watched Sierra and Mr. Green, who had now made friends with the K-9 who'd subdued him. "A fake camp or a real camp where he'd stayed and then used to throw us off his trail. He decided to do that days ago. The mine could be an easy place to be ambushed, or bombed, or too many other things I'd rather not think about. The point is that I don't feel good about staying here. But I don't feel good about leaving either. We thought we'd found him, Sheriff. Now…"

How…how had they ended up like this? They'd planned to track and find Raul, but instead they were here and Bryce could see no clear safe direction. Raul had made a fool of them. Bryce felt like a complete idiot.

God, please help. What's the right thing to do? I can't fail to protect her again.

"Dynamite!"

Sierra jerked her gaze to see Officer Kendall rushing toward her. "It's not old like some miner just forgot about it. It's new." He glared at Eric. "We have to get out of here."

She eyed the entrance. "I have a feeling that it's not going to be easy to leave. We should lay down some gunfire before we exit. Cover each other."

"This was his plan then. Trap us inside. He plans to blow the mine." Bryce turned narrowed eyes on Eric. "You said you didn't know anything."

"I don't." Eric's fear-filled expression confirmed his words. "I didn't know about the dynamite."

"You didn't explore the cave?" Kendall asked.

"I stayed in that tent hoping you would hurry and get here. I heard someone coming so I came out and that's when the dog attacked."

They rushed to the mine entrance but hung back in the shadows. Sierra's pulse pounded in her ears, and she choked back tears. She didn't want to die in here like this, taking Samson and Bryce and two more innocent people with her.

Bryce and Kendall shared a look with her.

"Whoever goes first is going to be a target," Bryce said.

"I suggest we send the dog." This from Kendall.

Sierra fisted her hands. "No! He isn't expendable."

"Is there a way for us to stay here and survive the dynamite?" Eric asked. "Or can we move it? Throw it out of the mine?"

"I didn't look closely, but my guess is that he's attached a detonator—maybe activated by cell signal or radio attached outside the cave. I don't know enough about explosives to help."

"What's he waiting for then?" Bryce asked.

Good question. "I'm not willing to wait around and find out if he's going to blow the mine," Sierra said. "I'll take my chances."

"No!" Bryce's iron grip stopped her from going any further. "You're a better shot than me. You've always been better. I need you to cover me. I'll try not to get shot as I make a run for it. I'll draw the fire. You can try to take him out. It's up to you if you send Samson after him too. But get out of the mine. Wasting time on more words could cost our lives."

Bryce released her, then rushed out of the cave, without giving them more of a heads-up. She didn't have time to aim, so she fired her weapon into the ground, hoping her gunfire might scare off anyone gunning to shoot them if they tried to escape the mine.

Bryce made it to a boulder and so far, no one had accosted him. No gunshots could be heard from outside.

Sierra made to step out, but Kendall held her this time. "No. He could be waiting for you. It's you he wants."

"In that case I'd better get out of this cave before he decides to blow it up—with you and Eric still in it. I'll draw the fire and then you take him out." She twisted from his grip and dashed out of the mine entrance toward the rock where Bryce waited. This time gunfire resounded. Samson barked.

"Oh, no, Samson!" She made it to the rock, her dog next to her. "Are you hurt? Did you get shot?"

Then he sniffed at her and groaned. The fire in her arm drew her attention and she spotted the blood. Dizziness prevented her from telling her dog to find and attack the man after her.

Bryce continued to shoot at the ridge above them. Gunfire resounded like she was in the middle of a shootout in an old Western movie. Only this was real. This was today. This was happening.

An explosion resounded as the ground rumbled beneath them.

"Look out!" Bryce shouted and covered her using his body as a human shield.

Antiseptic accosted her nostrils.

Sierra opened her eyes to a white sterile hospital room. Grogginess held her in place, but she lifted her head. That elicited pounding and her vision blurred. She looked down the length of her body and found her arm bandaged, but as far as she could tell there were no other injuries.

She was alone in the room. Sierra searched and finally found the call button and pressed it.

A few moments passed before a nurse appeared. "Oh, good. You're awake. How do you feel?"

"I'll let you know when you tell me what happened to the others." Bryce. Samson. Kendall. Eric.

The nurse's expression took on a pained look. "I'll need to call the doctor."

Sierra sat up in bed and slowly put her legs over the side.

"Oh you shouldn't do that. You're—"

"What? What am I? Looks like you patched up my arm." Sierra started pulling the IV out.

Another woman entered the room. "Ms. Young—"

"It's Deputy Young and I want to know what's going on. What happened to the people I was with? Why am I here?"

"Ma'am, if you'll just calm down, Sheriff Locke is on his way to explain everything. He wanted us to call him as soon as you came to."

This wasn't the clinic in Crescent Springs. "On his way? He has to be two hours…"

She was shaking her head. "He's here at the hospital."

The aide entered and started taking vitals. "And there's someone else here."

"I'll go get him," the nurse said.

Another man. Bryce or her father? Sierra's head spun. What had happened? She eased back onto the pillow at the aide's urging. The images blasted through her mind as the aide put a pulse oximeter on her finger. Checked her temperature and blood pressure, which she was sure was high at this moment.

Bryce stepped into the room, bruised and scratched from head to toe, but beautifully, wonderfully alive. His smile barely hid the concern in his gaze, but she'd always loved his smile and it reassured her now.

He was alive. Her heart still hammered as he approached and took her hand, leaning in close.

"Bryce, you're okay. Please tell me what happened. Please tell me if—"

"Everyone is okay. Everyone made it out alive, thanks to you. And by everyone, yes, I do mean Samson too. He saved us."

"Where is he?"

"Well they wouldn't allow me to bring him up here since he's not one of the therapy dogs, though he totally could be. He's staying with Barbara."

"And Dad?"

"He's out there in the waiting room."

"Why am I here?"

"Surgery on your arm." He gently touched her cheek. "You risked it all to save everyone else by drawing the gunfire so Kendall and Eric could escape. Raul got a few shots in and hit your arm. Don't you remember?"

"I remember not feeling anything and then the explosion. I don't remember anything after that."

"Samson's a hero. He's a multitalented dog, that's for sure. He helped pull us from the rubble. After the explosion some rocks and dirt fell on us."

"I remember you covered me. You protected me. I remember that now."

"Yeah, well, I couldn't budge or move. My foot was caught. Samson pawed and dug and nudged until I was free. But you were… You were unconscious."

"I can't believe I passed out."

"Sierra. You were shot." He opened his mouth as if to say more then held back. "Fortunately help was already on the way. I was—" his eye shimmered "—I was worried you weren't going to make it."

Was he going to cry? So much emotion poured from him that she had to look away. She closed her eyes as if tired. She *was* tired. Exhausted. Finally she turned her gaze on him—she simply couldn't look away for long.

"Let me guess. They didn't find Raul."

With a grim look, he shook his head.

"So much for our expedition. I doubt they'll let us search for him again."

Lord, why is this happening?

She'd been a good and upright citizen. She'd done the best job she could while she was a detective and now here as a deputy. Why did evil hunt her down? She couldn't help the tears that burned down her cheeks. Though her eyes were closed, she knew when Bryce sat on the bed. He gathered her in his arms.

"We have to stop meeting like this. You holding me because something's wrong." She said the words into his chest, but held on as if for dear life.

A throat cleared.

The sheriff again. "I keep interrupting you two, it seems."

Bryce released her. Sheriff Locke crossed his arms. "It's good to see you, Sierra."

Barbara stepped in behind him.

"Wait. I thought you were watching Samson?"

She smiled. "I am." She stepped aside and Samson barked as he bounded into the room. He rushed forward and practically jumped on the bed.

Sierra hugged his big fat head and he licked her face. What would the nurse say? "I thought he couldn't come in because he's not a therapy dog."

"I'm the sheriff's wife, and I say he's a therapy dog. I can see that you needed therapy. Bringing him was the right thing."

Warmth flooded her heart. All these people who cared. Dad poked his head in the room too. "Finally you're awake."

"Good to see you too, Dad. When can I get out of here?"

FIFTEEN

Six days had passed since they'd seen any sign of Raul. Bryce feared letting himself relax. Was this the quiet before the storm? Or had Raul used up the last of his determination to torture and eventually kill Sierra? Having failed, was it possible he'd decided to move on?

Bryce hoped, but again, he would stay alert.

Sierra had been released from the hospital the day after her surgery. He tried hard not to think of that moment when the dynamite had blown and rocks came down on them. He kept the details of that experience to himself. Sierra didn't need to know that she could have bled out before help had arrived, even before he was in a position to tourniquet her arm. The bullet had gone through the humerus and lacerated a vein. If it had hit an artery, she probably would have died. But help had arrived and whisked her away. Doctors repaired the vein and had given her blood to replace what she'd lost.

That was just another of too many close calls for comfort.

And now... Nothing from the villain in their life.

In spite of his wariness, Bryce had enjoyed the predictable uneventful last few days. As for Sierra's position as a deputy, she'd been put on a paid leave. With her injury it was best she wait a few weeks until the doctor okayed her to officially return to work.

But even if she'd been completely fit, Sierra wasn't going to return as a deputy until Raul was caught or proven to be far from this region of the world—that per Sheriff Locke, who said he would put her on desk duty if Raul was still at large by the time she was fully recovered. Sierra preferred working at the toy store if she couldn't get out there in the county.

So every day Bryce hung out at the toy store. Every day it was the same. Coffee and breakfast with Sierra and John, and then Jane arrived and they stocked toys and helped customers.

But today was different.

Sierra leaned against the wall outside at the back of the building and talked Bryce through training games with Samson. The sun shined down on the world and it seemed that no evil could break through. He knew better, of course, but they needed this moment of smiles and the feeling that all was well with the world.

Samson jumped around and played like a puppy, without seeming aware of how huge he was. He accidentally knocked Bryce on his rear. "Did you do that on purpose?"

Sierra's laugh was filled with joy. Only for this moment in time, and Bryce would treasure it. Samson held Bryce to the ground and he couldn't get up. He allowed himself a laugh too. "Okay, would you call your dog off? Come on, Samson. Come on, boy."

"Here." Sierra used the German command. Samson seemed to know this was more a game than actual training and he licked Bryce across the face and dropped drool for good measure.

Sierra offered her good hand as if to help him up. He grinned and considered pulling her down with him, but he didn't want to hurt her arm. He hopped up on his own and ended up standing close.

He stared down into her gorgeous blue eyes. It took all his willpower to keep from pulling her against him and kissing her thoroughly—after wiping off the drool, of course. He chuckled inside. He could live with weaving his fingers through her long golden hair, but Bryce held back.

If this was any other situation, Bryce would have already left.

John opened the door. "Sierra. I need your help."

"Sure, Dad. I'll be right there." She smiled and left Bryce outside with Samson.

"Come on, boy. Let's go inside too." Bryce needed to wipe the drool off anyway.

What am I going to do?

Bryce couldn't stay in Crescent Springs forever. He simply couldn't afford to keep renting a room in the hotel without dipping into his retirement. At some point too, he'd have to start building his business back up. He'd already turned down quite a few investigation jobs. Still he wasn't too worried. He had connections and believed he could drum up business again. He'd find a way to make it work, if that was what Sierra needed him to do.

Nothing was more important than protecting Sierra.

But it seemed as if Raul had disappeared. Law enforcement had scoured the area with no results, and eventually the number of searchers had decreased. Now it was a matter of citizens calling an eight-hundred number if they spotted Raul. The state had even used one drone. Just one. Sheriff Locke was trying to raise funds to buy one for the county, but politics interfered. Always politics.

So in the meantime, he was left with waiting and watching.

He and Sierra had both believed that Raul's incarceration was the only way she would ever be safe. But now what? Would they grow complacent and then he would strike?

Was that what he was waiting on?

Or maybe he'd moved on after his attempt to draw them into the mine and blow them to bits had failed. Maybe he'd decided his efforts were futile.

Still, a fugitive was out there. A dangerous fugitive who'd targeted Sierra.

Bryce sighed.

He'd move here if he could, but he doubted Sierra would allow him to stay and protect her indefinitely.

He pinched his nose and squeezed his eyes shut, wishing he knew what to do next. At the sink he grabbed a glass of water as if this were his place too. Sierra and John moved from the store back into the apartment in what bordered on a heated discussion.

"No, Dad. You don't need to do it. I'll do it. I can do it. I'm not an invalid."

"Well, at least have Bryce drive you then."

He downed the water, then said, "I heard my name. How can I be of service?"

"We need some supplies. Stuff we can only get in Montrose," Sierra explained. "It's about an hour's drive."

"She just doesn't want me to drive because she doesn't trust me."

"It's a treacherous road, Dad. I don't want to drive it either. Not in the winter. Are you up for driving the Million Dollar Highway, Bryce?"

Highway 550, aka the Million Dollar Highway. The only way to get to Montrose from Crescent Springs. It required one hundred percent concentration in the summer, but even more so during the winter.

"Of course. I might as well be of some use."

"Don't beat yourself up," she said. "It's better that we aren't getting shot at or stalked or attacked."

Sierra took a few steps closer and smiled up at him. "Don't try to deny it, you're bored out of your mind here at my little store in Crescent Springs."

"Me? Never."

And she was happier than he'd ever seen her in Boulder. Carefree, despite the knowledge that Raul was still out there. But he looked closer behind all the warm fuzzies and saw that the wariness remained. She couldn't so easily shake the fear.

He tugged his keys from his pocket.

John tossed him his own keys. "Take the truck so you'll have room for everything on the list."

Bryce grabbed his coat.

Sierra dropped her hand to Samson's big forehead and rubbed his fur. "You'll be fine here, Samson. You're such a good boy. I promise, as soon as my arm is good to go, it'll be you and me playing again."

"Hey, I thought we had a good time." He gave a fake look of disappointment.

She glanced up at Bryce and sent him a teasing smile. "Too good a time. I was jealous." She winked—her beautiful eyes bright and hair shining...

He shook off the thoughts.

"You ready?" she asked.

"As I'll ever be." He peered out the window. The beautiful day they'd experienced had disappeared and a dark, gray snow cloud had moved in quickly.

Outside the store, they trudged down the sidewalk to find her father's truck. He opened the door, started the engine and cranked up the heat. Then he took one side and Sierra took the other and they scraped the snow from the windshield.

Once inside the truck he steered them through the small town and headed out on the Million Dollar Highway. Sierra seemed oddly quiet considering her earlier cheerful mood. Almost as if she had something on her mind and wasn't ready to talk about it.

He was glad, actually, because he needed to focus solely on the road now. There was no guardrail. Nothing but a huge drop.

"Why were those supplies so important again? Scratch that. Don't tell me."

"Okay I won't. But I do need to talk to you about something."

Couldn't this wait for another time? But he kept that thought to himself. He'd wanted her to speak her mind earlier and now she was ready. But why did it have to be now when he needed to concentrate on these switchbacks? He wouldn't be surprised if they closed the road at some point today. He hoped that wouldn't happen at a point when the two of them would have to wait it out.

"So what's on your mind?"

He steered slowly around the curve in the road to stare down at a big RV coming toward him. Was there enough room for both of them on this narrow two-lane road?

"Raul hasn't targeted me in a week now. I think he

realizes it's taking too much of his time and energy and he's risking getting caught the longer he stays. The bottom line… You can't stay and protect me forever, Bryce. Even if I was paying you, I couldn't afford you forever. Just like you can't afford to work for nothing—not for much longer anyway. I think we both know that it's time for you to go home."

Bryce hugged the edge of the cliff as he slowly passed the RV in the opposite lane, the sheer stress of the situation combined with her words caused an ache in his chest. He couldn't breathe a sigh of relief once they'd successfully driven beyond that too-big vehicle—too big for this road, in his opinion.

"What? You don't have anything to say?" she asked.

"I'm thinking." He wasn't sure what he thought, except that he was surprised at the hurt that surfaced. She really wanted him to go?

A vehicle in the rearview mirror moving too fast for comfort drew his attention. "I'm not going to have time to respond. You need to hang on."

"Hang on. What? Why?"

"There's no way that SUV behind us is planning to pass. There's no passing here. I think…"

The white SUV didn't swerve into the left lane but continued pressing in behind them, faster and closer.

Bryce braced himself for impact even as he accelerated.

"Bryce!"

Heart pounding, she squeezed the armrests as though they could protect her.

The vehicle behind them bumped them slightly but Bryce continued to speed up so the impact was minimal. But he couldn't go much faster without their truck tumbling over the side. This road had no guardrail, but she doubted even a guardrail would protect them. They would go right through at this speed.

"What are we going to do?" Her voice was high-pitched with fear.

She risked a glance at Bryce. Tight lines carved his face as he concentrated on the road. She didn't know if he could get them out of this alive. If he could save them.

What could she do to help? Maybe keep quiet so he could focus. She looked around to see if she could spot anything they could use to their advantage. The road had been plowed but it had started snowing again after a beautiful blue-sky morning. Snow wasn't so bad but she felt the slight slipping every time the truck hit icy patches. Hitting one too fast could get them killed.

Lord, please help us!

"Brace yourself. He's gaining on us again."

"What? Well, can't you do something?" She regretted spewing out the words going through her mind.

"What would you like me to do? I take this too fast and we can't make the turns."

"I know, I know. Sorry. So what's your strategy then?"

"Stay alive."

"I'm glad to hear it." *Okay, Sierra. Just stop talking.*

"All I have to do is stay on the road beyond this next treacherous section and then our chances of escaping will increase."

She stared ahead at the huge straight-down drop into a rocky abyss.

"Here he comes again."

"That could cause us to nosedive over the ledge."

The vehicle slammed them from behind and Sierra's body jerked forward, the seat belt keeping her in place.

Bryce swerved around a corner fast, yanking the wheel to bring them back across the barely visible double yellow line into his own lane just in time to miss an oncoming vehicle. Loud honking ensued then fell away.

The vehicle was still coming. Still behind them. The driver was crazy and was risking his own life as well. Didn't he realize that? Did he believe he had it all under control or that he was invincible?

Or did he not care that he might die as long as he got to kill her in the process?

Sierra pressed her feet into the floorboard as though she was pressing the brakes and could slow the car— somehow it helped her psychologically. Her heart in her throat, Sierra was sure her life would pass before her eyes at any moment.

She'd thought she would die that night she'd looked into Raul's eyes as he'd pinned her to her bed and breathed his foul words of death, describing every evil thing he would do to her before he slowly killed her. She'd wanted to fight back but had been powerless. Instead she'd squeezed her eyes shut and turned her head away. Projected her mind anywhere but there at that moment, beneath the monster murderer.

Terror like she'd never known had paralyzed her.

What kind of cop was she anyway?

And now, she could almost feel that same terror bearing down on the both of them.

"I see it. I see what you're trying to make!" Up ahead, she could see mountain and trees on *both* sides so if they were run off the road, they could hit a tree instead of diving to their death. Still not a great option, but better than the road they'd have to pass through first, hugging the mountain on one side and dropping off hundreds of feet on the other.

"Unfortunately he sees it too. You might want to close your eyes, Sierra. Maybe even say your prayers."

"Oh, Bryce. Don't say that. Don't think like that." Though she was definitely already saying her prayers. But they were not prayers that one might say as their life ended. Instead, they were prayers of victory and desperation.

Save us God!

The impact thrust them forward and the truck slid across a sheet of ice.

Bryce shouted as he tried to gain control. "Come on!"

She risked a peek from her closed eyes. They were spinning—the ice had them and wasn't going to let go until it was much too late.

Nausea swirled in her stomach. Sierra screamed. Her heart stumbled around as though trying to find the right rhythm—the right response before they plunged to the bottom of the ridge. Time seemed to slow—she glanced at the movie playing before her.

The red mountain.

The snow.

The trees.

The beautiful and treacherous rocky drop.

Bryce had lost control and wouldn't get it back.

If she was going to die, she wouldn't close her eyes this time.

She spotted the vehicle that had sent them on the death spin sitting stopped in the middle of the road.

She caught a flash of *him*.

A glimpse of his face.

Felt the rage and fear he wanted to inflict on her.

The truck suddenly stopped, coming to rest against the rocky shelf that climbed above them instead of diving off the ledge and dropping a hundred feet or more. Her heart still pounding, she gasped for breath.

The nausea subsided.

"We're not going to die today, Bryce." Her words were breathy, but there was iron beneath them. "Get out," she said.

"Huh?" Bryce glanced her way, his face twisted in confusion.

"Get out of the truck."

SIXTEEN

Bryce did as he was told. She was thinking clearly and was right. If they remained in the truck they would be trapped. Now was their chance to escape. He threw open the door and clamored out. Pulled her across the seat to get out on his side, since she couldn't open her door—it was pinned against the rocky ridge looming over them.

"Come on." Together they ran around to the other side of the truck.

She pulled out her weapon, and so did he. Bryce noticed her pained expression as she tried to use both arms.

Gunfire ensued, only not from their guns.

Raul stood in the middle of the street—snow falling around him and on him, cold embracing him. The wintry backdrop and long, deadly fall mere feet behind him.

Sirens rang out in the distance. Someone had called 911, or had Sierra? He honestly couldn't recall, he'd been so intent on keeping the truck on the road.

But this would be over long before anyone could come to their aid.

He edged around the truck. A bullet pinged against it.

Sierra's hands pulled him back. "Don't get yourself killed. Don't do it, Bryce. Not for me."

"I'm pretty sure he's going to shoot us both if we let him. Like you said before, we have to be proactive."

They'd thought the man had moved on, but he'd shown up here today like he knew exactly where they would be. It was time—past time—to end this.

Then Raul emptied rounds into the vehicle as Bryce pushed Sierra back, back, back to the far side behind the front right tire. The truck provided good cover, but it wasn't foolproof. Some bullets were bound to make it through.

"I'm worried about any innocent people standing by. Cars are already lining up along both sides." He realized several were honking. He'd completely blocked out the sound as he focused on surviving.

Didn't they see a crazy man had a gun and was shooting?

"I really don't want to engage him in a gunfight in public like this," he said. "People could get hurt."

Bryce glanced to the ridge behind them. It opened up about ten yards away to trees and rocks—the portion of the road he'd been hoping to reach in the truck. Could they make it that far on foot before Raul was on them? And if they did, what would they do—just cower again? He wanted to stand out there and face off with this jerk, but his most important responsibility was to protect Sierra. Second to that, he wanted to keep any bystanders from harm.

Sierra had pulled out her cell and pressed it to her ear. "Sheriff," her voice shook. "We're pinned here on the highway. Raul is standing in the road shooting at us."

"Take him out!"

Bryce heard the words shouted over the cell. That was all he needed. What he'd been waiting for.

"You got it." He stepped away from the truck and aimed his weapon to shoot to kill, but Raul was nowhere to be seen.

"What?"

Raul wasn't in the vehicle. He… He'd just vanished.

A car at the end of the line of waiting commuters backed up, turned around and sped away. A man stood at the side of the road, his hands on his head.

Had Raul just hijacked his car?

A SWAT helicopter swept toward them and hovered in midair.

Bryce and Sierra put down their weapons lest there be any confusion about what had just happened. Bryce pushed her behind him.

"Call the sheriff again. Make sure he's communicating with these guys. Tell him that Raul took off in a red crossover—that he hijacked a car to escape."

"Okay." Sierra called again and explained. "Please tell them we're not the bad guys here. That he tried to kill us again and almost succeeded."

She ended the call and pressed her hand onto Bryce's shoulder.

Sirens grew louder, and a Colorado State Patrol vehicle expertly maneuvered around cars and parked next to the vehicle Raul had driven. It was probably also hijacked or at least stolen. What had he done with the driver?

Another vehicle pulled in behind the troopers. Sheriff Locke hopped out and rushed up to the state officers, telling them Bryce and Sierra had been attacked. His form was intimidating and he didn't back down even when facing off with state LEO. He approached, his expression filled with concern. "Are you okay?"

Bryce stepped aside for the sheriff to see Sierra for himself. She shivered and he turned to wrap her in his arms. "Give these guys your statement. We're out of my county now. Then I'll take you home."

"But… We needed supplies."

"All right. I'll take you into town and we'll get those, then I'll bring you back."

"Sheriff, that's too much trouble. You've done so much for me already. You have a big county to take care of—you shouldn't spend so much time on me."

He lifted his hat then sat it back on his head. "You're part of the people entrusted to me, Sierra. Not only that, you're one of my deputies. Now, come on. You guys are going to get hypothermia standing out here. You can sit in my vehicle and get warm."

A half hour later, they'd given their statements to the state officers. Bryce held his tongue on numerous occasions to keep from demanding some answers of his own. He wanted to ask why they hadn't already caught Raul Novack and put him back where he belonged.

Sheriff Locke would drive them all the way into Montrose to get supplies. While they waited on him to finish up a conversation with one of the patrol officers, Bryce sat in the back with Sierra. They watched as traffic once again flowed, only in a single lane around them. John's truck had been shot up and the engine was damaged, plus it would be used as evidence of this vicious attack.

Sierra's sniffles drew his attention. He should have been focused on her, but his adrenaline had long ago crashed and he was barely keeping it together himself. He brushed away tears from her cheeks. Her eyes widened as she swiped at him, refusing to give him the honor.

"I'm sorry. I wish I could stop crying."

Concern for her rippled through him. He wasn't sure he'd ever seen her so shaken, even the night that Raul had broken into her home.

"I thought we were going to die. The last time I felt like that, Raul was hovering over me, pinning me on my bed. So I just kept seeing his face and hearing his words."

She pressed her face into his shoulder and sobbed. Bryce held on to her with everything in him. "Shh," he whispered. He wanted to sob too, honestly. "It's good to get this out."

It was, wasn't it? Sierra was a strong person, but even strong people could be crushed, and it was best to let the pain out rather than to keep it inside. He knew that this was just the process that she had to go through.

Sheriff Locke finally climbed into the vehicle, and Sierra pulled away from Bryce. She looked up at him with swollen red eyes. "You need to leave."

They didn't have a chance to discuss her order right away. True to his word, Sheriff Locke had assisted them in getting supplies in Montrose and then ushered them back home where she could inform her father that his truck was toast. Once the county vehicle was unloaded, Bryce stood in the kitchen, looking like he was lost.

She understood. He was confused at her proclamation that he needed to leave. Sierra was spent. Her arm throbbed. She wanted to lie down, but she owed him an explanation.

"I have cowboy soup simmering in the slow-cooker

if you want some." Dad eyed them both but said nothing more. He didn't have to. Anger was evident in his features. Anger at Raul. He probably had plenty he wanted to say to Sierra too, but he held back for now.

"In a bit, Dad."

Bryce.

He had to go.

"Can I talk to you?" She ushered him over to the sofa. Dad had a big fire going. He disappeared upstairs. Good. He probably sensed she needed to have a heart-to-heart talk with Bryce.

Samson made sure she knew he wanted in on the conversation, planting himself right at her feet. She hugged his big head to her and kissed him. When she glanced up, Bryce was watching her.

Bryce.

He was everything she could ever want in a man. But she wouldn't subject herself to more pain.

And that's why… "You have to go, Bryce. You could have been killed out there today. You were going to sacrifice yourself for me. You would have… You would have died!" Sierra realized she was shouting but she continued. "You walked out into the middle of the street to shoot him. If he had still been standing there, you would both be dead. This isn't some Wild West reenactment." She couldn't take the look he gave her and shoved from the sofa. Samson whined.

Sierra moved to stand near the fire and rubbed her hands. Her arm throbbed even a week after surgery.

Still Bryce said nothing in response. Maybe he was waiting for her to get it all out before he made some argument to stay.

"I don't want you getting hurt on account of me. Protecting me at the cost of your own life. I can't have that on my conscience."

Bryce was behind her. She could feel his presence. She wanted to escape. She needed to escape. But she couldn't make herself leave. She leaned back into him, resting her head on his shoulder.

"Please… Just leave."

He gently turned her to face him. "You know why I can't," he whispered.

And then he kissed her. All this time they had fought it, and now he pressed his lips gently against hers. The emotion that poured from him was enrapturing, and more than she remembered from before. It took her breath away, and yet she knew he was holding back so much more of what he wanted to give.

She wanted to slide her hands over his chest and up around his neck and wrap her hands in his hair and pull him closer. How long had it been since they'd shared a kiss—years?

And why now were they finally giving in to that longing?

Back then, she'd pushed him away from her for emotional reasons. Now, it was so much more than mere emotion. "Bryce," she whispered breathlessly.

He eased from the kiss. "You want me to leave so you won't have to live with my death. But I can't have your death on my conscience, if I were to leave. I'm here until it's over. Whatever the cost."

And that's what scared her the most.

His breath tickled her cheeks. "And I know that I shouldn't have kissed you. I know why you won't let yourself love. You understand why I can't either. We're both broken in the same way."

She closed her eyes as he left her standing there next to the fireplace, listening to his footsteps.

He would leave now. Head to his hotel and perhaps get some rest.

As for Sierra, she wouldn't sleep after what happened today with Raul…and with Bryce.

She wouldn't sleep after that kiss. But he was right—they were both broken.

When this was over, he truly had to leave because she couldn't bear for him to stay. She might fall for him again and that was something she couldn't risk.

That night Sierra took forever to fall into a fitful sleep. She tossed and turned and would wake up and do it all over again.

A sudden shrill noise startled her awake. Gasping for breath she sat up and grabbed her gun, then realized her cell was ringing. She answered the call. "I'm here."

Silence met her on the line.

Then, "Sierra."

"Sheriff Locke, what is it?" The clock glowed 4:30 a.m.

"We got him." He was breathing hard. "We got him, Sierra."

SEVENTEEN

Bryce didn't like this at all.

But he was in it until the end, and so he stood with Sierra at the jail where Raul waited for transport back to the penitentiary. Sheriff Locke had procured a way for Sierra to see Raul, hoping to give her some closure.

Bryce could not believe she'd requested to see Raul. A clerk hit the buzzer to open the door. Grabbing Sierra's arm, he prevented her from entering. "Sierra, are you sure about this?"

"Yes." Her grim expression seemed set in stone. "Yes. I need to look him in the eyes and let him know he didn't get to me. He didn't kill me or destroy me. All his attacks were for nothing."

Together, they walked down the quiet hallway—a gray polished floor, contrasting with bright green cells and bars. Every county jailer's dream decor. Their shoes squeaked in the quiet. Two state officers escorted them.

Sheriff Locke also accompanied Sierra. Raul had come after his deputy, after all, and terrified his wife at his home and his friends in his county seat, and the man was now in his jail.

When they reached Raul's cell, the man sat on the

edge of a cot, hanging his head. Though he was jailed, his wrists and ankles were chained together ready for transport back to the penitentiary. Was that protocol for a dangerous, escaped convict finally retrieved, or were they making an exception for Raul Novack?

Raul lifted his head, his features somehow euphoric. When he spotted Sierra, a grin took over his face. He slowly got up and lumbered toward them. Bryce wished they weren't standing so close to the bars. He would remain with Sierra but he wished she would take a step back.

He understood why she couldn't. That would show weakness when she'd come here to show strength.

He stood close enough to her that he felt the slightest tremble in her body, and he put his hand closer to hers. Not holding it, just touching fingers. She responded.

Raul approached and held on to the bars, his chains clanking against them.

Sierra said nothing.

Had she planned to speak to him? Or just simply show him that he hadn't gotten to her?

Bryce wouldn't say anything, though he wanted to reach through the bars and do much more than say words to this man. He wanted to wrap his hands around Raul's throat. But that was the difference between him and this monster. Bryce would never act on such impulses.

Raul kept his grin in place. A grin that went all the way to his eyes. An evil grin.

"You're going to die."

Sierra's pinkie finger flinched.

"You're going to die, girl."

"We're all going to die," she said. "It's just a matter of when."

His laugh was sick. "And how, girl. You're going to die and I'm going to enjoy it."

"How's that possible now that you're once again in jail?"

He gave her a knowing look and just laughed. As if to dismiss her, he shuffled back to his cot, sat down and stared at the wall.

The officers ushered them back down the hallway. Sheriff Locke escorted them to his county vehicle.

Sierra didn't say a word. None of them did.

Once inside the vehicle they all sat in silence. Sheriff Locke didn't start the ignition. He just sat there.

Bryce knew exactly what he was thinking, but Bryce wouldn't say those words out loud.

"What do you think he meant?" Sierra finally asked. "When he told me I was going to die and that he was going to enjoy it?"

Sheriff Locke started the vehicle. "I think he's crazy, Sierra. I thought you needed the closure or else I never would have agreed to arrange this meeting. But now it's over. It's done with. He's going back to prison and will be under extra security. The best thing we can do is forget about him. Forget everything that happened. Put it behind us. You especially, Sierra."

She rubbed her arms. She sat in the front seat next to the sheriff, and Bryce in the back, so he couldn't hold her. He stared out the window and watched the trees pass by and the day grow colder and grayer.

It's over.

Just keep telling yourself that.

Back in Crescent Springs, Sheriff Locke dropped

them at the toy store. Bryce followed Sierra inside where she shared what had happened with her father and Jane—everything except Raul's words to her. John hugged her fiercely.

He gripped her arms. "Now you're free. He's back in jail. We don't have to think about him ever again."

If only it was that easy.

By going to face off with her stalker, Sierra had meant to make a statement, but in Bryce's opinion, things had gone horribly wrong.

She turned her attention to Bryce. "Let's take Samson for a good, long walk. It will be nice to do that without having to worry about someone attacking us."

He nodded. He hadn't taken his coat off yet, so was ready.

She led him out the back door of the apartment into blinding white. Fortunately someone had shoveled within the hour so they could easily walk.

Samson was leashed for the walk and they kept to the wooded lot, not encroaching into the National Forest. Bryce had so much he wanted to say to her about what had happened since the first day he'd been here, especially about today. He needed to process through his thoughts and he wanted that to happen with Sierra if only he could find a way to tell her. If only he could turn back time and prevent her from confronting Raul while he was behind bars. He wasn't so sure that Raul's threat had been idle, but how did he tell her that? He didn't want to scare her. This had to end. And it should have ended once the man was put behind bars.

Since Raul had threatened Sierra, Bryce had a reason to stay. He *should* stay. He wanted to stay to make sure that Raul's threat wasn't real—that Sierra was truly safe now. *That* was the only reason. It had nothing at all to do with being with Sierra—her bright blue eyes and golden hair. Her smile and her laugh. The way she loved on her dog, Samson.

Or the way she'd kissed Bryce back last night. Bryce struggled to push aside the emotions battling inside him. He struggled to find the words to express what he wanted to say to her.

Samson took his time, seeming to enjoy the pleasant relaxed pace of the walk. He moved from tree to tree to see what was what.

The quiet between Sierra and Bryce wasn't their usual comfortable silence. Tension seemed to waft off Sierra. That could be Raul's doing.

Or it could be Bryce's doing. He needed to jump-start a conversation. "When do you think you'll start training again?"

"Tomorrow, if possible."

"But…your arm."

"I'll make it work."

Not "we'll" make it work. It was now or never if he was going to convince her that he should stay on longer. "Listen, I think I—"

"It's time for you to go, Bryce."

Ugh. She hated the way those words sounded coming from her. Could she have worded this any worse? And the look on his face hurt her so much!

Stepping closer, she peered up into his handsome face. His silver-blue eyes and thick head of brown hair. "I want to thank you Bryce. No, wait. Those words are nowhere adequate. You saved me—so many times. I couldn't have made it through this without you. Of that much, I'm sure. But you don't have to stay with me now. You don't have to protect me. Raul is heading back to the penitentiary today."

Bryce's intensity overwhelmed her. She let Samson pull her away with the leash and averted her gaze to take in her surroundings of the beautiful San Juan Mountains.

Her home.

This was hard. So very hard.

"Sierra I'm not sure…" Bryce didn't finish.

"You're not worried about his threat, are you? Raul was just saying the words to freak me out." She paused to take in his expression. Serious. He was serious. And something more was behind his gaze.

It was that something more that she couldn't receive. Couldn't accept or explore. "I can't in good conscience ask you to stay. I would need to pay you if you stayed, and honestly I can't afford a bodyguard."

"You should know that your dad already tried to pay me."

"And you refused, of course."

"You didn't ask me to come. The way I look at it is that we're both in this together. We went through it together before and I would never leave you to go through it again alone."

"I can't thank you enough." She was repeating herself but she didn't know what else to say.

They stood close now. Much too close. Samson was sniffing the snow at their feet. They were probably the perfect picture for a romantic postcard.

Sierra saw in his eyes that he wanted to kiss her, but she also knew that he wouldn't.

"I'm glad you were here for me, Bryce. You're… It's

meant so much to me. I hope you know that I'll be there if you ever need me."

He nodded as if finally accepting that she was right and it was time for him to go. Regret clung to his expression, but he too, knew that the moment had come for him to pack and go home.

Again she averted her gaze and this time squeezed her eyes shut. Images of yesterday accosted her. Bryce shoving himself from cover to take Raul out once and for all.

For her...

Buck's death came back to her along with the grief.

If... If she allowed herself to care deeply, if she hadn't lost the man she loved before to a bullet he didn't deserve, then Bryce would be the man for her. But telling him those words wouldn't do either of them any good. It would only lead to more heartbreak.

She'd already hurt him once.

They finished walking Samson, discussing mundane things like the future of the toy store. Bryce was also considering becoming a dog handler for SAR rescues. As they walked back to her apartment, they laughed like the two old friends they were, but Sierra sensed the sadness that lingered between them.

Right now, they were two old friends who needed to say goodbye.

Two old friends who might never see each other again.

In the apartment, he crouched and rubbed Samson everywhere the dog enjoyed. "You're a good boy, Samson. Keep my girl safe, will you?"

My girl...

The endearment cracked her heart in a new place. Would that ever mend?

Sierra walked him out through the toy store. Bryce said his goodbyes to Jane and Dad. Sierra exited the store with him and stood on the sidewalk. Memories of their shared kiss surged through her, but she put those aside hoping she never thought of that kiss again.

Sierra stood on her toes and pecked him on the cheek. *Call me sometime*, seemed to be the natural thing to say, but she wasn't sure that would be a good idea.

His blue eyes were more silvery this morning as he peered at her. "Take care of yourself, Sierra. I'm just a phone call away if you ever need me. I'm in the hotel across the street until the morning." He winked.

Then he headed to his hotel to pack up and go back to Boulder.

Sierra stood outside in the cold letting the chill reach into her bones. Maybe it would chase the pain away.

Dad came out with her. "He's gone now?"

"Yeah." She shivered. "He'll leave in the morning so he won't be driving at night."

"Then what are you doing standing out here like you want to make him stay? Unless of course you do."

"No. I won't do that to him." Or herself. Parting ways the first time had been hard enough. A gust of wind blew cold over her along with snow from the rooftops.

Dad gently urged her back inside. "Are you going to be okay?"

"I think I'm going to turn in early." What would she do without Dad and Jane to pick up the slack on days like today? She could trust Jane to close up the shop with Dad. "I'll just go up to my room."

"Do that. I'll bring you some hot tea with your dinner in a bit."

"That would be nice, Dad."

Her heart throbbed along with her arm. Sierra might take one of the painkillers the doc had prescribed too.

Sierra woke and stared at the glowing numbers on the clock. Though it was still dark outside, it was already seven in the morning.

Bryce would probably wait at least until the sun came up to make that treacherous drive through the mountains back to Boulder.

Going to bed early and getting a long night of sleep hadn't removed the pain in her troubled heart. She and Bryce—they needed to talk about it. Talk it through. She'd thought she couldn't take the heartache of losing someone again and had pushed Bryce away. Well, she'd been right—she couldn't take the heartache of losing Bryce. The realization had been long in coming.

Maybe she didn't have to experience this pain. She wanted to avoid grief, the risk involved in loving someone like Bryce, but was letting Bryce walk away without even telling him how she felt any better?

Was that the answer? She thought the doubts would be gone by this morning, but they remained. Her pushing him away was definitely not the solution to regaining her peace of mind.

She had to catch him before he left. If she hurried, she could have breakfast with him and lay all her cards out there. Put them on the table.

Two old friends who potentially loved each other shouldn't leave things unfinished.

She groaned and rolled out of bed. Pulled her hair into a pony tail and finished dressing.

Downstairs, she was careful not to disturb Samson who snored loudly next to the fire. She didn't have time to walk him. She should probably text Bryce and invite him to breakfast. But what if he said no or put her off? She'd hurt him, after all. Better to just show up.

She entered the toy store front, more doubts warring in her mind. What if she put her heart out there and he tromped on it, told her that loving her wouldn't be worth the risk? That…that would be worse than what she was feeling now.

Come on, Sierra, have some courage.

Sierra stood in the dimly lit store and looked at her phone contemplating a text to him.

The door jingled. Sierra froze. Had Dad or Jane forgotten to lock the door last night?

"I'm sorry, but we're not open yet." Sierra tucked her cell in her pocket. Never mind the text. She lifted her gaze to face the muzzle of a gun.

EIGHTEEN

Bryce woke to his alarm, though it was still dark outside. By the time he dressed dawn would be lighting the skies over the mountain roads.

He rubbed his eyes.

Today he would go home.

But where exactly was home? Admittedly while he'd stayed here in Crescent Springs to protect Sierra, he'd kind of grown attached to the place. He'd actually started dreaming about a life with Sierra. Started believing she was finally ready to take a chance with him.

Because now he was no longer a cop but a private investigator and he could pick and choose his assignments and clients that wouldn't put him in the line of fire. She wouldn't have to be concerned about losing him like she'd lost Buck. Why hadn't he tried harder to make her see that?

Maybe subconsciously he'd become a private investigator in hopes of winning her back one day. So far he was doing a lousy job at that. His resolve that he wouldn't allow her to hurt him again crumbled away when he was with her. He wanted to take the risk with her.

She needed to know that, and she couldn't know unless he told her. He should have told her yesterday as they walked Samson and said their goodbyes. Those ridiculous goodbyes filled with unspoken emotionally charged words between them.

He threw off the covers.

Yes. Bryce was willing to risk the hurt all over again if it meant a chance with this woman who he'd never stopped loving.

Admit it!

He was so done with shoving his true feelings for her to the dark side of the moon. Somehow he had to convince her they needed to try again. Just… One more time.

He would stay here for her. It would be far from a hardship. This place was beautiful and peaceful.

He quickly dressed and rushed down the stairs of the small hotel. After his conversation with Sierra he could either check out or stay longer. Or find more permanent accommodations. Though wary, afraid to hope, he couldn't help the excitement that coursed through him. And as he pushed through the door of the hotel, dawn brightened the sky over the mountains as if reassuring him this truly was a new day and a new start for him and Sierra.

With a bounce in his step, he made his way over to the toy store. He'd planned to walk around to the back and knock since the store wasn't open yet. But he spotted lights on, so knocked on the door as he peered through the glass.

John emerged from the toys and let him in. "Morning, Bryce." The man had a quizzical look on his face. "What can I do for you?"

"I was hoping to speak with Sierra. Take her to breakfast."

John frowned. "To tell you the truth, I thought Sierra was with you."

"What? Why would you think that?"

"Well, she wasn't herself last night. And since she isn't here this morning, I thought she had gone over to find you and make things right between you."

While those words sounded good to Bryce, apprehension gripped him. "She's not here. She's not with me. Where could she be?"

"I don't know. Maybe she left me a note. Let's go back to the apartment."

"Or a text. Maybe she texted you where she'd gone."

In the apartment, Samson yawned and lapped at his water. Samson didn't appear concerned that his master and handler wasn't here. Surely he would have alerted John if there had been something to worry about. Bryce relaxed. She was probably talking to the sheriff about getting back to work. John had figured it wrong about how Sierra felt about Bryce.

John palmed his forehead. "Oh. I missed it. Right here on the table. She left a note."

He lifted an envelope and handed it to Bryce. "I was wrong. She left the note for *you*."

Why would she leave a note for Bryce? For all Sierra knew he was leaving this morning. But maybe she knew him well enough to know he would want to talk to her about staying one more time. Maybe that was why she wasn't here—so she wouldn't have to hurt him by sending him away again when he came for her.

His heart ached. He'd been rejected again without

even trying. Note in hand, he quickly opened it and skimmed the contents.

Bryce,
If you're reading this note that means that you're still here. Please know nothing can happen between us. Ever. I would like you to leave. If you don't leave town then it feels like you're more of a stalker than anything. I'm glad you were here to help me escape Raul, but that's over. I don't need you anymore.

"Oh." Bryce folded the missive and stuck it back in the envelope. He didn't want John to read it otherwise Bryce would have simply wadded it up and tossed it in the trash. Instead he stuffed it in his pocket.

"Well where is she?"

"It didn't say. Just…she was just saying goodbye. So I'll be on my way." He shook John's hand and told him to call if he needed anything.

Though John smiled, more of his frown stayed in place.

In a pain-filled daze he checked out of his hotel and loaded his vehicle. He sat in the seat and let it heat up, hurt squeezing his chest. Could she really view him like a stalker?

Why had he let himself care about her again?

He slammed the steering wheel.

I knew better!

She'd been stupid to not see this coming. She should have figured it out. Instead, she'd been caught completely off guard by her abductor—someone who hadn't been on her radar.

Just a little more. It has to work. Just one more try.

Gasping for breath, she growled in frustration and gave up. But she'd given up already too many times. She would try again.

Breathe in. Breathe out.

In. Out. In, out, in, out, in, out.

Okay now she was hyperventilating.

Calm down. You can do this.

She had to get out of here or she would die at the hands of her abductor. Sierra worked her wrists back and forth. They were tied together behind her around the chair back. It was painful to be tied in this position for so long, especially with her injured arm. The muscles in her shoulders and arms burned as if on fire. At least the circulation still flowed. She kept reminding herself that pain was good.

Okay. Again. She tried loosening the rope around her wrist. Rope seemed old-school when there was duct tape or plastic ties, but she would be grateful for small things. Wearing down plastic ties would be a lot harder. Even with rope, her skin raw and likely bleeding by now, sharp pains stabbed with each twist to try to pull one or the other hand out. To try to loosen up the rope.

Had they taught her how to escape this in cop school? If they had, she must have missed that day.

What they *had* taught her, was how not to get abducted. Being fully aware of one's surroundings and ever on alert was key. But she just hadn't seen this one coming.

The wind howled through the cracks in the window of the creepy old cabin in the woods, making it seem haunted. Old logs that had been stacked together to form a square room sometime in the last century added to the unnerving feel. Sierra wasn't in the market for an old cabin—she was desperately trying to escape. But someone had clearly made themselves at home here.

Was this where Raul had been staying before he'd been caught?

She shivered as cold fear wrapped around her. That and a heaping dose of chilled air as the temps dropped outside.

How many hours would she have to remain tied to the chair in this ancient, decrepit cabin? The fire had died out long before she'd been abducted and brought here. Again, she'd worked her wrists back and forth. Warm fluid spread.

Now she knew she was bleeding.

She had already tried to break the chair. That, she'd done first—to no avail. She'd merely left herself bruised and in pain and almost knocked herself unconscious. Her gunshot-wounded arm throbbed incessantly.

How was she going to get out of this?

I have to get out of here. She gasped. *God, please I have to get out of here. Please help me. This can't be it. This can't be the end.*

Because… Because more than just wanting to live, she wanted another chance with Bryce. She saw that now. Early this morning, she'd realized she should at least talk about her feelings with him, but now she didn't even want to talk about them. She didn't want to reason or analyze or discuss. The time for talk was long over.

If she ever saw him again she would run up and kiss him good and hard and convince him that she was the one for him. She'd been so foolish to push him away.

He'd walked back into her life and Sierra should have seen that for what it was—a sign.

Life was much too short to live in fear of loving because you were afraid you might lose someone.

She should have told Bryce how she felt about him when she had the chance.

And now it might be too late.

She'd been forced to hurt him all over again with that cruel, heartless note. Pain lanced through her heart.

Oh, Bryce... Please don't believe it. Don't believe a word of it!

Still, considering the history they shared, Sierra should accept the fact there was no chance he would read the note, if he even got it, and do anything but leave town.

If Bryce read the note, he wouldn't be coming to look for her.

And if he *didn't* read the note, he wouldn't be coming to look for her.

She'd made sure of that.

I'm going to die... But she wasn't ready to die.

She laughed hysterically at her desire to live. When did that ever make a difference?

NINETEEN

"Look, something's wrong, John. Please let me take Samson. He can help me find her," Bryce pleaded. He'd driven nearly ten miles out of town, gearing up to face a tumultuous drive in the increasing winter weather when it hit him like a cold smack in the face.

"Sierra didn't write that note. She would never be cruel like that, dismissing me as if she didn't even consider me a friend. And the words seemed stilted." Bryce thrust the note out for John to read.

He skimmed the contents then frowned. Did John believe the note was sincere—that this was truly Sierra's opinion of him? That notion cut him through and through, but he pushed the pain aside. Time to care later. Right now he needed to convince Sierra's father. But how? He scraped a hand around the back of his neck. Maybe he should go to the sheriff, except that would take more time. He was here now with Samson. If the dog couldn't catch a scent and someone had taken her, then what would they do?

Panic swelled in his chest. He fisted his hands. "Every minute you make me beg you could have one less minute left to save her. You come too. You can help me find her."

The man frowned, desperation filling his eyes. "You don't have to convince me, son. I know you're right. Sierra wouldn't have written this note unless she was forced. You go and I'll call the sheriff. But I don't know if Samson will take your commands."

"I don't know either, but I've watched Sierra. And I know the dog will want to find her. He seems anxious right now as though he senses something's wrong." Though admittedly the dog had only grown anxious since Bryce had come in and started stirring up trouble. "Let me try. If she's anywhere near then Samson will find her."

"But if you're right," John said, "and she's in danger, she wouldn't want you to put her dog in harm's way. That was one of the reasons she moved back here."

"What do you think, John? Are you okay with me taking the dog into a dangerous situation if it means saving Sierra?"

"Go. Find her. Just don't let her dog get hurt."

Bryce leashed Samson, afraid he wouldn't be able to call him back. He needed the dog sticking close to him on their search.

He grabbed Sierra's scarf to let Samson know that Bryce wanted him to find Sierra. He wasn't a trained handler but simply copied what he'd seen Sierra do. He rubbed the scarf over Samson's nose. "Find Sierra."

What was the German word Sierra had used? His brain too flustered—he couldn't remember. Then Bryce opened the back door to the woods. They could start there.

Samson nearly yanked his arm off as he escaped

through the door. Was it working? He cautioned himself not to get his hopes up. For all Bryce knew Samson had merely picked up on Sierra's previous excursion here. Bryce couldn't know and could be wasting time too. Then again, judging by Samson's urgency, he could very well lead Bryce to Sierra.

"I'm calling the sheriff." John shouted from behind.

Bryce followed the dog's urgent search through the deep snow, over fallen snow-covered logs, branches. Through the underbrush, and over frozen creeks. Samson veered south along the river where Bryce had fallen through the ice a few days back. Bryce feared the dog could lose the scent as he'd seen happen a few times—due to someone getting out on a snowmobile or because the snow-covered the tracks—but Samson continued on unhesitatingly.

Bryce sucked the cold air deep into his lungs—he might die of a heart attack before Samson found Sierra. But one thing he felt in his gut—the dog was on her scent.

"Good boy. Keep up the good work. Find Sierra."

God, please just let this storm ease up, and let me find her. Protect her. Protect Samson. Help me to find and save her.

He struggled to maneuver around boulders and over rocky outcroppings as Samson searched to catch a trace of Sierra's scent.

Lord, help us find Sierra.

Better yet, just have her call me on my cell to say that she's all right.

With the thought and prayer, he felt the buzz in his pocket. He didn't want to slow Samson down, so kept up with him as he dragged the cell out and tried to view it with numb, gloved hands.

"Hold up, Samson!" Probably not a command, but Samson whined, understanding just the same. He continued to sniff.

Bryce read the text from John.

Sheriff hasn't seen Sierra this morning. He'll help look around town and worst case, he'll organize a search party. She was supposed to talk to him today about coming back to work and didn't show up. Please find Sierra, son!

Finally, about an hour after they'd started, Samson alerted Bryce to a cabin. He tried to remember the command for Samson to sit and stay quiet. Bryce pulled his fingers from his gloves to ready his weapon, unsure if any part of his body would respond in this cold. If Samson could be trusted, Sierra was in that cabin.

And not by her own will.

What had happened? Who had taken her?

Keeping to the trees, he slowly approached the log cabin. Snow piled high on one side and he wondered about the reliability of the old structure. Dim light drifted from one dirty window. A branch hung low and scraped the window.

Bryce waited and listened, then slowly eased over to peek into the window, hoping the moving branch would help hide the movement. His heart lurched at what he saw. Sierra was tied to a chair, arms behind her back. Her ankles were tied too.

Her mouth had been stuffed so she couldn't scream—

as if anyone would hear her out here. Bruises covered the left side of her face.

And *Jane* stood over Sierra speaking. Bryce couldn't hear her words above the wind that was picking up. Seemed like they were going to get caught in a blizzard.

This was the moment of truth. Would Bryce be able to save her this time too, like he'd done in the past? Would he die for her? He was certainly willing.

To calm his pounding heart, he slowly breathed in a few icy breaths.

He sent up a silent prayer. *Lord, you never leave us nor forsake us. Be with me now as I go in to free Sierra. Keep her safe.*

Bryce wished he could simply command Samson to attack. But that could get the dog killed and Sierra would never forgive Bryce for putting her beloved pet in harm's way. Ideally, he'd wait for backup of the human variety, but there just wasn't enough time.

Jane's back was to him so Bryce took advantage of that and analyzed the room and surroundings. There wasn't any way he could enter the cabin through that one door without alerting Jane of his approach.

One step on that porch would probably give him away unless she thought the wind was causing the creaks. He could hope. The only good news was that the heavy wooden beam used to bolt the door was hanging down, and the door could be breached more easily. Still…

God, what do I do?

He considered his few options, indecision warring inside him. He didn't want Sierra to get hurt or killed when he entered. But he couldn't just stand there and watch her be harmed either.

Bryce had to act now.

* * *

Sierra stared at Jane, her eyes watering with pain. In her wildest dreams, she never imagined this would happen. Raul had been the tormenter in her dreams.

She hadn't known that he and Damien had raised a niece after her mother had died in a car crash. They'd changed her name and protected her from all connections to them. Her true name was Raven. But under the guise of Jane, she'd come to work for Sierra and planned out her revenge—long before her uncles had escaped and tried to do the same.

With Damien's death, Jane and Raul worked together to extract vengeance. And Jane had provided the hiding place for her uncle Raul at her own home right there in town.

Sierra wanted to heave to think that Raul's niece, Jane, who hated her so much, had been so close to her this whole time. She had been close to thinking of Jane as family more than an employee. Over time she would have. What about the guy Jane was dating? Did he know her true identity—and her true, cruel nature? The whole thing caused acid to rise in her throat. Raul had been even closer than she ever could have imagined.

He had eluded the police and the search dogs with his snowmobile and other tricks, but in the end he always returned to Jane's home without anyone being the wiser. That is, until he'd been caught coming back from his highway attack. That had been one desperate and stupid move on his part, to boldly stand on that road shooting at them when there was no real escape for him.

All Sierra could think was that he hadn't cared if he was caught, as long as he killed her. But he'd failed.

"And now I'm left to finish the job," Jane said. Her

entire demeanor had changed, and she looked like a dangerous and venomous person.

"It's been my show all along, really. Sure, Uncle Raul shot at you and attacked you, but I played the mind games. I ransacked the home while you and your good old dad were out."

That made sense, but Jane had seemed so concerned for her when she had called to inform about the break-in. Why hadn't Sierra sensed something in Jane or seen this coming? Why hadn't she figured it out when Raul had seemed to know her every move before she made it? Because Jane had informed him of all of her plans. She'd been listening closely to all Sierra's conversations even though she'd seemed to be busy at work and happy with her job. And when she wasn't at work, she'd lived in a bungalow in a wooded area on the edge of town where Raul could come and go without prying eyes. But she'd clearly found a remote and forgotten cabin to use in her plans to abduct Sierra.

"You have no idea how long I've been planning and waiting for this. Did you know that I followed you all the way from Boulder?" She giggled as if punch drunk. "And when you hired me for that part-time job helping out at the store, I knew that providence must be on my side."

Sick. Providence would never be on the side of a crazy like Jane.

Jane pulled the rag out of Sierra's mouth. "Well? Got anything to say to all that?"

Sierra moved her tongue around and tried to wet her parched lips. "Why now? You've been here for a year. Why did you decide… Oh, because your uncles escaped. But you didn't have to reveal yourself. Why continue? You'll only be caught just like Raul was."

That earned her another slap on the face. Jane must have been holding it all in this last year and waiting for the moment when she could unleash her pent-up anger. Again, nausea roiled inside.

"I knew that your boyfriend could end up staying. I wanted to keep taunting you, but I couldn't if he stayed. So I sent him away when I made you write that note. He must be miles away now and no one is coming to save you this time. My only regret is that my uncle—"

A disturbance drew their attention.

Bryce had knocked through the doorway. He pointed a gun straight at Jane.

"Step away from her and put your hands on your head."

Ignoring Bryce's demands, Jane laughed. "Well, well. You figured it out after all. I don't mind—I have to say that Plan B is just as exciting as Plan A. Now I get to kill those whom Sierra cares about the most right in front of her."

Jane darted away, dodging Bryce's bullet and producing a gun of her own. She aimed it at Sierra.

As if in slow motion, Sierra watched as a growling, barking Samson jumped on Jane but not before she fired her gun right as Bryce lunged in front of Sierra.

Samson and Bryce—she loved them both—tried to save Sierra. Jane was screaming. Samson subdued her with his massive form.

And now Sierra better understood what had happened. Samson had never liked Jane. Maybe he had even tried to alert Sierra, who continually trained him to trust Jane... So Jane had been able to march into

the store and abduct Sierra at gunpoint without anyone being the wiser.

Including her precious guard dog, Samson.

Tears leaked from her eyes.

"Call him off! Call your dog off!" Jane screamed.

Sierra ignored the woman. "Bryce, get up. Bryce,
are you okay?"

He groaned. Got to his feet then produced a knife.
Hands shaking, he cut her free. She rubbed her bleeding wrists. He cut her ankles free too.

"Are you all right?" she asked. "Wait, you're shot!"

He looked himself over. "No. She missed. Samson
changed her aim."

"You risked your life for me again, Bryce. You could
have died."

"It's all part of the—" he cleared his throat "—it used
to be part of the job."

He kept his intense gaze on her, a gaze that could
have been lifeless now since he'd once again risked his
life, willing to give it for her.

This was why she couldn't love because… Because
she couldn't take that pain of loss again.

But it was too late.

Sierra already loved Bryce.

Samson clamped down on Jane's arm to keep her
in place. Sierra's hands were numb from being tied so
long. "Do you have handcuffs you could secure her
with? And let's call the sheriff."

He nodded. Stumbled over to Jane and secured her
hands while Sierra tried to get a signal. Finally she
found one bar and left a voicemail. Then she texted
the information to the sheriff in case her words were
garbled. Sent the text to multiple people including Dad.

Samson relinquished his hold on Jane after Bryce restrained her with the rope she'd used on Sierra.

"Samson," Sierra called. "Good boy. You found me, didn't you?"

"And you, Bryce. You… You came looking for me. Why? That note I wrote—I figured you would be long gone and I would die here."

"The note didn't sound like you. Either that or I didn't want to believe you in which case that would mean I *am* a stalker."

Samson moaned, then suddenly struggled to stand. He ignored Sierra's commands for his attention. What was happening? What was wrong?

Panic slid around Sierra's throat.

Her dog collapsed at her feet.

"Samson? Samson!" She held his head up. His eyes were closed, but he still breathed.

Sierra gazed around the room. Had Samson gotten into something? She spotted the water bowl over behind where she'd been sitting. She hadn't been able to see it before.

No…

Maniacal laughing started from the table. Sierra gazed over at Raven. "What did you do?"

"It's all part of Plan B."

To kill those whom Sierra cared the most about—right in front of her. Bryce hadn't been shot, but Samson…

TWENTY

At the Crescent Springs Vet Hospital, where Samson lay on a table, they waited. A couple of chairs sat empty against the wall. Sierra couldn't sit while she worried about Samson. So she stood and leaned against the sterile decor, the fingers of one hand covering her mouth, the other hand held firmly in Bryce's. He was as concerned for Samson's well-being as Sierra was, and remained understanding and patient. She thought he might even be praying.

Sierra thought back to her experience at the cabin where Jane had taken her. To Bryce and Samson's heroic actions to save Sierra and capture Jane. Despite the blizzard brewing outside, the authorities had moved quickly for Sheriff Locke, deputies and Officer Kendall to get to the cabin to arrest Jane-Raven. They also brought with them an opioid antidote kit Sierra had requested. She couldn't know for certain that's what caused Samson's reaction, but Bryce had found a stash of pill bottles with painkillers on Jane. She finally admitted she'd crushed a few pills into the water as part of her Plan B in case Bryce and Samson decided to be heroes.

In this case, Sierra believed her.

How could Jane harm Samson like that? It took significant control not to unleash her rage on the woman. Unfortunately Jane was raised by two demented men and followed in their footsteps. But Jane was no longer Sierra's concern.

She focused her thoughts on Samson.

Proximity to Sierra had been dangerous to those closest to her, and now Samson could pay the highest price of all.

The vet, Harry Eubanks, had explained that dogs were trained to search for drugs and were more resistant to narcotics than humans, but those same dogs who could sniff out heroin could die from small doses of the synthetic opioids used for pain relief. Veterinarians, police and EMT's now regularly carried the kits to treat overdoses.

Harry listened to Samson's heart and lungs with his stethoscope. He peered up at Sierra. "It's been a couple of hours since the naloxone was administered to counter the drugs. All we can do now is wait."

"And pray," she said. She wouldn't leave his side until this was over, one way or another. *But God please let him wake up. Let the antidote work for him.*

She never meant for Samson to be put in danger. If Samson died because he'd come with Bryce to find and save her, she didn't know how she could deal with that.

As it was, she wanted so much to tell Bryce what she was truly thinking about the fact that he'd thrown himself in front of a bullet. But that conversation would have to wait. Now she was concerned for her best friend, Samson.

"He's going to be okay, Sierra," Bryce said. "Don't you worry. Samson's a strong one."

Sierra was keeping the faith, keeping the hope. She wanted to believe what Bryce said was true. She wouldn't argue with him about it. But when she glanced up and into his eyes, she saw the question in his eyes plain as day.

He feared that she blamed him for this. Bryce was the one to take Samson out to search for her, so in that respect he had put the dog in harm's way. But she didn't hold that against him—after all, if he hadn't used Samson, she would be dead right now. She'd been praying he would use Samson to find her.

"Tell me what you want me to do, Sierra. How can I help?"

She moved to the table and stroked Samson's fur. Harry was over at his counter working on his laptop. Close, but giving them space. "You're helping now. Just being here. Finding me."

Bryce's mesmerizing silvery-blue eyes held her gaze, and she didn't miss that they were filled with extraordinary pain.

"How can I ever thank you? If you hadn't come—"

"Then you don't... You don't blame me for using Samson to find you?"

Sierra took Bryce's hand. "How could I blame you for that? I tried to protect Samson the same way I tried to protect my heart. By avoiding the risks. I can't do that anymore. Samson saved us both today and I'll never forget that. He has to do what he was born and trained to do." She swallowed the tears welling in her throat. "Oh, Bryce, I was so afraid you were going to die. And for me. I had asked you to leave for a reason."

Her heart stuttered as she looked at him. She loved him. Yes, she loved him. She couldn't stop if she tried.

"But I didn't die." He took her other hand in his. "I hope… I hope you'll change your mind about me leaving."

Tears flooded her cheeks. Okay. Not good. She swiped them away. "I can't stop myself from loving you, Bryce, no matter if I'm afraid to take the risk. Even if you leave, I'll still love you." She stepped closer until her face was a few inches from his. She looked up at him, remembering that kiss.

Emotion stirred behind his gaze. "I'm right here with you. We're together in this and we can always be together if you just… Just say the word. I won't leave." He let his gaze drop to Samson who breathed peacefully on the table. "And as long as Samson approves, of course."

Samson moaned and barked and rolled up to sit.

"Samson!" Sierra and Bryce shouted in unison.

"Oh, Samson." Sierra hugged his neck. Then she peered at his face. "You're okay. You're going to be okay."

Harry was at his side in a flash and listened to the dog's heart and breathing again. "The antidote worked. He sounds good all around. I think you can take your dog home, boys and girls."

Samson hopped from the table. Harry poured water into a bowl and the dog lapped it up. Sierra crouched next to him, thrilled that he'd made it.

Samson licked her face, then Bryce's.

She laughed and then stood up. Bryce stood so close and she was drawn to him. She stepped into Bryce's arms. "I think Samson is giving his approval. His approval for… What did you mean when you said you wouldn't leave? Do you mean you're going to move out here to the middle of nowhere?"

He chuckled. "Only if that's okay with you."

"What are you really thinking?"

"I'm thinking I want to get a dog and have puppies with you and train them for SAR rescues. Anything to spend more time with you. I love you, Sierra. I thought my heart would stop when you said you loved me. What I'm really thinking… Okay, here it goes… I want to marry you. I've wanted that since the first year I knew you. What do you say?"

She stood on her toes and pressed her lips against his. Wrapped her arms around his neck and then up into his hair and pulled him closer to her, pouring all her answer into the kiss.

He broke away, leaving her breathless.

"Does that answer your question?"

* * * * *

Mary Ellen Porter's love of storytelling was solidified in fifth grade when she was selected to read her first children's story to a group of kindergartners. From then on, she knew she'd be a writer. When not working, Mary Ellen enjoys reading and spending time with her family and search dog in training. She's a member of Chesapeake Search Dogs, a volunteer search-and-rescue team that helps bring the lost and missing home.

Books by Mary Ellen Porter

Love Inspired Suspense

Into Thin Air
Off the Grid Christmas

Visit the Author Profile page
at Harlequin.com for more titles.

INTO THIN AIR

Mary Ellen Porter

Many are the plans in a man's heart,
but it is the Lord's purpose that prevails.
—*Proverbs* 19:21

To Eldridge, for always believing in me,
even when I doubted myself. Your love, support
and unfailing encouragement are the foundation
of all my achievements.

To my children, Skylar and Trey.
No mother could be more proud than I am of you;
you make me smile every day. May you find
God's special purpose for your lives within
your hopes and dreams.

And to my sister, Shirlee McCoy, whose ten years
of persistent and "gentle" prodding resulted in this
book. Smart. Talented. Tenacious. Stubborn.
A definite combination for success. It's finally
my turn to say "Me, too." Thank you for
never letting me forget my dreams. This one's for you.

ONE

It was a passing glimpse, no more. A young teen walking slowly along the edge of the darkening side street, a violin case tucked in the crook of her arm, her face illuminated by her cell phone screen as she furiously texted, aware of nothing but the phone in her hand.

The van made even less of an impression, the driver all but invisible as the vehicle passed Laney Kensington's Jeep Wrangler.

Both should have been easy to ignore, but they nagged at Laney's mind—made the hair on the back of her neck prickle. Laney told herself it was just her imagination getting the best of her—but she couldn't simply drive on.

Call it intuition, call it divine intervention—Laney called it never wrong.

She'd never ignored it on a search. She wouldn't ignore it now.

She glanced in the rearview mirror, pulse jumping as the van swung a wide U-turn and headed back toward the girl. Laney did the same, stepping on the gas, her Jeep surging forward.

The slowing van closed in on the girl. She finally

looked up, eyes widening as a figure jumped out and sprinted toward her. The violin dropped from her arms and she tried to run.

Too little, too late.

The man was on her in a flash, hand over her mouth, dragging her toward the van. In seconds they'd be gone. One more child missing. One more family broken.

Not today. Not if Laney could help it.

Although it had been years since she'd last prayed, Laney found herself whispering a silent plea to God, begging Him for help that deep down she knew would never come. She'd learned a long time ago that the only one she could depend on was herself.

Putting her trust anywhere else was just too risky.

The van was right in front of her, and there was only one thing Laney could think to do to stop the kidnapping. She braced for impact, ramming the front of the van with her Jeep in the hope of disabling it. In the back seat, Murphy yelped at the jarring stop; there was no time to comfort the dog.

Leaping from the Jeep, Laney threw herself at the would-be kidnapper. His weight off-balance from the struggling child, he tumbled over. The girl went with him, her high-pitched scream piercing the still air. Laney snagged the girl's hand, yanking her to her feet.

"Run!" she shouted, but the kidnapper was on his feet again, snatching a handful of the girl's shirt and dragging her back.

"Back off!" he commanded, his voice chilling.

Laney slammed into him again, this time with so much force they all fell in a tangled mass of limbs, pushing and grabbing and struggling. The kidnapper grunted as Laney kneed him in the kidney. His grip on the girl loosened, and Laney shoved her from the heap.

But the kidnapper would not let his prey go without a fight. He reverse punched Laney, propelling her backward. She tumbled onto damp grass, her head slamming into hard earth. She had a moment of panic as blackness edged in. She could *not* lose consciousness. She willed herself up, lunging toward the struggling pair as they neared the van. Laney yanked the guy's arm and slammed her foot into the back of his knee. He cursed, swinging around, the girl between them.

"I said *back off*!" he growled, his dark eyes filled with fury, his hand clamped firmly over the girl's mouth.

Laney eased around so that she stood between him and the van. She saw that the girl was still fighting against his hold, but her efforts were futile. She met Laney's eyes, the fear in her gaze something Laney knew she would never forget.

It's okay, Laney wanted to say. *He's not going to take you. I won't let him.*

"Let her go," Laney demanded.

"I don't think so." The man glanced just beyond Laney's shoulder, a cold smile curving his lips.

The girl stilled, her eyes widening.

Laney knew without even looking that someone was behind her.

Her blood ran cold, but she turned, ready to fight as many people as it took for as long as she had to. Eventually, another car would come, someone would call the police, help would arrive. She just had to hold the kidnappers off long enough for that to happen.

A shadowy figured jumped from the van's open door.

Laney had the impression of height and weight, of dark hair and cold eyes, but it was the gun that caught and held her attention. Although the gunman was shorter and more wiry than his stocky partner, the firearm in his hand made him far more lethal.

"Don't move," he snapped, the gun pointed straight at Laney's heart.

Laney stopped in her tracks, hands in the air in a display of unarmed surrender.

She wanted him to think she'd given up; she needed him off guard. She had to get the gun out of his hands, and she had to free the girl.

"Get the kid in the van before someone else comes by," the gunman ordered his accomplice.

"What do we do with the woman?" the other man asked as he dragged the child around Laney, grunting and tightening his grip as the girl's sneaker-clad foot caught his shin.

"Get rid of her. She's a loose end. No witnesses, remember?" The words were spoken with cold malice that sent a wave of fear up Laney's spine.

No cars coming, nothing to hide behind. No matter what direction Laney ran, a bullet could easily find her. If the girl was going to survive, if *Laney* was going to, the gunman had to be taken down. Laney braced herself for action, waiting for an opening that she was afraid wouldn't come.

Please, she prayed silently. *Just give me a chance*.

The girl grunted, trying to scream against the hand pressed to her face. They were close to the van door, so close that Laney knew it was just a matter of seconds before the girl was shoved in.

"Bite him!" she yelled.

"Shut up!" the gunman barked, glancing over his shoulder to check on his accomplice's progress. That was the opening Laney needed. She threw herself at his gun hand. He cursed, the gun dropping to the ground. They both reached for it, Laney's fingers brushing cold metal, victory right beneath her palm. He slammed his fist into her jaw and she flew back, her grip on the gun lost in a wave of shocking pain. A dog growled, the harsh sound mixing with the frantic rush of Laney's pulse.

Murphy! She'd not given him the release command, yet he raced toward them, teeth bared.

The man raised the gun. Laney tried to scramble out of the way as he pulled the trigger. Hot pain seared through her temple, and she fell, Murphy's well-muscled body the last thing she saw as she sank into darkness.

Grayson DeMarco rushed through Anne Arundel Medical Center's fluorescently lit hallway, scanning the staff and visitors moving through the corridor. He'd been working this case for almost a year. He'd dogged every lead to every dead end, traveling from California to Boston and down to Baltimore, and he'd always been a few steps behind, a few days too late.

Sixteen children abducted. Four states. Not one single break.

Until tonight.

Finally the abductors had made a mistake.

A young girl was missing. The police had received her parents' frantic call less than thirty minutes after a woman had been found shot and unconscious on the sidewalk, a violin case and cell phone lying on the grass near her. The case had the missing girl's name on it.

Grayson had been called immediately, state PD moving quickly. They felt the pressure, too; they could see the tally of the area's missing children going up.

Like Grayson, they could hear the clock ticking.

They'd found a gun at the scene, spattered with blood, lying in the small island of grass that separated the sidewalk from the street. Grayson hoped it would yield useable prints and a DNA profile that could possibly lead him one step closer to the answers he was searching for.

He prayed it would, but he wasn't counting on it.

He'd been to the scene. He'd peered into an abandoned Jeep, lights still on, driver's door open. He'd opened the victim's wallet, seen her identification— Laney Kensington, five feet three inches and one hundred ten pounds. He'd gotten a good look at the German shepherd that might have been responsible for stopping the kidnappers before they were able to kill the woman. He'd pieced together an idea of what might have happened, but he needed to talk to Laney Kensington, find out what had really gone down, how much she'd seen. More importantly, he needed to know exactly how valuable that information might be to the case he was working.

Time was of the essence if Grayson had any chance of bringing these children home.

Failure was not an option.

A police officer stood guard outside the woman's room, his arms crossed over his chest, his expression neutral. He didn't move as Grayson approached, didn't acknowledge him at all until Grayson flashed his badge. "Special Agent Grayson DeMarco, FBI."

"Detective Paul Jensen, Maryland State Police," the

detective responded. "No one's allowed in to see the victim. If that's why you're here, you may as well turn around and—"

He cut the man off. "We don't have time to play jurisdiction games, Detective. As of tonight, three kids are missing from Maryland in just under six weeks."

"I'm well aware of that, but I have my orders, and until I hear from my supervisor that you're approved to go in there, you're out."

"How about you give him a call, then?" Grayson reached past the detective and opened the door, ignoring the guy's angry protest as he walked into the cool hospital room.

The witness lay unconscious under a mound of sheets and blankets, her dark auburn hair tangled around a face that was pale and still streaked with dried blood. Faint signs of bruising shadowed her jaw, made more evident by the harsh hospital lights. A bandage covered her temple, and an IV line snaked out from beneath the sheets. She appeared delicate, almost fragile, not at all what he was expecting given her part in the events of the night. Fortunately, as fragile as she appeared, the bullet had merely grazed her temple and she would eventually make a full recovery.

Unfortunately, Grayson didn't have the luxury of waiting for her to heal. He needed to speak to her. The sooner the better.

He moved toward the bed, trying to ignore the pine scent of floor cleaner, the harsh overhead lights, the IV line. They reminded him of things he was better off forgetting, of a time when he hadn't been sure he could keep doing what he did.

He pulled a chair to the side of the bed and sat, glancing at Detective Jensen, who'd followed him into the room. "Aren't you supposed to be guarding the door?"

"I'm guarding the witness, and I could force you out of here," the detective retorted, his eyes flashing with irritation and a hint of worry.

"What would be the point? You know I've got jurisdiction."

The detective offered no response. Grayson hadn't expected him to. Policies and protocol didn't bring abducted kids back to their parents, and wasting time fighting over jurisdiction wasn't going to accomplish anything.

"Look," he said, meeting the detective's dark eyes. "I'm not here to step on toes. I'm here to find these kids. There's still a chance we can bring them home. All of them. How about you keep that in mind?"

The guy muttered something under his breath and stalked out of the room.

That was fine with Grayson. He preferred to be alone with the witness when she woke. He wanted every bit of information she had, every minute detail. He didn't want it second-or third-hand, didn't want to get it after it had already been said a few times. He needed her memories fresh and clear, undiluted by time or speculation.

Laney groaned softly and began to stir. Just for a moment, Grayson felt like a voyeur. It seemed almost wrong to be sitting over her bed waiting for her to gain consciousness. She needed family or friends around her. Not a jaded FBI agent with his own agenda.

He leaned in toward Laney. Though only moments ago she had appeared to be on the verge of waking, she had grown still again.

"Laney?" he said softly. "Can you hear me?"

He leaned in closer. "Laney?"

She stirred, eyes moving rapidly behind closed lids. Was she caught in a dream, or a memory? he wondered.

"Wake up, Laney." He reached out, resting his hand gently on her forearm.

She came up swinging, her fist grazing his chin, her eyes wild. She swung again, and Grayson did the only thing he could. He ducked.

TWO

"Calm down," a man said, his warm fingers curved around Laney's wrist. She tried to pull away but couldn't quite find the strength. Her head throbbed, the pungent smell of antiseptic filled her nose, and she couldn't manage to do more than stare into the stranger's dark-lashed blue eyes.

Not the kidnapper's eyes. Not the eyes of his accomplice. She wasn't lying on the pavement in the dark. There was no Jeep. No van. No struggling young girl with terror in her eyes. Nothing but cream-colored walls and white sheets and a man who could have been anyone looking at her expectantly.

"What happened? How did I get here?" she asked, levering up on her elbows, the hospital room too bright, her heart beating an erratic cadence in her chest.

"A couple of joggers found you lying on the sidewalk," the man responded. "Do you remember anything about tonight?"

Anything?

She remembered *everything*—heading home from Murphy's training session, seeing the girl and the van, struggling and fighting and failing. Again.

"Yes," she mumbled, willing away nausea and the deep pain of failure.

"Good." He smiled, his expression changing from harsh and implacable to something that looked like triumph. "That's going to help a lot."

"Help who?" Because her actions tonight certainly hadn't helped the girl or her family. Overwhelming sadness welled up within her, but Laney forced it back. She had to get a grip on herself. She had no idea how long she'd been unconscious, what had happened to Murphy, or most importantly, if the police even knew a child had been taken.

"I'm Special Agent Grayson DeMarco with the FBI," the man explained. "I'm hoping you can help with a case I'm working on."

"I'm not worried about your case, Agent DeMarco. I'm worried about the girl who was kidnapped tonight." She shoved the sheets off her legs and sat up. Her head swam, the pain behind her eyes nearly blinding her, but she had to get to a phone. She needed to tell Police Chief Kent Andrews what had happened. They needed to start searching immediately if there was any chance to save the child. And there *had* to be a chance.

"The girl *is* my case—and several other children like her," Agent DeMarco responded. "The local police are at the scene of the kidnapping. They're gathering evidence and doing everything they can to locate her, but she's not the only victim. If you've been watching the local news, you know that."

Because he seemed to expect a response, Laney nodded, realizing immediately that was a mistake as pain exploded through her temple. Her stomach churned.

"Lie down." Somehow Agent DeMarco was standing, his hands on her shoulders as he urged her back onto the pillows. "You're not going to do anyone any good if you're unconscious again." The words were harsh, but his touch was light.

Laney eyed him critically. She'd been working around law enforcement—local as well as Secret Service and DEA—for much of her adult life. She knew how the agencies operated. The FBI wouldn't be called in on an isolated, random child abduction.

"I'm fine," she muttered, pushing the button on the bed railing until the mattress raised her to a sitting position.

"You came within an inch of dying, Laney. I wouldn't call that fine." He settled back into the chair, his black tactical pants, T-shirt and jacket making him look more like a mercenary than an officer of the law.

She gingerly fingered a thick bandage that covered her temple and knew Agent DeMarco was right. "Murphy must have thrown his aim off."

"Murphy is the dog that was found at the scene?"

"Yes, I need to—"

"The local police have him. I was told he was being brought back to the kennel."

"Told by whom?" she asked. Agent DeMarco was saying all the right things, but she didn't know him, hadn't seen any identification, still wasn't a hundred percent convinced he was who he said he was.

"Chief Kent Andrews. He'll probably be here shortly. He's still overseeing the scene."

"I'd like to speak with him." She and Kent went back a couple of years. She often worked with the Maryland State Police K-9 team, correcting training issues with both the dogs and their handlers in an unofficial capacity.

"You will, but I need to ask you a few questions first."

"How about you show me some ID? Then you can ask your questions."

The request didn't surprise Grayson. He'd been told that Laney knew her way around law enforcement and that she wasn't someone who'd blindly follow orders. While working with the state K-9 team as a dog trainer, her skills with animals and the trainees alike had garnered the respect of the police chief and his men. More than that, Grayson got the distinct impression that Kent Andrews really liked Laney as a person and wasn't surprised at all that she would put herself in danger to help another.

"Sure." Grayson fished his ID out of his pocket, handed it to her.

She studied it, her wavy hair sliding across her cheeks and hiding her expression. She didn't trust him. That much was obvious, but she finally handed the ID back. "What do you want to know?" she asked.

"Everything," he responded, taking a small notepad and pen from his jacket pocket. "All the details of what happened tonight. What you saw. Who you saw. Don't leave anything out. Even the smallest detail could be important."

"I was on my way back from Davidsonville Park with Murphy when I saw her."

"Was she alone?"

"Yes. She was walking by herself. I always hate seeing that. I can't even count the number of kids my team and I have searched for who were out by themselves when they disappeared." She pinched the bridge of her nose and frowned. "Sorry, I'm getting off track. This headache…" She shook her head slightly and winced.

"Want me to call the nurse and get you something for the pain?" He would, but he didn't want to. He needed her as clear-headed as she could be.

She must have sensed that. She rested her head on the pillow. "That would be nice, but I'm not sure I'll be any good to anyone filled with a bunch of painkillers."

"Don't suffer for your cause, Laney. If you need pain medication, take it."

She smiled at that, a real smile that brightened her eyes and somehow made the smattering of freckles on her cheeks and nose more noticeable. She was pretty in a girl-next-door kind of way. He tried to imagine her taking on a guy with a gun. Couldn't quite do it. "I hate taking narcotics," she muttered. "I'll ask for Tylenol later."

He wasn't going to argue with her. "You saw the girl walking alone," he prompted her.

"Yes. I was headed home. A van was coming toward me in the opposite direction. We passed the girl at nearly the same time."

"Passed her?" He'd assumed she'd driven up as the girl was being abducted.

"Yes. The van made me think of the news reports of other abductions in the area. I glanced in the rearview mirror and saw the van U-turn. I did the same." Laney looked away as if unable to meet his gaze. "Unfortunately, it reached her first. She was texting and didn't even see them coming."

"Could you see the color of the van?"

"Not initially, but I got a good look at it when I rammed it with my jeep. It was a dark charcoal gray. My front fender probably scraped off some of the paint. It will have a fresh dent on the front passenger side…" Laney's voice faltered.

"Did you see the person who grabbed her? Can you describe him?" he asked, every cell in his body waiting for the answer. If she saw the guy, if she had a description, if there was DNA on the gun, they'd finally have something to go on.

"I had a pretty clear view. There were streetlights and the headlights from my Jeep."

"Tell me what you remember. Don't hold anything back." Grayson urged.

"He was about six-foot-one with the build of an ex–football player—beefy but not in great shape anymore. His hair was dark brown and cropped close, like a military cut. He was wearing jeans with a black hooded sweatshirt and black work boots. He had brown eyes and an olive complexion. I saw part of a tattoo on the back of his neck, sticking out from the collar of his sweatshirt, but I didn't get a good look at it." She paused, frowned. "He wasn't alone. There was another guy in the van. He came out to help. He was shorter— I'd guess about five-foot-ten. Thin—like a runner's build. His hair was light brown, nose slightly crooked. He was the one with the gun."

Grayson scribbled notes furiously. "What about their ages?"

"Early to mid-thirties. Both of them."

"Did either speak?"

"Both did, but they didn't call each other by name." Too bad. That would have been another lead to follow.

"What about accents?"

"None that I could distinguish."

"Did the girl seem to know her kidnappers?"

"If she knew them, it didn't show. As far as I could tell, she was an arbitrary target, but the way the van was parked would have made it nearly impossible for anyone on the street to see the kidnappers. It seemed random…but not."

"How so?"

"Like they were trolling the streets looking for someone, but once they picked a target their actions were deliberate—no hesitation—like they'd done the same thing before. If I hadn't been there, the girl—"

"Olivia Henley. She's thirteen. She was on her way home from her weekly music lesson. Her parents reported her missing shortly after the joggers found you." He wanted Laney to have a name to go with the face. He wanted her to know that there was a family who was missing a child. Not because he wanted her to feel guilty or obligated, but because he wanted her to understand how serious things were, how imperative it was that she cooperate.

"Olivia," she repeated quietly. "If I hadn't been there, she would have disappeared, and no one would have known what happened." She paused, her face so pale, he thought she might lose consciousness again. "If only I had done something differently, maybe she wouldn't have been taken."

"You did what you could, which is more than most would."

"But it wasn't enough, was it?" She leveled her gaze at him, surprising him with the depth of anger he saw reflected in her eyes. "That little girl is gone, Agent DeMarco. Her bed will be empty tonight."

Grayson recognized and understood her frustration. So many children went missing every day, and not all of them would make it home. He knew that better than most. "Not because of you, Laney. Because of the kidnappers."

"That's no consolation to her parents." Laney closed her eyes. "I wish I could have saved her."

"You still might be able to. If you're up to it, I'd like you to meet with a sketch arti—"

"I'm up to it. Let's go." Before the words were out of her mouth, she was up from bed, the white cotton sheet draped around her shoulders like a cape as she wobbled toward the door, the IV pole trailing along behind her.

"I didn't mean now," he said, taking three long strides to beat her to the door and slapping his palm against it so that she couldn't open it. "And I didn't mean you should walk out of here with an IV line attached to your arm, either."

"Then bring the sketch artist here." She turned to face him, swaying a little in the process. "The sooner you have an image of these guys, the sooner everyone can be on the lookout for them. If you really think Olivia can be saved, there's no time to lose."

She was right, of course. About all of it. There was only one problem with her plan, and it was a big one.

"We're not bringing the sketch artist here," he said, leading her back toward the bed. "You'd better lie down before you fall down."

She dropped into the chair instead, her face ashen, her eyes a dark emerald green against the pallor. "Why *not* bring the sketch artist here?" Her voice had lost some of its strength, but she hadn't lost any of her determination. "We're wasting time talking when we could be—"

"As far as the kidnappers know, you're dead, Laney," he said, cutting her off.

"What?"

"Dead. Deceased. Gone."

She rolled her eyes. "I know what you meant, Agent. I want to know *why* they think I'm dead."

"You were shot. Murphy might have distracted the shooter, but you went down. You were bleeding enough to make anyone think you'd been mortally wounded. The joggers who found you were a couple of teenage girls. They panicked, called 911 and reported a body. No one knows who you are or that you survived except the first responders and the hospital staff treating you, and they've been asked to keep it quiet. As far as the media and the public are concerned, Jane Doe was shot and killed on Ashley Street at approximately seven-thirty this evening. I'd like to keep your identity quiet for as long as possible."

Laney frowned. "Protecting my identity is the last thing we need to worry about."

"I disagree."

"Maybe you should explain why."

Grayson hesitated. Andrews had assured him that Laney was as good as they came, loyal and trustworthy. Even so, Grayson was reluctant to divulge too much. He was used to working alone. Putting his trust in God and his own abilities above all else. He had this one perfect lead, and he didn't want anything to keep it from panning out. "For now, I need you to trust that I'm making the best decisions I can for you and Olivia."

"For now," Laney agreed, struggling to her feet. "But you need to know that I'm not going to spend much time sitting around this hospital room while you make decisions for me. That's not the way I work."

She jabbed the call button on the bed railing, and he had visions of her walking out of the hospital in the mint-green hospital gown, the bandage on her forehead a glaring testimony to her injury. If the kidnappers were hanging around hoping to hear rumors confirming Jane Doe's death, they might catch a glimpse of Laney and follow her home. That was the last thing Grayson wanted.

He was all too aware that his biggest hope just might lie on the slender shoulders of Laney Kensington. If she could identify the kidnappers, he would be one step closer to saving Olivia—and the other children. He needed her help. And to get it, he had to give her some measure of trust.

"Then tell me how you *do* work," he offered. "And, let's see what kind of a compromise we can reach."

"I'm not looking for compromise. I need to know what's going on. Let's start with what you've got on these kidnappings."

It went against his nature to give her the information. He'd been keeping everything close to the vest. The less media coverage about the kidnappings, the better, as far as he was concerned. He was closing in on the perps. He could feel it, and he didn't want to risk scaring them off. He needed them to feel comfortable and confident. Their cockiness would be key to bringing them down.

On the other hand, he couldn't risk having Laney go maverick on him. If what the police chief had said about her was true, she knew enough about search and rescue and about police work to be dangerous. He had no doubt that she understood she could walk out of the hospital and away from him altogether. He had nothing on her and no legal means to keep her where she was. And if the kidnappers caught even a glimpse of her, the damage would be done. She'd gotten a good look at the kidnappers. He could only assume they'd gotten a good look at her, too. Once they knew she was alive, how quickly could they find her if they put their minds to it?

"Okay," he finally said. "Just have a seat and I'll tell you as much as I can."

She hesitated, her face drawn. Finally she complied, dropping back into the chair and fixing all of her attention on him.

"Well?" she prodded.

He pulled a chair over and sat.

They were knee to knee, the fabric of his pants brushing against the sheet she'd wrapped herself in, the IV pole just to the side of her chair. She looked young and vulnerable, her life way too easy to snuff out. That thought brought memories of another time, and for a moment, Grayson was in different hospital room, looking into another pale face. He hadn't been able to save Andrea, but he was going to do everything in his power to make sure Laney survived.

THREE

"What I am about to tell you is sensitive," Agent De-Marco said. "I need your word that you'll keep it confidential."

"Of course," Laney agreed.

"Good, because you're the only witness to a kidnapping that is connected to the abduction of two other children over the past six weeks."

"That's not a secret, Agent. It's been in the news for a few weeks." In fact, those abductions—one outside of DC and the other in Annapolis—had been nagging at her when she saw the van on Ashley Street.

"There have also been similar clusters of child abductions in two other states."

She definitely *hadn't* heard that before. "How many children are we talking about?"

"Thirteen others, so far. Not including the three from this area."

"Sixteen kids missing? I'd think that would be all over the news."

"It has been. Regional news only. The first seven disappeared from the Los Angeles area over a four-month period. The next six disappeared from the Boston vicinity in just under three months. In many cases, there were reports of a dark van in the area around the time of the abductions."

"Just like the van tonight."

He nodded. "Your description is the most detailed, but other witnesses mentioned a dark panel van. Unfortunately, no one has seen the driver. You're the first witness we have who's seen everything—the van, the missing child, the kidnappers. It's the break I've been waiting for, and I don't want anything to jeopardize it. We need to keep the fact that you survived quiet for as long as possible. The less the kidnappers realize we know, the easier it will be to close in on them."

"I understand. I won't tell anyone."

"It's not as simple as that. The kidnappers are aware that you were shot. They could have followed the ambulance to the hospital. They could be waiting around, hoping to hear some information that will confirm your death or refute it."

"Why would they bother? I saw them, but I don't know who they are."

"You've worked with law enforcement for years, Laney. You understand how this works. They tried to silence you to keep you from reporting what you witnessed. If they see that they failed, they may try again."

"But is sticking around to kill me really worth the risk when they could just skip town with the kids and disappear?" That's what she thought they'd do, but she wasn't sure how clear her thinking was. Her head ached so badly, she just wanted to close her eyes.

"This trafficking ring is extensive," Agent DeMarco explained. "We've had reports that the children are being transported overseas and sold into slavery. This is a multi-tier operation that isn't just being run here in the United States. There are kids missing in Europe, in Canada, in Asia, and each time, the kidnappings occur in clusters. Five, six, seven kids from a region go missing, and then nothing."

"Except families left with broken hearts and no answers," Laney murmured, the thought of all those kids, all those parents and siblings, all those empty bedrooms and empty hearts making her heart ache and head pound even more.

"Right." Agent DeMarco leaned forward, and Laney could see the black rim around his blue irises, the dark stubble on his chin. He had a tiny scar at the corner of his left brow and a larger one close to his hairline. He looked tough and determined, and for some reason she found that reassuring.

"Olivia's abduction makes the third in this area," Agent DeMarco continued, "but if their pattern holds, they plan to target more from the surrounding area before moving the kids."

"It seems a safer bet for them to cut their losses and move on," she said doubtfully.

"We're talking money, Laney. A lot of it. Money is a great motivator. It can turn ordinary men into extraordinary criminals."

"And kidnappers into murderers?"

"That, too." He stood and paced across the room. "This is a business for them, with schedules to keep and deliveries to make. I'm certain the children are being held somewhere while they wait for prearranged transport out of the country. Moving them to another location would also risk exposure. You were shot tonight because they can't afford any witnesses. They need to buy time to get their quota of children ready for de-livery. With you dead or incapacitated, the immediate threat of exposure is gone."

"So as long as they believe I died, it's business as usual."

Agent DeMarco nodded, returning to his chair, and leveling his gaze on her. "The longer it takes for the kidnappers to realize you survived, the better it will be for everyone."

"Not for Olivia," she pointed out, that image—the one of the girl, her eyes wide, begging for help—filling her mind again. She'd failed to save her, and that knowl-edge was worse than the pain in her head, worse than the nausea. "She's terrified and alone. She doesn't care who knows what. All she cares about is getting home."

"You're wrong. It does matter for Olivia," Agent De-Marco responded. "There's a chance that we can reunite Olivia with her family, but only if the kidnappers aren't scared into moving early. All we have to do is find Oliv-ia's kidnappers, and we'll find her. We'll find them all."

His words made her heart jump, and she was almost ready to spring up from the chair and start looking in every place they could possibly be. "Then why are we sitting here? Why aren't we out searching for them?"

"Chief Andrews said you'd ask that," he responded, a half smile curving his lips. "He told me to assure you that he has a K-9 team working the scene."

But Laney knew they'd not find much. Olivia had been driven off in a van. Even her retired search dog, Jax, who had been one of the best air scent dogs in the country, wouldn't be able to pick up her scent under those circumstances.

She recognized that, but still, she wanted to be in on

the action in a way she hadn't wanted to be since the accident that took her teammates' lives. The accident that had prompted her to leave her search-and-rescue work behind and put Jax into early retirement. The thought stole some of her energy, and she sank back against the chair. "That's good. If there's something to find, they'll uncover it."

"That's what I've been told. You've been working with them for a while?"

She had. For nearly two years now. She volunteered her time to ensure high-drive, problem dogs were given the chance to succeed. She'd helped train several dogs that had been like Murphy—problematic but with obvious promise. Although Kent made repeated offers to make her role with the department more permanent, she was reluctant to fall back into the stressful life of a contract employee. Besides, her own clients kept her busy enough. "Unofficially. I own a private boarding and training facility in Davidsonville. Murphy is the most recent in a line of MPD K-9s I've worked with."

"Murphy." His smile broadened. "He's quite a dog."

"He's quite a problem child, but we're working on it."

"He came through for you tonight," he pointed out.

"Yes. Though technically, he's supposed to leave the vehicle only on command."

"Well, in this case, it's a good thing he didn't."

"I think seeing the gun set him off. We just started working with firearms last week, and he's making good progress." Better than she had hoped. She was pleased at how quickly Murphy was improving after being booted out of the MPD K-9 program once. He was a little high-energy and distractible, but he possessed the important shepherd traits—intelligence and loyalty.

Agent DeMarco smiled. "Andrews and the K-9 handlers certainly seemed happy the dog came through for you."

She forced herself out of the chair, every muscle in her body protesting. "Speaking of which, I need to talk to Kent. I don't suppose you have my things?"

"Purse? Cell Phone? House keys?"

"Yes."

"They've been collected as evidence. Your Jeep was impounded, too. And your clothes—" his gaze dropped from her face to the cotton hospital gown "—were also taken as evidence."

"I guess I'll be flagging a taxi in this hospital gown," she responded. She wasn't going to stay in the hospital any longer than necessary. Her business was thriving. That meant plenty of work to do at the kennel. She was hoping that would keep her mind off her failures. She didn't need to spend months mourning what she hadn't been able to do for Olivia. She'd been down that path before, and it hadn't led to anything but misery.

"Leaving in a hospital gown isn't going to work. It's a surefire way to get the wrong people's attention. When you leave, we're going to do everything possible to make sure no one notices you."

"That's going to be really difficult with—"

There was a sudden commotion outside the door, a flurry of movement and voices that had Agent DeMarco pivoting toward the sound.

"Stay there," he commanded, striding toward the door and yanking it open.

His broad back blocked Laney's view, and she moved closer, trying to see over his shoulder. A police officer stood in the doorway, back to the room.

"Ma'am, I told you no one can enter without permission," he said to someone Laney couldn't see.

"Ridiculous," a woman responded, the voice as familiar as the morning sun.

Great-Aunt Rose. Someone must have called her.

"Aunt Rose, don't—" Laney began.

Too late. Rose somehow darted through the blockade of masculinity, slipping past the officer.

Agent DeMarco stepped to the side, letting her by. Obviously he wasn't worried about a five-foot-nothing octogenarian. The officer, on the other hand, looked quite disgruntled.

"Do you want me to cuff you, ma'am?" he shouted.

"Don't be silly, boy. I'm too old. You'd break my brittle wrists." Rose smoothed loose strands of silver hair back into her neat bun, then brushed invisible lint from her beige slacks. Her gaze settled on Agent DeMarco for a moment before her focus shifted to Laney.

"You're awake! Thank the good Lord for His mercy!" she cried, hefting an oversize bag onto the bed.

"Yeah," the officer sputtered. "She's awake, and I'm going to lose my job."

"Now, why would you go and do something like that?" Aunt Rose asked, completely unfazed by the commotion she'd caused. Typical Rose. Always in the midst of trouble and never quite sure why.

"My aunt is notorious for getting what she wants," Laney cut in. "I'm sure Chief Andrews will understand the position you were in."

"He might, but I don't," the officer responded irritably. "But I guess as long as she's your aunt, I'll go back to my post."

He returned to the corridor, closing the door with a little more force than necessary.

"You've annoyed him, Aunt Rose," Laney said.

"And you've annoyed me. Getting yourself shot up and tossed into the hospital and interrupting a perfectly wonderful book club meeting," Rose responded. She touched Laney's cheek and shook her head. "What in the world happened? I mean, Tommy said you'd been shot…but I figured he's so old, he probably got it wrong."

"Tom is barely sixty, Aunt Rose, and you know it." Laney sighed. Her aunt and the deputy chief of police Tom Wallace had never hit it off. She'd have to remember to thank him for calling Rose. The poor guy tried to avoid Rose as often as possible.

"But he acts like he's a hundred, 'bout as fun as a stick in the mud. Remember that picnic at the kennel last year? He—"

"Aunt Rose, please. I'm not in the mood for trips down memory lane," Laney said, her head pounding with renewed vigor.

"Are you in the mood to sit down?" Agent DeMarco asked, taking Laney's arm and urging her to the chair she'd abandoned. "You look like you probably should."

She settled into the chair, watching with horror as Rose peered up at Agent DeMarco. If Laney's brain had been functioning at full capacity, she'd have found a way to refocus her aunt's attention. As it was, all she could do was hope that Rose didn't say anything she'd regret. Or, more to the point, that *Laney* would regret.

"You must be that FBI agent Tommy told me about," Rose said with a smile.

"Yes, ma'am. Special Agent Grayson DeMarco."

"Well, I'm too old to be remembering all those names and titles—what's your mama call you?"

Agent DeMarco smiled at that. "She calls me Gray."

"Well, then, Gray it is, and you can call me Rose. None of those niceties like 'ma'am'…that just makes me feel old." Rose plopped down in the chair Agent DeMarco had vacated only moments ago.

"How'd you get here Aunt Rose? I hope you didn't drive," Laney said. The thought of Rose speeding down Route 50 was not especially comforting.

"Of course not. You know my license was temporarily revoked after that unfortunate incident at Davis's Plant Emporium. Really, I don't understand why everyone was so upset—it was only a couple of bushes and some potted plants, after all…but that's neither here nor there." Rose shook her head and patting Laney's knee. "Tommy drove me. Kent sent him to pick me up. I imagine Tommy will be along soon." She lowered her voice to a decidedly loud whisper. "I made him drop me off at the door so no one would see us walk in together— that's how rumors get started. Before you know it, the whole congregation will be saying I was arrested or some such nonsense."

"Rose," Agent DeMarco said, "did Deputy Chief Wallace explain that we need to keep the details of this situation quiet?"

"Yes, yes. He explained. No need to worry about me. My mind is a steel trap, and my lips are sealed." Rose put a hand up as if waving away the agent's concerns, then turned to Laney. "So, how on earth did you get yourself shot?"

Was Laney allowed to mention the kidnapping? She

didn't know, so she kept it brief. "I witnessed a crime and tried to intervene."

"I bet you weren't carrying that mace I gave you last Christmas, were you?" Rose frowned. "That stuff's supposed to be powerful enough to stop a bear in its tracks. A criminal would probably have a hard time aiming at you with that in his eyes. I've got my can of it right in that bag. Anyone tries to come at us, I'll take him down."

Grayson would almost have liked to see that.

Laney's aunt looked about as old as Methuselah, but she moved like a woman much younger. He could picture her reaching into the bag, yanking out the spray and taking down a kidnapper.

A quick rap at the door and a young female doctor walked in, followed closely by Deputy Chief Tom Wallace. Grayson had met him at the crime scene, and he'd liked the guy immediately. Though old-school and by-the-book, he didn't have any compunction about sharing information with the FBI.

"Agent DeMarco," Wallace said, "the chief said to let you know they've finished with the crime scene. He's going to the precinct to make sure the blood and finger prints on the gun are expedited for processing."

"Thanks, Deputy." So far he liked the way Chief Andrews handled things, and he wasn't surprised that Andrews was taking a very personal interest in the case. "I may head that way myself after Laney is discharged."

"*If* she's discharged," Wallace replied. "The *doctor* will decide that and *then* we can come up with a plan for getting her out of here."

They weren't going to do anything. Grayson had a

plan, and he was sticking to it. He didn't bother telling Wallace that. The doctor was already leaning over Laney, flashing a light in her eyes, asking about pain level, nausea, dizziness. Laney answered quietly.

"We did an MRI when you were brought in. I'm happy to report that there's no fracture and no hemorrhage in the brain," the doctor said, tucking a loose strand of black curly hair behind her ear and pushing her glasses up on her nose. "You do have a concussion, and the effects of that can last for a while. Expect the headache to linger for the next few days. I can give you some prescription-strength Tylenol to take the edge off the headache, or something stronger if you think you'll need it."

"Prescription-strength Tylenol's fine."

The doctor marked something in her chart. "You were really fortunate, you know. If that bullet had traveled a different trajectory—just a half an inch in any direction—the outcome would have been very different." She tucked her pen in her lab-coat pocket and her clipboard under her arm. "There's really no need to keep you here overnight, assuming there's someone at home to monitor you."

"I'll be with her," Rose piped up.

The doctor looked over at Rose, then back at Laney, an almost indiscernible look of concern crossing her face. "Do you two live alone?"

"Oh, we don't live together," Rose responded. "I like my space. But I'm happy to stay with her for a few days."

"I see." The doctor frowned. "Maybe it *would* be best if you stayed here overnight, Laney." Her gaze jumped to Grayson. "Unless you two—"

"No!" Laney said quickly, cheeks reddening. "He's a—"

"Law enforcement." Grayson cut in.

"I see," the doctor responded. "It's no problem to let you stay here tonight, Laney. We can monitor your condition—"

"I'll be fine, doctor. I'm sure I'll sleep better in my own bed," Laney insisted.

"Well, if you're certain, the nurse will be in momentarily to remove the IV. She'll give you written wound-care instructions and your medication, then wheel you out."

"I think I can make it out without a wheelchair—" Laney began, but the doctor was already walking out of the room, with Deputy Chief Wallace close behind. Grayson figured they would discuss Laney. Though he was curious to know what they were saying, he was more interested in making sure Laney stayed safe, so he didn't follow. He just waited as Rose hovered over Laney, chatting incessantly, while a nurse arrived and removed the IV. Grayson spent the time counting the seconds in his head until he could get Laney safely home.

The nurse handed Laney discharge instructions and a bottle of pills and went to look for a wheelchair.

A few seconds later, Wallace returned. "Looks like you're clear to go, Laney. Once the nurse gets back, I'll roll you out and—"

"How about you take Rose, and I'll take Laney?" Grayson suggested.

"Now, wait just a minute," Rose protested. "I'm staying right here with my niece until she leaves this building."

"Rose," Laney interrupted. "Don't argue. Just do what you're asked so we can get things moving. I want to get out of here quickly, and I don't really care how it happens."

Rose's face softened. "Of course, love. But don't you worry. I'll have Tommy bring me to your house. I'll be there when you get home." Rose began to turn away but stopped. "Oh, I almost forgot, I brought you some clothes and your spare house keys. They're in the bag on the bed. Do you need help dressing?"

"I'll manage."

"Then I guess I'll see you at home. Come on, Tommy." She grabbed Wallace's arm and dragged him to the door.

"That's your cue to leave, too," Laney told Grayson quietly. She'd regained some of her color, but she still looked too fragile for Grayson's liking. He wasn't completely happy that she was being released tonight. He would have preferred she stay in the hospital under guard until they found the kidnappers, but since that wasn't going to happen, escorting her home was the next best option.

"I thought we agreed that we're going together."

"We may be leaving together, but I'm not putting on my street clothes while you're standing in the room." She reached into the bag Rose had brought and pulled out what looked like a huge pink sweater. "Great," she muttered.

"Don't like the color choice?"

She turned the sweater so he could see the front. A giant white poodle with fuzzy yarn fur stared out at him.

"Nice," he said, swallowing a laugh.

"If she brought me the matching leggings…" She pulled out bright pink leggings covered in white dog bones. "She did."

"A Christmas gift?"

"Birthday. Two years ago. Needless to say, I've never worn them. Typical Rose, bringing them for me when she knows I have no other option but to put them on."

Grayson smirked. He wasn't into fashion, but even he could see why a person would not want to be caught dead in that getup.

Then the smirk died on his lips, the thought sobering him instantly. The truth was that if he wasn't vigilant, that is exactly what could happen to Laney Kensington.

"You have options," he said. "It's that or the hospital gown. Pick your poison."

"Right." She pulled the outfit to her chest. "I'll change in the bathroom."

It took her longer than it should have. She might have told the doctor she was feeling okay, but Grayson wasn't buying it. Her eyes had been glassy, her complexion still a little too waxy. If she passed out in the bathroom, he wouldn't know it.

"Laney?" Grayson rapped on the door. "You okay?"

"Fine." She opened the door, her body covered from neck to ankle in pink and white.

He shouldn't have smiled. He knew it, but he couldn't stop himself.

"Wow," he murmured as she met his gaze.

"And not in a good way, right?"

"You almost make it work."

She offered a wan smile and sighed. "I'm not worried about making it work. I'm worried about everyone in the hospital catching a glimpse of me in it. If we're trying to slip out of here undetected, this outfit isn't going to help."

"I can fix that," Grayson said, shrugging out of his jacket and setting it on her shoulders. She slipped her arms into the sleeves, and he tugged the hood up over her hair, his fingers grazing silky skin.

That he noticed surprised him. Since Andrea's death, he'd devoted himself to his job. There wasn't room in his life for anything else.

He stepped back. The jacket hung past Laney's thighs, the sleeves covering her hands.

"It's a little big," he said.

She scowled, pulling at the pink leggings. "Not big enough, I'm afraid."

He laughed. "Well, at least the poodle is covered."

"There is that." She grabbed Aunt Rose's bag from the bed. "Do you think if I press the button, the nurse will come any faster? I'm ready to get out of here."

"You can give it a try," he responded. He was anxious to leave, too. He had an uneasy feeling that said things weren't going to go down as smoothly as he wanted them to.

Laney jabbed the call button. "Really, I think a wheelchair is silly. I'm perfectly capable of—"

The lights went out, the room plunging into darkness. No light seeping in under the door. No light filtering in from behind the curtain. When he'd driven in, Grayson had noticed construction signs for a new wing—perhaps the power outage was related to that. Unfortunately, he couldn't afford to assume anything.

"What's going on?" Laney whispered.

"I don't know," he responded, grabbing her hand and pulling her close to his side. "But, I can tell you this. We're not waiting for the wheelchair."

FOUR

Laney's nerves were on edge, her vision adjusting to the darkness as Agent DeMarco guided her toward the door. It flew open as they reached it, and Detective Jensen barged in. The door slammed shut behind him. "What do you make of this, DeMarco?" His voice was low and tense. His hand rested on his holstered revolver.

"Could be a power outage from the construction that's going on or—" the agent glanced at Laney "—something less innocuous. It's hard to say, but I don't like it. We need to get Laney out of here."

"You have a plan for doing that without attracting too much attention?"

"Laney and I will leave now, through the hospital service entrance on the ground floor. I'll take care of getting her home. You call Chief Andrews and fill him in. We're going to need a couple of guys down here to investigate—we need to know for sure what caused this outage."

"Do you really think this power failure could be connected to the kidnapping?" Laney interjected. "It seems like that would be a lot of trouble to go through."

"How much trouble is too much trouble if it's going

to keep a multimillion-dollar operation running?" Agent DeMarco asked.

It was a good question. One that Laney couldn't answer. Agent DeMarco struck her as levelheaded and calculated, completely focused on the investigation. If he thought the hospital's power failure could be staged by the kidnappers, she wouldn't write off the idea.

"Are you sure you don't need me for backup?" Detective Jensen asked, brows furrowed in concern.

"I'd rather you stand your post. Act like you're still guarding the room. Make note of everyone that comes by—hospital employee, electrician, patient—everyone," Agent DeMarco replied.

"Will do." Detective Jensen pulled the door open, stepping out of the way, and Agent DeMarco pressed a warm hand to the small of Laney's back.

"Stay close," he said as he led her into the hall.

She didn't need the reminder. She planned on staying glued to his side until they exited the building. The emergency generator must have turned on. The hallway wasn't quite as dark as the room had been. A row of red lights illuminated the area, providing just enough light to see down the corridor to the dimly glowing exit sign.

A nurse made her way down the corridor, peeking into rooms as she went, calling reassurances to patients, inquiring about the occupants' welfare. Other than that, the hallway was empty, the stillness of the hospital unsettling. Agent DeMarco took Laney's elbow, urging her toward the stairwell.

"We're going to have to take the stairs," he said, wrapping his arm around her waist, pulling her closer to his side, the protective gesture somehow reassuring. "We're on the eighth floor, do you think you'll be able to make it?"

"Yes, I'll be fine." She didn't have a choice.

"If you need to take a break, let me know. If you get dizzy or—"

"How about we just go?" she cut him off, because the longer they stood around talking, the more her head ached and the less energy her legs seemed to have. They were on the eighth floor, which meant navigating seven flights of stairs down to the ground floor. She was fit and healthy. She had to be to train dogs the way she did. On most days, she could sprint up ten flights of stairs and barely break a sweat. This wasn't most days.

"Just remember," he responded, opening the stairwell door and ushering her onto the landing, "you pass out and I'll be carrying you out of here like a sack of potatoes, not worrying about maintaining your dignity."

"If I pass out, dignity won't be first on my priority list."

But neither of them would have to worry about it, because there was no way she was passing out in the stairwell like some damsel in distress. That wasn't her style. It was bad enough she was forced to make a covert escape from the hospital in tight, itchy leggings and a fuzzy poodle sweater. She wasn't going to do it lying over Agent DeMarco's shoulder.

Not if she could help it.

By the time they reached the fifth-floor landing, she wasn't sure she could.

Her head throbbed with almost every jarring step. She was dizzy and nauseated. The only thing that kept her on her feet was the horrifying vision of herself slung over Agent DeMarco's shoulder, her puffy sweater–

clad torso slapping into his back as he jogged down the stairs.

Just five more flights of stairs. Four more. She counted them off in her head, forcing herself to take one step after another. She'd do everything she needed to do to buy the FBI and the MPD some time if that meant there was a chance of finding Olivia and the other children.

Her feet seemed leaden, every step more difficult than the one before, but she kept going, because she didn't want the image of Olivia's fear-filled eyes to be the last one she had of the girl. She wanted to see photos of her being reunited with her family, wanted to see her smiling and happy and playing the violin she'd been carrying when she was abducted. She wanted this time to be different. She needed a happy ending for Olivia. An ending she'd not been able to offer her teammates' families...

She stumbled, her legs nearly giving out.

Agent DeMarco's grip tightened on her waist. "Do you need to sit for a minute?" His voice rumbled close to her ear, his breath ruffling the fine hairs near her temple.

"No. I'm fine," she lied, and kept walking.

Laney was lying, and Grayson knew it.

He wouldn't insist she sit down, though. He wanted her out of the hospital, and this stairwell, as quickly as possible. If that meant carrying her out, so be it.

Voices drifted into the stairwell as they neared the third-floor landing. Grayson tensed, wary of who might be approaching. He didn't believe in coincidences, and a power outage at the hospital while the key witness to a kidnapping was in it would be a big one. It was possible the construction crew had knocked out the power, but he wasn't counting on it. If the kidnappers were responsible for the power outage, they might be on a fact-finding mission, hoping to discover who Laney was and whether or not she was actually deceased.

If they already knew she was alive, Grayson had a new problem. Namely that someone who knew Laney had survived had leaked the information to the kidnappers. Though he hoped it wasn't the case, a leak could explain why the kidnappers always seemed one step ahead.

Laney stumbled again. He pulled her closer, steadying her.

"We're almost there," he murmured, leading her down the stairs as quietly as possible. By the time they reached the second floor, she was visibly weak, her hand clutching the railing as she took the final step onto the landing.

Even in the dim red light, he could see the paleness of her skin, the hollows beneath her cheeks. Her eyes were glassy, her skin dewy from perspiration. She might have the will to make it out of the stairwell, but he wasn't sure she had the strength.

He pulled the hood from her head and pressed a palm to her forehead. Her skin was cool and clammy, her breathing shallow and quick. "Maybe you'd better sit for a minute."

She backed away from his touch, squaring her shoulders and yanking the hood back up over her hair. "I appreciate your concern, but if we stop every time I feel light-headed or dizzy, we might not make it out until morning."

Her matter-of-fact tone left no room to argue, so he stayed silent. Now was not the time for a struggle of wills.

"Three more flights to go," he pointed out, and he thought he heard her sigh quietly in response.

It was taking forever to reach ground level, but then, Grayson wasn't the kind of guy who liked to do things slowly. He liked to have a plan in place and execute it with efficiency and as much speed as was prudent.

In this case, that meant going at a snail's pace.

It would have been quicker and easier to carry Laney the rest of the way down, but she wouldn't have appreciated it, and he needed her cooperation.

Somewhere above them, a door opened and shut with a bang.

How many floors above? he wondered. Four? Three?

Grayson stilled, listening. A quick shuffling of feet, then nothing.

Ten seconds passed.

Twenty.

The stairwell remained eerily silent. He didn't like it. Someone was up there, still and listening, and he had a hunch it wasn't a hospital employee. If he was right, his witness's identity had been compromised. Peering over the railing, he scanned the stairwell below, its dark corners untouched by the dim emergency lights. There were now only two flights between them and escape. Multiple doors that the enemy could enter. He and Laney were vulnerable here, sandwiched between whoever had entered above and anyone who might be waiting below.

If there had been any other way out of the hospital, he would have selected it over the stairwell. Experience had taught him stairwells were prime locations for an ambush. A gunman above, a gunman below, and a person could be taken out in an instant.

Caught between floors, they had no choice but to continue down. He doubted Laney would make it up even one flight of stairs. Meeting her eyes, he held a finger to his lips, then guided her quickly down.

On the ground floor below, another door opened. He could hear heavy footsteps coming their way.

Not good.

Grayson had no intention of being caught in the middle of an ambush. Better to go on the offensive—meet trouble one-on-one. Grayson urged Laney down to the first floor landing, gently pushing her into the shadows. Drawing his gun, he peered over the rail.

A shadowy figure ascended the steps quickly, the barrel of a gun glinting in the dim emergency lights. From above, footsteps echoed loudly as the second person rushed down the stairs.

Grayson needed to act now. And it wouldn't be by the book.

If he announced himself, he'd lose the element of surprise. If he took a bullet, Laney would be easy pickings.

There's no way that was happening.

He had to time it perfectly. The gunman slowed as he neared the landing, cautiously stepping around the corner, gun first. In one quick motion, Grayson cracked the butt of his service weapon on the guy's wrist, eliciting a startled howl of pain and sending the gun clattering down the stairs.

The guy turned back—whether to flee or retrieve his gun, Grayson couldn't be sure. Reaching out, Grayson grasped a handful of the guy's sweatshirt and brought his gun forcefully down on the man's temple. The blow sent the man crumpling to the ground in a motionless heap.

Grabbing Laney's arm, Grayson pulled her forward, ushering her around the fallen assailant. The unmistakable pop of a silenced pistol echoed in the stairwell, a bullet slamming into the concrete wall a foot from Grayson's head. He shoved Laney forward, placing himself between her and the gunman as they raced down the last few steps to ground level.

He shoved the door open, scanning the hallway and the open door of the room beyond. Backup lights illuminated the hospital's laundry room, the huge cavernous area the perfect cover for anyone who might be lying in wait. Footsteps pounded on the stairs above, the second gunman moving in quickly.

Grayson dragged Laney into the hallway, shielding her from any threat that might be waiting.

"This way." He motioned toward a glowing neon exit sign pointing them to their escape route. They ran toward the far wall, turning the corner as the stairwell door slammed open once more.

Grabbing Laney's hand, he sprinted toward the exit. He knew she was struggling to match his pace, but slowing down wasn't an option.

Right now he couldn't worry about anything but getting her to safety—as safe as any place could be for the only witness against a very large, very lucrative crime ring.

They barreled through the exit door into the employee parking lot.

"Come on," he encouraged her. "I parked my car out here."

* * *

Agent DeMarco didn't let go of Laney's hand as they ran through a near-empty parking lot. Silver streaks of moonlight managed to break through the intermittent cloud cover, providing some visibility beyond the shadows of the building. Too much visibility if their pursuer ran out of the building behind them. Laney shuddered at the thought.

She didn't want to be within sight of that door if it opened and the gunman appeared.

Her body was wearing down, though. No matter how much she wanted to keep sprinting along beside Agent DeMarco, she wasn't sure how much farther she could go. Her legs shook, every pounding step across the pavement making her head throb.

She stumbled, and his grip on her hand tightened.

"You can do this," he urged her.

Maybe she could.

If wherever they were heading was closer than a few steps.

They rounded the corner of the building, putting brick and mortar between themselves and the door. She wanted to feel safer because of it, but fear pulsed through her veins, churned in her stomach. They had no idea how many men were after them—or where their attackers might be lying in wait.

A sudden clatter from around the building, like a can kicked across pavement, had Agent DeMarco snagging the arm of the jacket she wore, yanking her behind a large metal Dumpster.

"Stay hidden. I'll be right back," he ordered before easing around the Dumpster and moving soundlessly into the night. She stood still, keeping as quiet as possible. Listening. She could hear nothing but the deafening rush of her own blood in her ears. Without Agent DeMarco, she felt exposed and vulnerable. Releasing the breath she hadn't realized she was holding, she tried to shake off that feeling.

She'd worked under stressful, even dangerous, circumstances in the past, and she'd never had to rely on anyone to get her through them. She couldn't allow herself to rely on Agent DeMarco, either. Playing the part of the victim just wasn't her style. After all, if something happened to him, she would have to take care of herself.

And she would. She'd been doing it her whole life.

She'd realized at age eight that her mom was powerless to protect either of them from her father's violent outbursts. Laney had been forced to take on that role. She'd learned to protect them both. This was no different. She needed to be ready. She needed to assess the situation herself. Plan her escape route should anything go wrong.

She eased out from behind the Dumpster, peering into the darkness. Nothing. The night seemed too still, the parking lot too dark. Dozens of cars were there, the streetlights off, the moon temporarily hidden by clouds.

A shadow moved at the edge of the lot, a deeper darkness in the gloom.

She jerked back, heart pounding wildly.

"Good choice," someone whispered, and she jumped, spinning toward the voice.

Big mistake. Blood rushed from her head, and she swayed.

Firm hands cupped her waist, held her steady as she caught her balance.

She looked into Agent DeMarco's face. "Where did you come from?" she whispered.

"I was circling around to get a location on him. I also told you to stay out of sight."

"I did."

"You didn't." His hands dropped away. "I had you in a position of cover. You walked out where anyone could see you."

"It's dark."

"Ever heard of night-vision goggles?" he asked. "Because someone who has money enough to run a kidnapping ring the size of the one we're dealing with has money for all kinds of things the average Joe might not have at his disposal."

She hadn't thought about that, but she wasn't going to admit it.

"Did you see him?" she asked.

"He's headed in the other direction—toward the visitor's parking lot, but it won't take him long to figure out we're not there and double back." He grabbed her arm, leading her toward the parking lot. "Come on. Let's not lose our head start."

FIVE

The investigation had been compromised, and Grayson needed to find out who was responsible. But first, he needed to get Laney as far away from the gunman as possible.

He'd already called the local PD. Officers would be on the scene soon. They could deal with the gunmen. Grayson would deal with protecting Laney.

"You live in Davidsonville, right?" Grayson asked, laying his cell phone in the center console.

"Yes." Laney glanced over at him. "The quickest way is Route 50 to the 424 exit—that road is a straight shot to my community."

"I don't think we'll go the quickest route," he said as he stopped at the darkened signal lights on Hospital Drive. He'd seen the gunman moving through the parking lot, could have taken a shot at him, but he had no idea how many others there might be, and he couldn't afford to take any chances.

"Why not? The sooner we get home, the happier I'll be," Laney responded, leaning forward in her seat, scanning the darkness as if watching could keep trouble from coming.

"I don't want to risk anyone following us." He turned left on the main road, heading away from her house.

She looked over her shoulder, eyeing the empty road. "I hadn't thought about that."

"Then, it's good we're together," he responded. "Because anyone who'd take a couple of shots at someone while she's with an FBI agent isn't going to hesitate to follow us."

"He might not have known who you were."

"Maybe not." But Grayson thought the perp did. Whoever the kidnappers were, they seemed well connected. Somehow, some way, they'd found out that Laney was alive.

"But you think he did?" she asked.

"I don't know, but I'm not willing to take chances with your life."

"What about Olivia's? If the kidnappers know I'm alive, they may move her now. If they're desperate enough, they may do worse."

He'd had the same thought. He didn't like it any more than Laney seemed to. "She's a high-priced commodity. I doubt they'll do anything that will compromise their bottom line."

"You doubt it, but you don't know," Laney said with a sigh. "I should have—"

"You should have stayed behind the Dumpster when I left you there." He cut her off, because he understood the regrets she had, the guilt. They wouldn't do Olivia any good. They wouldn't do Laney any good, either.

"We've covered this ground before," she responded wearily.

"And now we'll cover it again. I need you to understand what we're dealing with. You have to listen to the precautions I suggest and take them seriously."

"I understand…"

"I don't think you do. You're my only witness, Laney. The key to closing a case I've been pursuing for over a year."

"Wow," she said drily. "I feel so…special."

That surprised a laugh out of him. After speaking with Andrews, he'd known Laney was a force to be reckoned with. He hadn't expected her to make him smile, though. "You should. I gave you my coat. I'm taking you for a moonlit drive."

"You're saving my life," she added quietly.

"You saved your own life. Or maybe Murphy did. You'll have to thank him." He glanced in the rearview mirror. Nothing. No sign that they were being followed. He wasn't sure that meant anything. If the perps knew their witness was alive, they might also know her identity. He drove into a cul-de-sac, waited a few seconds, drove out again. Still no sign of a tail.

His phone vibrated, and he answered it quickly. "De-Marco here."

"It's Kent Andrews. I'm at the hospital."

"What'd you find?"

"No sign of either of the perps. The fire marshal is here assessing the damage from the electrical fire that caused the power outage. He's calling in the arson investigator. Looks like the wiring in the circuit panel was tampered with. Someone went through a lot of trouble to make it look like faulty wiring, but the fire chief isn't buying it. How's Laney doing?"

Grayson glanced at Laney.

She smiled, and something in his heart stirred to

life, some gut-level, knee-jerk reaction that surprised him as much as his laughter had. "I'll let her answer," he responded.

That was Laney's cue to speak, and it should have been easy enough to answer Kent's question. The problem was, she wasn't sure how she was doing.

"Laney?" Kent prodded.

"I'm fine," she managed, and Kent let out a bark of laughter.

"You were shot in the head. You're not fine."

"In a couple of days, I think I'll be good as new."

"That's a relief," he said, "You had us all worried. Murphy was beside himself, by the way. Wouldn't let anyone near you, even the patrolman who responded to the scene. Luckily he was wearing his MPD collar, so a K-9 handler was called in. He backed down on command." Laney could hear the smile in Kent's voice. "He did real good tonight."

"Yes, he did." She smiled at the thought of the overly excitable dog, of the hours she'd spent working with him, determined to make him into the K-9 team member she thought he could be. She hadn't been sure it would work. Not every dog was capable of the focus required, and Murphy had already flunked out of the K-9 training program once. Now there was hope. All the hard work on both their parts was finally paying off. "Where is he now?"

"He's at headquarters being pampered. The guys bought him a huge steak and brought a dog bed into the office for him. He thinks he's a king or something. Never seen that dog look quite so proud of himself."

Laney laughed. "Good for him." Before tonight, you

couldn't have paid a K-9 handler to work with Murphy. A couple more weeks and he'd be ready to enter the program again.

"We'll take good care of him until you're ready to have him back. Don't you worry."

"You can bring him by tomorrow. I don't want any breaks in his training routine. He's almost there."

"Are you sure? Wallace reported back the doctor's orders for you to take it easy for a few days." The concern in Kent's voice was obvious. The guy was gruff and abrupt most of the time, but he had a heart of gold.

"I won't overdo it. Riley and Bria both work tomorrow, so I'll have plenty of help at the kennel."

"You're not going there tomorrow," Agent DeMarco said so abruptly, she nearly jumped out of her seat belt.

"Going where?"

"To the kennel."

"Of course I am. It's my job."

"You think your job is worth dying over?" DeMarco responded, and Laney frowned, all her fatigue washed away by a wave of irritation mixed with anxiety.

"Of course not, but I have to live my life."

"Have your crew do the work at the kennel tomorrow," Kent cut in. "That will be the safer. As a matter of fact, maybe you should be in a safe house until we find the guys who are after you. What do you think, DeMarco?"

A safe house?

Laney hadn't even given that scenario a thought. She'd agreed she wouldn't take unnecessary chances, but she wasn't sure she was willing to put her life on hold. After all, if the kidnappers knew who she was, they could have just waited for her to arrive home rather than cause an elaborate power outage at the hospital.

"I think we can wait on that," Agent DeMarco responded. "If the kidnappers knew her identity, they would have waited at her place, taken her out there." Hearing her own thoughts spoken aloud, imagining men skulking in the shadows of her house, made her blood go cold.

"Are you sure waiting is the best decision, DeMarco?" Kent asked.

"No. But I *am* sure there's a leak, and since I don't know if it's in my house or yours, I can't be certain Laney will be any more protected in a safe house than she would be at her own house, under guard."

"Okay. I'll send an officer over. He'll be there when you arrive.

"Thanks, Andrews."

"Laney's one of us. We'll do whatever's needed to keep her safe."

"Understood. When do you think you'll be wrapping things up over there?"

"About an hour. We're waiting for copies of the surveillance video and questioning the security guard."

"Did he see anyone in the area?"

"He says he didn't." Laney could hear the hesitation in Kent's voice.

"But you're not buying it?" Grayson asked.

"It's just a gut feeling, but no." Kent said. "We're going to make an excuse to get him down to the precinct for more thorough questioning."

"I think I'll get someone to run a background check on the guy. Can you email me his information?" Grayson asked.

"Sure, but the hospital does a thorough background check before they hire someone. I think you'll find that his record's clean."

"I'm more interested in the state of his bank account."

"You think he was hired to set that fire—or look the other way?" Kent asked, his Boston accent thicker than usual. He'd transplanted from New England years ago, but Laney had noticed that the faster he talked and the more enthused he was about the subject, the thicker the accent became.

"I just want to be thorough," Agent DeMarco replied.

"And yet, you didn't ask me about his work record."

"I take it you checked?"

"Absolutely," the chief said, sounding almost gleeful. "His logs check out, but he's been reprimanded previously for sleeping on the job. Ideally the surveillance videos will give us a good look at what really transpired while he was on duty tonight."

"I like the way you think, Andrews," DeMarco said as he veered onto Route 50. "Do you mind if I drop by the precinct while you're questioning the guard?"

"That's not a problem."

"Then I'll head over after I get Laney settled."

"See you then." Kent disconnected, and Laney laid her head back against the seat, tempted to close her eyes just for a minute. She was that tired. So tired she didn't care that she might start snoring loudly while a good-looking FBI agent sat beside her.

"You still with me?" Agent DeMarco asked.

"Where else would I be?"

"Dreaming?"

"Good idea. I think I'll give it a try," she responded,

and then she did exactly what she'd been wanting to do, closed her eyes, the pain still pulsing through her head as DeMarco sped along the highway.

Grayson found Wynwood easily, driving into Laney's well-established, affluent neighborhood and glancing in his rearview mirror as he turned onto her street.

Nothing. The road was empty. Just the way he wanted it.

Laney groaned softly, asleep, but obviously not pain-free.

He didn't wake her. Just followed his GPS coordinates down the quiet street. Grand brick homes sat far back from the street, their large lots sporting well-manicured lawns and decorative plants. Nothing wild or unkempt about this place. People who lived here were affluent and not afraid to show it.

It was a nice community. Pretty. Well-planned.

Laney shifted in her seat, and he glanced her way. She'd pulled his jacket close, her hands barely peeking out of rolled cuffs. It reminded him of a spring evening long ago, the scent of rain in the air, the refreshing coolness. Reminded him of Andrea, her senior year of college, his jacket around her shoulders as they lay on a blanket watching the sunset. He'd proposed to her that day, and she'd had the tiny diamond ring, the best he could afford, on her finger.

"Our access road is on the right, just after that set of mailboxes," Laney said, her voice rough with sleep. It jarred him from memories that he tried hard not to dwell on.

The past was what it was. He couldn't change it.

He could only move forward, do everything in his

power to be the man God wanted him to be, do the work that had been set before him.

"Where?" He could see nothing but thick foliage that butted up against the narrowing road. This end of the neighborhood had fewer houses and was less polished, but there was beauty in the overgrown fields that stretched out on either side of the road.

"See those tall bushes?" She gestured to the left. "And the mailboxes? Just slow to a crawl. You'll see the access road when you're almost on top of it."

He did as she suggested, barely coasting past the mailboxes until he spotted the road, a long gravel driveway lined with mature trees.

He drove nearly a quarter of a mile down the gravel road before the first house appeared. A quaint one-story cottage with white shutters and a wraparound porch, it was nothing like the other houses in the neighborhood. The moon had edged out from behind the clouds, its reflected light shimmering across a small pond set off to the left. Tall trees cast dark shadows across the gardens and neatly cut yard surrounding the building—perfect hiding places for an assailant. Despite his confidence that they'd not been followed from the hospital, Grayson wasn't comfortable with this setup at all.

"Perfect," he muttered under his breath, imagining all the ways someone could approach the house unnoticed.

"It really is," Laney agreed. Apparently she hadn't heard the sarcasm in his voice. "My great-grandfather built it. At one time, he owned all the land in the neighborhood. When my grandfather sold a portion of the land, he kept the cottage and the main house. Aunt Rose lives in the cottage. I'm at the main house."

"Which is where?" he asked. The location of the cottage wasn't ideal. Maybe the main house was in a less secluded spot.

"Just keep following the driveway. It veers past the cottage. The house is another quarter mile in."

The headlights of the sedan flashed across thick woods and heavy foliage as Grayson drove past the cottage.

The "main house," as Laney had called it, looked to be a slightly larger version of Rose's cottage. Same wooden shingles, same white shutters and a very similar porch. Its single-story layout meant that all rooms of the house could be easily accessed by an intruder. Worse, it sat in the middle of a clearing that looked to be approximately twenty acres in diameter and was surrounded by woods on three sides, making it a surveillance nightmare.

Grayson pulled up to Laney's darkened home and turned off the engine. "What's in the back of the house?"

"The kennels, agility course and covered training pavilion." Laney tried unsuccessfully to suppress a yawn. "Would you like a cup of coffee before you head out?" she asked.

"I'll pass on the coffee, but let me take a quick look around the property while I wait for the officer to arrive."

"Sure. I'll turn on the outside lights for you."

"Hold on," he said, but she was already opening the door and stepping out of the car.

By the time Grayson had grabbed his flashlight from the glove box and exited his vehicle, Laney was halfway up the stone walkway to her house. For someone who'd nearly died, she moved fast, making her way up the porch stairs. He wasn't sure how long it would take her to realize she didn't have the bag her aunt had packed for her. Rose had said the keys were in it, so he grabbed it, heading up the porch steps after her.

She was patting the pocket of his jacket as he reached her side. The hood had fallen off her head, and her auburn hair looked glossy black in the darkness, her face a pale oval. "I hope I didn't leave my keys at the hospital," she said, plucking at the fuzzy sweater as if the keys might be hiding in there.

"Didn't Rose mention she'd put your spare set in the bag?" He held it out, and she took it, offering a smile that made her look young and a little vulnerable.

"Oh, that's right. Thanks." She dug the keys out, said good-night and walked inside. Seconds later, the porch light went on, casting a soft white glow across most of the yard. He saw the front curtains part slightly and wondered if it was Rose or Laney who peeked out.

He waved to whoever it was, then turned toward the yard. A large sign sat to the left of the driveway. He flashed his light across it, reading Wagging Tails Boarding and Training Facility. Flower beds around the sign and in front of the house were similar to those surrounding Rose's cottage. A cool breeze carried the faint scent of pine and honeysuckle. Above the sound of the rustling wind, Grayson detected the crunching of leaves and underbrush in the woods to the left of the house. He turned the corner of the house just in time to see the last of a small herd of deer returning to the safety of the woods.

He trained his flashlight back toward the house, inspecting the grass and mulch beds for signs of disturbance.

Nothing.

The window screens were all in place. Floodlights shimmered over the expanse of yard between the house and the kennels. He was impressed by the setup. There was a very large agility course with tunnels, beams, ladders, hoops, cones and platforms at various heights connected by tight netting. The kennel looked as if it could accommodate twenty dogs, with each dog having its own inside space and an exterior fenced-in run. The dogs were in for the night. One or two barked as he walked around the structure, checking doors. Everything was locked.

Next to the kennel, the covered pavilion was also fenced in. He walked around the training facilities, shining his flashlight into the darker corners of the yard and toward the woods. All was quiet. Peaceful. Almost idyllic.

Satisfied that there was no one lurking in the shadows, Grayson turned back toward the house. Laney was safe, at least for the moment. Yet he felt uneasy at the thought of leaving her alone, even for a quick trip to the precinct. He tried to shrug it off. She wasn't in protective custody. At this point, there were limits to what he could do to keep her safe. But Grayson was used to pushing the boundaries, and he knew that if he wanted to solve this case, bring the kids home, and keep Laney safe, he was going to have to think outside the box to do it.

He wasn't sure what that would mean, what it would look like, but he knew one thing for sure—he would do anything necessary to protect his only witness.

SIX

Agent DeMarco was still outside. Laney could see his light bouncing along the tree line near the kennels.

Jax, her six-year-old Australian shepherd, and Brody, her ten-year-old Belgian Malinois, were too happy to see her to notice the stranger out in the yard. Both followed her through the kitchen, tails wagging as they waited patiently for her to acknowledge them. She took off Agent DeMarco's jacket, tossed it over the back of a wooden chair and called the dogs over. They sat in front of her, tails thumping as she scratched behind their ears, murmured a few words of praise. Both barked as a car pulled into the drive. Must be the officer Kent had sent over. That would mean that Agent DeMarco would be heading out soon.

Good. There was something about him that made her…uncomfortable.

Maybe it was the way he studied her, as if she were the secret to some great mystery he had to solve.

She almost laughed at the thought, because that's probably exactly what she was to him.

The only witness to Olivia's kidnapping, the one person who could identify the kidnappers and potentially help put them behind bars.

She tugged at the itchy sweater as she headed toward her bedroom. She needed to take off this getup. Now. Not only because it looked ridiculous but also because it was probably the most uncomfortable outfit she'd ever owned. There was definitely wool in the sweater. Perhaps if she threw it in the washer and then put it through the dryer on high, it would shrink so badly it that wouldn't be fit for anything but the Goodwill bag. She smiled at the thought, but who was she kidding? Even the homeless wouldn't grab this outfit off the rack. The dogs followed her down the hall toward her bedroom.

The door to the guest room at the end of the hall opened, and Aunt Rose popped her head out. "Oh, you're home, dear. Don't you look nice."

Laney ignored the compliment. Aunt Rose meant well, but she had questionable taste at times. "It's after eleven, Aunt Rose. You didn't have to wait up for me."

"I was just catching up on my devotional," Rose said. "Let me grab my slippers and robe and I'll be right out."

"There's really no need…" But Rose shut the guest room door before Laney could get her sentence out. She sighed, hurrying into her room before Rose could reappear. She immediately peeled off the offending tights and sweater, letting them drop to a heap on the floor, then changed into some comfortable yoga pants and her old University of Colorado sweatshirt. A glance in the mirror showed she still had a few faint streaks of blood on one side of her face, and the bruise on her jaw was starting to turn from red to blue. She carefully peeled back the bandage. A thin line of five staples started at her temple, disappearing into the hairline. Only about a half inch of the scar would be visible when healed. The rest would be concealed by her hair.

A shadow passed outside her bedroom room window, and Brody growled deep in his throat. Laney's pulse quickened—then she shook her head, chastising herself for being so jumpy. Agent DeMarco had probably decided to take another look around. She pulled back the curtain, peering out the window. There was no sign of him. Or anyone else.

"It's okay, boy." Brody had always had a protective streak in him—surprising since he had failed his temperament test for the Secret Service as a puppy. Too laid back, they'd said.

She'd been under contract with the company that supplied the puppies and had been given first choice for adoption. She'd seen the potential in him and had turned him into a top-notch search dog, cross-trained in both air scent and human remains detection. He was her first partner. In the years they'd worked together, they'd logged more than a hundred searches in the Colorado wilderness and had twenty-eight live finds to their credit. His hips forced him into early retirement at the age of six. By then, Jax was already trained and operational as an air scent dog. She'd worked exclusively with Jax then, only retiring him after the accident—and before he was able to complete his human-remains detection training.

She knew both dogs missed the work, so she regularly ran training exercises on the weekends with the neighborhood children. That training was all the "action" any of them saw these days. She hadn't been on a real search since that last find. The one that left three teammates dead.

Shaking off the thought, she went into her bathroom, ran a comb through her hair and scrubbed traces of blood from her face.

The doorbell rang, and she hurried to the foyer. Both dogs barked three times and remained at her heel—their signal for a visitor. Laney pointed to the cushions in the corner of the family room, as customary when visitors arrived, and gave the command "place." The dogs immediately sat, eyes trained on Laney, waiting for the next command. She peered out the peephole, saw Agent DeMarco standing on the porch and opened the door. "I take it everything's clear?" she asked.

He nodded, his eyes scanning the room before his gaze settled on her. "You changed." He smiled, and she was drawn to the dimple at the corner of his mouth. "That look suits you." Her face warmed under his scrutiny. For once, a quick comeback failed her.

"Don't you have a security system out here?"

Laney gestured toward the dogs. "There's my security system."

"Dogs are a great deterrent, but I'd feel a whole lot better if you had a top-notch alarm." He turned, inspecting the deadbolt on the front door.

"It would be a waste of money, Agent DeMarco. Aside from some recent vandalism and petty theft in Wynwood, we've never had much crime out here. It's a long walk down that access road in the dark, and we'd hear a car coming up the gravel drive before it could reach us."

"A walk down the gravel driveway in the dark versus announcing their presence and a lifetime in prison? How do you think a criminal would weigh that?"

"Point taken."

Grayson turned his attention back to her. "I see the bandage is gone."

He closed the small gap between them.

"Do you mind if I look?" he asked, gesturing to her temple.

She shook her head, and then he was in her space, and she was breathing the fresh scent of the outdoors mixed with something dark and undeniably masculine. "Go ahead," she responded, her voice just a little rougher than she wanted it to be.

He gently lifted her hair, his warm fingers lightly brushing her forehead. Laney's cheeks heated as he studied the wound.

Finally, he let her hair drop back into place. "The scar shouldn't be very noticeable once it heals."

"I'm not worried about it. I'm alive. That's way better than the alternative."

"Agreed." He smiled, absently fingering the scar on his left brow.

Had he received it in the line of duty, or was it a battle scar from some childhood antic? She didn't know him well enough to ask, but neither scenario would surprise her. He seemed determined and relentless. Those traits were likely to get a kid into all kinds of trouble.

"But I've found that women can be a little more self-conscious about scars on their faces than most of the men I know," he said.

She shrugged. "We all have scars. Some just run deeper or are more visible than others."

She took a seat on the overstuffed, well-worn leather reclining chair that still smelled of her grandfather's cherry tobacco. She breathed in the scent. Felt herself calming at the memories of him. This home, and her grandfather, had often been her refuge as a child, avoiding her father's drunken rages and her mother's frequent bouts of depression. In her teens, she'd spent more time at her granddad's house, helping him with the kennels and the dog training, than she'd spent in her own home. His passing last year had left a void no one could fill.

Laney looked at the dogs, who were eyeing Agent DeMarco with interest. "The dogs want to say hello. Do you mind?"

"Not at all. I love dogs."

Laney gave a quick hand signal with the word "break." At her command, both dogs bounded off their pillows and headed over to Agent DeMarco, tails wagging. He smiled, rubbing them behind the ears.

"The Aussie is Jax, and the Mal is Brody."

"They're great."

"Thanks." Laney smiled. "They love attention—they'll sit there all night as long as they're getting petted. Do you have a dog?"

"No." Agent DeMarco smiled. "I've thought about getting one, but the truth is, I work too much. It wouldn't be fair to leave it home alone all the time."

"Dogs do need companionship."

"Laney!" Rose called. "Is someone here?"

She had to know someone was. Despite her age, she had perfect hearing. "Yes. We're in the living room."

"Who is it?" Rose asked, sashaying into the room wearing a fuzzy teal robe and a muted pink granny nightgown. Laney might have believed that she'd just rolled out of bed and hurried down the hall, but every hair on Rose's head was in place. She had powder on her cheeks and pink lipstick on her lips. She smiled sweetly as she spotted Agent DeMarco. "Oh, I didn't know you were here, Gray."

"I was looking around outside and decided I'd check in before I left."

"Would you like a cup of tea?"

"No, thank you. I'll be heading out in a minute."

"Maybe you could give Aunt Rose a ride back to her place?" All Laney wanted to do was get in bed and fall asleep. She definitely did not need Aunt Rose flitting about, making herself "useful." As much as she loved Aunt Rose, the woman had more energy than three people combined, and Laney wasn't sure she could handle that tonight.

"What?" Rose responded with a frown. "I'm staying here tonight, remember?"

"There's no need. I don't plan on doing anything but sleeping. I'm sure you'd be more comfortable in your own bed."

"Well, that's a thought, but it's not going to happen," Rose said, grabbing the bag from the foyer floor as she entered the family room. "You heard what the doctor said—you shouldn't be alone for a few days."

"The doctor was speaking out of an abundance of caution."

"She was speaking out of genuine concern for your well-being!"

"I agree with Rose," Agent DeMarco interjected.

"And that's supposed to make me concede?" Laney asked, shooting him a sideways look.

"I once knew a man who got knocked in the head by a piece of shrapnel," Agent DeMarco said. "He thought he was fine until he wasn't."

"If you're going to tell me he keeled over and died, I'm not going to believe you."

"I was going to tell you that he ended up in the hospital in a coma for two weeks, but your version is a lot more compelling."

If she hadn't been so tired, if her head hadn't been aching so badly, she might have smiled at that.

"That's settled, then," Rose stated matter-of-factly. "There is no way I'm leaving you here and having you fall into a coma. You look a little flushed. Have you taken your painkiller yet?"

"No, I haven't had a chance. I'll take some in a minute."

"You'll take some now." Rose rifled through the bag, pulling out the bottle of pills. "I'll get a glass of water. Stay put." She hurried off.

Which left Laney and Agent DeMarco alone in the family room.

That should have been fine. She was used to being around male law enforcement officers.

But it felt odd having him there, eyeing her somberly.

"What?" she finally asked.

"I got word that the sketch artist flies in at one-fifteen tomorrow. I'll have her here between two and three, depending on traffic."

"That seems a long time to wait…"

"She's worth the wait. The best in the nation." Agent DeMarco studied her. She felt her face flush under his scrutiny. "Are you sure you're going to be up to working with her?"

"I'd work with her now if I could."

"Just take care of yourself between now and then."

"You've got to make sure your key witness stays

healthy, huh?" she joked. Only Agent DeMarco didn't look like he thought it was funny.

"I need to make sure *you* stay healthy," he responded. "You're important to my case, but you're also a civilian, and it's my job to make sure you stay safe."

"It's not—"

He held up a hand. "It's late. You need to rest, and I've got to meet Andrews at the precinct. Stay inside. Don't leave the house for any reason—not to walk the dogs, not to run to the grocery store, not to check the mail. Not for anything."

Having never been one who liked to be told what to do, Laney tried to control her annoyance at his demanding tone. She'd been making her own decisions since she was eight and was accustomed to weighing her options and deciding the best course of action for herself. In the end, she was the one who had to deal with the consequences of her choices. "Agent DeMarco, I appreciate your concern, but…"

"Call me Grayson, or Gray. Your aunt already took the liberty, so it only seems fitting that you do as well."

"Fine, Grayson. I appreciate your concern, but let's not forget there's an officer parked right outside."

"Don't be lulled into a false sense of security. Remember, if someone manages to get to you, they'll get to your aunt, too."

He had a point, and she'd be foolish not to consider it. If something happened to Laney, if she was shot or wounded or attacked, Aunt Rose would run out to help. "Okay. I'll stay close to home." She had a few board-and-trains in the kennel, but that was a short walk from the house.

"Glad to hear it." His gaze jumped to a point beyond

her shoulder, and he smiled. "You're just in time, Rose. I've got to head out of here."

"I found your jacket hanging over a chair in the kitchen." Rose handed it over. "And Laney's business card is in the pocket. Just in case you need to reach her."

"Aunt Rose!" Laney protested, but Grayson was already walking out the door, pulling it firmly shut behind him.

She crossed to the window and pulled back the curtain just enough to peek outside. She felt foolish doing it, like a teenager mooning over a secret crush, but she still watched him stop and chat with the officer before getting in the car, anyway. Her work cell phone buzzed, but she ignored it. Probably Kent checking in on her.

It buzzed again, and she sighed, letting the curtain drop and grabbing the phone from the coffee table. She had two text messages from a number she didn't recognize. Curious, she opened the first one. Get away from the window, and save this number in your contacts. Gray.

The second one said, See you tomorrow afternoon.

That made her smile. She was still smiling as she said good-night to Rose and headed to her room.

SEVEN

Laney usually slept with her windows open in the early fall, but after Grayson's warnings, she thought it best to keep them closed. It was nearly midnight by the time she pulled the comforter around her and lowered her head onto her soft down pillow. She closed her eyes against the dull ache in her temple. Even after Rose had retired to the spare room and the house had grown quiet, Laney found herself shifting restlessly in her bed, sleep evading her despite her exhaustion. It seemed like hours before she was finally lulled to sleep by the soft breathing of her dogs.

She woke with a start, blood rushing loudly in her ears with every beat of her heart. She lay still, trying to control her breathing, listening for some sign of what had yanked her from her sleep. The silence was deafening. Pale silver moonlight streamed in through a sliver of an opening in the curtains, casting its eerie glow across her bedroom walls and floor. The blue numbers on her digital alarm clock announced the time as two-fifteen.

Suddenly Brody emitted a low growl. Rising from his spot on the floor, hackles up, he walked toward the window. Soon Jax was beside him, a silent sentry focused on the window. A small scraping sound caught her attention—like a tree branch brushing softly against the screen or the siding. But there were no trees outside her window. *Was someone there?* A dark shadow outside the window blocked the moon's light for a brief instant, and she knew. Something—or someone—*was* there.

She grabbed her cell phone, hands shaking as she found Grayson's number and dialed. He picked up on the first ring.

"Grayson?" Laney whispered. "It's Laney."

"Laney." His voice was instantly alert. "What is it?"

"I'm not sure." Her voice trembled as she tried to keep from being heard by whoever was out there. "The dogs are growling, and I thought I saw a shadow pass by my window." She paused, listening. "I'll admit I'm a little on edge after tonight, so I might be overreacting… It could just be the officer looking around. Should I go check?"

"No," Grayson answered quickly, voice firm. "I'm on my way. Stay away from the windows. Call 911, wake up Rose, and turn on every light in the house. If it's the officer, we'll sort it out in a hurry."

"Okay, I'll do that now—" A muffled thud interrupted her, followed by a sudden shout from down the hall.

Aunt Rose!

"Oh, no!" She gasped, dropping her phone as she launched herself from the bed with a yell. "I'm coming, Aunt Rose!"

Heart in her throat, she ran toward the door, grabbing her mace from the dresser and rushing down the hall, the dogs at her heels. Flinging the guest room door open, she barged in, mace at the ready, prepared for the worst.

The window was wide open, screen missing. The curtains flapped in the breeze. Bright silver illuminated the room.

And a man. Dressed in dark clothing and wearing a ski mask.

He advanced toward Rose who was backing toward the wall, mace in hand. Ducking his head, the intruder shielded his face with one hand to avoid the foam mace shooting out from Rose's special-edition breast-cancer-awareness canister. The mace did actually have as good a range as the canister, and Rose, had claimed. Unfortunately, Rose's aim was not as reliable. From the amount of foam on the floor, wall, and intruder himself, there couldn't be much left in the canister.

The intruder must have known it. He snagged Rose's nightgown, jerked her toward him. Something glinted in his free hand.

Laney's pulse jumped. A gun.

Without thinking, she rushed toward them, bare feet slipping on the hardwood floor slick with foam mace. The dogs followed her in.

"Halt!" Laney commanded the dogs to keep them out of the mace. The dogs stopped immediately at the emergency command. Both Rose and the intruder looked her way.

Aunt Rose ineffectively pelted the man with her small fist and the mace can, her face flushed and angry. Foam mace covered the left side of the intruder's ski mask. Though his left eye was squinted shut, he glared at Laney with his unaffected right eye. It was then he caught sight of the dogs behind her and hesitated.

"Brody. Jax. Danger." On her command, the dogs growled. "Don't move, or you'll be dog food," she yelled, mace at the ready.

It was a bluff, a scare tactic. Jax and Brody were search dogs, and not cross-trained in protection. But their teeth were bared, their growls menacing. The man stilled. "Put your hands where I can see them and step away from my aunt." Laney's calm command belied her terror for Rose. Years spent working with dogs that were far more sensitive to moods than the average person had taught her to control her emotions.

The man released Rose, shoving her away from him and taking a step toward Laney, hands raised, gun still in his grasp. Glancing first at the door, then toward the window as if calculating his likelihood of a quick getaway, he took yet another step closer.

Could this be one of the kidnappers? If he was, Laney couldn't afford to let him get away. He could lead them to Olivia and the others. She needed to figure out how to detain him until help arrived.

"Drop the gun," she ordered, her gaze and the can of mace trained on him.

"That's not gonna happen," he sneered, teeth gleaming behind the ski mask as he stepped forward. Brody's growls turned to a menacing bark.

"Don't move another step," she warned him. "I mean it."

Behind him, Rose quietly sidled around the wall to the dresser. Grabbing a large vase of flowers and hoisting it over her head, she launched it with as much force as she could muster. Unfortunately she wasn't very strong, and the water-filled vase was heavy. It hit him near the base of the neck, covering him with flower petals and water as it deflected off his shoulder and smashed to the floor—shards of glass mixing with flowers, foam mace and water.

The man cursed, quickly turning on Rose. In a blink, she grabbed the empty mace canister and pitched it at the intruder. He deflected it easily, rushing toward her as she scrambled across the bed in an attempt to evade his reach.

She wasn't fast enough.

He grabbed Rose's ankle. She cried out, kicking him ineffectively with her other foot.

Not wanting to inadvertently spray Rose with the mace, Laney frantically scanned the room for something she could use as a weapon. Anything to give them a fighting chance until help arrived.

A lunge whip Laney used to evaluate play drive in puppies rested by the closet. Snatching it up, she furiously slashed at the man's head and hands with the heavy nylon cording. The last hit left a welt on the bare skin between his gloved hand and his sweatshirt sleeve, causing him to release his grip on Rose.

He angrily grabbed at the whip as it angled down toward his head, trying to yank it from Laney's grasp, but it was slick with foam mace.

Jerking it back, and ignoring biting shards of glass under her feet, Laney rushed toward the intruder. The only other weapon she had was the mace, so she brought the canister down with force on the side of his head and ear. Letting out a howl, he cursed again and came around swinging. Laney ducked. Scrambling backward, she narrowly avoided the blow. Her feet lost purchase on the slippery floor and flew out from under her. She landed on her backside, the jarring force sending pain shooting through her body all the way up to her aching head. She felt dizzy, sick, and then he was on her, one hand on her throat, the other pointing the gun. She lifted the mace, pointed and prayed.

Gravel crunched under the tires and pelted the bottom of Grayson's sedan as he sped along Laney's drive. It had been several minutes since Laney had called, and time wasn't on his side. It took only seconds for a life to be snuffed out. Grayson knew that all too well.

Pulling his car to an abrupt stop in the front drive, he noticed the officer in a heap by the open driver's-side door of the marked car—head bleeding, gun holster clearly empty. There was no time to check his condition.

Leaving his emergency lights flashing, Grayson rushed to the front door, the distant approach of another car on the gravel road giving him hope that backup was on the way.

The house was locked tight. He'd never be able to break down the solid oak door. Knowing that the sliding glass door to the kitchen was his best bet, he ran the length of the porch, vaulting over the railing and sprinting around the corner of the house.

"Laney! Rose!" he called out, racing toward an open window and the scuffling sounds of a struggle mixed with barks and growls.

"Gray! In here! Help!" Rose's voice.

Hoisting himself up, he dropped through the window, into the room.

Laney was on the floor, wrestling with a man for a gun. One of the dogs had a hold of the man's pant leg.

The other dog was by Laney, barking and growling furiously. Rose was doing her best to help, pelting the intruder around the head and neck with a boot.

"Get back, Rose!" Grayson yelled, rushing forward as the man wrenched the gun from Laney's grasp and rose to his feet, turning the gun on her.

The quiet click of the trigger, then nothing.

No bullet. No blood.

And no way was Grayson giving the guy a second chance. He rammed into him. Hard. They were both thrown off-balance as Grayson grabbed for the guy's gun hand, twisting it around until the perp had no choice but to drop the gun. It clattered to the hardwood floor.

"Aunt Rose—get the lights!" Laney called out.

Balling his fist, Grayson slammed it into the guy's ribs, then quickly followed that blow with an uppercut to the jaw.

The lights flicked on, and Grayson dodged a punch. Then another. His opponent was slower, half-blinded by mace. But Grayson still had the image of Laney at the barrel end of the gun in his mind. Still heard the click of the trigger. He had no mercy as he returned the attempted blows with an onslaught of punches to the perp's face and ribs.

The guy dropped to his knees with a grunt.

Grayson helped him the rest of the way to the floor with a hard shove, then pressed his knee into the guy's back.

Reaching for his cuffs, he saw Laney going for the gun. "Leave it," he cautioned her.

Laney stopped short. Dressed in black yoga pants and a tank top, her feet were bare and bloody. Smudges

of mace lined her bruise-covered jaw. Her hair fell in
wild, tangled waves around her face. "What do we do
now?" she asked, worrying her bottom lip. Somehow
she managed to look both tough and vulnerable.

"There's a police cruiser pulling up to the house.
You two meet the officers at the door and bring them
back to me."

Ten minutes later, he and Laney were seated at the
kitchen table while Rose busied herself making a pot
of tea. Laney's foot was elevated. A paramedic used
tweezers to extract small shards of glass. Grayson was
certain it hurt, but probably not as much as being shot
had. And she'd come close to having that happen again,
close to dying.

She winced as a larger splinter of glass was removed.

"You holding up okay, Laney?" he asked, his eyes
turning toward the suspect who'd been read his rights
and brought to the kitchen to be cleaned up. His ski
mask had been bagged as evidence, along with a glass-
cutter and some duct tape. The only other thing he'd
had on him was a folded piece of paper with Laney's
address printed on it.

And the gun. He'd taken it from the patrol officer
after he'd knocked the guy out.

"I'm great," she responded, and Grayson turned his
full attention back to her. She had the greenest eyes
he'd ever seen.

"You're lying," he replied with a soft smile.

"Maybe a little." She flinched as the paramedic dug
another piece of glass from her foot.

One of the officers was none-too-gently wiping remnants of the mace from the intruder's face with a wash-
cloth. Grayson wished he'd hurry. Having the guy who'd

tried to kill Laney in the same room had to be disconcerting for her.

There was a flurry of sound from the foyer. Then Kent Andrews rushed into the kitchen with Deputy Chief Tom Wallace right behind him.

"What have we got?" Andrews asked Grayson. In his early fifties, Andrews was a fitness buff who made the gym part of his job. Grayson had brought him into the case six weeks ago when the first Maryland victim, an eight-year-old girl from Annapolis, had disappeared. Since then, Andrews kept an open line of communication between the MPD and Grayson. Though Grayson was used to working alone, he appreciated another set of eyes on the case file and ears on the streets.

"White male. Possibly late twenties, early thirties. No ID on him, and he won't give his name." Grayson sighed. "He's lawyered up, not talking."

"Typical."

Grayson nodded in agreement. "The officers are cleaning him up. Quite a bit of mace squeezed through openings of the ski mask he was wearing. We're hoping either Laney or Rose will recognize him."

"Any signs of an accomplice?" Wallace asked.

"Not that I could see. He appears to be working alone. How's the officer?"

"He's conscious. Paramedics are loading him into the ambulance," Andrews said. "He's a little fuzzy about what happened, but we surmise the suspect staged a distraction and attacked after the officer got out of the car to investigate, obviously stealing the gun while the officer was down."

"It was fortunate the safety was on and the perp didn't have a clue," Grayson replied.

Andrews nodded. "Right now we're canvassing the area to see if we can tie a vehicle to him. It stands to reason he either lives or is parked somewhere in the community and came up the gravel road."

"That's my thought, too," Grayson agreed. "Though there's still a slight possibility he has a car and driver waiting for him, or a scheduled pickup time with an accomplice."

"Agreed. This property backs right up to Route 2, I've got two cars searching," Andrews offered with a glance at the suspect, whose back was to them. "But the underbrush is heavy this time of the year, and he looks way too free of thorns, burrs or dirt to have taken that route."

"Sounds like you've got all the bases covered. I was going to see if I could call in some agents if you didn't have men to spare."

"This case is our number-one priority right now. We'll do what needs to be done." Grayson recognized the sincerity and determination in Andrews's tone.

"I know you will." Grayson cast a glance at Laney. "And by the way, this wasn't a random break-in. He had a piece of paper with Laney's address folded up in his pocket."

"He's as good as he's gonna get, Chief, but his eyes are still a little swollen shut." The officer grabbed the suspect by the arm, yanking him toward the kitchen table. Grayson took a good look at the suspect. The officer was right. The perp's eyes were red and irritated. The mace had done a job on him. The punch he'd taken to the face hadn't helped, either.

Grayson stood up, grabbing the suspect's other arm

and turning him toward Laney. "Do you recognize him?"

Laney shook her head. Sighed.

"No." She bit her lip, resting her head in the palm of her hand. Grayson could see Laney was as disappointed as he was. If this had been one of the kidnappers, they would have been one step closer to finding Olivia and the other children. Instead, they had another mystery on their hands. Who was this guy, and how was he connected to the case?

"Rose, how about you?" Grayson asked. Rose came around from the kitchen counter, walked right up to the suspect and gave him a once-over.

"He doesn't look familiar." Rose took one step closer, peering up at the suspect, and Grayson thought he felt the suspect twitch. "Nope. I've never seen him before."

"Get him out of here," Andrews said to the uniformed officers.

He then turned back toward Grayson. "What do you make of this, Agent?" Chief Andrews asked.

"It's got to be connected to Olivia's abduction."

Andrews nodded his agreement. "Can I speak with you in the foyer for a moment?" he asked.

Leaving Laney and Rose in the company of Deputy Chief Wallace, Grayson joined Chief Andrews in the foyer. "Here's what's bothering me about this. There have been a number of home invasions in the surrounding area lately. Same MO—a glass cutter and duct tape have been used to cut a pane of glass from a window so the robber can reach through to open the lock. We've kept the method out of the media."

Grayson hadn't been aware of that similarity. The implications were not good. He knew this break-in hadn't been random. If it had been, the perp would have aborted when he saw the uniformed officer outside. Besides, the slip of paper with Laney's name and address made it clear that she'd been specifically targeted. But someone obviously wanted the break-in to look like it was connected to the recent home invasions.

Someone with access to law enforcement files.

"I don't like this, Andrews."

"I know where you're going with this," Andrews said quietly, "and unfortunately, I'm thinking the same thing. There's a leak somewhere, and whoever it is has access to MPD files."

"Can you pull the files from the break-in cases? We can review them to see who might have had knowledge of the abduction and shooting tonight."

"Yeah, I'll do that, but I know every man in the precinct, and I can't think of one who would want Laney hurt."

Grayson knew Andrews wanted to believe that his men were honorable, but unfortunately, things were not always as they seemed. "You could be right. I'd also like to send a forensic expert down here to triage your computer networks. It's possible that your networks have been hacked—that you have a leak, but it's not from one of your own."

"Your forensics expert can have full access. I'll let our IT guy know he's to cooperate fully."

"Thanks. I'll have my laptop triaged, as well." Even though Grayson hoped the leak wasn't in his own house, the fact remained there *was* a leak—either in the local PD or the FBI—and he had to check out every possibility. He'd kept his suspicions to himself, sharing them only with his supervisor, Michael King, and his friend and mentor, retired FBI profiler Ethan Conrad. Like Grayson, both men were reluctant to believe the leak was in the FBI. But they'd agreed he had to look at all scenarios equally.

"Has anyone taken statements from Laney and Rose?" Andrews inquired.

"Not yet."

"I'll do that now."

"Can you step up patrol in the area until sunrise?" Grayson asked. "I'm going to stay here until then if Laney agrees. I've also asked Special Agent in Charge Michael King to authorize FBI protection starting tomorrow."

"There will be a car on this property until morning, Agent. With two officers," Andrews stated matter-of-factly, glancing into the kitchen, where Laney and Rose were quietly talking. "There's no way I'm leaving Laney's safety to chance."

"Then that makes two of us," Grayson said. And judging from the events of the night, he suspected that keeping Laney and her aunt safely out of trouble might be more of a challenge than Andrews thought.

EIGHT

An hour after the police carted the suspect away, Laney sipped a cup of now-cold tea and waited to be asked the same questions another fifty times. She was pretty sure that was how many times she'd already been asked them.

She wasn't annoyed by Kent's thorough interview. She was exhausted. She eyed the police chief as he paced across the room, pivoted and headed her way again.

"So," he continued, "what you're saying is that—"

"I've never seen the man before. I don't know why he broke into the house. I don't know what he wanted. Aside from the fact I tried to stop a kidnapping, I can't think of any reason why anyone would want to hurt me or my aunt."

Grayson snorted, and Laney was pretty sure he was trying to hold back a laugh.

He hadn't said much since the interview began, just leaned against the counter, nursing a cup of coffee and eyeing her intently.

She'd tried not to notice.

It had been difficult.

The guy exuded masculinity, confidence, kindness. All the things she'd have wanted in a man if she'd actually wanted a man in her life at all.

"Sorry to keep asking you the same questions, Laney," Kent said. "But sometimes things become clearer the more we go over them."

"I think this is all pretty clear," she responded, standing on legs that felt a little weak and walking to the sink. She washed her cup, set it in the drainer. She felt… done. With the questions, with the interview, with what seemed like an endless night.

She needed to sleep. She wanted to pull the curtains back from the window so she'd be awakened by the sun rising above the trees. Sunrise was always her favorite time of day. It reminded her of new beginnings, second chances.

"I think she's had enough," Grayson said quietly. No demands. No commands. But there was no doubt he was saying the interview was over.

She almost turned around and told him that she could take care of ending it herself, but she was too tired to protest. The past few years had been tough, digging out of the hole of mourning and guilt, rebuilding her life into something that resembled normal. It had worn her down. So had all the events of the past ten hours.

"I guess I have everything I need. You get some rest, Laney." Kent patted her shoulder, the gesture a little awkward and rough but strongly sincere.

"I will." She forced a smile and walked him to the door.

She thought Grayson would leave, too, but he just waited while she said goodbye to Kent, didn't even make a move toward the door as she waited with it

open wide. The sky was dark, dawn's glow not yet peeking above the trees.

"You should probably go, too," she said, and he shook
his head.

"I don't think so."

"What's that supposed to mean?"

"It means that he wants to help me with this cross-
word puzzle," Aunt Rose said as she looked up from the
dining room table. "I'm stumped, and I've heard that
FBI agents are very intelligent."

"I'm not sure that's true in my case," Grayson said
with a smile. "But I'll be happy to help if I can."

Laney didn't have the energy to argue with either
of them. Shutting the door, she retreated to the family room.

Not only was she exhausted, but her headache was
returning, the dull throb making her stomach churn.

She dropped into her grandfather's chair and pulled
one of the handmade quilts across her lap and shoulders. Grayson and Rose were discussing which five-
letter word best fit Rose's puzzle, and she let her eyes
close, let herself drift on the quietness of their voices,
the gentle cadence of their conversation.

It felt…nice to have other people in the house. Paws
clicked along the wood floor, and she opened her eyes
to see Grayson crossing the foyer from the dining room
into the family room, Jax and Brody at his heels. The
dogs seemed to have taken a liking to the FBI agent.

"It's been quite a night," he commented as he sat on
the couch across from her, the dogs taking their spots on
the dog beds in the corner. "How are you holding up?"

"Pretty well, all things considered." She smiled.

"God was watching out for you and Rose tonight, Laney." Grayson ran a tanned hand through his hair.

Laney admired his conviction, but it was one she had a hard time sharing. She'd gone to Sunday school every Sunday as a child, had prayed every night for her mother to get better. To be stronger. To leave her father. And every day those prayers went unanswered. As she'd gotten older, she'd stopped praying and started acting. She'd had to rely on her own ingenuity and street smarts to protect them both from her father.

"We definitely got lucky," she agreed.

"I don't believe in luck. Everything happens for a reason. The good and the bad. All the events of our lives, big and small, shape us into who we are. Prepare us for our purpose." He fingered the scar over his brow absently, and Laney again wondered how he'd gotten it. It was definitely an old scar, its jagged ridges faded. It didn't detract from his good looks, but rather gave his face more strength of character. He looked real. Not like some politician, musician, or model. Like a man who would risk his life for what he believed in.

"I hope you're right," she said, because she wanted to believe the way he did. She wanted to think that everything she'd been through had brought her to the place she was supposed to be. That was hard, though, with the weight of guilt on her shoulders, the sorrow heavy in her heart.

"I'm going to bed." Rose announced, standing on threshold of the foyer and the dining room. "A good night's sleep is important to keep the mind sharp."

"Good night, Rose." Grayson remained seated on the couch.

"I need to get some sleep, too," Laney admitted with

a yawn. She hoped he would pick up on her not-so-subtle hint as she headed toward the foyer to let him out. "I guess we'll see you in a few hours, then…"

"I'm not leaving." Grayson's voice was firm.

"I'm afraid I have only one spare room, and Rose is using it."

"I'll be fine on the couch. The sun will be up in a few hours, and I'd just as soon keep watch on the house until that happens."

"Well, I personally think that's a good idea," Rose interjected. "I'm a little too tired to take on another intruder tonight—plus my can of mace is depleted. I'll get the blankets and the extra pillows." Without waiting for Laney's response, Rose headed down the hall.

"Well, then, I guess it's settled," Laney agreed, not wanting to admit, even to herself, that she felt better knowing Grayson would be down the hall. "If you'll excuse me, I need to go grab the pillows from the top shelf before Aunt Rose takes it upon herself to get on the stepladder—we definitely don't need another trip to the emergency room tonight."

Grayson woke with a start.

He was up and on his feet in seconds, the pile of blankets Rose had given him falling to the floor. No sign of any danger, and the dogs weren't barking.

Something clanged in the kitchen. A pan or pot, maybe.

He thought it might be Rose, and he went to join her, stopping short when he spotted Laney standing at the sink. The early-morning sun cast gold and amber highlights through her silky hair as she put on the coffee and popped an English muffin into the toaster. Jax and Brody acknowledged him with brief glances, then continued sitting patiently by the counter, watching Laney's every move.

"Good morning."

Though he spoke softly, Laney gasped and turned toward him, clearly startled.

"I'm sorry," he said. "I didn't mean to scare you."

"It's not your fault. I was lost in my thoughts. I guess I'm a little on edge, that's all." She grabbed two dog bowls and a bag of food from the pantry. "Would you like a muffin or some coffee? I've just put on a pot," she asked while preparing the dogs' food.

"A cup of coffee would be great. And I'd like to grab a quick shower later this morning if you don't mind."

"Of course. Fresh towels and soap are under the cabinet in the hall bathroom. Unfortunately, I don't have any clean clothes that would fit you…"

"I keep spare clothes in a duffel in my car."

"Then you're all set. And feel free to help yourself to anything you need from the visitor kit I keep in the bathroom. Sometimes clients will stay overnight when they drop their dogs off, and I like to be prepared."

"That's not a surprise."

"What's that supposed to mean?"

"Just that you seem like the kind of person who prefers to have a plan in place."

"This from the guy that keeps spare clothes in a duffel in his car?" she retorted, placing the dogs' bowls down by the sliding glass door. Neither dog moved from its spot. Eyes trained on Laney, they watched as she crossed the room to the coffeepot and grabbed two mugs from the cupboard.

She glanced at the dogs. "Break," she commanded, and both went for their food.

"They're really well-behaved," he commented.

"Dogs need to understand their boundaries and limitations. Consistency in reinforcing those things is the key." She poured coffee into the mugs. "Milk or sugar?"

"Black is fine."

She leaned against the counter, sipping her coffee. Dressed in beige tactical pants, work boots and a white, long-sleeved T-shirt with the Wagging Tails Boarding and Training logo on it, it was clear she was ready to work. "Heading out to take care of the dogs?"

"It's what I do."

"Not without an escort."

"You're welcome to come along, but I've got some training to do, so I may be a while."

"How long have you been a dog trainer?"

"Professionally, since I was about nineteen—it helped pay my college living expenses—but I've been training dogs since I was eleven. I picked it up from my grandfather. He's the one who started this training facility. He mostly trained police dogs for protection work and drug sniffing back then. Some of my best childhood moments were spent in the kennels with the dogs." Her smile lit her eyes. "But then, what kid wouldn't like playing with dogs all day?"

She pulled her hair up in a ponytail, tying it off with an elastic band she'd worn around her wrist. She wore no makeup, the bruise at her jawline now a bluish green; the end of the red, jagged bullet wound and one staple were clearly visible at her temple near her hairline, but none of it detracted from her quiet beauty. She had an inner strength and calmness about her that he was sure was part of her success as a dog trainer. Grayson had always believed dogs to be perceptive about people's character and moods.

"I've got to head out. My staff will be here by eight to help open the kennels, and I have a potential new client coming at nine for a puppy evaluation—it should be interesting because I've never worked with a Leonberger before. Her name is Maxine."

Grayson had never even *heard* of a Leonberger. "Do we have time for me to grab my laptop? I've got some case files I want to go over."

"Can you do it in two minutes?"

"It's out in my car. I can do it sixty seconds."

"Challenge on," she responded, lifting her wrist and staring at her watch.

He made it back with the laptop in fifty seconds, because he was pretty sure she wouldn't wait the entire sixty.

She was still in the kitchen, the sunlight still playing in her hair.

He thought he'd like to see her outdoors, working with her dogs, doing what she did best.

And that wasn't a good thought to be having about his key witness.

"So what are you planning to tell your staff about your injuries?" he asked, because he needed to get his mind back on protecting Laney. Even though it seemed certain her connection to the case had been leaked, he still thought it wise to downplay her involvement, to keep the reason for her injuries quiet.

"I think explaining your presence, and that of the patrol car, could be just as difficult, actually. What would you suggest?"

"For now, let's blame your injuries and police protection on the break-in and call me an old friend."

"We can try it, but I'm not good at subterfuge. If they start asking questions, that story will fall apart quickly."

"Well, I guess you'll have to keep them too busy to ask questions."

"That part probably won't be much of a problem." She opened the sliding glass door, letting the dogs out into the yard.

Grayson followed Laney to the kennels, where she busied herself filling water bowls with a two-gallon jug. She had released most of the dogs, about fifteen in all, into a fenced enclosure in the center of the kennel that appeared to be an indoor training area. The morning quiet was now broken with lots of barking, yapping, jumping and running around. He noticed one dog, a large Rottweiler, remained in its enclosure. "What's wrong with that one?" he asked out of curiosity.

"He's here as a board-and-train. He's a rescue, but he's dog-aggressive and hard to control on walks. He's improved since he's been here, but I don't trust him to play unsupervised yet."

"That's too bad."

"He's young, and he's smart. His new owners love him. He'll have a happy ending." She smiled.

A door opened at the back of the facility. A girl, about fifteen, came out, hands filled with two buckets overflowing with metal dog bowls. An older teen boy was behind her, pushing a cart piled high with dog food.

"Guys, I'd like you to meet Grayson DeMarco. He's an old friend. Grayson, this is Riley Strong and Bria Hopewell, my staff."

Riley stepped out from behind the cart, extending a

hand to Grayson. "Nice to meet you," he said, pumping Grayson's hand just a little harder than socially acceptable. Not at all threatened by Riley's obvious territorial gesture, Grayson smiled.

"The pleasure's mine," he countered, returning the handshake. He had no doubt Riley knew he was no match physically for Grayson, but he appreciated the kid's protective posture and wondered if Laney recognized his obvious devotion to her.

Bria stepped forward, pushing her glasses up on her nose and extending her hand, as well. She was taller than Laney, about five-six, and way too skinny. Her natural blond hair was pulled up into a ponytail, the bangs falling into her eyes. She barely met Grayson's eyes as she mumbled, "Nice to meet you," before dropping his hand like a hot potato. Grayson had seen kids act like that before, and usually for a reason other than severe shyness. He made a mental note to ask Laney about Bria's story later.

"What's up with the cop car outside?" Riley asked.

"We had a break-in last night, and Chief Andrews thought it would be safer to leave some officers here." A red flush crept into Laney's cheeks. She was right. She was possibly the worst liar Grayson had ever seen. The kids didn't seem too perceptive, however, accepting her explanation and going about their task of feeding the dogs.

"You're welcome to use my office if you need a place to work, Grayson. Here, let me show you where it is."

"This is a nice setup," he commented, following her through the facility.

"I renovated when I took over the business from Granddad about two years ago."

Grayson noticed a sprinkler system in the ceiling, and cameras in the corners focused on the training ring.

"You have security cameras in your kennels but won't get an alarm in your house?" Grayson asked. It seemed to him that her money would have been better spent equally on the house and the kennel.

"The cameras are for recording training sessions only. They're not set up for around-the-clock monitoring."

Grayson's phone vibrated on his hip. "Mind if I take this?"

"Why would I? You've got work to do, and so do I. My office is this way." She led him past the reception area, down a small corridor that ended at an office and storage area as Grayson answered the phone.

"DeMarco."

"Andrews here. The arson investigator is wrapping things up. He'll have the official report to us this afternoon, but the fuse at the hospital was deliberately blown. He confirmed his initial assessment of arson."

Just as Grayson had expected. "What about the surveillance video?"

"No one was in or around that area except the security guard. I've sent a patrol car out to his house to bring him to the precinct for further questioning," Andrews said.

"Good. We need to press him. Any ID yet on our perp from the break-in?" he asked, meeting Laney's eyes. She looked worried. She should be. It was obvious the kidnappers knew she had survived. There was no doubt the blown fuse, the intruder, all of it were connected with the intent of finding and silencing her.

"Prints were a match for Stephen Fowler," Andrews

continued. "Two-time loser. Just released nine months ago after serving a four-year stretch for B&E. His car was parked at his parents' house in the neighborhood, but they claimed they'd not seen him since his release. Father seemed pretty angry over a stolen family car a few years back—claims he'd cut off all ties. Mom may be maintaining contact without telling dad, but I don't think either had any knowledge of his actions last night."

"Fowler say anything useful?"

"No. He's still clammed up. It doesn't look like he'll be able to make bail. Maybe another night in jail will loosen his tongue."

"Maybe. We could definitely use a break. Right now I'm pinning all my hopes on Laney being able to ID a suspect," Grayson said.

"Do you think we should reconsider moving her to a safe house?" Andrews asked.

"The problem is, I don't know who to trust. I'd feel better if she was here, with a combination of police and FBI protection for the next few days."

"I'll support that. I'll rotate officers out front," Andrews said. "Any word on the FBI protection detail?"

"Best case scenario, tonight or tomorrow. I'll stay around until we get more people lined up."

"I'll be by in a few hours to drop Murphy off. You can let me know then if you think we need to take additional precautions."

Grayson checked his watch. "Actually, I've got the sketch artist flying in soon. If you're going to be here, I'll feel better about leaving Laney to pick the sketch artist up from the airport. My plan is to bring her directly here—the quicker we get the sketches done, the better."

"That won't be a problem," Andrews said. "You still planning to bring in that computer-forensics guy? Because if you're not, I'm calling someone in. If there's a leak in my department, I want to know it."

"She's coming, but she's not a guy. I called in a favor and got the leading cyber-forensics investigator in the country." He didn't mention that Arden was his sister. No need for that. Andrews would figure it out soon enough.

"She's FBI, too?"

"No. She's brains for hire. An independent contractor. But I know I can trust her, and that's all that matters right now."

Grayson said a quick goodbye and disconnected.

"Well?" Laney demanded, her eyes deeply shadowed, the bruise on her jaw purple and green against her pale skin.

"I think you heard most of it. The arson team confirmed that the fuse box had been tampered with, and the perp from the break-in is still not talking. Kent's planning to bring Murphy…"

A sudden commotion in the kennels, followed by a reverberating crash and a piercing scream, had Grayson on high alert, hurrying toward the office door. "Wait here," he ordered Laney as he rushed into the kennels, pulling the door shut behind him.

Drawing his gun, he raced to the indoor training ring, scanning the facility for the source of danger.

He didn't have to look far.

Near the entry of the indoor training facility, a brown-and-black mass of fur on legs was excitedly pulling on its leash. It must have weighed a good seventy or eighty pounds. The poor owner was putting all his strength into holding it at bay as it wagged its tail excitedly and tried to reach Riley and the food cart. It had already managed to barrel over Bria, knocking her off her feet and scattering metal dog bowls all over the concrete floor. Riley was trying to pull her up, one eye warily trained on the furry menace.

Unexpectedly, the pup pulled free, launching himself in a ball of unbridled excitement toward the teens and the food cart. Grayson cringed, but it was like watching a train wreck about to happen. He just couldn't look away.

Footsteps pounded on the ground behind him, and he whirled around, ready for danger. Laney was there, wild auburn curls flying around her face, eyes wide with surprise. She held a long metal pole, her knuckles white from her grip on it.

"I guess," she said, as he turned back and saw the furry beast had its head in a bucket of dog food, "that is Maxine."

NINE

Maxine was a darling, but she was a wild one.

Laney barely managed to get her back into her own-ers' SUV after the evaluation was done.

They drove away, waving wildly, probably in grati-tude that Maxine hadn't killed Bria or Riley.

Maxine stuck her head out the side window, her tongue lolling out.

"I can't believe that thing is only five months old." Grayson commented.

"She's cute, isn't she?" Laney asked.

"Cute? I don't think anything that big can be called cute."

"Beauty is in the eye of the beholder," she responded absently, turning to clean up the mess left in Maxine's wake.

"You shouldn't have come running out of the office. You know that, right?" Grayson asked, helping right the cart and scoop what was left of the food back onto it.

"What was I supposed to do? Cower in my office, hoping and praying that the screams weren't my staff members being slaughtered?"

"You thought they were being slaughtered, and you

came outside with this?" He lifted her grandfather's old catching pole, a tool used to control vicious, potentially dangerous dogs. It was a five-foot-long aluminum rod with a grip on one end and a retractable noose on the other.

She had never used one herself, and in all the years she had worked with her grandfather, she had never seen him use one, either. But when she'd prepared to leave the office to find the source of the screaming, it had been the only potential weapon within her reach.

"It made sense at the time." She shrugged, her hair sliding along her neck and falling away from the wound on her head. She'd almost died trying to save a stranger. It shouldn't surprise him that she'd come running to rescue her employees.

"It would have made more sense to stay where I left you. I have a gun, Laney, and I'm trained to take down criminals."

"And I'm trained to take care of the people who work for me. I'm not going to sit back and let them be hurt because I'm too afraid to act." Her voice shook—she hoped he didn't notice.

"Okay," he said, sounding less like he truly agreed and more like he simply didn't want to argue with her.

"What's that supposed to mean?" she asked, her voice laced with suspicion.

"It means you're exhausted. And you need some rest."

"I need to meet with that sketch artist."

"She'll be here this afternoon."

"But will that be soon enough? The kidnappers know I'm alive. They may move Olivia and the other children sooner rather than later."

"Moving them early would take a lot of coordination and effort," he reminded her, but she heard the doubt in his voice. She knew he'd hoped to lull the kidnappers into a false sense of security by making them believe she was dead. Since that plan had fallen through, he had to be just as worried as she was that the abductors would decide to cut their losses and leave the area with the children they'd already taken.

"That doesn't mean they won't do it, and once the kids are out of the country, they may never be found."

"I suspect they have a quota of children to meet, and the kidnappers are not going to jeopardize their payday just yet. Not until they've exhausted all other options."

"As in tried everything to get rid of me?"

"Something like that. Come on. Let's go back to the house. You're looking a little pale."

She had a feeling he was being diplomatic. If the aching exhaustion she felt was any indication, she probably looked like five miles of rough road. "I'm feeling a little pale, too, but I have dogs to take care of."

"Your staff can handle it." He pressed his hand to her lower back, urging her to the house.

He looked even more worried when she didn't bother to protest.

They walked to the house silently, her steps slow and a little unsteady. The adrenaline that had shot through her when she'd heard the screams of her staff was fading, leaving her drained and hollow. When she'd heard Bria and Riley calling out, her heart sunk with the certainty that she had—once again—put the people who trusted her in harm's way. Now her mind was filled with dark memories and all she wanted was to crawl into bed and hope that sleep would push those memories away, at least for a little while.

"You know what?" she murmured without looking at him. "I think I'm going to lie down for a while."

She didn't give him a chance to say he thought it was a good idea. She just walked down the hall and into her bedroom, closing the door behind her.

Sunlight tracked along the ceiling, the house filled with noises. Rose's voice. Grayson's. The television blasting *The Price Is Right*. Dishes clanked, and the sweet smell of fresh baked treats filled the room. The dogs sniffed at the closed bedroom door. She could hear their quiet snuffling breaths, but she was too tired to let them in. She allowed herself to drift in that sweet place between waking and sleeping, that soft spot where memories didn't intrude and circumstances didn't matter so much.

Someone knocked on the door. "Laney," Rose called. "Do you want some tea?"

It was Rose's cure-all, and most times Laney would humor her aunt by having a cup. This wasn't most days, and she kept her eyes closed, pretending to be asleep as the door swung open.

"Laney, dear?" Rose whispered. The floorboards creaked as she approached the bed, and Laney caught a whiff of her aunt's lavender body wash. "Are you awake?"

"I'm trying really hard not to be," Laney muttered.

"Oh. Well, then, I'll just leave you to it. That good-looking FBI agent is sitting in the living room having one of my famous cinnamon rolls. I thought you might like one, too."

"First of all," Laney said, finally opening her eyes, "you know his name is Grayson. Second, your famous cinnamon rolls come from a can, so I'm not sure how you can even call them yours or famous."

"They *are* famous, Laney. The commercials for them are all over the television. I made them. Therefore, they are mine," Rose huffed.

"I'm sure several million other people have also made them." Laney sat up, her entire body achy and old-feeling. "You didn't just come in here to ask me if I wanted a cinnamon roll. What's up?"

"I'm worried about you," Rose admitted, sitting on the edge of the bed and placing a hand on Laney's thigh. "Since when do you lie around in the middle of the day?"

"Since I got shot in the head?"

"Don't try to be funny, Laney. This isn't the time for it."

"Really, Aunt Rose. You don't need to worry. I'm fine."

"The bruise on your jaw and the staples in your scalp would say differently."

"What they say, Aunt Rose, is that I survived. That's a great thing. Not something to make you worry."

"I always worry about you, dear. Ever since that unfortunate incident—"

"I think I *will* have one of those cinnamon rolls." Laney stood so abruptly, her head swam.

"You can't keep running away from it forever, Laney." Rose grabbed her arm, her grip surprisingly strong for a woman of her age. "Eventually, you're going to have to do the hard work of letting go."

"I have let go." She just hadn't forgotten, would never forget.

"Then maybe what you really need is to grab on to something worth believing in." Rose planted her fists firmly on hips that sported bright pink running pants.

"I suppose you're going to tell me what that is?"

"*I* suppose that *you're* intelligent enough to figure it out yourself! But maybe not, since you've spent the past few years hiding in your safe little house, ignoring God's calling for your life!" She flung the last over her shoulder as she huffed out of the room.

Laney sank onto the bed, her muscles so tense she thought they might snap. She didn't like to talk about what had happened in Colorado. She didn't like to think about it. Of course, she still thought about it almost every day. How could she not? She'd lost three well-trained team members. Not just team members. Friends. All of them gone in a blink of an eye and the wild heaving of an avalanche. She rubbed the back of her neck, tried to force the memories away.

They wouldn't leave her. Despite what she'd said to Rose, she hadn't let go. She *couldn't* let go. She'd been responsible for her team, and she'd failed them.

There was nothing that could change that, nothing that could bring back the lives that had been lost.

Not even giving up search and rescue, a quiet voice inside reminded her.

She ignored it. She'd made the decision to retire Jax. It had been the right one to make. She was doing good things with her business, and she didn't see how that could be construed as ignoring God's calling.

Whatever that calling might be.

She frowned, eyeing the old family Bible that sat on her dresser. It had belonged to her grandfather, and he'd given it to her a few weeks before his death. She had opened it once, to read verses from it during his funeral. She touched the cover. Ran her fingers over the embossed letters that read *Travis Family Bible*. It was smooth as silk, decades of being handled and read leaving the old leather soft. She'd believed in God for as long as she could remember. What she hadn't believed was that He cared, that He had a purpose and a plan for her life.

Aunt Rose, though, was convinced otherwise.

So, apparently, was Grayson.

Laney wanted to believe it. She wanted to know everything that had happened would eventually lead her to the place she was supposed to be.

"Everything okay in here?" Grayson asked from the open doorway. He'd showered and changed into a clean set of black tactical pants and a black T-shirt with the FBI logo. Her breath caught as he smiled. He looked good. Great, even. And she'd have to be blind not to notice it.

"Yes."

"Then why did Rose stomp into the kitchen muttering something about stubborn nieces? You're not planning your escape, are you?"

"Not hardly." She laughed, her hand falling away from the Bible, the soft feel of its cover still on her fingers and in her mind. "She's just annoyed with me."

"Why?" He walked into the room, and it felt smaller, more intimate.

"Because I retired from search and rescue," she admitted, sidling past him and moving into the hall. The last thing she wanted was Grayson DeMarco in her bedroom.

"I read about that," he responded.

She stopped short, turning to face him. The hall was

narrow, and they were close. She could see the stubble on his chin, the dark ring around his striking blue irises. "Where?"

"A local paper did a story about you a couple of years ago, remember?'

"Yes, but I didn't think anyone else did."

"I did a little research while you were resting and found it. I told you I planned to work this morning."

"I'm not sure I like that you were digging into my past. As a matter of fact, I'm pretty positive that I don't like it at all."

"I wasn't digging. I was doing background checks on everyone involved in the case."

"You need a background check on a witness?"

"Not every witness is an innocent bystander, Laney," he responded, eyeing her. "Now that I'm thinking about it, Rose was also muttering something about grumpy nieces."

"I am not grumpy!" Laney protested, even though she probably was.

"Sure you are. Sleep deprivation will do that to a person. Come on." He took her arm, his strong fingers curving around her biceps, their warmth seeping through her cotton shirt. "A little sugar will perk you right up."

"I don't need—"

"What you need," he cut her off, his expression serious, "is to let go and let someone take care of you for a while." He began leading her to the kitchen.

It was the second time in just a few minutes that someone had told her she needed to let go.

Maybe it was time, she thought, but she wasn't sure she knew how.

TEN

The cinnamon roll was surprisingly good, despite the slightly burnt edges. The conversation was better.

Grayson was funny and intelligent, and Laney would have been lying if she said she hadn't enjoyed spending time with him. But Grayson's easy banter couldn't belie his concern. He was reluctant to leave, even after Kent arrived with Murphy, who'd greeted Laney like a long-lost friend before eying Grayson suspiciously until introductions were made. Grayson had finally given her a stern reminder to stay in the house and left for the airport.

With Grayson gone, Laney tried not to watch the clock, counting the minutes until he'd return with the sketch artist. The armed officers in Laney's drive, plus the curtains pulled tightly closed throughout the house, were blatant reminders of the danger she was in. If that wasn't enough, the nagging headache and various aches and pains she had would have been.

She watched as Rose popped opened another container of cinnamon rolls. Despite her cheerfulness, she looked tired, her skin a little pale, her hair a little less bouncy than usual.

"Why don't you let me do that, Aunt Rose?" she asked, and Rose scowled.

"You think I'm too old to handle this?"

"I think that if I'm tired, you must be, too."

"Well, I am, but Grayson would probably enjoy a few more piping hot cinnamon rolls when he comes back, and you've never been all that good of a cook."

"This isn't cooking," Laney said, taking the can from her's hands. "And you know that Grayson has only been gone forty minutes. If we bake these now, they won't be hot when he gets back."

"Truth be told," Rose admitted, "I want one. I stress-eat, dear. That's how I got these." She patted her hips, and Laney laughed.

"You've got nothing. Now, sit down. I'll take care of the rolls."

She helped her aunt to the chair, anxious to get her off her feet. The woman had more energy than most twenty-year-olds, but she wasn't twenty, and she could easily overdo it.

Once Rose had settled into the chair, Laney opened the container, peeled out the rolls and placed them in the baking dish. After sticking them in the oven, she did a half dozen other things that were everyday and easy. All the while, her heart slammed against her ribs. Her throat was dry. Every minute, she expected something to scratch against the kitchen window, someone to kick in the kitchen door.

Sure, they had armed police officers outside, but that hadn't made any difference the previous night.

As if thinking about it made it happen, the back door flew open.

She screamed, the sound choking off as she saw a police officer standing in the doorway.

"Sorry about that, ma'am," he said, his gaze shooting to a spot just past her shoulder. She glanced back and saw Kent on the kitchen threshold.

"What's going on?" he asked, his tone cold, his eyes icy. Maybe he thought the police officer was a threat. Whatever the case, the young officer swallowed hard, took a step backward.

"Mills Corner store and gas station has just been held up at gunpoint. Dispatch has called us in since we're the closest officers. You cool with us going to the scene, Chief?"

Kent hesitated, then nodded. "Go ahead. Call in to dispatch to have a couple of officers head out here to fill in, though. We don't want to take any chances."

"Will do!" He raced back outside. Seconds later, the sound of a siren blasted through the afternoon stillness.

"I don't like this," Kent said with a scowl, pacing to the front window and pulling back the curtain. Murphy, sensing his anxiety, was instantly at his side. "That gas station is so far off the beaten track, it's nearly impossible to find if you don't know where to look. It's too much of a coincidence that it just happened to be robbed today. Call those kids back from the kennel, Laney. I'm going to take Murphy with me and do a sweep of the property. Make sure everything looks clear. Let the kids in, lock the door and stay inside."

He snapped a lead on Murphy, issued a command and opened the sliding glass door.

As soon as he disappeared from view, Laney texted Bria and Riley, telling them to come to the house. The chief was right. The little gas station had been around for as long as Laney could remember, and as far as she could recall, it had never been robbed before. The mom-and-pop store offering cheap prices on junk food and milk didn't look like much. It certainly didn't look like much money could be found there.

Riley knocked on the sliding glass door, and Laney opened it, waving the teen inside. Bria was right behind him, her eyes wide. "What's going on?" she asked. "More trouble?"

"Not yet," Laney responded, keeping her tone calm. She didn't want to scare her employees.

"Meaning you're expecting trouble?" Riley asked. "Because if you are, I want to go home and get my hunting rifle."

'There's no need for that," she cut him off. "We're not even sure there's actually any trouble."

"Then Bria and I should go back to the kennel. We've got a lot of work to do." He opened the slider, stepping outside. One of the kenneled dogs barked, the frantic sound a warning that Laney recognized immediately. Trouble. Danger.

She met Riley's eyes. "Was everything okay when you left?"

"It was fine," he responded. "We were…" His voice trailed off as a wisp of gray smoke spiraled up from the corner of the kennel.

The scent of it followed, wafting into the kitchen, stinging Laney's nostrils.

"Fire!" she shouted. "Rose, call 911! There's a fire at the kennel."

Rose grabbed the kitchen phone while Laney raced out the sliding glass doors toward the kennel, Riley and Bria close behind. They needed to get the dogs out first and then worry about containing the damage to the kennels.

"You guys get the hose and meet me by the outdoor dog runs. We're about to put the emergency evacuation system to the test. Remember, under no circumstances do either of you go into the facility." Her mind racing, Laney knew she could be walking into a trap. As much as she wanted to get the dogs out safely, she could not endanger either Riley or Bria to do it.

Laney was at the kennel entrance in moments. She'd had an emergency release switch designed to open all the dog runs at once. She'd tested it after it was installed but had never needed to use it again.

Throwing the facility door open, she rushed in. Smoke billowed from under her office door. So far the flames were contained behind it. Laney knew the sprinkler heads would activate only with direct heat. There were two sprinkler heads in her office. She hoped they would contain the fire. She pulled open the dog run control panel and yanked down the emergency release lever. The grinding sound of the gates opening was an immediate relief. Now it was just a matter of getting into each run, putting a leash on the dogs and taking them to the outside training pavilion until help arrived.

A shadow passed across the open door.

Was someone there? "Kent?" she yelled, hoping the chief had finally arrived. The property was large, but there was no way he'd missed the thick cloud of smoke that was engulfing the area.

"It's Riley," the teen responded. "I thought you could use an extra set of hands."

"I told you not to come in the kennel," she snapped

as Riley appeared at the threshold. She didn't want him to become an unintended target.

A sudden movement behind Riley caught her eye.

A man ran toward the entrance to the kennels, a base-ball cap pulled low over his face, a tire iron in his hand.

"Riley! Look out!" Laney warned, rushing toward him. Riley turned, ducking and bringing his arm up in an attempt to block the blow from the tire iron. Though his arm took the brunt of the blow, the tire iron still caught him on the side of the head. He crumpled to the ground in a heap.

"No!" Laney cried out as the man roughly nudged Riley with his foot, stepping callously over the body of the unconscious teenager.

She couldn't see the man's face, but something about him was eerily familiar. He had the same wiry frame and runner's build as the gun-wielding kidnapper. A familiar fear ran up Laney's spine as he advanced toward her, tire iron poised for attack.

Glancing around, she saw the catching pole resting against the front desk where she had left it that morning. Wielding it like a sword, she swung it at him. He dodged back to avoid the blow. She swung again, the tip of the pole hitting his hand.

"You're going to pay for that!" he growled.

He lunged forward, the tire iron arcing toward her head.

She ducked, swung the pole again. He grabbed the end and tried to rip it from her hands.

"Laney! Where are you?" Kent called from the other side of the kennels.

"Here, Kent! Quick! Help!"

At the sound of Kent's voice, the man dropped the

catching pole and darted toward her. The tire iron whizzed through the air.

She felt it glance off her arm as she ran toward Kent's voice.

She thought she'd feel it again, slamming into the back of her skull or the side of her head. She was sure that at any moment, the man would be on her.

Instead, she felt nothing. Heard nothing. She glanced over her shoulder and saw him disappearing into the woods.

She was safe.

But she didn't feel safe.

She felt terrified.

Kent called out again, and she managed to respond, her heart in her throat as she turned back and knelt beside Riley. He groaned, his eyes fluttering open. He was alive. She was thankful for that. She had to keep him that way. Keep Rose and Bria safe.

A task that seemed to grow more difficult by the hour. If something happened to any of them, she'd never forgive herself. She was all too familiar with that scenario. Her failure to protect them would haunt her dreams. And her waking hours.

A fire truck, an ambulance, two police cruisers and a K-9 unit were still in the yard when Grayson navigated the gravel road. Andrews had called and briefed him on the attack and Grayson's mind was racing as he parked quickly, jumping out of his sedan and opening the passenger door for the sketch artist.

"Slow down," Willow Scott demanded, her curly blond hair pulled into a loose bun, the hairstyle matching her no-nonsense business suit perfectly. "Rushing isn't going to change what's already happened," she said, her long stride easily keeping up with his as he jogged toward the house.

"Moving slow isn't going to keep more from happening," he growled, frustrated with himself, with Kent, with the two officers who'd left their post to respond to the falsified report of an armed robbery.

The door flew open as he jogged up the porch stairs, and Kent Andrews appeared, a streak of soot on his cheek and a scowl deepening the lines in his face. "This the sketch artist?" he asked, gesturing to Willow.

"I am," Willow responded, moving past him and into the house, adjusting a bag of art supplies she had slung over her shoulder. "Where's the witness?"

"In the kitchen. She thinks the guy who was out here today might be one of the kidnappers from last night."

"How'd he get away?" Grayson asked.

"I'm pretty sure he had an accomplice parked out on the highway. Murphy and I scoured the woods. No sign of anyone, though Laney clearly saw him disappear into the trees."

"That's unfortunate. I really want to ID these guys quickly," Grayson responded.

"Well, if Laney is as good a witness as you think she will be, we'll be able to run a sketch through the system before the day is out," Willow interjected. "If the partial prints or DNA profile from the gun recovered at the scene pan out, your case will be airtight—and if either of the kidnappers is in the system, we'll have a positive ID in no time."

Grayson was banking on it. The FBI's new facial recognition program was able to compare surveillance images and even sketches against the FBI's national database of mug shots in minutes. That's why he'd brought Willow in. She'd had a hand in developing the system and the highest hit ratio of any artist using it. "Let's hope both perps have criminal records."

"There's a good probability they do. You don't get involved in this type of crime overnight. I'm betting these guys are career criminals."

"Let's get this done, then." Grayson said, leading the way to the kitchen.

The house bustled with activity. Firefighters, police and ambulance personnel were all milling around, eating freshly baked chocolate chip cookies that Rose was passing around on a platter. Despite the cookies, the air was still ripe with the scent of smoke, the sliding glass door open, cool air tinged with a hint of moisture drifted in.

He scanned the room and found Laney seated in a chair at the table. She caught his eye and smiled. She looked young, her hair scraped into a ponytail, her eyes shadowed. "You made it back," she said.

"Better late than never, I guess." He took a seat beside her, the acrid stench of smoke heavier there. Though her clothes were smudged with soot, her face and hands looked freshly scrubbed.

"You're not late," Rose cut in. "You're just in time for a cookie." She handed him one, and Grayson ate it.

It tasted like dust. Or maybe mud.

"Good?" she asked, beaming as she held out the platter. "Have another."

"Thanks, but we've got a lot of work to do. Maybe you could—"

"Say no more!" she interrupted. "Bria and I will check on the dogs, but we'll go see Riley first. He's conscious but the paramedics want him assessed at the hospital. His parents just arrived and they're planning to head over there with him. Bria, grab that platter of cookies in case anyone needs a snack."

Seconds later, Kent had cleared the rest of the room, then joined firefighters and police outside. Willow took a seat on the opposite side of Laney, smiling as she introduced herself. She was good at what she did. Great at it, and part of that gift was in her ability to make the witness feel comfortable and confident.

She emptied her bag of supplies onto the kitchen table.

Grayson had seen her in action before, but he pulled up a chair and watched, anyway. He needed this sketch to match something in the database. Despite the police presence, he was worried. Laney had been attacked again. Both times she'd been under the protection of the MPD. Both times, he was not around.

Had the attacker known Grayson would be at the airport picking up the sketch artist? The timing of the fire seemed to indicate that, but only a few people had known when Willow would arrive.

Was the leak in the FBI or in the local PD? It was a question Grayson needed answered. Until then, he'd be taking extra precautions. And unless it was absolutely necessary, he wouldn't be leaving Laney's side.

He'd confirmed the FBI protection detail had been processed and should arrive before the day was out. It couldn't come quickly enough for Grayson.

His phone vibrated, and he glanced at his caller ID. Ethan Conrad.

Good. Grayson needed to run a few things by him. Though retired, Ethan remained an influential and well-connected force in the FBI. He had lobbied for Grayson to be assigned the kidnapping ring case when the Boston field agent stepped down. He'd been Grayson's sounding board during the past few months, helping him weed through and make sense of dozens of reports and reams of information from field offices in California and Boston.

Grayson didn't bother excusing himself, didn't want to interrupt the flow of Willow's work. Instead, he stepped out the sliding glass door. "Grayson here. What's up?"

"Just making sure Willow arrived as scheduled. I spoke with Michael this afternoon, and he's antsy to get a sketch of the perps into the system."

"Same here," Grayson responded. "Willow's working with Laney Kensington now. The sooner we can identify our suspects, the better. There've been additional attempts on Laney's life."

"I thought you requested twenty-four-hour protection."

"I did. MPD's been covering so far and FBI is on the way. But our perps seem to know my schedule, and they use it to their advantage." He explained briefly, and Ethan sighed.

"Your theory seems accurate, then. We've got a leak. In the bureau or in the police precinct."

"I'm inclined to think it's in our office. Who else would have known what time Willow would arrive?"

"Anyone with access to airport databases can search for a name and find out when that person's flying in or out of a city. Willow is one of the most sought-after sketch artists in the country, and this kidnapping ring is savvy enough to pinpoint who you'd likely bring in and follow that person's activities. It would be easy enough to figure out what time she'd be arriving."

He was right, but Grayson couldn't shake the feeling that the leak was somewhere in the FBI's house. "I've got Arden coming in to take a look at the computer system at the local police department. If any information is being filtered out or in there, we'll know it."

"You've got that right." Ethan chuckled. "She won't miss anything."

"Do you have time to look through some case files for me, see if there's something I missed?" Grayson asked.

"Send the files to me over the FTP site. I'll grab them from the server and start reading through them tonight."

"Thanks. And Ethan, let's keep our suspicions quiet. If the leak *is* a federal agent, we don't want to give him a chance to cover his tracks."

"You know me better than that. I'll call if anything jumps out at me from the files. In the meantime, stay focused. This kidnapping ring has got to be stopped before any more families are destroyed."

Disconnecting from the call, Grayson paced the length of the back deck. He didn't want to believe the leak could be one of their own. But he couldn't afford to bury his head in the sand. *Someone* was leaking information to the kidnappers. There might be a computer hacker accessing the online systems, but the information the perps had went deeper than that. They seemed to know who would be where, and when. There was no way for them to know so much without an informant.

Worse, Grayson was beginning to believe the head of the child trafficking ring might be hiding behind an FBI badge. The cases spanned three states and international waters. It was possible someone in the state PD was on the payroll, but there was no way that person was the mastermind. It had to be a nationally connected source, and the FBI was the only agency working this case. The thought wasn't a reassuring one, and Grayson wanted to ignore it.

He couldn't. Children's lives were at stake. Families were at stake. Laney's safety was at stake.

He walked back into the kitchen. Laney was still at the table, eyes closed as she said something to Willow. Was she visualizing the perps? Trying to bring their faces into better focus?

Maybe she sensed his gaze. She opened her eyes, glanced his way and offered the kind of smile that seemed to say she was glad he was there.

She was a strong woman, determined, hardworking, energetic and obviously willing to sacrifice her safety for the safety of others.

So why had she retired from search and rescue? His cursory search of national databases hadn't revealed much. She'd retired early from her work, but the article he'd read hadn't said why. He wanted to know. Not because it would help with the case, not because it mattered to the outcome of his investigation, but because he wanted to know more about Laney.

He wasn't sure how he felt about that, but it was a truth he couldn't deny, one that he carried with him as he crossed the kitchen and settled in the chair next to her.

ELEVEN

Laney tried to focus on Willow Scott's work as Grayson took a seat beside her.

It shouldn't have been difficult. Her elegant hands deftly moving across the paper, Willow was bringing Laney's description to life. The work was fascinating, her questions as detailed as her drawing.

Yes. Laney definitely shouldn't have had any trouble keeping her eyes on Willow and her sketch. Unfortunately, Grayson was difficult to ignore. Especially since he'd pulled his chair a little closer, his arm brushing hers as he leaned in to get a closer look at the sketch.

She met his gaze, her heart doing a strange little flip when he smiled.

"So," Willow said, turning the drawing pad toward Laney and forcing her to refocus her attention. "How's this match with what you saw?"

Laney's breath caught in her throat. The charcoal drawing looked like a black-and-white photograph of the gun-wielding kidnapper.

"Wow, that's him." Laney didn't think it could be any more perfect—down to the small scar on his left cheek and the slightly crooked nose. Willow had captured him perfectly.

Grayson leaned over to look at the drawing, his closeness oddly comforting. "I'll run this through my scanner and feed it into the facial recognition system while you work on the sketch of his accomplice."

Carefully tearing the page from her pad, Willow handed it to Grayson. "Let's stretch and grab a drink of water, Laney. Then we'll do the next sketch."

"There's probably some homemade raspberry iced tea in the fridge if you're interested," Laney offered, her focus still on the sketch. The guy looked mean, and she could almost picture him slinking through the kennels, setting fire to her office. Had he been the man on her property? She thought so. And it wasn't a comforting thought.

"That actually sounds good," Willow replied. "I'm a Southern girl at heart, and we do like our iced tea." Willow chatted with Grayson about new updates to the FBI facial recognition system as Laney grabbed the pitcher of tea from the fridge and tried to pour it into a tall glass. Her hands were shaking so hard, the tea sloshed over the sides of the glass, spilling onto the counter.

"Let me help with that," Grayson said, reaching around her, his chest nearly touching her back as he steadied her hand. The tea poured into the glass without a drop spilling, and Laney handed it to Willow, her cheeks warm, her heart racing.

Not because of the sketch. Because of Grayson.

The man was messing with her composure, and she didn't like it.

"Thanks," Willow said, not a trace of Southern accent in her voice. She took gulp of the tea, tilting her head back just enough for Laney to catch a glimpse of a thin scar extending from the bottom of her jaw horizontally across her neck. Even to Laney's untrained eye, it would have been a significant injury. Life-threatening, even. And definitely intentional.

She turned away, not wanting Willow to know she'd been staring.

Whatever had happened, it had been a long time ago. The scar was faded and old.

"Here." Grayson thrust a glass of tea into Laney's hand. "I think you need this. You look a little done-in."

"Gee, thanks," she responded, sipping the tea as she dropped back into her chair.

Willow and Grayson were still on their feet, both of them tall and fit. They looked good together, seemed comfortable with one another. For all Laney knew, they were dating. Good for them. Laney had better things to do with her life than devote it to a man. Her mother had done that. She'd spent her entire adult life trying to please a man who couldn't be pleased. Laney's dad had been a good-looking charmer.

When he wasn't drunk.

Most of the time he was. Behind closed doors, he was a mentally and physically abusive husband and father. Laney had watched her mother lose herself to depression, and she'd vowed never to be in the position where being with someone meant losing herself.

"Okay." Willow's voice jogged Laney out of her thoughts. "I'm ready if you are."

Within an hour, Willow had completed the second sketch. It was eerie how much the charcoal drawing resembled the man. Somehow Willow had even managed to capture his menacing stare.

In the family room, Grayson had set up his portable scanner and laptop.

Jax, Brody and Murphy were lying by the coffee table, watching him work, when Willow and Laney brought him the second sketch.

"This looks great," he said. "I'll get it scanned and entered into the system."

"How long will it take to get the results?" Laney asked.

"That depends. There are thousands of mug shots in the national database. If we don't get a hit there, the system will ping other participating statewide databases according to a query I've set up. This search will run against the California, Boston and Maryland databases first, then hit the rest of the states until all databases are exhausted." He carefully laid the second image down on the scanner. "I'll queue up the next query to run when the first is complete."

The dogs barked, announcing a visitor.

"Place," Laney commanded, going to the door. An overweight, balding man dressed in a blue uniform that read Carlston Construction stood on the threshold. With barely a glance at Laney, he began his practiced spiel. "Good afternoon. I'm here to replace a pane of glass in a window…" he said, flipping through a clipboard of invoices, oblivious to Grayson, who had followed Laney to the door.

"Looks like…back window. Double-paned glass." He looked up, finally seemed to notice Grayson and took a step back. "I do have the right house, don't I?" he asked, looking down at his invoice again.

"We've got a broken window in the back, but I didn't call in an order to have it fixed."

"It was called in by Rose Cantor."

Rose hadn't returned from the kennel. Laney suspected she was camped out in a lawn chair, reading one of her romance novels while Bria tended to the dogs.

A police officer approached the door. "Want me to show him around back, Agent DeMarco?" he asked, and Grayson nodded.

"Yes. Don't let him leave without a guarantee that window will be fixed tonight. It poses a security threat."

"Yes, sir."

The look on the contractor's face had Laney thinking he'd replace the entire window, not just the broken pane of glass, to keep Grayson happy. Of course, she'd be glad to have the window fixed. They'd nailed a sheet of plywood across the window last night, but that brought with it other concerns in case of a fire—a real consideration in light of today's events.

Grayson's laptop dinged twice as they returned to the family room.

Willow looked over at them, a grin spreading across her face. "We have a hit—with a 94 percent accuracy rate, Grayson."

Laney rushed over. Two images—Willow's sketch and a photograph of a convict—were on the screen.

"That's definitely him." She couldn't contain her smile. They had identified one of the kidnappers. That meant they were a step closer to finding the missing children and closing down the child trafficking ring.

"You were the perfect witness, Laney," Grayson said. "I knew you'd be the key to identifying the kidnappers."

"Willow was the key. If she hadn't been able to sketch what I saw—"

"Let's give credit where credit's due," Willow countered. "You managed to really see this guy and commit his face to memory. That's hard to do, even under the best of circumstances. I consider myself fortunate to get a 75 percent likelihood of a match."

"And that's a high average." Grayson added, saving the image to his laptop.

"What do we do now?" Laney asked.

"We put out an APB on David Rallings Jr. Tonight."

The sun was low in the sky, the air crisp. Grayson sat on the porch swing, rocking with one foot. The three dogs had followed him out, and after a brief romp around the yard, they had each found a place on the porch to relax in silence. The windows were open, the aroma of chicken and freshly baked Pillsbury rolls wafting through the screen, mixed with the scent of honeysuckle and pine, nearly masking the now faint smell of smoke. Light chatter and low bouts of laughter came from the kitchen where Laney and Willow were helping Rose prepare dinner.

In any other circumstances, this would have been an idyllic fall afternoon, the evening quiet and relaxing.

He was tense, though, anxious to hear from the local PD. The APB on David Rallings had been issued, and Grayson was hopeful they'd be able to bring the guy in for questioning soon. They had a name, a last known address. And a lengthy criminal record with multiple charges for assault, robbery and domestic violence. He'd served jail time five years ago, but had been clean—or just avoided being caught—ever since. Kent had sent officers to Rallings's house, and they were procuring a search warrant.

Things were coming together.

Unfortunately, there had been no match on the second suspect. They might have an ID soon, though. If

Rallings wasn't at his house, if he couldn't be located, both sketches would be released to the media on the ten o'clock news.

The dogs came alert to the sound of tires on gravel, lifting their heads simultaneously, eyes focused on the driveway.

A candy-apple-red 1965 Camaro rounded a curve in the drive.

Arden. Finally.

He loved his sister, but her fear of flying made it difficult for her to move from location to location quickly. But he'd choose her any day over a more accessible computer expert.

She'd driven ten hours, from a contract job in Georgia, to make it to Maryland this morning, heading directly to the precinct to examine their system. He wondered what she'd found, but was certain if something was there, she'd know it. She was a genius, graduating from high school at fourteen and from college with a master's degree by the time she was eighteen. Focused and independent, she marched to her own drum. That was one of his favorite things about her. Unfortunately, along with the genius IQ came some quirks that didn't necessarily endear her to everyone.

She came up the walk, a backpack slung over her shoulder. With her black shoulder-length hair, fair skin and blue eyes, she looked much like their mom.

"Hi, Gray. Mom said to tell you you'll be in hot water if she doesn't hear from you before the week is out." She grinned, stepping into his embrace.

"Is that the way you greet the brother you haven't seen in six months—with threats from Mom?"

"Hey, don't shoot the messenger." She brushed a

hand over her hair, sweeping thick, straight bangs from her eyes. It was a new look. One that had probably taken her a year to decide on.

"You look great, kid."

"Flattery won't get you anywhere. You owe me big time, and you know I'm keeping track."

Grayson laughed. "I'm sure you are."

"What's with the dogs?" she asked, bending down to scratch each behind the ears.

"Two of them belong to my witness, Laney. The other is a dog she's training for the MDP."

"Laney, huh? Chief Andrews told me about her this morning. He thinks highly of her."

"I do, too."

"Hmmm…guess I need to meet her, then." With that, she walked into the house without ringing the doorbell or knocking. That was pure Arden. No qualms about walking into other people's space, barely any acknowledgment of the boundaries most people lived inside. It wasn't that she didn't understand the rules. She just tended to ignore them unless it was absolutely necessary to do otherwise.

He followed her into the house and wasn't surprised when she made a beeline for the kitchen. Arden loved cars, computers and food.

Laney and Willow were slathering butter on slices of bread. Rose was tossing a salad. Hopefully she'd had nothing more to do with the cooking. If her burnt cinnamon rolls and mud-like cookies were any indication, the woman should be kept far away from meal preparations.

Inhaling deeply, Arden dropped her backpack on the floor.

"Something smells good. Do you have room for one

more?" she asked, taking a seat at the kitchen table before she was invited to do so.

Grayson shook his head.

"Of course there's room," Rose said, setting a plate in front of her. "But get yourself out of that chair and help first. If you want to eat, you've got to work. Get the tea from the fridge and some glasses from the cupboard to the right of the sink."

Laney looked horrified at Rose's barked instructions, and Willow tried hard to squelch her snicker.

Arden laughed outright.

That was another thing Grayson loved about his sister. She knew how to laugh at herself. "Laney. Rose." Grayson gestured toward Arden as she got up to do as she'd been told. "This is my sister, Arden. She's the computer-forensics specialist I told you about."

Laney and Rose smiled in greeting. "Nice to meet you," Laney said. "Make yourself at home here."

"And you remember Willow..." Grayson began.

"Hey, Willow," Arden interrupted. "It's been a while. How's the facial-recognition system working out?"

"Perfectly. Which you know. So stop fishing for compliments," Willow responded with a smile, setting a platter of roasted chicken in the middle of the table.

"Not fishing. Making sure the program I designed works," Arden responded, reaching for a piece of bread and getting her hand slapped away by Rose. "Got paid a lot of money to do it, and I want to be sure the FBI is happy with the return on their investment. I've been toying with some upgrades to speed the processing, mostly by giving it the ability to read multiple file formats without conversion."

"I didn't know upgrades were in the budget." Grayson cut in, trying to steer away from the more technical discussion that was sure to ensue once Arden got on a roll.

"They aren't. I just feel it's not the best product I could have delivered. The first set of upgrades will be on me." Arden tried to snag a cookie from the jar on the counter, and Rose sighed.

"Young lady, we haven't even said our grace yet."

"Oh. Right. Let's do that, then." Arden sat, and everyone else followed suit.

"Grayson," Rose asked as she took a seat opposite him, "would you be willing to do the honors? And if it comes to mind, pray for my niece and her safety. She's too stubborn to listen at times, and we—"

"Rose!" Laney nearly shouted. "Enough!"

"Enough what, dear?" Rose asked with an innocent smile.

"Let's pray," Laney responded, and Grayson was pretty sure she mumbled *before I kill someone* under her breath as everyone bowed their heads.

When he finished praying, he leaned close to her ear and caught a whiff of freshly baked rolls and something flowery and sweet.

"Murder is a capital offense," he whispered, and she choked on her sip of tea.

He patted her back until she stopped coughing and thought about leaving his hand right where it was—resting between her shoulder blades, his fingers just touching the edges of her ponytail.

"So, Laney," Arden said suddenly, her voice a little too loud in the quiet room. "My brother tells me you're a dog trainer."

"That she is," Rose interjected. "Probably the best in the country."

"Let's not exaggerate, Aunt Rose." Laney shook her head.

"No," Arden argued. "Your aunt is right. I thought you might be the Laney Kensington from Colorado, and you are, right?"

"Yes," Laney said, her voice tight, her expression unreadable.

"I've read all about you," Arden said through a mouthful of buttered bread.

"I'm sure there wasn't all that much to read."

"Sure there was. Up until the past couple of years, you were in the news all the time."

Uh-oh. Here she goes, Grayson thought. Arden had a photographic memory…and no filter. "I saw a picture of you, Brody and a family you and your team pulled off the mountain—they ran an article about you being the youngest dog handler on the Colorado Wilderness Search and Rescue Team."

Laney couldn't hide her surprise. "I thought that article only ran locally. Were you a Colorado resident?"

"Oh, no. I liked reading good news stories when I was a kid, so I developed an app that collects and downloads good news from more than three hundred online publications worldwide."

Grayson knew the real reason Arden had developed that application. At thirteen, she'd worried too much about the state of the world—the news stories would keep her up all night. In typical Arden fashion, she'd decided the best way to stop worrying about the bad news was to read only the good. She'd never told anyone but Grayson that, and he'd kept her secret. For her to even admit to the app…she was up to something.

"That must be a lot of reading each day," Willow interjected.

"Surprisingly, no. People would rather read about calamity, so that's what news reporters cover," Arden countered. "Anyway, when I saw that article, I put you and your team into my search engine so I could follow your adventures—they were pretty cool. Volunteers risking their lives to save others. I have tremendous respect for people like you."

"Um, thanks. But I gave that up a couple years ago." Laney's face had gone ashen, but of course Arden wouldn't stop.

"It's a shame. I read that you and Brody had the highest success rate for live finds of any dog-and-handler team in the nation."

"Those stats were probably inflated," Laney responded. "Besides, I retired Brody when he was six—bad hips."

"Do you think he misses the work?" Arden asked.

"At times."

"Do you?"

"No. I lost the passion for it, so it was better I walk away. You have to be on point for wilderness search and rescue. People's lives depend on your ability to stay focused and do your job."

It was a practiced answer, and Grayson wondered what the real reason was.

"What about Jax?" Arden pressed.

"What do you mean?"

"I read he was even better than Brody. Do you think he misses it?"

"Lay off with the twenty questions, Arden. Laney's had a rough couple of days." Grayson figured the direct approach would be the only chance of making his sister realize she was treading on thin ice.

"Sure. No problem." Arden grabbed another piece of bread. "I miss reading those stories, though. They were some of the best. It's a shame that avalanche killed your teammates. Must have been hard on you, huh?"

"I think," Laney said, pushing away from the table, "I'm done." She headed to the foyer.

Grayson got up to follow her.

TWELVE

She needed some air, because she felt like she was suffocating. She unlocked the front door and yanked it open.

"Not the best idea, Laney," Grayson said quietly.

She turned to face him. "I have to check on the dogs."

"You have to stay safe," he responded, opening the coat closet and taking out her jacket. He dropped it over her shoulders, lifting her hair out from under the collar. "So if you need to check on the dogs, I'll go with you."

"You have your sketches and an ID. I'm not necessary to the case any longer, so maybe it's time for me to keep *myself* safe."

"Still grumpy?" he asked.

"No."

"Then I'll just assume my sister's comments upset you."

"They didn't." Not really. It was the memories that upset her. The guilt.

"Arden has no boundaries, but she doesn't mean any harm."

"I know." Laney walked outside.

The sun was just falling below the horizon, golden

rays resting on leaves tinged with gold and red. A hint of smoke still hung in the air, mixing with the crisp fresh scent of early fall. That she was there to enjoy the beauty of it was a matter of chance or circumstance. That's what she had always believed, because it had been too hard to believe that the God who had allowed her mother to be beaten and mistreated actually cared about the world or the people He'd created.

Her grandfather had disagreed. Rose disagreed, her years as a missionary in Africa sealing her belief in God's grace and mercy, His direction and guidance.

"You're sad," Grayson said, pressing a hand to her lower back and guiding her down the porch stairs.

"Not really. I just wish…"

"What?"

"That I had the kind of faith you have. The faith Rose has. The kind that says everything is going to be okay. No matter how bad things seem."

"Is that what you think my faith tells me?" he asked, his hand slipping from her back to her waist as they walked side by side. She could almost imagine that they were more than an FBI agent and his only witness. She could almost imagine that he was worth pinning hopes and dreams on, worthy of putting her trust in.

"Isn't it?"

"No." He stopped, urging her around so they were face-to-face. "It doesn't tell me that everything will be okay. It just tells me that no matter what happens, *I'll* be okay. Life is tough, Laney. No matter how strong my faith, no matter how much I believe, that doesn't change the fact that I'm living in a sinful and fallen world. Bad stuff happens." He frowned, touching the very edge of her head wound. "People are hurt. People are kidnapped. People die. I can't stop that from happening, but I can do everything in my power to make sure the people responsible pay for their crimes."

"Your purpose, huh?"

"Exactly." He smiled and started walking toward the kennels again.

It took two hours to check on the dogs, give them playtime and attention and settle them for the night. It was her normal routine, one she'd carved out of the ashes of her old life. She loved it, but on nights like tonight—with the early fall air touching her cheeks and the crisp hint of winter in the air—she longed to be out on the trail again, working with a team, searching for the missing. Grayson moved beside her as she fed the last dog, locked the last kennel.

"Done?" he asked.

"Yes. It takes a while. I'm sorry if I pulled you from your job."

"Right now, you're my job."

"Your job is to find Olivia and the other children."

"I'm working on that, too."

"Do you think it's really possible they'll be found?"

"I am going to do everything in my power to make it happen."

"If I'd been able to keep them from getting Olivia—"

"Don't," he cut in.

"What?"

"Don't play that 'if only' game with yourself. Regrets don't do anything for anyone. As a matter of fact, they usually just keep us from doing what we could and should and *would* accomplish if we weren't so caught up in the past."

"Did Rose pay you to say that?" she asked, because she'd heard the same thing from her aunt more than once.

"No." He laughed. "Why? Have you heard it one too many times?"

"Maybe."

"Because of what happened with your team?"

She stopped short at his words, her heart slamming so hard against her ribs, she thought it might burst. "That's something I don't talk about."

"Maybe you should," he countered.

"Maybe. But not tonight."

"Okay," he said simply. He didn't say any more. Didn't press her to tell him what had happened. If he asked Arden, he'd get the truth, but Laney doubted he'd ask. She had the feeling that he'd wait until she was ready to tell him.

She liked that about him, the patience, the willingness to allow her to reveal what she wanted when she wanted. She liked *him.*

Moonlight painted the grass gold. Crickets chirped a constant melody. And Laney? She felt oddly at peace. Just for a moment, she allowed herself really to believe that Grayson was right. That everything happened according to God's plan. Her childhood, career choices, and search-and-rescue successes and failures all converging to make her into the person God needed her to be.

And that maybe, just maybe, Olivia was in her path last night for a reason.

And maybe that reason was to bring Olivia and the others home. With hope in her heart, she silently prayed for the strength to see it through.

* * *

Laney looked beautiful in the moonlight.

The thought was one that Grayson couldn't allow himself to entertain. Eventually, the kidnapping case would be closed. Laney would no longer be part of his investigation.

And then what?

He knew what he should do. Walk away. Let Laney go her way while he went his.

But there was something about Laney, something that he couldn't ignore. Something he wasn't sure he wanted to ignore.

It had been ten years since Andrea had died. Murdered by a stray bullet that deep down Grayson knew had been meant for him. Her death, a month before their wedding, had been a wake-up call for Grayson. He'd doubted his purpose, second-guessed his career choice. He'd finally come to terms with the reality that his future, his calling, this life he had chosen, did not come without sacrifice. A wife and family of his own were not in his future. He'd been selfish to try to have that with Andrea—a selfishness that had led to her death. He didn't have the time to devote to a family. His job required that he miss birthdays, anniversaries, holidays. That wasn't fair. Not to anyone.

He wouldn't ask another woman to understand the demands of his work, his drive to be successful, not even someone like Laney.

She might understand his single-minded dedication to his work, but she had her own guilt, her own memories, her own reasons for doing the work she did. She didn't need anything else laid on her.

He led her to the sliding glass door, opened it and ushered her inside.

"Gray, is that you?" Arden called from the family room.

"Yes."

"Well, what took so long? I've been done for like… an hour!"

"Have you found anything?" he asked as he and Laney joined her.

Rose was on the recliner, a colorful quilt covering her equally colorful pajamas, nose buried in her devotional. Willow sat on the couch beside Arden, a glazed look on her face. She'd probably spent the past two hours listening to every excruciating detail of Arden's next project.

"Malware," Arden said, her gaze on Gray's laptop. "None of the data you've sent or received via email can be trusted. The malware is very sophisticated."

"Can you disable it?"

"Is there anything I can't do on computers?"

"Way to be vain, sis."

"Vanity is about beauty. I'm confident. But I'll admit, this is going to take some time. Simply put, someone set up a duplicate email account to intercept all your messages before you received them."

"Can you tell if anything was modified or removed?"

"Unfortunately, no. Because the full files were never saved to your hard drive, not even to your temp files, there is just no way to run a recovery program."

This was bad news. This was Grayson's official FBI email account; he trusted it and the data he received from it.

"Is there any way to tell how long this has been going on?

"I knew you'd ask that." Arden smiled. "It appears the duplicate account was set up about in January."

"So my email has been compromised for nearly a year?" Just about the time he was assigned to the case. Grayson didn't like the coincidence.

"Is there any way to trace who's been accessing the account?" he asked.

"I think so, given time. But until I do, any data you send over this account is in jeopardy. Anything you receive is suspect. You'll have to decide what's more important—to have a secure email account, or to track the hacker on the other end. We can close this account down now, but that means whoever is on the other end will know you're onto him."

"I need to know who's accessing my account." Pacing the length of the family room, Grayson outlined his plan. "I'll call the IT team tomorrow and request a new email account, but will keep this one open. Until I get the new account, I'll do everything the old-fashioned way." He glanced at his watch. "It's too late tonight, but tomorrow I'll call the local PD in California and Boston to request faxes of their case files. I can compare them with versions that were emailed to me."

"You think those files were tampered with?" Willow asked.

"I think there's got to be a reason someone hacked into this account."

He looked up at Laney. "Do you have a fax-machine number I can use, or should I have everything sent to Chief Andrews?

"I have a fax at the reception desk in the kennels. The fire didn't reach there, so it should be fine. Aunt Rose gave you one of my business cards. The number's on it."

"Be careful, Grayson," Arden added. "Make sure you contact someone you trust—otherwise the hard copies may be modified, as well."

"Got it covered."

"There is also the slim possibility that the duplicate account was set up by an FBI system administrator. If that's the case, I won't have much time to complete my forensic investigation—I'd expect him to disable the mirror account, leaving no trace. I'll do what I can tonight, but there is no guarantee I'll be able to track this back."

"Well, Arden," Willow interjected. "it's been great seeing you again, but it sounds like you're planning to work most of the night on this thing and I've got a flight out tomorrow at ten. I think I need to find a hotel room and crash. I caught the redeye last night so I could get here as early as possible, and I'm beat."

Rose looked up from her reading then, glasses perched on her nose, "What's this I hear about hotel rooms when I have a perfectly good cottage just down the drive?"

"I wouldn't want to impose, Rose." Willow said.

"No imposition. I'm staying up here with Laney. My place is a bit smaller, one bedroom. But there's a pullout couch and clean sheets in the linen closet." She stood, folding the quilt neatly over the recliner. "I'll walk you down now. Arden can join you later."

"I'm sure I can find it on my own…"

"I'm sure you can, too," Rose cut her off. "But I need the stretch. I've been cooped up all day and some fresh air will do me good."

Laney frowned. "Aunt Rose, it's too dangerous for

you to be walking outside alone right now. Maybe Grayson should—"

Rose sighed. "You young people ought not argue with your elders. Haven't you learned it's futile?"

Arden snickered at Rose's statement.

"Besides, who says I'm gonna be alone?" She started toward the kitchen. "I have two fresh chicken sandwiches and some raspberry tea prepared for the officers out front. I'm sure one of them will escort me down the drive and back in payment for a nice dinner." She emerged from the kitchen, lightweight blue jacket zipped over flowered pajamas, white Keds on her feet and a small picnic basket in her arms. "I threw in some cookies for good measure."

Grayson grimaced. Maybe he should warn the guys before they bit into one of them.

"Of course," Rose continued, "if I had my mace, I wouldn't have to go through the trouble of bribing a police officer with food. Come on, Willow. Let's get out of here."

She was out the door before Willow could make a move to follow.

"Well," Arden said.

"Well, what?" Grayson responded, his gaze on the open front door and on the officers who were being handed chicken sandwiches.

"I like that old lady. She's pretty cool."

"Get back to work, sis." He sighed as Willow walked outside and closed the door.

THIRTEEN

Laney toyed with the idea of sleeping in her very comfortable, yet extremely ugly, fuzzy frog pj's—a Christmas gift from Aunt Rose that, surprisingly, Laney actually used. But she did not want to be seen in public wearing them. Given the last twenty-four hours, she could not even begin to wonder what might interrupt her sleep.

Instead of the fuzzy pj's, she threw on a clean pair of yoga pants and a soft Under Armour T-shirt. Glancing in the mirror, she sighed at her reflection. With her hair pulled back into a loose braid, the staples at her hairline were not quite hidden and still inflamed. Her fair skin, made all the more pale from lack of sleep and worry, only served to accentuate further the unattractive yellowish-green bruise that shadowed her jaw.

It could be worse, she thought wryly, dropping onto the bed. She could be dead.

In the corner of her room, Murphy made himself comfortable between Jax and Brody. No doubt happy that he was not relegated to his usual kennel for the night, the younger dog lay upside down, belly showing, legs in the air, snoring. Head resting on Brody's back and a foot splayed over Jax's, he wiggled in his sleep. Brody let out a huff, but both dogs, friendly to a fault, accepted Murphy—at least for the night.

Good. Laney wanted a peaceful night's sleep. She needed one, because she was starting to think things she shouldn't. Things about Grayson, about her future, about maybe reconnecting with her old purpose, her old mission.

She frowned, touching the old family Bible again.

She wanted what her grandfather and aunt had, what Grayson had.

"Please, just show me what you want me to do," she whispered.

Brody opened one eye, gave a quiet little yip.

She smiled, turning off the light and lying down. She didn't think she'd be able to fall asleep with the events of the past twenty-four hours swirling in her head, but she must have. The next thing she knew, someone was pounding on the door. Loudly.

"Laney? You awake?"

Grayson. She knew the voice, could hear the urgency in it as she tumbled out of bed and across the room, nearly killing herself as she tried to rush to the door. She flung it open. "What's going on? Is it Rose?

"No. Nothing like that."

"Then what?"

"I just got a call from Kent. We finally got the search warrant and entered David Rallings's house."

"Did they find anything?"

"They're still processing the scene, but a car registered to David Rallings Jr. was found on the premises. Inside, the television was blaring, and there was a half-eaten dinner on the table. The front door was open, screen door unlocked. No sign of Rallings or of foul play. Andrews figures that he was tipped off and knew they were coming for him."

"Okay." She wasn't sure why Grayson had thought it necessary to wake her to tell her that.

"There's more, Laney," he said, his expression grim. "Prince George's County Police are reporting a John Doe floating in the Patuxent River. Possible robbery victim. No wallet or ID on him."

Laney knew where this was going, and it wasn't good. "Rallings?"

"He fits the description, but the police haven't been able to find any family to identify him. They'll take prints at the morgue, but it will likely be tomorrow before they can search the databank and get a positive ID. I don't want to wait until tomorrow, Laney. If Rallings is dead, someone is afraid we're getting too close. If that's the case, there's every possibility the kids will be moved sooner rather than later."

"You want me to identify him, don't you?"

"I want you to do what feels comfortable and right. Identifying a body that's been in the water isn't pleasant, and I—"

"I've found drowning victims, Grayson. I've pulled them from rivers and ponds. Older people. Toddlers." They'd been the worst. They were the ones she hadn't been able to forget. "I think I can handle this."

He nodded, glancing at his watch. "I'll meet you in the family room. I need to call Andrews and tell him we'll be at the morgue before midnight."

Laney grabbed her oversize Colorado Search and Rescue sweatshirt from the closet, pulled it over her T-shirt, slipped into her shoes and followed him into the family room. He stood near the window, speaking quietly into his phone.

Arden was still on the couch, Grayson's laptop balanced on her thighs, several devices spread out on the coffee table. She had earbuds in and was bobbing her head to some song only she could hear. She didn't look up as Laney approached.

"Arden?" Laney touched Arden's shoulder, and Arden nearly jumped out of her skin.

"Wow! Man!" She tore the earbud from her left ear. "You scared me."

"Sorry, I just wanted to let you know I'm leaving with Grayson."

"Yeah. He told me," Arden responded, her gaze sliding back to the computer screen.

"I don't want to wake Rose to tell her. If she comes looking for me, can you let her know where I've gone?"

"Sure." Arden replaced the earbud and went back to work.

"Ready?" Grayson asked, shoving his phone into his pocket and taking Laney's elbow. "Andrews said he'll meet us at the morgue in twenty."

"What else did he say?"

"That the security guard who was at the hospital the night of the power outage may have skipped town. His girlfriend called the police to report that he never made it home from work last night. She's suspected him of cheating, so she went straight to the bank to clean their account out. Unfortunately, he'd already been there. Took every bit of the six hundred dollars they had and deposited it into a personal account." He paused as he opened the door and ushered her out onto the porch. "He also transferred ten thousand dollars that she had no idea was there. She was very willing and very able to give us a bank statement. The money was deposited by wire transfer. Half of it twenty minutes before the power outage. The rest after."

"Can Kent trace the transfer?"

"He did. It came from an overseas account. No way to find out who the account holder is. Andrews put out an APB on the security guard. Hopefully we can stop him before he goes too far underground."

"Or before he ends up in the Patuxent?"

"That, too."

The temperature had dropped, and dark rain clouds shadowed the moon. Laney could feel the moisture in the air. There'd be a storm soon. She hoped that wherever Olivia and the other kids were, they were warm and dry. More than that, she hoped that they'd be home soon. She *prayed* that they would, because she had nothing left but that. No power to change anything, no hope that identifying the body would bring them any closer to stopping the kidnappers. All she had was the feeling that maybe she'd spent her life putting her hope in the wrong things, that maybe she'd spent too much time believing in her own strength and power and not enough time relying on God's.

"Better get in," Grayson said as he opened the passenger door and helped her into his car. "The storm is almost on us."

He closed the door as the first raindrop fell.

The pelting rain made it difficult to drive as fast as Grayson would have liked. Even with the wipers swishing back and forth at full speed, visibility was still impaired. Laney was quiet in the seat next to him, her hands fisted in her lap.

"What are you thinking?" he asked, breaking the silence.

"That Olivia and the other two kids might be out in this mess."

"I doubt the kidnappers would risk the health of their sales product."

"Is that really all those kids are to them?"

"If it weren't, they'd never have taken them in the first place."

"That's sad."

"Lots of things in life are, but there's good stuff too. Like your dogs."

"And your sister."

"And food that Rose doesn't cook," he said, hoping to lighten her mood.

She laughed. "Poor Rose. She has an overinflated opinion of her cooking."

"She's a good lady, though."

"She is. I didn't see much of her while I was growing up. She and her husband were missionaries. She came home on furlough, but it wasn't enough for her to make a difference."

"Make a difference in what?" he asked, turning onto the main highway. They should be only ten minutes from the morgue, but it would take a little longer with the rain. Grayson hoped the medical examiner would stick around.

"My life," Laney said so softly that Grayson almost couldn't hear her. "She's always felt guilty about that. I think it's why she lives in the cottage instead of a retirement home with all her friends. She says she'd be bored there, but I know she'd be happy. Dozens of people around her all the time, plenty of things to do."

"You don't feel guilty about that, too, do you?"

She didn't respond, and he took her silence for assent. "Rose would tell you to get a grip. You know that, right?"

"Rose tells me lots of things. If I listened to all of them, I'd have blond hair and sixteen pairs of bright pink jeggings."

"And twenty of those fuzzy sweaters?"

"Exactly." She shifted in her seat, and he knew she was studying his profile. "Do you think they'll find anything at Rallings's house? Assuming he's dead, there's no hope of questioning him."

"Everyone leaves something behind." How valuable it would be remained to be seen, but Grayson was certain they would find something.

"They killed him because I identified him."

"Guilt again, Laney? Because it's totally misplaced. They killed him because he put their operation at risk."

In the center console, Grayson's phone vibrated, the name Ethan Conrad flashing on the dashboard media system. Grayson accepted the call. "Grayson here."

"Gray, it's Ethan. I got your message but was poring over the files you sent."

"I called to tell you to hold off, Ethan. The integrity of the files has come into question. My system's been hacked."

"Are you sure? Only a skilled hacker could get into the FBI system."

"Arden confirmed it."

"I guess you're sure, then. These guys may be more powerful than either of us imagined."

"I agree."

"It sounds like you're getting close. Be careful." Grayson could hear the concern in Ethan's voice.

"Don't worry, Ethan. I learned from the best. I can take care of myself."

"I know you can, but I think I'll take a trip out that way tomorrow and take a look at the police files on all the cases if you can set it up with the chief. Maybe I could talk to a few people, shake up a few leads."

"I think you'd be wasting your time, Ethan."

"Its possible, but I'd feel better doing something."

"Okay, I'll talk to the chief about it and call you in the morning."

"Sounds good." Ethan paused. "You're like a son to me, and I can't lose another one. Be safe." The connection ended before Grayson could respond.

"He sounds like he cares a lot about you," Laney commented.

"We go way back. He was my best friend's stepfather. Married Rick's mom when Rick was only seven. His own dad walked out on them when Rick was a toddler. Rick idolized Ethan, joined the bureau because of him."

"What happened to Rick?"

"Murdered. It was our first major case. We were both twenty-five. He called me and told me he'd had a breakthrough, but that it wasn't safe to talk over the phone."

Grayson remembered that night like it was yesterday, the loss of Rick and Andrea on the same day had been a blow he almost hadn't recovered from. He hadn't shared the story with many, but he had the sudden urge to tell Laney. He needed her to know. Understand how dangerous his life really was, not to him, but to those he loved.

"That night I'd picked up my fiancée from the elementary school where she worked. We'd been out for dinner and a movie, celebrating that the wedding planning was done and the date was in less than a month. I was on my way to drop her off at her parents' house when Rick called. He said it was important, sounded frantic. Andrea insisted we go, saying she'd wait in the car and grade some papers while Rick and I talked."

He glanced at Laney. Shadows of rain from the windshield ran over her face, and she looked soft and lovely, but strong in a way Andrea had never been. "When we got there, Rick was nowhere to be seen. I heard the first shot before it hit Andrea. It smashed through the passenger-side window. She fell into my lap, unconscious. Her blood…" He stopped himself. He could still smell the coppery scent of it. "It was an ambush. The second shot broke the windshield, narrowly missing me. The glass shards flew into my face."

"The scar over your eye?" she whispered.

"Yes."

"I drove to the hospital, only two blocks away. Andrea was still breathing, but the damage to her brain was irreversible. Telling her parents was the hardest thing I've ever had to do." They hadn't blamed him. Just cried for their daughter. "Her parents pulled her from life support that evening, after our families had said their goodbyes. She was twenty-three."

Later that night, after she was gone, her father had pulled him aside. *Find who did this to our girl, Gray. Find him and make him pay.*

"I'm so sorry, Grayson."

"I learned later that Rick was dead before we even arrived at the warehouse."

"Did you ever find out who did it?"

"Yes, no thanks to me. I was a basket case, but Ethan stepped in. He examined Rick's case files, traced his cell calls—he solved the case." And he'd made the guilty party pay.

"No wonder this case has him worried," she said.

"It has me worried, too, Lancy, but for different reasons."

They fell silent then to the rhythmic cadence of the rain and windshield wipers, each lost in thought.

He glanced in the rearview mirror. In the distance, lights from another vehicle were approaching from behind.

Fast.

Grayson's grip on the steering wheel tightened as he stepped on the accelerator. These weren't ideal conditions for evasive driving, but he'd work with what he had. The old Bowie Race Track was a half mile ahead. Used now as a practice track only, it would be locked up for the night, but he could pull in the drive to let the car pass. If he made it that far.

If not, there was a ditch on one side of the road and the Patuxent River on the other. Neither a good option.

He glanced in his rearview mirror again. The car was approaching at a dangerous speed. They weren't going to make it to the racetrack.

He eased up on the accelerator. One of three things was about to happen. The guy would swerve around them and speed on, he'd slam into the back of the sedan or he'd pull up beside them and fire off some shots.

Better for Grayson to keep his speed down and retain control of the car than for him to try to outrun the vehicle in these conditions.

"Grab my phone, Laney. I want you to call 911."

FOURTEEN

Laney fumbled for Grayson's cell phone, making the call as he navigated the dark, winding road. She glanced out the back window as she spoke to the 911 operator, doing everything she could to keep her voice calm, her thoughts clear.

There was definitely a car behind them. It was definitely gaining fast.

"Don't look back, Laney. Keep your eyes and head forward. Hold on to the armrest."

Controlling her panic, she did what he asked.

"Shouldn't you speed up? He's gaining."

"I will. I'm waiting for the right moment."

Trusting Grayson, she watched the road ahead, the phone falling from her hand as she clutched the armrest and center console.

Grayson's gaze rapidly switched from the road ahead to the rearview mirror and back again. "Here he comes!"

Grayson hit the accelerator and the car lurched forward as the other vehicle slammed into the bumper. The sedan fishtailed, but Grayson maintained control. They were in the center of the two lanes, a curve fast approaching. If another vehicle was coming around the bend, they'd be in serious trouble.

Grayson slowed, getting back in the right lane. "He's coming again."

The impact was stronger this time, the other driver catching on to Grayson's evasive tactics. The sedan accelerated around the corner, Grayson struggling to maintain control. The tires couldn't find traction on the wet pavement. The car spun out, coming to a stop sideways in the middle of the road. The other driver was coming right for them.

Grayson would take the brunt of the impact. "Look out!" Laney screamed.

Grayson stomped on the accelerator, angling the car back into the street and speeding forward just before impact. The other car slammed into the back fender of the much larger sedan.

Pop, pop, pop.

A bullet pierced the rear windshield, exiting through the rear passenger's side window.

Laney heard a fourth gunshot even as Grayson pushed her head to her knees.

"Keep down!" he shouted as he accelerated into the next curve. Two quick shots and the car fishtailed out of control.

"He's taken out the rear tire!"

Laney braced for impact as the sedan careened off the road and into thick foliage.

Grayson struggled to steer the car between two big trees, missing each by mere inches. Laney could only grip the armrest in horror, flinching as branches and leaves smacked the car and windshield. The car jostled down the embankment, sideswiping a large tree and mowing down saplings before skidding sideways, the passenger's side slamming into a fallen tree, air bags exploding.

Grayson looked over his shoulder; Laney followed his stare. The other car's headlights were above them, at the road's edge.

"You have the cell phone?" Grayson asked, his voice calm.

"I dropped it!" She sounded nearly hysterical. She took a deep breath, tried to calm her frantic breathing.

"Check the floor. See if you can find it."

She did what he asked, reaching through pebble-like pieces of broken glass. There! She felt the smooth surface and rectangular shape of the phone.

"Found it!" Laney thrust it into his hands.

As he zipped it into his jacket pocket, Laney shoved at her door with everything she had. "It's wedged against a tree. Does yours open?"

He tried it. "No, it's jammed." He grabbed her hand, squeezed gently. "We'll go out through the window. Hurry."

Cold rain pelted her face and hands as she exited the vehicle and nearly fell headfirst into the roots of the fallen tree. Grayson squeezed out the window after her.

"Where—" she started to ask, but he pressed his fingers over her lips.

"Listen." He breathed the word near her ear, the sound more air than anything.

She froze, tried to hear above the frantic pounding of her heart.

Branches cracked, leaves crackled.

Someone was coming.

Grayson's hand slid from her lips, slipped down her

shoulder and her arm until their hands met, their fingers linked. He didn't speak, barely made a sound as he led her quickly away from the car. The pouring rain muffled any noise they made, and she thought that maybe they had a chance of escaping.

There was no light. Nothing to guide their steps. Her eyes tried to adjust to the darkness, but the shadowy trees hid roots and rocks and fallen branches that seemed determined to trip her.

More than once, Laney stumbled over the unforgiving terrain.

They headed downhill, away from their pursuer and toward the Patuxent River. Rushing water drowned any sound of their pursuer but served to mask Laney and Grayson's progress, as well. Somewhere in the distance, sirens screamed. The police must be on their way.

She wasn't sure they'd arrive in time.

As close as she and Grayson were to civilization, they were cut off from everything.

Grayson pulled out his cell phone, "No signal," he muttered, shoving it back into his pocket. He tugged her close, pressed his lips to her ear, his breath warm against her chilled skin. "When we reach the bend in the river, we'll head up. There's help on the road. I can hear the sirens."

She nodded, clutching his hand as he led her around a curve in the river. From there, they climbed through thick foliage, clutching branches and trees to boost themselves up the steep, rain-soaked ravine.

Leaves had begun to fall for the season, making the ground cover slippery. Laney's feet went out from under her, and Grayson tightened his grip, pulling her back up.

The sound of sirens grew louder, but Laney could

barely hear them. She was panting too loudly, her lungs screaming, her head pounding.

She'd thought she'd recovered from her concussion, but her climb up the hill was proving otherwise. What should have been easy was agonizingly difficult, her feet sticking to the ground with every step, her arms shaking as she tried to pull herself up.

Grayson stopped short, Laney bumping into him from behind.

"What—"

"Shh," he cautioned, pulling her around so that they were side by side.

And she saw the problem.

She couldn't miss it.

Eight feet high with six inches of barbed wire across the top, the chain link fence might as well have been Mount Everest.

"We have to go back," she hissed.

"We have to go over, the race track is on the other side of this fence," he responded, scaling the fence easily and tossing his jacket over the barbed wire. "Come on," he urged, reaching down for her hand.

If he'd been anyone else, she would have said no. If he'd been anyone else, she would have come up with her own plan and trusted it to get her out of the trouble they were in.

But her gut was telling her she could trust Grayson. If there was a way out, he would find it.

She was feeling weak. She wasn't sure she could make it, but she climbed the first few links of the fence and managed to grab his hand.

Behind her, something crashed loudly in the brush.

She panicked, trying to scramble up, her feet slipping

from the fence, her body dangling as Grayson clutched her hand and kept her from tumbling down.

"Get your feet back on the fence," he barked, and she somehow managed to do it.

Seconds later, she was beside him, looking straight into his eyes.

"This is the hard part," he murmured, his gaze jumping to some point beyond her shoulder. "I'll go over first, and then I'll help you. If you don't move fast, that barbed wire is going to slice through the jacket and into your skin. Be careful!'

He was over the fence in a heartbeat, and then it was her turn. She grabbed the barbed wire, wincing as it dug into her hands.

"Move fast. The weight of your body is going to sink that barb in deeper if you don't," Grayson encouraged her from the other side of the fence.

She nodded, her brain finally kicking in, all the panic suddenly gone. She'd done similar acts before, scaling rock walls to find the missing, climbing fences to check ponds and quarries. Only this time, the safety ropes were nonexistent, and there was a gun-toting maniac behind her.

The movement in the brush was growing closer, and it was human.

Grayson could hear whoever it was stopping every now and again to listen for signs of its quarry. Laney was scaling the fence more slowly than he would have hoped, but he was mostly relieved she'd made it this far. Her breathing had been labored during their ascent to the fence. It was obvious she was tired. But she never complained. Not one word. She just attempted to stick with him as if her life depended on it.

And it probably did.

Laney precariously straddled the jacket-covered barbed wire.

"Easy…" he cautioned, putting a hand on her arm as she maneuvered her second leg over.

The sound of their pursuer grew louder with every passing moment. He wanted to hurry Laney along, drag her down the fence and onto the solid ground.

If she fell, though, she could break a leg, sprain an ankle, slowing them even further.

She finally got solid footing on the links on the other side of the fence, then reached for the jacket and tugged.

"Just leave it," he hissed. "They're coming!"

"Your phone…" She gave the jacket one more firm tug and it broke free, but the jerking motion sent Laney careening backward.

He grabbed her shoulder, nearly losing his grip on the fence as he caught her.

A branch cracked in the woods on the other side of the fence, and Grayson was sure he saw a sapling sway.

"Let's go!" He scrambled down the fence, then reached for Laney's waist. "I've got you. Drop!"

At once, she released her grasp, falling into his arms, just as a quick pop sent a bullet whizzing by his head.

"Go!" He pulled his own gun, firing off a shot as he shouted for Laney to run. She took off, and he followed, zigzagging through the thick stand of trees that bordered the fence and surrounded the racetrack on all sides. Emerging from the trees, they sprinted across tall grass, coming upon a three-and-a-half-foot wooden railing surrounding the dirt racetrack. Laney was already tumbling over to the other side of it as Grayson reached her.

Across from them, the starting gates and now-rickety spectator stands stood sentry, shadows of a once-popular winter racing venue.

"Hurry. We need to get across the track and find cover. I hope the police heard the gunshots and are heading this way."

They made it to the center of the track, unkempt with overgrown grass and weeds. The footing was uneven in places, holes in the ground threatening to twist an ankle, but they didn't slow their pace until they'd crossed the muddy track again and reached the next wooden rail. By the time their pursuers had cleared the stand of trees, Laney and Grayson were out of range. Grayson could see them racing toward the railing, two dark figures against the gray night.

Ducking behind the empty spectator bleachers, Grayson took stock of the situation. There was really no good place to hide. Every structure surrounding the track allowed entry from too many directions, and with two men after them, that left too many opportunities for ambush.

Beside him, Laney tried to catch her breath.

"Can you make it to the covered horse bridge?" he asked, pointing to the shadowy structure at the top of the hill, behind the bleachers.

She nodded, pushing a strand of wet hair from her eyes. "I can make it."

"Okay. I'm going to distract them. On my signal, you head for the bridge. Wait for me there. If we can get to the stables on the other side of Race Track Road, we'll have a better shot of getting a jump on them rather than the other way around." Putting on his jacket, Grayson removed his phone. "Take my phone. When you reach the bridge, check for a signal. If you get one, call Andrews and tell him to let the local police know that we're at the racetrack. They're looking for us, but if they don't look in the right place…" He didn't finish. There was no need. Laney knew what was at stake.

The men had already reached the overgrown center of the oval track and were steadily gaining on them.

"Let's give them a reason to proceed with caution," Grayson muttered, taking aim at the lower leg of the closest man. He wanted them alive, because he wanted whatever information he could get from them.

He wanted to live more. He wanted Laney to live.

One shot in the leg, and the guy went down. The other guy dropped too.

"Go!" he commanded Laney, firing a shot at the ground near the second guy's head.

Laney ran, sure that she had a huge glow-in-the-dark target plastered to her back.

At any second she expected to feel a bullet sear through her flesh.

She heard the loud pop of another shot as she reached the wooden bridge. Built nearly thirty years ago, it served as safe passage for Thoroughbred horses and their trainers across busy Race Track Road. The bridge was separated down the middle by a tall fence. Signs marking the exit and entrance gave clear directions to those passing through.

Laney veered to the right, choosing the entrance sign. Since Thoroughbred horses tend to be skittish, there were no windows in the bridge. Completely protected from the elements on all sides with the exception of the entrance and exit, the structure was eerily dark inside. Her footsteps echoed across the dry wood, breaking the silence as she pulled out Grayson's phone, checking for signal. Three bars. Better than none.

Making her way to the other side of the bridge, she dialed Kent's number. A shot rang out, startling her; she could only hope it was Grayson doing the shooting. Heart racing, she peered around the corner of the bridge. Shadows of the now-empty stables loomed directly ahead and to her left, a parking lot to her right. She hit the call button, putting the phone to her ear. It rang once, twice, a third time.

"Please. Please pick up." Laney whispered to the darkness.

"Andrews here."

"Kent, it's Laney."

"Laney, where are you? We expected you twenty minutes ago."

"In the covered bridge on Race Track Road and headed for the stables. We were shot at and our car was driven off the road and into an embankment. We left the car and were followed to the racetrack. We heard sirens close by. I called 911, but I don't think they know exactly where we are."

"Is DeMarco with you?"

"He's trying to keep the gunmen from advancing on us." The words were rushed, frantic-sounding even to her own ears, but she wasn't certain how much time she'd have before she'd need to take off for the stables.

"How many gunmen?"

"Two." Laney lowered her voice. Footsteps pounding on the dirt indicated someone was approaching the bridge. Fast. Was it Grayson or someone else?

"I've got to go. Someone's coming."

She disconnected the call.

Holding her breath and pressing herself into a dark corner of the bridge, she waited, watching the entrance, praying Grayson was the one who'd appear.

Finally, a shadow appeared, tall, broad, moving with a confidence she recognized immediately.

"Thank You, God!" she whispered, rushing to Grayson, throwing herself into his arms.

She wasn't sure who was more surprised. Her or Grayson.

His hands settled on her back, his fingers sliding across her spine.

"You okay?" he asked, his breath ruffling the air near her ear.

"Yes. And I got the call out to Kent."

"Good, but we're not out of danger. One of the guys is wounded, but he and his buddy are still on the move," Grayson whispered, pulling her in the direction of the stables. "If the police know our location, we just have to hold the perps off until help arrives."

Water pooled in small divots and dips in the ground as they left the bridge behind, the saturated ground sucking at Laney's soaked running shoes, leaving an easily traceable impression in the earth.

"We're leaving footprints," she whispered, following Grayson into the first of the two stables in the far corner of the training facility. Smelling of wood and hay, the interior was mostly dry, its windows having been shuttered against the elements.

"I know. I'm hoping they'll follow our tracks into

this stable and waste time searching for us in here—we're headed out the back and will hide in the next stable over."

Huddling in one corner of the hayloft, arms wrapped around her legs, knees drawn to her chin, Laney strained to hear signs of their pursuers. Grayson's jacket, resting over her shoulders where he left it before taking his place in a stall below, offered necessary warmth, but she still shivered slightly with fear. A few minutes ago, the men had burst into the first stable. She had clearly heard doors slamming and wood banging, then nothing.

The hayloft, now mostly empty, spanned the middle of the stable, allowing hay to be thrown down from both sides into the walkway below. Grayson had placed a loose piece of plywood in front of her, leaning it against the wall, near other boards, tools and buckets. From her hiding place, she was just able to turn her head left and right, having a clear view of both rear and front of the stable. Below her, Grayson was hidden in shadows.

The front door creaked open. A man ducked in, pressing himself to the darkened corner of the wall. Remaining still, Laney controlled her breathing and waited. Grayson had explained that he wanted to catch one or both men alive. This was potentially a chance for them to get another lead in the case.

Laney trained her gaze on the man's position. Unmoving, he stood as if waiting. Hair prickled on the back of Laney's neck, and she turned just in time to see the second man drop soundlessly through an unshuttered window toward the back of the stable.

An ambush. Did Grayson know?

There was no way to warn him without giving her

position away. Laney looked around for something, anything to arm herself with. Settling on a heavy rubber-ended mallet, she crept from her hiding place to the edge of the loft, Grayson's jacket sliding soundlessly from her shoulders. Peering down, she kept the second man in sight. A scuffling commotion behind her was met with a gunshot. Then another.

The second man rushed forward, gun drawn. It was probably an eight-foot drop, but Laney didn't hesitate. Pulling herself to a crouching position, hammer in hand, she leapt for him. He caught sight of her at the last minute, trying to duck while pointing his gun at her, but Laney's momentum carried her forward too fast, her knees slamming into his chest. They fell to the ground, his gun clattering against the stable wall, his body cushioning Laney's fall.

She scampered off him, trying to elude him. His calloused hand grasped her wrist, pulling her back toward him. Hammer in hand, she turned, intending to bring it down on his head. Raising his forearm, he blocked the blow, yelling in pain as the hammer smashed against bone.

Behind her, a gun exploded, its echo merging with the sound of screaming sirens. Outside the stable, car doors slammed and a dog barked.

Help had finally arrived.

Grayson rushed forward, yanked Laney back, and pointed his firearm at the attacker. "Don't move!"

In that moment, both the front and back doors of the stable burst open.

"Police. Drop your weapons!"

Laney froze, dropping her mallet.

"FBI!" Grayson shouted, throwing one hand in the

air and slowly placing his gun on the ground. "Don't shoot!"

Kent Andrews and five officers converged on the scene, guns drawn.

"You two okay?" Kent asked, his gun trained on the man who lay on the floor.

"Barely," Grayson muttered, lifting his gun from the ground.

That's when the gunman moved, his hand snaking out as he reached for his weapon.

"He's going for his gun!" Laney cried.

The guy rolled to his side, the gun clutched tightly in his hand, his eyes gleaming.

Grayson shouted Laney's name, tackling her to the ground as the first bullet flew.

A quick succession of returned fire from the officers ended before Laney and Grayson had even hit the ground.

FIFTEEN

The rain had subsided, leaving in its place a cold chill that permeated the thick evening air. Grayson felt it to his bones as he led Laney out of the Prince George's County Morgue.

Despite the jacket he'd thrown over her shoulders, she was shivering violently, her teeth chattering as they walked into the parking lot.

He'd managed to keep her from being shot. Barely.

Grayson was worried. With three dead suspects, a probable arsonist on the run, a stolen car and one jailbird refusing to sing, Grayson was pinning his hopes on the idea that the search of David Rallings Jr.'s residence would yield some new clue. "You doing okay?" he asked, and Laney nodded.

"Aside from being half frozen to death, I'm fine."

"I may be able to help you with that," he responded, and she eyed him dubiously.

"If you're talking about a repeat of that hug—"

Her comment was so surprising, he laughed. "I wasn't, but now that you mentioned it, I don't think I'd mind a repeat performance."

"Grayson—"

"Tell you what," he said, reaching Andrews's police cruiser and popping the trunk. "How about we just worry about getting you warm?" The chief had given him the keys and told him that he and Laney could wait in the car. It had been as obvious to him as it had been to Grayson that Laney was at the end of what she could handle. She'd identified the deceased, answered a couple of dozen questions. Now she needed to be bundled up in a blanket and left alone.

Grayson grabbed a blanket from the emergency kit in the back of Andrews's car and wrapped it around her shoulders.

She didn't speak as he opened the passenger door and eased her into the front seat.

"Laney?" He touched her hand. It was ice-cold, her complexion so pallid he was surprised she was still conscious.

"I told you, I'm fine." But her voice broke, and she turned away, a single tear sliding down her cheek.

He closed the door, then walked around the car, slipping into the driver's seat.

Grayson started the car and got the heat going, then turned toward Laney.

"It's okay to cry after you see something like that."

"I'm not crying." She swiped another tear from her cheek.

"Your eyes are just leaking all over your face?"

"Something like that," she responded with a trembling smile.

"Do you want to tell me why?" he asked.

"I like you, Grayson. You know that?"

"You sound surprised."

"Maybe I am. I guess I didn't expect to…" She shrugged.

"What?"

"Ever meet someone who was as passionate about what he does as I am about what I do. You were great tonight. Calm and smart."

"Not smart enough. Both our perps are dead. I wanted to bring them in alive."

"I'd rather have you alive. And me." She shivered and tugged the blanket closer around her shoulders.

"You didn't answer my question," he prodded.

"About why I'm crying? I guess it's because three men are dead. They weren't good men, but they were human beings. And I guess it's also because I'm worried that their deaths mean we'll never find Olivia and the other children."

"It's not your job to find them," he reminded her gently, taking her hands, holding them between both of his, trying to warm them.

"Maybe it is, Grayson. If I had a location, I could take Jax and we could—"

"Laney, you don't have to be the responsible one all the time."

"I don't know how to be any other way," she replied softly.

"How about, just for now, you close your eyes and trust me to take care of the situation? I won't let you down." Even as the words rolled off his tongue, he knew he shouldn't have said them. He couldn't make any promises or guarantees. Not even for a night.

But deep down, he felt the need to say them. He wanted her to feel safe. More than that, he wanted to protect her. The alternative was unthinkable.

Chief Andrews rapped on the glass near Grayson's head, and he opened the door and got out. "Everything taken care of?"

"The medical examiner is getting prints from the deceased. Neither was carrying identification." Andrews looked tired, his eyes deeply shadowed. "I'll get you two back to Laney's place. She needs her rest. I'm afraid you'll have to ride in the back."

"No problem." Grayson slid into the back of the cruiser.

"You have any idea who knew you were coming out here tonight?" Andrews asked as he pulled out of the parking lot.

"Could have been someone at your office. Could have been someone with the FBI. Which means we're right back where we started."

"I just don't get it. The shooter is dead. The accomplice can't be identified through the facial recognition system. And even if we find a match later, the damage is done. Laney's already given us all the information she knows. Why continue to try to harm her?"

"I don't think it's just about Laney anymore. I believe we're getting close to the guy who's calling the shots. He's trying to buy time whatever way possible."

"You could be right," Andrews agreed. "If they can take out the lead investigator and the only material witness to the crime at the same time, the investigation could be set back a day or two."

"Just enough time to get the required number of children needed for the next delivery and stick with the pre-arranged shipping plans," Grayson said.

"It's also possible there's something significant in

Rallings's place. We've got someone looking through his computer files now."

"I'm really hoping you're right, Andrews. But either way, I have a feeling we're on the verge of breaking this case wide open."

The ride home was short and, thankfully, uneventful. The house was dark as they pulled up to it. A patrol car guarded in the driveway. A black sedan was also in the driveway, its occupants concealed behind tinted windows. The FBI protection detail had arrived.

Laney didn't wait until Grayson and Kent got out of the car. She opened her door and hurried up the front steps. The door opened before she reached it. Arden stood silhouetted in the opening.

"Looks like you lived," she said without preamble.

"Yes. I guess we did." Laney sidled past her, the dogs wagging their tails happily as she entered the house.

"I heard all about it on the news. Crazy stuff. Bullets flying and two people dead. Called the chief to see if you and Grayson were involved. Glad it wasn't you or my brother in those body bags." She retreated to the couch and the laptop, shoving earbuds back in her ears.

Laney left her there. She wasn't in the mood for conversation. She was tired and cold. Thankfully, Rose was in bed, her door closed. Laney crept past the guest room and walked into her own.

Jax followed her, dropping down on the floor near the foot of her bed. She knelt down, putting her arms around his furry neck. He whined softly, and she knew he sensed her mood, felt the same need for action that she did.

"For someone who's nearly frozen, you move fast," Grayson said from the doorway.

"The car ride warmed me up."

"And what didn't get warm from the ride, Jax is taking care of?" He sat down next to her on the floor, his body close enough that she could share his warmth too. "He's a good-looking dog."

"I think so. The pick of the litter, and a gift from a team member." Remembering eight-week-old Jax brought a smile to her face. "Jeremy's mom bred Aussies. Jax's play drive was so good, even at eight weeks old, that Jeremy convinced his mom to let me have him."

"That was a generous thing to do."

"Yes. It was. She still sends me Christmas cards every year, and I send her pictures of Jax on his birthday."

"No pictures for Jeremy?"

"Jeremy died two years ago." She was quiet for a minute after that, thankful that Grayson didn't interrupt the silence, that he let her have the time to pull her thoughts together. It gave her the strength to continue. "We were best friends all through college, and he joined me in search-and-rescue training because he was jealous of the time I spent there. He was the flanker on my team. One of the best I ever had. Later he qualified with his own dog."

"Sounds like a good guy."

"He was."

"And after he died, you didn't want to work search and rescue anymore."

"I didn't, but not just because of him." She hesitated. This wasn't something she spoke about. Ever. But

Jax's warm weight rested against her left side and Grayson's warm presence was to her right, and the words just spilled out. "I lost two other team members that day. It shouldn't have happened. We were on a routine search—three hikers had been reported lost on the peak. The conditions were good for a find that day. The temperatures were relatively mild."

It had started like any other search. Working with local law enforcement, she'd mapped the search sectors based on the victims' supposed area of travel. "Tanya and Lee were Jeremy's flankers that day. Ironically, when I mapped the sectors, I took the steeper, more treacherous sector because Tanya was three months pregnant and tired a little more easily. I was working the east perimeter of my sector, which bordered Jeremy's sector, when I heard the first rumbling echoes of the avalanche. I called a warning to the team and base," Laney's voice broke. "But it happened so fast, not everyone was able to clear the area."

His arm slid around her shoulders, and he pulled her closer to his side. "You can't blame yourself for that."

"I try not to, but there's no one else to blame," she responded, her hand lying on Jax's soft head, her head resting against Grayson's shoulder.

"There is no one to blame. Nature is a hard taskmaster. There isn't a search-and-rescue professional alive who doesn't know it."

He was right. Her head knew it, but her heart was a different story.

Taking a breath, she fought to control her emotions, still raw after all this time. "It's easy to say when it isn't your team. I've heard it from everyone, and I still can't forget that I was the one who put them in that position and that I lived while they died."

"I don't think they would want things to be different," Grayson said, smoothing hair from her cheek, his fingers warm against her skin. "As a matter of fact, if they were standing in your shoes, if they were the ones who'd lived and you'd died, they'd be mourning your loss, wishing they could have taken your place."

"But they aren't here, Grayson," she said, and the tears she'd been holding back spilled out. "I am, and I can still remember every minute of the search, every second that ticked by in my head. I can remember digging them out and trying so desperately to breathe life back into them." Laney wiped the tears from her eyes, but the vivid memory of that day stayed with her, a picture in her mind, unblurred by her tears and not lessened by time.

Grabbing Laney's shoulders, Grayson turned her to face him, pulling her into a silent embrace. The soft scent of rain and pine trees mingled with a hint of aftershave. Relaxing into him, her tears fell freely. Tears for Jeremy, Tanya and Lee. Tears for herself. For the first time, she let someone else share the enormous weight of their deaths. Not just anyone, but Grayson. A stranger to her a mere day ago, yet her life was now inexplicably tied to his.

"Do you think I don't understand?" he asked gently. "After Andrea died, everyone told me it wasn't my fault. That everything would be okay. But the truth is, I knew it wasn't my fault. And yet I couldn't help feeling her safety and well-being were my responsibility. I had promised her forever when I gave her that ring, and we never got a chance to start our lives together—

to raise the children she always wanted. It wasn't okay. Her death will never be okay. There will always be a place in my heart for her, and I'll always carry regrets. But I've learned to give them to God. Not to dwell on them. Not to lie in bed at night, reliving that day, playing the 'what if?' game. I've grown stronger through her life and death—Andrea wouldn't have wanted it any other way."

He pulled back and looked into her eyes, gently brushing tears from her cheeks.

"You honor your friends every day by your strength, your kindness and your life. Let God bear the burden of their deaths while you rejoice in what you shared together. The good times. Not the bad ones."

Looking into his ocean-blue eyes, Laney could almost believe that was possible.

SIXTEEN

Morning came quickly. The antique grandfather clock in the corner chimed 6:00 a.m., but a soft clatter from the kitchen and the scent of coffee brewing told Grayson he wasn't the first to wake. Yawning, he rose from the couch and stretched. Some coffee would do him good. He'd had a restless sleep, haunted by nightmares and memories, and by the nagging feeling that he was missing something.

He'd spent a couple of hours looking through his files again, familiarizing himself with every word, making a list of every cataloged clue, every person who'd worked on each case, every interview, hoping that when the originals were faxed to him, it would be easier to pick out deleted information. He'd start making phone calls to Boston and California this morning, both local PD and the original FBI case agents. Hopefully he'd have the files in his hands this afternoon.

In the kitchen, Rose looked up from her task of pouring herself a cup of coffee.

"Here." She held the cup out. "It looks like you need this worse than I do. I'll pour myself another."

"Do I look that rough?"

She laughed, green eyes twinkling. "Well, let's just say you look as if a good, strong cup of coffee and a shower wouldn't hurt."

"Well, what a coincidence, because I was just thinking about both."

"Were you thinking about a slice of coffee cake? I've got some right here."

He hesitated, and she laughed again. "No worries, Gray. It's not homemade."

"I wasn't—"

"Of course you were." She cut a slice of coffee cake and put it on a plate. "Everyone who knows me knows I can't cook. I'm not one to give up, so I keep trying. Plus—" she looked around and lowered her voice "—I love to see the expressions on people's faces when they bite into something I bake. And watching them try to dispose of the food while I'm not looking? Priceless!"

"You're incorrigible, Rose," he said, sipping the coffee and letting the hot, bitter brew wipe away some of his fatigue.

"I am," she responded. "But I like you. So I won't make you eat any more of my homemade treats."

"Do I smell coffee?" Laney came around the corner into the kitchen, dressed in her work gear, hair pulled back in a high ponytail. Jax, Brody and Murphy were at her heels.

"Good morning, love," Rose said cheerfully. "I just made a pot, and I've got coffee cake to go with it. Fresh from Safeway. That sweet little Willow took my car and bought some groceries last night. There are a lot of mouths to feed in this house."

"You're up early, considering you didn't get to bed

until after one this morning," Grayson commented as Laney sat at the table.

"You're one to talk," she countered. "You were still clicking away on your computer when I finally dozed off."

He nodded to concede the point. "What are your plans for today?"

"Bria is coming by this morning to help with the dogs. I need to run the board-and-trains through their paces today. I really don't like skipping a training day. I told Riley to take a few days off." Adding a generous portion of cream and sugar to her coffee, she took a sip. "You?"

"Well, after last night's incident, I don't have a car. The FBI is supposed to send me another one when the protection detail shift change occurs. But you're stuck with me until then."

The back door slid open and Arden entered, carting a backpack full of equipment and her laptop. Dropping her bags on the ground by the table, she barely remembered to say hello before starting in. "Is there any coffee cake left, Rose? I tried a piece last night, and it was delicious. Since my brother is a pig when it comes to things like cake, I thought I'd better hurry over before he finished it."

"I'm surprised *you* didn't finish it off last night, Arden," Grayson said as Rose placed a piece of coffee cake on a plate in front of her.

"I would have," Arden said, "but Willow told me she'd cut off both my hands if I touched it again before morning."

"You left for Rose's cottage before Laney and I were

done talking, so I didn't get a chance to ask you what you found."

"Well, I haven't identified the hacker yet, but I'm pretty sure he's a hacker for hire."

"How do you know?" Grayson was almost afraid to ask since it was early, and Arden's technical speak could be quite off-putting at times.

"Well, he used some very sophisticated binary obfuscation techniques to prohibit reverse engineering that could identify the original malware commands and potentially lead to his identity. Fortunately for you, I'm familiar with all of the techniques used. Even more fortunately for you, one of the techniques can be traced to only four people in the world."

"How could you possibly know that?"

"Because I created it, and I limited distribution with a signed nondisclosure agreement."

Grayson was starting to get excited—he didn't know much about binary obfuscation or reverse engineering techniques, but he understood that the pool of potential hackers just got a whole lot smaller. "So, are you telling me that we can narrow the hacker down to three people?"

"I'm telling you we can narrow the release of the technique to three people. One could be the hacker, but it is just as feasible that one of them could have sold the technique illegally, in violation of the ten-year nondisclosure agreement."

"Well, that still seems promising."

"It is. I need to analyze my findings this morning, and I should have a name for you early this afternoon."

Getting up from his chair, he hugged Arden, then kissed her on the cheek. "Way to go, kid. I knew you would come through for me." His sister blushed under his public display of affection.

"Don't blow it out of proportion, Gray. You know Mom would kill me if I left you hanging—and Dad might help."

"I love you, too, sis." he countered, winking.

Winking back, she polished off the last bit of her slice of coffee cake. "All that late-night work sure did build up my appetite, Rose. I don't suppose you'd mind giving me another piece of that cake?"

Rose snorted, cutting another slice and placing it on Arden's plate. "Are you ever not hungry, child?"

"No. I don't think so."

Grayson laughed, stretching. "The apple definitely didn't fall far from the tree. Everyone in our family likes to eat. I'm going to hit the shower."

He turned to Laney, leaning down so that he could speak close to her ear. "Wait for me before you head to the kennels. I'll only be a minute."

Grayson's "minute" turned into thirty. Good thing Bria wasn't scheduled to arrive until seven.

Laney sipped her second cup of coffee, picking at the coffee cake that Rose had set in front of her. She wasn't hungry, but she knew she needed to eat. She had a lot to do, and doing it without nourishment would be foolish.

"My brother thinks highly of you," Arden said through a mouthful of toast. "What do you think of him?"

"Not very tactful, are you?" Smiling, Rose sipped her coffee. Then she turned to Laney. "But, since I'm curious, too, I won't chastise you for it."

A blush crept into Laney's cheeks. The answer

should be simple, really. She hardly knew Grayson. He was obviously a good agent. A man of strong faith. A solid, dependable person willing to put his life on the line for her. She should feel respect for him—and nothing more.

"Umm… I think he's great?" It came out as a question. Stuffing her mouth with a bite of the coffee cake, Laney hoped to avoid another uncomfortable question.

"Good." Arden smiled with a conspiring glance at Rose.

Laney didn't like the direction she thought this conversation was about to take. It was hard enough to get the upper hand with Aunt Rose, but Laney suspected Arden would give her aunt a run for her money. She was thankful when a knock at the door set the dogs off. She excused herself to answer it.

"Good morning, Laney. Is Grayson up?" Kent asked, stepping into the house.

"He's in the shower."

"Not anymore." Grayson rounded the corner of the hallway, towel-drying his hair and carrying his dirty clothes. "What's up, Andrews?"

"There's been a development. I'm on my way to the scene of a possible kidnapping. The MO is different, but I'm not taking any chances. Deputy Wallace is en route, and I've got units dispatched. We've called in the Greater Maryland Region Search and Rescue Team. Since you're not due to get your replacement vehicle until later this morning, I thought I'd check to see if you want to ride along."

"I'm not sure I'm comfortable leaving Laney here."

"You need to go," Laney cut in. There was no way she wanted him babysitting her when he should be out in the field rescuing an abducted child. "I'll be fine. There are two FBI agents and two officers outside."

Grayson hesitated, then nodded. "Okay. Tell me what the situation is, Andrews."

"A group of fifth graders was on an overnight field trip at Arlington Echo last night. Four kids woke up before their chaperone and snuck out to find some poison ivy to shove in another kid's shoe."

"Nice," Laney said.

"Yeah. Not. One of the kids, ten-year-old Carson Proctor, got separated from his buddies. They were calling to him, trying to help him find the way back, when he started yelling for help. The other kids saw him being carted off into the woods."

"Arlington Echo is more than two hundred acres of forest," Laney said. "The kidnapper was on foot. He could still be out there with the boy. How many resources is the search and rescue team bringing?"

"Unfortunately, they have only two deployable dogs in the state right now. Seems the rest of the team is in New Jersey at the National Search and Rescue Conference. My guys are going to act as flankers since there's no telling if the guy is armed," Kent responded.

"Two dogs are not enough dogs to cover all that ground."

"We're calling other teams in the area, Laney. It's just going to take time to get them here."

"We don't have time," she responded, her heart thudding painfully.

Laney knew what she had to do, but she was almost too scared to say it.

She took a deep breath, thinking about what Grayson had told her. She couldn't keep mourning her team members' deaths. She had to start celebrating their lives. The best way to do it was to carry on with the work they'd been doing when they'd died. "I'm bringing Jax out of retirement."

"Since when?" Grayson asked, his gaze sharp.

"Since right this minute." She opened the hall closet, pulling out an orange Coaxsher search and rescue pack. "I've got my ready pack here. I just need to fill the water bladder and I'll be set to go." She did it quickly, ignoring her aunt's questioning look and Arden's incessant chatter. Ignoring Grayson's worried look and Kent's excited one.

"Tell Bria I was called away, Aunt Rose. Tell her to feed the dogs. I'll be back when I can."

Laney grabbed a red lead off a hook in the closet.

The situation was critical. They needed to find the child, and the kidnapper, and they needed to do it quickly. Laney was pretty sure that if they missed this opportunity, it might be too late for Olivia and the rest of the children as well.

But she was scared out of her mind, terrified that she'd make a wrong decision, cause someone to be injured or killed.

She had to trust herself.

No. She had to trust God. He'd see her through this.

She wanted to believe that.

She would believe it.

"Jax, come."

Jax darted to her and sat at her feet, immediately giving her all his attention. Fastening the lead on his collar, she looked at Murphy and Brody.

"Sorry, boys, not today." Then she followed Grayson and Kent out to the patrol car.

* * *

The patrol-car sirens and lights were blasting as the cruiser sped down Route 2 toward Arlington Echo. The FBI detail was ill-equipped for a search, so they stayed behind to watch for signs of trouble at the house. Laney was quietly looking out the window as the scenery whizzed by. Jax, his head resting on her lap, was sprawled across the backseat. Laney absently petted his silky ears.

Grayson wondered what Laney must be feeling, headed to a search for the first time since the avalanche. From the tension in her face, he guessed whatever she felt, it wasn't good.

They reached Arlington Echo in under ten minutes and pulled into the lot where a table had been set up as a base. To Grayson, the scene looked a little disorganized, perhaps even chaotic. There were children, camp counselors and adult chaperones standing around the perimeter of the woods behind a line of bright orange flagging tape. Men and women in uniform stood near the table and milled around the parking lot.

They were waiting for direction, and apparently Laney planned to be the one to give it.

She jumped out of the car and hurried to the table. She had a compass hanging from her belt, along with a map pouch and a bottle of what looked like baby powder.

It took her about ten seconds to get people organized.

Two other dog handlers were suddenly at the table, photocopied pictures of the missing boy in their hands, listening as Laney explained how they'd sector off the area.

Grayson watched with interest as the dog handlers

studied their maps, jotting notes on pads small enough to stuff in the pockets of tactical pants.

Andrews approached the group, giving clear-cut rules for engagement. They weren't just dealing with a missing child. They were dealing with a kidnapper.

The chief gave out the assignments. "Sector one is for team one, composed of Kensington, DeMarco and Reese. Sector two is team two with Collins, Gentry and Pinkerton. And sector three is team three with Henderson, Graft, Wilfred and Davis. Any questions?"

"Which comms channel will you broadcast from?" The question was asked by a member of the volunteer search and rescue team.

"Set your radios to channel two. Maintain radio silence as much as possible. The suspect doesn't want to be found. If he hears you, he will go into hiding—or worse, he'll go for an attack. You need to be clue-aware, look for fresh tracks, articles of clothing, anything that could belong to our suspect or victim. Okay, unless there are any questions, I need you to get started," Andrews said, dismissing the group.

Grayson made his way over to Laney. She'd spread out her map on the car hood and was marking a point on it. Glancing over her shoulder, he could see she had drawn a circle for base. "Looks like I'm with you," he said.

"Can you find our other team member? I think his name is Reese. I want to go over our search strategy and get started quickly."

"I'm right here." An armed parks and recreation officer approached, a small pack on his back. He introduced himself, "I'm David Reese.

Laney stepped forward, extending her hand. "Pleased

to meet you. I'm Laney Kensington. This is Grayson DeMarco. Have you had any prior search experience with dog handlers?'

"No, ma'am, but I've been on wilderness searches before without dogs."

"Good. There are three things to remember. First, don't pet or feed the dog when he's got his vest on. Second, keep up. And third, never get between the dog and the handler. Understand?"

Grayson and Reese nodded.

"Cool." She smiled, and Grayson could see that she was in her element, completely comfortable with what she was doing. "Take a look at this map. This is our sector. We'll check the wind when we get closer, but at first glance I'm inclined to follow this stream, because the terrain is relatively flat compared with the surrounding areas. With a seventy-pound kid in tow, the kidnapper will likely be looking for the path of least resistance." Laney folded the map and put it in her plastic map case, then used her compass to orient her map. "There's bottled water at the base. Both of you grab some. We'll be traveling fast, and you'll become dehydrated quickly. I'll vest up Jax, and we'll get moving."

SEVENTEEN

It felt like coming home.

Every detail of the preparation, every whiff of pine needles and outdoors, every sound of dogs barking and people calling to one another felt as comfortable as a well-worn cardigan.

Laney led the way through a small clearing, moving into the tree line and the edge of their sector. She knew where they were heading, but she paused there to orient her map once more.

Beside her, Jax was visibly excited. He knew this wasn't just training. He always knew. She'd never been sure if it was because he was so in touch with her moods, but Jax's entire demeanor was different on a real search than during a training exercise.

She bent over, scratching him between the ears. "We're about to start, buddy. Just need to do one thing first."

Shrugging the pack from her back, she dug into the front pocket, pulling out a Leatherman.

"What are you doing?" Grayson asked, leaning over her as she opened the knife.

"I need to cut the bells off Jax's vest. They'll give him away if the kidnapper is in our sector. Jax works fast and he ranges, so he'll be out of our sight sometimes. I use the bells to help me keep track of the direction he's traveling and the area he's covered. This time, we'll work without them." She sliced off the bells and stuffed them deep into her pack. Finally they were ready.

Her pulse raced, her heart tripping all over itself.

This might be like coming home, but that didn't mean she wasn't nervous about it. She took a deep breath, removed Jax's lead and placed that in her pack as well.

"Are you ready, Jax?"

He snuffed his agreement, tail wagging his excitement.

"Go find!"

At the search command, Jax was off, into the woods and out of sight.

Laney took off after him, Grayson and Reese two steps behind.

The trees offered plenty of shade from the early October sun, but the Maryland humidity was heavy, and it was tough navigating through the dense, thorny underbrush. They'd walked less than three minutes before coming upon the stream that served as a natural border for their sector. Jax was relentless in his work, making large circles around handler and flankers, nose to the air as they moved quickly forward, Laney leading them on with quiet confidence. Grayson was amazed at the speed at which they were covering ground.

But he was still worried that they weren't moving fast enough.

The kidnapper was on the run. It had been nearly forty minutes; if he was not already out of the woods, he was nearing the road, slowed only by what must feel like the growing weight of a child. After all, seventy pounds of dead weight would be challenging for any-one to cart through brush and over uneven ground as the heat and humidity of the day settled in the woods. Surely he would have to stop and rest.

Of course, if he had a weapon, he'd likely be forc-ing the child to walk through the woods himself, but then they'd have to go at the pace of a frightened ten-year-old.

Laney put her hand up. "Wait."

Grayson and Reese stopped dead in their tracks.

Laney's complete focus was on Jax.

"What is it?" Grayson asked

"He's caught scent. It's faint—I can tell he can't pin-point the origin." Laney pulled her GPS from the large pocket of her cargo pants, "I'm marking the spot where Jax first showed interest." She released white powder from her puff bottle into the air. "The wind is pushing the scent across the creek. It's hitting the side of this hill and circling up. Scent forms a cone of sorts, stronger near the person and weakening as it gets further away, but sometimes the air movement can push it into a bar-rier where it gets trapped, leaving a heavy scent pool with no subject. This is when the handler has to read the dog and use whatever scent theory they know, and try to work out where the subject might actually be."

"What are you thinking?" Grayson asked. Could the kidnapper be somewhere close by, hiding until they passed?

"I think he's either picked up the kidnapper and vic-tim, or he's picked up the scent of another dog team working the other side of the stream." Reaching for her radio, she called base.

"Go ahead, team one."

"Permission to go direct with team two."

"Team one, you have the frequency."

"Team two from team one."

"Go ahead, team one."

"Jax is picking up scent on the border of my sector. It's faint. Judging by the air current, my best guess is it's coming from across the stream in your sector. Are you working the vicinity?"

"Negative, team one. We're at the west end of our sector, near the lake."

"Copy. To be sure he's not picking up our victim or the perp, I'm going to cross the stream to see if the scent pool is stronger. I'll probably go about fifty meters in. If he picks up scent, I'll follow. If not, I'll return to my sector. I'll let you know when I've left the area."

"Copy, team one."

Holstering her radio, she backtracked about fifteen paces, checking the wind, then headed to the stream.

"Jax, this way." Looking over her shoulder, she gestured to Grayson and Reese. "Guys, stay close. Keep your eyes and ears open. My gut is telling me someone is across the stream, just upwind of us. Could be a random hiker, but one thing is certain. It's not a member of the search team."

Grayson and Reese followed single file behind Laney and Jax as they crossed the ankle-deep stream. The water, somewhat cloudy after the rain, moved swiftly over slippery rocks and a muddy stream bed.

Jax paused, lapping up some of the cool water. Bending down, Laney splashed the water under his belly. "Okay, this way Jax, go find!"

Jax paused, his head popped up in interest, nose to the wind, and he was off. Laney went after him, keeping up a fast jog over uneven ground, dodging tree branches and ripping away from thorny brush that reached out to grab her as she passed. Unencumbered by a pack, Grayson stayed on her heels. Reese fell back slightly, Laney's pace combined with the weight of his pack proving too much for him.

For a moment they lost sight of Jax. Laney stopped abruptly, motioning for them to do the same. The distant sound of the dog jumping quickly through the brush was met with another sound.

Something large was moving in the same general direction.

All at once, the second movement stopped, and the distinct sound of the dog running toward them grew closer.

Standing stock-still, Laney waited. Seconds later, Jax bounded into view, tongue lolling, ears back, at a full sprint. Launching himself in the air, straight at Laney, his front paws hit her in the torso before he landed in front of her, tail wagging.

"Show me!" Laney commanded, and Jax quickly started off again.

All three raced after Jax, crashing through the vegetation, jumping over downed branches. But there was no way they could keep up with the agile little Australian shepherd. It seemed to Grayson that Jax was well aware of this. He constantly circled back, ensuring Laney was right behind him.

Bursting through thick underbrush into a clearing,

Jax stopped, then began circling the area—nose to the wind, taking in short quick snuffs of air.

"Grayson." Laney's voice was hushed. "The subject was here, but has moved. He's likely hiding. Jax is trained for this scenario—we sometimes see it with lost children and Alzheimer's patients. They are found by the dog and then move before we can get to them."

Fascinated, Grayson watched Jax work. The dog sniffed the ground, the trees, the air, looking for the scent. Even untrained, Grayson could tell when he found it. His head popped up again and his tail fanned out. In a flash, he was off. They followed him through a particularly thick stand of trees and brush and watched as he approached a large downed tree, its exposed roots jutting out, nearly four feet high in places.

A perfect hiding place.

Scampering up the downed trees limbs, Jax was quickly up and over the obstacle. Laney seemed poised to follow, but Grayson grabbed her arm, jerking her back toward him. He was about to have her call Jax back when a shot rang out.

Was Jax shot? Was he hurt, confused? Looking for her?

She had to get to him. Laney tried to shrug free of Grayson's grip, but he held tight as he ordered Reese to drop his pack.

Movement in the brush to their left had Grayson pushing Laney to the side, drawing his weapon. Bursting through the brush, Jax rushed forward, intent on indicating the re-find.

She hated to do it, but for his own safety, she gave the emergency stop command using the hand signal and whispering, "Halt."

His stop was immediate. He dropped to the ground in a down position.

Tapping her chest twice, her silent recall signal, she motioned Jax to her.

Once Jax was by her side, the reality of the situation hit her hard. There was someone on the other side of the log, and he was armed.

Reese had dropped his pack and unholstered his weapon. Grayson drew them in a close circle, whispering, "Laney, mark our coordinates on your GPS, then take Jax back through the stand of trees. Move quickly and make noise as you go. When you reach the stream, take cover and call base for backup. Reese, you circle around the fallen tree as quietly as you can from the left. I'll take the right. Don't be seen. Try to get in a position where you can see the shooter—when Laney is out of earshot, he may make a run for it. Be ready."

Reese nodded.

Laney turned to go, but Grayson grabbed her arm and pulled her close. "Don't come back until I call you."

She nodded her understanding, but he didn't let her go. His gaze was dark, his ocean-blue eyes filled with concern.

He cupped her cheek, his fingers rough and a little cool. "Be careful, okay?"

She swallowed down words that she knew she shouldn't say, words about friendship, about connection, about wanting to know that this wouldn't be the last time she'd ever see him.

"You, too," she whispered to his back as he quietly headed for the downed tree.

She headed in the opposite direction, crashing through the underbrush.

"Jax, come!" she yelled, and the dog followed.

She reached the other side of the trees, took cover behind a giant oak and called for backup, providing the coordinates to base. Her voice shaking, she made sure the other dog teams understood they should stand down and stay away from the sector.

"Laney?" Kent's voice came over the radio.

"Go ahead, Kent."

"We have four officers stationed on the road in your vicinity—we're sending them in now. Stay where you are until they get to you."

They arrived quickly, slipping through the woods almost silently. Only Jax's soft huff of anxiety warned her before they appeared.

"Where's the perp?" a tall, dark-eyed man asked. She was sure she'd seen him before, had probably worked with him at some point.

"Follow me, and be as quiet as possible." Laney led the officers around the thickest part of the brush in an attempt to keep down the noise. They followed her one by one, in silence. She stopped, the fallen tree fifty feet in front of their location, roots snaking out four feet in every direction, ensnared with thick underbrush. Turning to them, she whispered, "The suspect is holed up behind that downed tree." She pointed. "Agent DeMarco went to the right, Officer Reese to the left. They intended to get a visual of the suspect and wait for backup."

"Okay. We've got it from here. I want you to take cover behind that stand of trees, then radio base that we are here and in position."

Laney nodded. Then the officer in charge turned to

his guys. "Radio silence from this point on." Several of the officers turned their handheld radios off.

Laney crept to the stand of trees, finding a hiding place under a particularly thick bush. Then she called base, confirming the team's position. Motioning Jax to sit by her, she absently petted his head while she waited for something to happen. Anything.

Suddenly a voice broke the silence. Grayson's voice.

"This is the FBI. You're surrounded. Throw out your weapon and release the child."

"I'll kill the kid if you come any closer."

"Not before we kill you, so how about you make it easy on yourself? Send the boy out!" Grayson's last statement was met by a warning shot from the suspect.

It was then that Laney noticed the brush moving near the bottom of the fallen tree, where thick weeds and saplings were growing up around it. Could there be another way for the suspect to get out? If so, Grayson and the other officers were not in a position to see the suspect escape. Seconds later, a blond head popped out.

A child's tear-streaked face appeared as the boy pushed through the thick brush. Giving Jax the signal to stay, she grabbed her Leatherman out of her pack and opened it. She eased across the space that separated her from the tree and saw the boy's eyes widening with surprise as he spotted her. Holding a finger to her lips, she signaled him to stay quiet as he came out of the opening under the tree and stood. An adult's tanned hand was visible through the brush, grasping the boy's ankle. Laney readied herself, watching the brush move, the leaves rustle.

Was she the only one who noticed the movement?

Suddenly, the kidnapper's head and other hand

pushed through the opening. That hand grasped a gun. He never released his hold in the boy's ankle as he snaked through the brush. The child stood still, blue eyes wide with fright, trained on her. Laney didn't intend to let the kidnapper make it out from under the tree. She took two steps closer and stomped with all her might on his hand.

He cursed, the gun dropping from his slack hand.

She kicked it away and grabbed the boy's arm, yanking him from the kidnapper.

"Run!" she screamed.

EIGHTEEN

Hoisting himself quickly to the top of the downed tree, Grayson could scarcely believe what he was seeing. Hadn't he told her to stay by the creek? To wait in safety until he called her? She hadn't, and she was about to be taken down by a guy who looked like he'd gladly drag the knife from her hand and use it to slit her throat.

Grayson scrambled over the tree and tackled the guy as he lunged for Laney and the boy.

They all went down in a heap, tangled in weeds and thorny brush.

The guy was big. Maybe six-foot-four, muscular.

And angry.

He pushed himself to his knees and threw a punch; Grayson dodged it, the man's knuckles barely grazing his jaw. Grayson managed to land a well-placed blow to the man's cheek. The guy fell backward, knocking into Laney as she scrambled to her feet, grabbing the boy under the arm to drag him from the fray.

She stumbled. Falling to her knees, she shoved the boy out of reach. The kidnapper's arm shot out and grabbed Laney's calf. She tried unsuccessfully to kick him off while Grayson punched the guy in the back.

The man cursed but didn't relinquish his hold on Laney. He yanked her toward him across the brush like a rag doll. Grayson heard Laney gasp. Her chest hit the ground first, knocking the wind out of her.

Grayson landed a quick blow to the perp's head, and then another. Other than a faint grunt, there was no acknowledgment that the hits had any effect on the guy. Behind Grayson, the other officers were crashing through the brush to help.

The man relentlessly dragged Laney toward him, ignoring the kicks from her free leg.

Grabbing the guy in a choke hold, Grayson yanked him backward. Still he refused to release Laney.

Laney looked up, meeting Grayson's gaze over the perp's shoulders. He recognized the anger and determination he saw there. Without warning, she sliced her pocketknife across the guy's hand. With a howl, he let go of her leg.

She scrambled away and rushed to the boy, who stood watching wide-eyed by a tree. Grayson tightened his grip around the guy's neck. Reese nudged in beside Grayson, taking cuffs from his belt. He snapped them onto the suspect's wrists and pulled him to his feet.

"Hey! That crazy chick cut my hand! I need a medic!" the perp howled.

"You'll get one." *Eventually*, Grayson thought, but he didn't say it.

He was too busy striding to Laney's side, taking the knife from her hand. "Are you nuts?" he nearly shouted. "You could have gotten yourself killed!"

"What was I supposed to do?" she asked, touching the hair of the little boy who was clinging to her waist, his head buried against her abdomen. "Let the guy escape with Carson?"

"What you were supposed to do was stay away," he reminded her. "Until I told you differently."

"If she had," the boy said, shooting Grayson a dark look, "she couldn't have rescued me."

"I didn't rescue you. Jax did," Laney said. "Want to meet him?"

"Who's Jax?" Carson asked.

"I'll show you. Jax, come," Laney called, and the dog bounded out from the underbrush.

"He's so cool!" Carson dropped to his knees to pet Jax, his face suddenly animated. "When we saw the dog the first time, that guy made me hide under that tree with him so the dog wouldn't know where we went. He said I had to stay quiet or he'd kill me."

Grayson kneeled on the ground next to Carson. "So you did what he said, right?"

Nodding, Carson hugged Jax. "I was afraid of him. He was mean. He tried to shoot the dog, but I hit his arm so he would miss."

Laney went to her knees too, enveloping the boy and dog in a big bear hug. "Thank you for saving Jax."

"I knew Jax was good. We learned about search dogs in Boy Scouts. I knew he would bring me help, and he did."

"Yep, he did his job well. Now he gets his reward. Do you want to help me give it to him?" Laney asked.

"Sure, what is it?"

She pulled out two orange balls, squeaking them.

Jax turned toward the sound, ready to run.

"He gets playtime with his favorite toy for a job well done."

She chucked the ball as far as she could, and they both laughed as Jax rushed forward, jumping up and snatching it out of the air before it hit the ground.

Squeaking it in his mouth, the dog returned, dropping the ball at her feet as she launched the next one in the air.

"Grab that ball, Carson, and throw it as soon as he brings the other back—let's see who gets tired first, him or us!"

Grayson was betting on the two of them, since the ball of energy that was Jax showed no sign of stopping anytime soon.

Watching the woman who would likely never fail to surprise him, laughing and playing with the dog and the boy in the midst of what should have been a very traumatic day for all, Grayson realized Laney's affinity for dogs translated to children as well. Her fearless confidence and her empathy for the helpless attracted both to her. And right now, with this boy, she was managing to single-handedly end his bad day on a good note.

Although there were many people who had worked together to find and rescue Carson, Laney and her hero dog Jax would stay with the boy always. As he grew older and recounted this story, Laney would always be in it. His own fearless protector.

Funny. Grayson's story about the day would be the same.

Empty of the million little details that had made the rescue successful, and filled with hundreds of images of a woman he knew he would never forget.

Noon, and Laney was exhausted.

She should probably get up from the porch rocker

and go inside, but she was too tired to move. Grayson and Kent were a few feet away, talking to the two FBI agents assigned to her protection detail for the next few days. The sun had grown warmer, but dark clouds rolled in on a humid breeze, threatening rain.

Tonight would mark forty-eight hours missing for Olivia.

Two days of tracking one clue after another, but never seeming to get closer to the answers they needed to bring Olivia home. Laney was frustrated, irritated, antsy to see progress made on the case.

She had sensed some frustration in Grayson, as well. He hadn't been happy that the kidnapper's interrogation had been put on hold to treat his hand. Laney was sorry that the interrogation would have to wait, but she couldn't say she completely regretted the bone-crushing stomp to his hand that had apparently broken two fingers. She didn't regret cutting him, either. He'd deserved it, and worse, as far as she was concerned. She only hoped that Grayson and Kent would be able to uncover some link between this kidnapping and the others.

One thing was certain. Today's kidnapper was not the same man who took Olivia.

Kent and Grayson came up the porch stairs, the two FBI agents right behind them. "Laney, if it's okay with you, we'd like to use your house to have the FBI agents work with Arden and me on reviewing some of the case files that were faxed over this afternoon…the more eyes the better," Kent said.

"Make yourselves at home," she responded, gesturing to the front door.

The three other men walked inside.

Grayson stayed put, his gaze on Laney.

"You don't really think I'm going to leave you out here alone, do you?" he asked.

"I was hoping."

"Tired of all the people in your house?" He reached for her hand, tugging her to her feet.

"Tired, period." She would have stepped away, but he pulled her closer, looked straight into her eyes.

"From the search?"

"From everything."

"Was it hard?" He traced a line from her ear to the corner of her jaw, his hand sliding down and resting on her nape. He kneaded the tense muscles there.

"Stopping the kidnapper?" she asked, her mind more on his touch than on his questions.

"Going back to search and rescue."

"It was as easy as taking my next breath," she admitted, and he smiled.

"I thought it would be."

He opened the door and let her walk inside ahead of him. They followed the sound of voices into the dining room.

Arden was there, Kent and the two FBI agents a few feet away, watching as she systematically stacked documents on the table.

Arden placed the last piece of paper in the pile and finally looked up.

"There. I've organized these records by date and placed the original records we received today via fax in front of the records Grayson downloaded from his system. This is how I propose we tackle the review." She was interrupted by Grayson's phone.

He glanced at his caller ID and frowned. "Excuse me, everyone. I need to take this call."

Laney watched him walk away and fought the urge to follow. It still bothered her that she was relying on him so completely, but not as much as it might have a couple of days ago. She realized now it was okay to accept help when needed. And deep down, she knew she would be all right when he was gone. Even though a small part of her would be sad to see him go, she would always be grateful for what he'd done. Not just protecting her, but helping her get back to the person she wanted to be.

She'd taken the first step in moving on. She'd brought herself and Jax out of retirement. Maybe it was time to take the next step and join another search and rescue team here in Maryland. When this was over, she'd have to thank Grayson for helping her remember that some things were worth fighting for.

"DeMarco," Grayson said, pressing the phone to his ear. If it had been anyone else, he wouldn't have taken the call, but it was Ethan, and Grayson would do anything for his friend.

"Gray, its Ethan. How are things going?"

"We might have something to go on. We stopped a kidnapping today. The perp will be brought in for questioning after he's released from the hospital."

"Do you have evidence that he's connected to the other kidnappings?"

"No."

"Could be coincidental."

"You know how rare stranger abductions are, Ethan."

"I do, but rare doesn't mean they don't happen," Ethan responded, a sharp edge to his voice. That surprised Grayson. In the years he'd known Ethan, he'd never known the man to be short-tempered or impatient.

"Either way, I have to look at every possibility."

"Right." Ethan laughed it off, any hint of impatience suddenly gone. "I actually didn't call to argue. I wanted to let you know it will likely be another day before I can get to the Maryland precinct—Judith's brother's in town, and she needs me to hang around and play host. If you can send me records, I can start to go through them for you."

"We've got a group of people comparing the hard copies with the electronic files I've been working with for months—I can have someone scan them in and send them to you if you think you'll have a chance to look at them."

"I'll make the time, Gray. Send them my way when you can."

"Thanks, Ethan, I'll talk to you soon." Grayson disconnected, less satisfied with the conversation than he usually was when he spoke to Ethan for some reason he couldn't quite define.

He shook off the unease, walking back into the dining room and taking a seat next to Laney.

"Great. You're here," Arden said. "Ready to work?" She handed him a stack of files. "This is our West Coast file."

Grayson started skimming the reports. Everything matched up until he reached the fifth page. There he found a name he hadn't seen before.

Ethan Conrad. Called in for consultation.

That's what the file said.

Why had Ethan failed to mention the consulting services to Grayson? Could there be a simple explanation? Maybe. But it didn't seem possible that he'd just forgotten. Even if he had, why was the information in one file and not the other? "Who has the original Boston files, months one and two?" he asked.

"I've got them," Kent said.

"Was any consulting company listed in the reports?"

"Not a company, but a man was mentioned. It was an FBI profiler, I think…here it is, Ethan Conrad."

Grayson skimmed the page, comparing this entry to the California entry.

Arden looked up at the mention of Ethan's name, catching Grayson's eye. "Ethan consulted on both those cases?"

"Yes. And that information was deleted from the doctored files."

"What about here in Maryland?"

Grayson grabbed the Maryland files, skimming them for Ethan's name, relieved when he didn't find it. Perhaps there was a legitimate reason for Ethan's involvement. "Nothing in Maryland."

But then, Grayson thought, there was no need to consult here in Maryland. Grayson had discussed the case at length with Ethan after taking over for the agents in Boston at Ethan's recommendation.

They talked almost daily, about everything. Ethan was a sounding board. A trusted advisor.

Could he also be a callous criminal?

Grayson's mind raced. He'd known Ethan for years, trusted him like family. There had to be another explanation.

Kent Andrews's phone rang.

He answered, his gaze focused on Grayson.

He was going to have to share his suspicions with Andrews. He had no choice. He had to run this lead down. If Ethan was innocent, he'd understand.

Andrews's phone conversation took less than a minute. When it was over, he smiled. "Good news, Grayson. We finally have a jailbird that's ready to sing."

"The suspect is talking?"

"Not just talking, singing like a jaybird! He said he was paid five grand to snatch a kid."

"Who paid him?" Grayson asked.

"A guy he met while incarcerated—David Rallings Jr."

"So our floater paid him to snatch a kid..."

"Yep, and deliver the kid to an access road near Camp Cone."

"Camp Cone is up there near Glenn Arm, isn't it?" Laney asked.

Grayson didn't answer.

He was too busy thinking, reaching a horrible and inevitable conclusion.

He'd spent a lot of summers at Camp Cone. He knew it well. The property was a little wild, a little rugged. He'd hunted squirrel there, hunted turkey, done all the things young boys liked to do.

And he'd done them all with Rick, because the property they spent their summers on, the little cabin where they used to stay, it belonged to Rick's parents. It belonged to Ethan.

He stood, pushing away from the table with so much force, his chair toppled over.

"Grayson?" Laney stood, touched his arm. "Are you okay?"

"It's pretty difficult to be okay when you've just realized that you've been betrayed by one of your most trusted friends."

"What do you mean?" Kent asked.

"Ethan Conrad owns property near Camp Cone."

Kent frowned, glancing at the report he still held. "The former FBI profiler? The same one who's listed as a consultant in these files?"

"He's not just listed there." Grayson set his paper down and pointed to the name. "He's listed here, too. But his name was taken out of the reports when they were tampered with. The hacker didn't want us to know that he was involved."

"Anyone else find his name in a report?" Kent asked.

"It's here," Laney said quietly.

He didn't have time to feel sorry for himself. Didn't have time to sit around moping. Ethan was one of the most intelligent men he knew, but even intelligent men made mistakes. "There's a cabin on Ethan's property, and an outbuilding used for hunting—either of those would be the perfect place to keep a bunch of kids," he said. "Arden, can you print me out a few topographical maps of the Glen Arm/Camp Cone area? And Kent, we'll need a search warrant to go on private property."

"I'll make some calls."

"How long do you think it will take?"

"A few hours? Maybe a day, tops—if we can convince them it's necessary."

"That's a long time if you're one of the kids he's kidnapped."

"I'll try to put a rush on it," Kent assured him.

"Good." Grayson glanced at the name, felt fury clogging his throat. "Because I suspect we found our leak, and the sooner we plug it, the happier I'll be."

NINETEEN

Later that evening, after poring through files with Arden and the FBI agents, Laney retreated to her room, claiming exhaustion.

Earlier, Kent had gone to the precinct to see if he could call in some favors and help expedite a warrant on Ethan's property. Grayson was trying a different tactic. He'd driven away over an hour ago, determined to convince a reluctant judge to issue a search warrant.

He'd left Laney behind.

Grayson had thought it would be safer.

It would have been. If she'd actually intended to stay there.

Low voices and murmurs of activity carried down the hall to her room. Rose was clanging in the kitchen while the others worked in the dining room. Laney carefully removed the screen from her bedroom window. When she was done, she retrieved her small search-and-rescue day pack from the floor beside her bed, shoved a pilfered topographical map of Camp Cone in it, then turned off the light, dropping the pack out the window to the ground. Grabbing her work cell phone from the charger on the dresser, she shoved it into her cargo pants pocket. The sun had just set below the horizon. The grass was damp from the late afternoon showers.

Laney's heart raced. Climbing onto the windowsill, she dropped to the grass. The night was quiet. So far, so good.

Laney knew Grayson would not approve of her intent to give her FBI and MPD babysitters the slip.

She also knew that the chance of Grayson getting a warrant on a respected, retired FBI agent based on the circumstantial evidence they'd collected was slim. She'd heard the agents talking about it being a pipe dream that a warrant would be provided in time to rescue the kids.

But Laney understood law enforcement and probable cause. If she and Jax happened to be hiking in the area and came upon something that could point to the children, Grayson would have all the probable cause he needed for an official search.

She was determined to make sure that happened.

Olivia's life was at stake.

Shrugging the pack onto her back, she whistled twice. She heard the soft pad of Jax's feet in the yard behind the house before he raced around the corner and sat attentively in front of her. "Good boy," she whispered. Patting her thigh twice, the signal for heel, she started off at a quick jog. Jax kept pace by her side. Laney ran through the trees, sticking close to the edges of the woods.

She needed to get to Aunt Rose's house and borrow her car.

Rose kept the keys to her 1974 Hornet hatchback on a peg in the garage. So as long as the keys were there, borrowing the car would be easy. Laney just hoped the Hornet would make the hour-long drive to Camp Cone.

As far as she knew, Willow was the first person to drive the car in months, and she'd taken a five-minute drive to the grocery store.

Of course, it was a bit premature to worry about the car breaking down when she first needed to get into the garage. Laney was counting on finding the spare house key in its usual spot—buried in the topsoil under the decorated stone turtle in the back flower bed. Hurrying across the well-manicured back yard, she found the turtle right where she'd expected it to be. Beside her, Jax's ears perked up, standing at alert. His eyes watched the corner of the house. Someone was coming.

She jumped back into the shadows. There was no time to get the key. The soft sound of footsteps on the grass grew closer. "Laney?" As usual, Aunt Rose's whisper was scarcely a decibel under a yell.

"Shh!" Laney responded quickly. "Aunt Rose, what are you doing out here?" she hissed.

"Looking for you, of course." Reaching in her pocket, she pulled out a car key on a small fuzzy dice keychain. "I thought you might need this."

"How'd you know I was here—and why on earth are you carrying around a key to a car you can't legally drive?"

Aunt Rose planted her hands on her hips. "First of all, after the last break-in, I didn't want to leave the key where it could be so easily found—James is a classic, you know?" James, of course, referred to Rose's car. As Rose told the story, she'd purchased it the summer after her husband Peter died, because they'd watched James Bond together and he'd been fascinated by the aerial flip the car performed in the movie. Thankfully Rose had not yet attempted to duplicate that flip.

"Secondly," Rose continued, "I heard Gray and Kent talking to those agents, too. I'm not deaf, you know. As soon as I heard that they probably didn't have enough evidence to get a warrant, I knew exactly what you were going to do."

Lifting the stone turtle, Rose buried her fingers in the dirt below, coming up with the spare key to the garage. She absently wiped the dirt off on her pants. "Here you go."

"Does this mean you approve of the plan?" Laney asked, unlocking the garage and opening it.

Rose shook her head and sighed. "I'm not saying it's the smartest thing to do, mind you, but I know I won't be able to talk you out of it. You have too much of the Travis blood in you. Much more than your mama ever did, God rest her soul."

Taking the keys, Laney embraced her aunt. "Thanks, Aunt Rose."

"Honey, I know you've always worried that you might end up like your mother, but even as a girl, your mama was never strong. Not like you."

Shaking her head vehemently, Laney argued, "I'm not strong, I just try to do what needs to be done."

"Because you have an inner strength, girl. The grit and moxie your mom never had—that comes from here and here." She pointed to her head then her heart.

"Mom did her best."

"No doubt, but she married the wrong man."

"I know, and the sad thing is, I can see how it happened. My father could be a real charmer at times—you just never know what lies underneath."

"Laney, I think deep down you know that's not true.

Some men are exactly as they seem. For instance, your grandfather—my brother—and my own husband."

"I'm sorry I never got a chance to meet Uncle Peter."

"Me, too, but I won't romanticize him—he was far from perfect. God knows none of us are perfect. But he tried to live God's plan for his life. That one simple act of faith made him perfect for me. Maybe you'll find the same to be true with Grayson."

"Aunt Rose, Grayson and I are just…" What were they? Working together? Friends? At times it seemed she'd known him forever. But really, did she know him at all?

"You can protest all you want, but you can't deny the attraction. But don't you think on it now. God's plan will unfold in its own time." She gave Laney a quick hug. "Give me two minutes before you start the car. I'll distract them with my new batch of grandma's whoopie pies."

"I love you, Aunt Rose."

"I know, and I love you, too."

Opening the car door, Laney motioned Jax inside. "Jax, place." Tail wagging, he hopped into the car.

Pausing at the entrance of the garage, Aunt Rose looked back over her shoulder. "Be careful, Laney. And leave the lights off until you get to the end of our drive. That's what I always do." Grinning, she was gone.

Grayson wasn't happy. He'd just left the judge's house—*without* a search warrant for Ethan's property. Despite the case Grayson had presented, the judge reasoned that Ethan appeared to have been a legitimate paid consultant on the cases, and that those records could have been doctored by anyone to cast the blame on Ethan. Furthermore, Camp Cone was a public park, backing up to several private properties, and since there was no evidence directly linking Ethan to any of the victims or suspects, the probable cause was not there. The judge sympathized but told Grayson he needed to make a stronger case for a warrant to be issued.

Grayson had a decision to make. He could follow the rules and keep searching for more substantial evidence to link Ethan to the crimes, or he could search the property himself, perhaps finding the kids, but knowing that anything he found couldn't be used in a court of law.

For the first time in his life, Grayson was thinking about breaking the law.

There had to be a way around this. There must be a way to rescue the kids and still bring Ethan to justice.

Ethan, who'd recommended Grayson for the case in the first place, then used his relationship with Grayson to monitor the progress the bureau was making and plan his next move. Grayson tamped down his fury. Rage wasn't going to help him figure things out. It wasn't going to make things easier. He needed to stay calm and cool-headed if he was going to beat Ethan at his own game.

And that must be what this was to his mentor—a money-making game that he had been playing and winning for far too long.

What was worse, logic dictated that this wasn't Ethan's first venture into organized crime. Grayson wondered when Ethan had turned. Had Rick's death sent him over the edge? Or worse, could he have had something to do with Rick's death? And Andrea's?

The thought turned his blood cold. Grayson had always wondered how Ethan had wrapped up the case of Rick's murder so quickly, so cleanly. The perpetrators had died trying to keep from being taken into custody, and there'd been no one to interrogate. There was no telling how deep Ethan's betrayal ran, but Grayson wanted the chance to ask him.

His cell phone vibrated. Kent's name and number scrolled across the dashboard display. He grabbed the phone, his hand shaking with the force of his anger. "DeMarco here."

"Laney's gone. She took one of the topo maps and Jax with her."

"What? How? There are four armed law enforcement officers at the house, and her Jeep is still in the impound lot!"

"She snuck out through her bedroom window while the FBI agents were in the kitchen with your sister and Rose. They were going through the case files, and she said she needed to lie down—"

"That should have been their first clue that she was up to something!" he snapped.

"Don't shoot the messenger, DeMarco," Andrews bit out. They were both tense, both disappointed with the judge's decision regarding the search warrant.

"The good news is," Grayson said, trying to calm himself down, "she couldn't have gone far without a vehicle."

"You're assuming she doesn't have one."

"Where would she get…" Grayson paused, realizing just how easy he and everyone else had made Laney's escape. "Rose."

"Rose admits to handing over the keys to her '74 Hornet hatchback, then distracting my officers with a plate full of whoopie pies and milk. Both of my guys are now complaining of stomach pains. I swear she's a menace with the baked goods."

Grayson's grip tightened on the steering wheel. "I'm not sure I care about your officers' stomach problems. How long ago did Laney leave?"

"She's been gone about ninety minutes."

"She's had more than enough time to get to the Camp Cone area, then. Has anyone heard from her since?"

"No. I tried to call her work cell. No answer."

Grayson banged the steering wheel, his frustration making him reckless. "What was she thinking?"

"According to Rose, Laney went to get us our probable cause."

That wasn't what Grayson wanted to hear. It wasn't what he wanted to think about. Laney and Jax searching Ethan's property couldn't lead to anything good.

"I just left the judge's house," he growled. "I can be at Ethan's property in less than fifteen minutes. I'm turning around now."

"I'm on my way with two patrol cars. We'll be there in thirty minutes, tops."

Disconnecting the call, Grayson tried Laney's work phone. Straight to voice mail.

He drove faster than he should have, faster than was prudent, speeding toward Camp Cone. Dozens of memories flashed through his head. All the times Ethan had seemed interested, concerned, helpful, he'd been playing Grayson for a fool.

He managed to make it to Camp Cone Road in thirteen minutes. It wove through an older, established neighborhood and dead-ended at the park entrance, where visitors could gain free public access during park hours. Grayson was betting that Laney would pick that as her entry point.

The access gate would have been locked at sunset, but Laney could easily have parked in the small lot and walked in. From there, she'd have to navigate about twenty acres of heavily wooded parkland to get to the boundary of Ethan's property.

Remembering how quickly and easily Laney and Jax had navigated the trees and brush during the morning's search, he was confident that she was well within Ethan's property line already. He was equally confident that he was ill-equipped to trail her through the woods.

No, he'd need to take the direct approach. He'd enter the property through Ethan's driveway and have a look around. At this point, he had no other choice.

The conditions were perfect. Temperature mild. A light, consistent breeze. Jax was definitely in scent. According to the compass and topographic map, they were less than fifty meters north of a man-made structure, possibly the hunting cabin that Grayson had mentioned. According to the map, it bordered the southern corner of Ethan Conrad's property. Laney decided that direction was as good as any to start. After all, if Ethan was hiding three children on the property, he'd need a secure place to keep them—a building away from the main house would be the best bet.

Laney didn't use a flashlight and did not turn on the lights on Jax's vest. Luckily, the night sky was clear, the almost full moon illuminating the woods. Jax's head popped up, and he stopped, nose to the wind. Over the light wind rustling through the trees, Laney thought she heard voices.

"Jax, come," she whispered. For a second Laney thought he wouldn't listen; she could see the reluctance as he looked at her, as if to say, "But the human is right there! Just a few more steps."

Laney touched her open hand to her chest, reinforcing her voice command with the hand recall command. This time Jax came.

"Heel," she said softly. They made their way slowly through the trees in the direction of the voices. The edge of the tree line was heavy with thick brush that made silence difficult. Jax moved through it easily, but Laney's clothing and hair caught on branches that snapped as she pulled away. Hidden within the tree line, she could just make out the outline of a very small, old outbuilding. Perhaps a one-room hunting cabin or large shed. If there were windows, she couldn't see them on the wall that faced her. No door, either, so she had to be looking at the back or side of the structure.

She crouched at the very edge of the trees, Jax beside her, his body tense with excitement. She scanned the clearing beyond the trees and spotted the source of the noise. Two men stood to the right of the structure, talking quietly. From her vantage point she could make out that the shorter of the two had a bald head. The other, bigger man was partially concealed by the building.

Headlights splashed light across a gravel drive choked with weeds. An uncomfortably familiar-looking dark panel van rolled toward the building, the driver guiding it into a position about a foot from the structure. He hopped out, then hurried to join the other men. Were they about to move the children? She would need to get closer if she hoped to learn anything. Both men disappeared around the corner of the structure.

She reached down and hoisted Jax into her arms, then took one slow, deliberate step at a time toward the edge of the tree line. She made it to a spot that was cater-corner to the sliding panel door of the van. Setting Jax back on the grass, she gave him the hand motions for "down-stay" and crept toward the front of the structure.

She smelled cigarette smoke before she saw the third man. Seated in a folding camp chair, his back to her, he held the cigarette, its butt glowing orange in the darkness. Behind him, an open door revealed the black interior of the structure. Was someone in there?

"Hey!" the man called out, and she jumped, sure she'd been seen. "Hurry it up with those kids! We don't got all night to move them."

"They're not cooperating, so how about you get yourself in here and do something to help?" a muffled voice called from inside the structure. One of the three men she'd already seen? Or a fourth person?

"Do I gotta to do everything?" the man with the cigarette called back. He took a deep drag on the cigarette, tossed it onto the ground and crushed it under his foot. "You tell those brats I'm coming in. One more complaint from them and I'll set this whole place on fire with them in it."

"You don't do squat!" A man appeared in the doorway, and she recognized him immediately. The man who'd grabbed Olivia.

Silently pressing herself to the shadows of the building, she held her breath, praying that she wouldn't be seen.

"I do plenty. But if I got to help you load the brats, I'll help. Ship departs Baltimore at 6:00 a.m. We don't got a lot of time," the man said.

At that moment, the third man came out of the out-building, spouting a string of obscenities. He was bald, older than the other two, and smaller, but somehow more threatening.

"How about you two stop chatting and get back to work? In two hours, you can take your money and go your separate ways. For now, you'd better stick to the plan. Get in there and search the hold room for any evidence they may have left behind. We leave in ten. Either of you girls wants to slack off now, I can arrange for you not to leave at all."

The three entered the structure. The door slammed shut behind them.

Rushing to the tree line where Jax patiently waited, Laney pulled her cell phone out and powered it up. She had less than ten minutes to figure out how to stall the men. If they left, she'd have no way to follow them. She'd parked Aunt Rose's car a good twenty-minute trek back through the woods.

She could call 911 or she could call Grayson. She made the decision quickly, dialing the number and waiting as the phone rang twice.

"Laney! Where are you?" Grayson voice boomed through the phone.

"I'm at Ethan Conrad's property, and the kids are here."

"You've seen them?"

"No, but I saw Olivia's kidnapper and the van with the dented front end. The kidnappers are moving the kids to the Port of Baltimore. They'll be shipped out from there."

"When?"

"All I heard is that the ship leaves at six. I'm not sure

what time they'll be loading the kids, but they're planning to leave here in ten minutes."

"I'm on my way. So is Andrews. I need you to get back to the woods and stay out of sight."

"Grayson, if I do that, the kids will be gone before you get here."

"And we'll have people at the Port of Baltimore waiting for them."

"The Port of Baltimore is huge. You'll never find them."

"Don't argue, Laney!" he growled. "You've given me the probable cause I need. Now step aside and let us handle things."

"I'll…stay safe," she said. "I've got to go. They'll be out with the kids any minute."

Laney disconnected and turned off the phone before shrugging out of her day pack.

Reaching into the front pocket, she pulled out a plastic Ziploc bag containing her NASAR-required first-aid kit. It included three extra-large safety pins. Fishing them out, she returned the rest of kit to her day pack. If she could wedge a safety pin or two firmly into a tire's valve stem, the air would be released slowly, possibly causing a flat tire before the men reached the port. She knew she had only minutes to make this work.

Ducking behind the front passenger tire, she quickly unscrewed the tire's valve cover. Then, using the tip of the safety pin to push down the valve core, she wedged in the pin to keep it from popping up. It held, but felt loose, so she shoved in the second pin. Better, but it would likely not hold when the tire began rotating at sixty-five miles an hour. Grabbing her last safety pin from her pocket, she opened it and forced it between the first two pins.

Solid. Holding her finger over the air valve, she could feel the slight but steady rush of air pushing out. The question was, if it held, how long would it take before the van was inoperable?

The door to the building was flung open. "I'll be at the van. Get those kids ready to move," someone called out.

Laney was out in plain sight with no choice but to run.

She darted away from the van, aiming for the tree line and Jax.

She didn't make it.

He was on her in an instant, tackling her to the ground so hard, every bit of air was knocked from her lungs.

He grabbed a fistful of her hair and yanked her head up so he could look at her face. "You!" he spat.

"What's going on?" The bald man stepped outside, two children beside him.

"Nothing I can't handle." The kidnapper pulled out a gun, pressed it to her head.

"Are you nuts? Put that thing away. We kill her here and there will be blood evidence everywhere. That happens and Conrad will put a mark on each of us. We'll be dead by sunrise."

The kidnapper cursed but hauled Laney to her feet. "I guess you've got a better plan?"

"Sure do. We sell her. Just like we're doing with the kids. We needed five live bodies. Now we've at least got four."

"Right. Fine. Whatever." The kidnapper shoved her toward the van with enough force to knock her off her feet.

She went down hard, her palms skidding along gravel, bits of dirt digging into her flesh.

A fast-approaching vehicle barreled down the access road, high beams blinding. Laney could only pray it was the cavalry.

TWENTY

Grayson assessed the situation as his car barreled toward the old hunting cabin, high beams on in an attempt to blind the suspects.

Two men were loading kids into a van.

Laney was on the ground. He could see her clearly, and for a moment, he thought the worst.

Then she popped up and tried to run toward the trees.

A man grabbed her around the waist and hauled her toward the van. Another man jumped into the driver's seat.

Hitting the brakes, Grayson flung open the driver's door, pulled his service revolver and trained it on the guy who was manhandling Laney. "FBI. Throw your weapons down and put your hands in the air."

A third man ran out of the building and fired a shot at Grayson.

Laney screamed. Out of the corner of his eye, Grayson saw a brown-and-white ball of fur in a bright orange vest running in. Jax took hold of the kidnapper's pants leg while he struggled to push Laney into the van.

"Do something about this mutt!"

The bald guy turned, taking aim at Jax.

"No!" Laney yelled. "Jax off. Away!"

Jax immediately let go, backing away, the bullet missing him by mere inches as Laney was shoved in the van. The door closed behind her.

The man in the doorway of the building fired another shot. Grayson aimed and pulled the trigger.

The man went down, and the van took off, leaving the fallen kidnapper where he lay.

Grayson couldn't shoot at the van and risk a stray bullet hitting Laney or one of the children.

The perpetrators weren't as worried about that.

One of them leaned out the passenger side window and fired another shot at Grayson as the van barreled past. Grayson dove for cover, but the bullet dug into his shoulder, before he hit the ground. Pulling himself to his feet, he called in his location and the direction the perps were heading.

Blood oozed from the wound, but he didn't feel any pain. Couldn't feel anything but rage and fear.

"Jax, come!" he called.

The dog rushed to his side, looking up at him.

Grayson scooped him into his arms and deposited him on the passenger seat of his car.

His cell phone rang as he sped after the van. He took the call.

"DeMarco. Go ahead."

"It's Kent. I've got dozens of men heading to Conrad's place. Do you have Laney?"

"They've taken her and the kids to the Port of Baltimore," Grayson answered. "I'm headed there now."

"All right. I'll divert my guys there," Andrews acknowledged. "Do you still need resources at Ethan's property?"

"Send a patrol car and an ambulance. We've got one perp down." He didn't mention his own wound. It didn't matter. All that mattered was closing in on the van and getting Laney and the kids out of it safely.

"Will do."

"Can you also send someone out to Conrad's full-time residence? He's in Silver Spring." Grayson rattled off the address. It was as familiar as his own.

"Consider it done," Kent confirmed. "Do you have a visual on the van?"

"Not yet, but I'm moving fast."

"Where do you want us to meet you?"

"The Maryland Port Administration offices on Pratt Street. Someone's going to tell me which ships are leaving Baltimore at 6:00 a.m., and from which docks."

Grayson had been driving at a fast pace for about twenty minutes without seeing the van. That worried him. Had Ethan changed the plans? Had he caught wind of what was going on and decided to move the kids somewhere else? Taking Charles Street, Grayson exited to Pratt Street, where he would meet Andrews.

And there it was.

Abandoned on a side street, the panel van had one pancake-flat tire.

Pulling up behind it, he got out and touched the hood of the vehicle. Still warm.

He crouched near the tire. Safety pins had been jammed in the stem.

Laney. She'd put herself in jeopardy to sabotage the van. A smart move, too, since the Port of Baltimore was one of the largest ports in North America. There was no way the perps could parade around the docks with four hostages in the middle of the night and not draw attention to themselves. They would need another vehicle to get the kids and Laney to the loading dock undetected.

Another vehicle didn't just happen. They'd have to find one.

Which meant that they'd stash the kids and Laney somewhere close by.

He tried the van door and found it unlocked. Laney's cell phone lay on the floor. He left it there and put in another call to Andrews.

He gave the location of the van, his communication quick and to the point.

They didn't have time to waste.

When he finished, he walked back to his vehicle. Jax, still in his bright orange vest, waited there, the equivalent of a homing beacon. "You want to work?" he asked the dog.

He was rewarded by an enthusiastic thump of the tail.

"Good. Me, too." He lifted the dog out of the vehicle, ignoring the stabbing pain in his shoulder as he set him on the ground, then issued the command as he'd seen Laney do. He pointed to the van. "Jax, place!"

Jax leapt inside and immediately seemed to pick up on Laney's scent, going right to her cell phone with a little whine, then pressing his nose in all the rear seats of the vehicle.

Finally, when it was apparent Laney was not in the van, Jax sat down beside her phone, looking sadly at Grayson.

"Where's Laney?" Grayson asked.

At the sound of her name, Jax cocked his head. His ears perked up.

"Laney?" he repeated. He knew Jax was an air scent

dog, not a tracking dog. He could only hope Jax understood what Grayson was asking him to do.

Jax barked and stood, tail wagging, tongue lolling. Grabbing Laney's phone, Grayson put it up to Jax's nose. When he was done sniffing, Grayson dropped the phone in his pocket. "Jax, go find Laney!"

Grayson didn't have to tell him twice. Jax leapt from the van, put his nose to the ground, then to the wind, then back to the ground, and started across the street, heading straight toward a warehouse. Grayson could see the door had recent damage, as if someone had taken a crowbar and pried it open. Testing it, he found it unlocked. He drew his service revolver and stepped into the dark interior.

It was almost pitch black and a little cool in the storage room where Laney and the kids were waiting.

Laney pressed her ear to the door, trying to hear into the warehouse beyond their prison. She was pretty sure at least one of the bad guys was in the vicinity. The other had gone to find a new vehicle. He hadn't been happy when the tire went flat.

Laney had the bruise on her cheek to prove it.

She couldn't feel the pain of it. All she could feel was the panicked need to escape the room, to get the kids to safety, to make sure that Grayson was okay. She tried the door handle again. Locked. Still.

There had to be a way out. Had to be.

She turned back to the kids, felt something slap against her thigh, felt a moment of hope so pure and real that she nearly shouted with the excitement of it.

Her emergency penlight. She always carried it on

searches. She yanked it from her cargo pocket and flashed it across the three huddled kids.

"Don't worry," she said. "I'm going to find a way out of this."

She hoped.

She shone the light on the floor and pointed it into the dark corners. Boxes lined the walls and took up most of the floor space. Trails of rat droppings and dust dotted the old tiles. There was only the one door, but maybe there was a vent she could shimmy through, some other way of escaping. She flashed the light onto the ceiling. Old 1970s panels threatened to fall out of the drop ceiling.

Perfect!

Laney knew that if she could get to the top of the wall and push up a tile, all that would separate her from whatever was next door would be more tiles. She thought about dropping straight into the warehouse, but she didn't know where the kidnappers were. Four lives depended on her escaping without notice—including her own. She could climb over the support beam and drop into the next room. Ideally find an unlocked door there and move into the warehouse, where she'd find a way to smuggle the kids out.

She turned the light back in the direction of the kids.

They looked terrified, their faces streaked with grime, tears and, in some cases, a few bruises. Olivia was hugging a girl who looked much smaller and younger than she was. Laney recognized her from the Amber alerts and news stories surrounding her abduction. Eight-year-old Marissa James. The dark haired, slim boy standing beside them was eleven-year-old Adam Presley.

"I need you guys to help me move some of those boxes to the corner," Laney whispered. "We need to stack them so I can climb up."

She flashed the light so they could all see the area.

The kids moved quickly and more quietly than Laney expected.

Fear was a powerful motivator.

It didn't take long to create a sturdy platform. "I'm going to climb through," she whispered. "Once I make it to the other side, I'll unlock the door."

"Why can't we all climb through?" Adam asked. "If you go and don't come back—"

"I'll come back."

"But if you don't," Olivia whispered, "we're stuck."

"I will either open this door and get you out or come back through the ceiling. Either way, I'm not leaving anyone behind." She meant it. And she hoped she could follow through.

If something happened, and she was killed...

It was a thought she couldn't dwell on. God was in control. He saw. He knew. She had to believe that He'd act.

Laney said a quick prayer as she hoisted herself to the top of the storage room wall. She removed the drop ceiling tile, carefully handing it down to Adam. Using her penlight, she peered over the wall into an office space. It was empty. Pocketing her light, she started to formulate the best plan for lowering herself down to the next room.

The telltale sound of clicking of paws moving rapidly across the concrete floor grabbed her attention.

Could it be?

Had Grayson and Jax somehow found the warehouse?

And where was the kidnapper with the gun?

Her question was answered when the guy lumbered into the office, closing and locking the door behind him, then quietly peering through the blinds of a window that opened into the warehouse.

Jax was out there. Laney knew it, and she thought Grayson was with him. She hoped he was. She'd overheard one of the kidnappers say he'd shot him. If he was in the warehouse, he'd survived, but he was also a sitting duck. There were windows in the interior office wall that looked out into the warehouse. If Jax and Grayson walked by where the kidnapper could see them… Her blood grew cold at the thought.

She scrambled back down into the storage room.

"New plan," she whispered to the kids. "The kidnapper is in the room next door. I'm heading into the warehouse. I'll open the door when I get to the other side. When I do, everyone needs to leave single file and quietly. Hug the wall to the right, hold hands and stay together."

Removing her boots so her drop to the floor would not be heard, she climbed through the open ceiling tile and sat on the top of the wall. It was a good eight-foot drop. She lowered herself until she was hanging by her hands, her socked feet dangling about three feet from the floor. Holding her breath, she prepared to let go.

Keeping to the edges of the open warehouse, Grayson followed Jax toward a row of offices. Jax looked up.

Grayson followed his gaze and saw a pair of legs dangling from an open panel in the ceiling.

Laney!

He rushed forward, touched her ankle.

She let out a bloodcurdling scream, and the silent warehouse suddenly turned to chaos. Kids screamed from the other side of a closed door. Distant footsteps pounded on old tile.

Grayson yanked hard enough to pull Laney down, catching her as she tumbled into his arms.

"Grayson!" she cried, throwing her arms around his neck. "I thought you were dead."

"Not yet, but we both might be if we don't get moving."

"The children!" She broke away and unlocked and opened a door.

Three kids emerged, all of them in various states of hysteria.

An office door opened. The kidnapper rushed toward them, gun in hand.

"Everyone down!" Grayson hollered.

Laney, the children and even Jax hit the floor, leaving the gunman an easy target. Grayson got off his shot first. The man went down. But there had been two men in the van earlier. Where was his accomplice?

Thundering footsteps were getting closer, and Jax growled, sensing danger before any of them could see it.

Grayson scooped up the smallest child in his left arm, wincing as she latched onto his wounded shoulder. There was cover of sorts near the edges of the warehouse, where the shadows were deepest and machinery crowded the floor.

"Come on!" he urged.

Laney grabbed the hands of the other two children and followed Grayson closely.

Somewhere in the distance, a door opened and closed. Feet tapped on concrete. Not one set of footsteps. Several. Grayson was maintaining radio silence, but he'd called the warehouse location in, and he knew the cavalry had arrived. He just had to keep the kids and Laney safe until Andrew's men could take Conrad's remaining thug down.

Hugging the shadows, he led them down a shelf-lined corridor, toward the emergency exit.

Behind them, a commotion ensued—shouts and gunshots as the remaining kidnapper met the cavalry.

Kicking open the emergency exit door, Grayson led them to the alley, where the flashing red and blue lights of the first responders were a welcoming sight.

They were met by police and paramedics, who took the children from their arms and ushered them to the safety of an ambulance.

Laney turned to Grayson, her eyes drawn to the blood dripping down his arm from his wounded shoulder.

"You're hurt!" She motioned to a paramedic, who grabbed her bag and headed toward them.

"It's not serious."

But Laney insisted he push up his sleeve and allow the paramedic to take a look.

"You've got a nasty gash," she said, removing a sterile pad and some gauze from her medical kit. "You need to have this properly cleaned and sutured. Looks like you've lost a considerable amount of blood, so I can't clear you to drive yourself."

Just then, Kent and two officers came out through the warehouse door, ushering the handcuffed kidnapper out into the alley and the waiting patrol car.

Kent jogged over to him as the paramedic finished field-dressing the wound and called for a gurney to be brought over. "Well, DeMarco, it looks like you're a little worse for wear."

"It's just a flesh wound. I'll be fine." Especially now that he knew Laney and the children were safe.

A second paramedic wheeled over a gurney. "It's time to go, sir."

Grayson sighed. "It looks like we're in for an ER visit," he said, reaching his hand out to Laney.

"We?"

"If you think I'm leaving you here on your own, you can forget it." He rubbed her palm with his thumb. "With your track record, that's much too risky—I need a vacation before I allow you to pull me into the next case."

Laney smiled, shaking her head. "I guess I had that coming." Her green eyes filled with laughter as she followed along for the ride.

TWENTY-ONE

Almost two weeks later, thanks in part to the computer forensic work Arden had performed on both the FBI networks and Ethan Conrad's personal computers and cell phone, there was enough physical and forensic evidence to get an indictment against Ethan and seventeen other accomplices. Charges spanned from murder to child trafficking. The previous night, Ethan, who had been stopped after crossing the border into Mexico and extradited to Maryland, had been charged with three counts of child abduction in Maryland, plus the thirteen others in Boston and California.

That was great news. Laney was glad Ethan was behind bars where he'd be unable to tear another family apart.

She smiled as she brushed her hair into a high ponytail and fingered the purple scar near her hairline. The staples had been removed, but it would be a while before the scar looked less raw and angry.

She didn't care.

All that mattered was that Olivia and the other kids were safe, and that there was hope of more children being recovered.

That Grayson…

She smiled again, because thinking about him always made her do that.

He'd recovered from his gunshot wound.

It might take a little while longer for him to get over Ethan's betrayal. Ethan's computer logs had revealed that he'd also been part of a money-laundering scheme his stepson had discovered. When Rick had confronted him, Ethan had killed him. Fearing that Rick had revealed information to Grayson, Ethan made an attempt on Grayson's life, too. His bullet had missed its mark and killed Andrea instead. Pinning the murders on two high-level gang members, he closed up the case while Grayson mourned his fiancée and friend, then continued, without missing a step, with his mentorship of Grayson.

It was a sad story that had come out in bits and pieces of forensic information—bank account records, phone records, the testimonies of some of Ethan's coconspirators.

Since the children had been recovered, there had been a whirlwind of activity—interviews with the press, law enforcement, judges and a prosecutor. Between that and work, Laney barely had time to think, but when she did, she found herself thinking about Grayson. Obviously he'd spent some time thinking about her, too. He called or visited almost every day. He'd even made it to the ceremony that morning.

Laney glanced at Jax, smiling at the little medal attached to his collar. The FBI had honored Jax, Arden and Laney for their part in recovering the children.

"But you're the only one who got a medal, Jax," Laney said, walking out onto the porch and taking a seat on the swing. Jax padded along beside her and found a comfortable spot in the sunlight. They'd trained hard the day before, and they were both tired. It was worth it, though. Being out of retirement made Laney feel more alive than she'd felt in years.

A car drove toward the house, and Laney recognized it immediately. Grayson had said he'd stop by when he finished work for the day.

One thing she was learning about him—he always kept his word.

Jax stood as the car parked, excited to see his new friend.

Grayson jumped out, his black hair gleaming in the sunlight, his face soft with his feelings for her.

He walked up the steps and took both her hands in his. "I've been waiting to do this all day," he said, pressing a sweet kiss to her lips.

She would have begged for more, but Jax nosed in between them, looking up with dark eyes and a silly grin.

"He looks great in his medal," Grayson said with a grin.

"Yes." She laughed. "He's been strutting around shamelessly since they put it on him."

"You, on the other hand," he said, "don't need a medal to look great. You're beautiful in fuzzy dog sweaters and weird leggings, with staples in your head and bruises on your face. You're beautiful out in the field with sunlight dappling your hair. And you're beautiful here, with your hair up and your face scrubbed clean."

"Grayson, I…"

"Don't make me stop, Laney. I might chicken out.

There's something I want to tell you. I need to tell you. When I lost Andrea, I decided that was God's way of showing me that my plans for a family had to take second place to my career. For the past ten years, I've dedicated myself to this purpose God had for me." He touched her cheek, his fingers trailing down to her collar bone and resting there. "But something happened two weeks ago. It took a punch in the jaw from a pretty girl to bring me to my senses."

Laney laughed. "Yeah, sorry about that, but in my defense, I was concussed."

He smiled. "I had decided that because Andrea was taken from me, I wasn't meant to have a wife and family—to make promises to a woman that I might not be able to keep. I convinced myself it was God's plan for me to focus solely on my career, but the truth is, I was protecting myself from the possibility of finding someone and possibly losing them. I didn't want to hurt again the way I'd hurt when I lost Andrea. Her death left a hole in my heart."

"I'm so sorry, Grayson."

"I don't want you to be. I want you to know that you woke me up to the possibility that God might intend more for me. Everything happens according to plan, Laney, and meeting you, working together on this case, was all part of His plan.

"I can't promise you happily-ever-after, because the future isn't written in stone. But what I can promise you, Laney Kensington, is that if you take a chance on me, I will put your needs before my own, and I will protect you, and cherish you for the wondrously special and unique person that you are, for as long as I live."

Looking into his ocean-blue eyes, she saw the sincerity in them. His faith and strength of character were a constant, steadfast testament to who Grayson De-Marco was. And she knew that she believed him and trusted him with all her heart. Something that she never thought possible. She felt a tear fall before she realized she was crying.

He gently whisked the tear away with the pad of his thumb. "Why are you crying? Have I said something, done something…"

She shook her head and smiled. "I've never believed in happily-ever-after, Grayson, and I wouldn't believe anyone who offered it to me. But then again, I never used to believe in tears of joy, either, but you just wiped one off my cheek."

He kissed her then, gently, pulling her into his arms, then resting his chin on her hair. "Who knows, Laney? Maybe one day we'll both believe that happily-ever-after really is possible."

"Truthfully," she answered, "I think I already do."

* * * * *

WE HOPE YOU ENJOYED
THIS BOOK FROM

LOVE INSPIRED SUSPENSE
INSPIRATIONAL ROMANCE

Courage. Danger. Faith.

Find strength and determination in stories
of faith and love in the face of danger.

6 NEW BOOKS AVAILABLE EVERY MONTH!

SPECIAL EXCERPT FROM

LOVE INSPIRED SUSPENSE

INSPIRATIONAL ROMANCE

*When someone tries to take an infant from her ranch,
foster mother Isabelle Trent gets caught in the would-be
abductor's deadly sights. With her ranch hand, Brian
"Mac" McGee, at her side, they will do anything to
protect the baby.*

Read on for a sneak preview of
Peril on the Ranch *by Lynette Eason,*
available July 2021 from Love Inspired Suspense.

Isabelle Trent woke with a start. She lay still, trying
to figure out what had jarred her just as the sun was
beginning to make its way above the horizon. She'd
forgotten to pull her curtains closed before she'd fallen
into bed with a half-finished prayer on her lips.

Maybe it was just the light that had disturbed her.

A faint cry reached her. A cry that sounded like…a
baby? A kitten?

The sound grew louder, and it came from the
wraparound porch.

Finally, she identified it.

A baby.

With a soft gasp, Isabelle hurried forward to unlock
the French door and step outside.

At her feet, an infant was strapped into a carrier. "Oh,
my sweet little one." Isabelle released the straps and
scooped the tiny body, blanket and all, into her arms.

Movement from the edge of the porch caught her attention. "Hey, who's there?"

The slow-moving sun only revealed the silhouette of a man simply standing there. Not moving. Just watching. Unease crawled through her. "Hey, is this your baby?"

Still, he stayed silent. He looked back over his shoulder one more time, then seemed to make up his mind about something. Her nerves jangled and alarm shuddered through her. He took a step toward her and Isabelle spun. Holding the infant in the crook of her left arm, she twisted the knob with her right hand and pushed the door open just wide enough for her to slip through. She shut the door and locked it.

He moved as though to leave, then turned back, dark eyes on hers. He came toward the glass door, reaching for the knob. Isabelle whirled and raced to her bedroom to snatch her phone from the nightstand. She dialed 911 and hurried back to the den area to see the dark-clad figure pacing in front of her door. Quick as lightning, he spun and slammed a fist on the wooden part of the door. The noise jarred the infant, who let out a wail.

"911. What's your emergency?"

"Someone's trying to get in my house."

Don't miss
Peril on the Ranch *by Lynette Eason,*
available July 2021 wherever Love Inspired Suspense
books and ebooks are sold.

LoveInspired.com

LOVE INSPIRED
INSPIRATIONAL ROMANCE

UPLIFTING STORIES OF FAITH, FORGIVENESS AND HOPE.

Join our social communities to connect with other readers who share your love!

Sign up for the Love Inspired newsletter at **LoveInspired.com** to be the first to find out about upcoming titles, special promotions and exclusive content.

CONNECT WITH US AT:

Facebook.com/LoveInspiredBooks

Twitter.com/LoveInspiredBks

Facebook.com/groups/HarlequinConnection

LISOCIAL2020

Get 4 FREE REWARDS!

We'll send you 2 FREE Books plus 2 FREE Mystery Gifts.

Love Inspired Suspense books showcase how courage and optimism unite in stories of faith and love in the face of danger.

FREE Value Over $20

YES! Please send me 2 FREE Love Inspired Suspense novels and my 2 FREE mystery gifts (gifts are worth about $10 retail). After receiving them, if I don't wish to receive any more books, I can return the shipping statement marked "cancel." If I don't cancel, I will receive 6 brand-new novels every month and be billed just $5.24 each for the regular-print edition or $5.99 each for the larger-print edition in the U.S., or $5.74 each for the regular-print edition or $6.24 each for the larger-print edition in Canada. That's a savings of at least 13% off the cover price. It's quite a bargain! Shipping and handling is just 50¢ per book in the U.S. and $1.25 per book in Canada.* I understand that accepting the 2 free books and gifts places me under no obligation to buy anything. I can always return a shipment and cancel at any time. The free books and gifts are mine to keep no matter what I decide.

Choose one: ☐ **Love Inspired Suspense Regular-Print** (153/353 IDN GNWN) ☐ **Love Inspired Suspense Larger-Print** (107/307 IDN GNWN)

Name (please print)

Address   Apt. #

City   State/Province   Zip/Postal Code

Email: Please check this box ☐ if you would like to receive newsletters and promotional emails from Harlequin Enterprises ULC and its affiliates. You can unsubscribe anytime.

Mail to the **Harlequin Reader Service:**
IN U.S.A.: P.O. Box 1341, Buffalo, NY 14240-8531
IN CANADA: P.O. Box 603, Fort Erie, Ontario L2A 5X3

Want to try 2 free books from another series! Call 1-800-873-8635 or visit www.ReaderService.com.

*Terms and prices subject to change without notice. Prices do not include sales taxes, which will be charged (if applicable) based on your state or country of residence. Canadian residents will be charged applicable taxes. Offer not valid in Quebec. This offer is limited to one order per household. Books received may not be as shown. Not valid for current subscribers to Love Inspired Suspense books. All orders subject to approval. Credit or debit balances in a customer's account(s) may be offset by any other outstanding balance owed by or to the customer. Please allow 4 to 6 weeks for delivery. Offer available while quantities last.

Your Privacy—Your information is being collected by Harlequin Enterprises ULC, operating as Harlequin Reader Service. For a complete summary of the information we collect, how we use this information and to whom it is disclosed, please visit our privacy notice located at corporate.harlequin.com/privacy-notice. From time to time we may also exchange your personal information with reputable third parties. If you wish to opt out of this sharing of your personal information, please visit readerservice.com/consumerschoice or call 1-800-873-8635. **Notice to California Residents**—Under California law, you have specific rights to control and access your data. For more information on these rights and how to exercise them, visit corporate.harlequin.com/california-privacy.

LIS21R